More Praise for
SOUTH OF THE BIG FOUR:

"Stellar . . . a rich harvest . . .
Neighbor Kurtz has sown a great tale."
—*Indianapolis News*

"A marvelously layered story . . . rich in its sense of place,
full of consistent but unpredictable characters . . .
Kurtz has written a Midwest novel, to be sure,
but it is also much more."
—*Chicago Tribune*

"Kurtz has done for rural Indiana
what Richard Russo does for rural New York State,
creating an intimate portrait of a time, a place,
and a way of life threatened with extinction
by the forces of economics and change . . .
This is a fine debut; Kurtz is an author to watch."
—*Library Journal*

"An exceptional literary debut . . .
This is an unvarnished portrait of the family farm,
an exploration of the faces of love, and—most of all—
an examination of the strength of loyalty and the land.
Kurtz is a fine writer."
—*Booklist*

"Riveting . . . a wonderful, compelling first novel . . .
clear-eyed and open about what it takes to live this life
and why it is disappearing . . . Kurtz is a master of detail . . .
He tells the stories of these people and this land
with a deft, believable touch."
—*Albuquerque Journal*

"A stirring book . . . The novel's strength is
the flesh-and-blood characters Kurtz has created.
He remains true to them throughout . . .
You want to savor every word."
—*El Paso Herald-Post*

SOUTH OF THE BIG FOUR

BIG FOUR

DON KURTZ

AVON BOOKS ◆ NEW YORK

VISIT OUR WEBSITE AT
http://AvonBooks.com

All characters appearing in this work are fictional. Any resemblance to real persons is coincidental.

Portions of this novel, in somewhat different form, appeared in the *Iowa Review* and *Puerto del Sol.*

AVON BOOKS
A division of
The Hearst Corporation
1350 Avenue of the Americas
New York, New York 10019

First Avon Books Trade Printing: August 1996

AVON TRADEMARK REG. U.S. PAT. OFF. AND IN OTHER COUNTRIES, MARCA REGISTRADA, HECHO EN U.S.A.

Printed in the U.S.A.

OPM 10 9 8 7 6 5 4 3 2 1

For
Mel and Lorene
and
my mom and dad

Acknowledgments

The author wishes to thank Kevin McIlvoy, Antonya Nelson, Rita Popp, Paula Moore, Anne Marie Mackler, and Steve Chilton for their suggestions and encouragement. Special thanks to Mel and Lorene Myers, Frances and Lester Kurtz, and especially to Ann Gutierrez, for her love, spirit, and wisdom. Thanks too to my editor Jay Schaefer, and to the National Endowment for the Arts for its generous support.

SOUTH OF THE
BIG FOUR

PART I

I can still remember the drawing from the book we used in our high-school Vo-Ag class, a map of these United States and their farm products. Corn-Hog Belt was what the bold letters read, running across Iowa and Illinois to end just above us there in Haskell County. Underneath, a tiny man in overalls stood next to a round-backed Hampshire hog.

In north-central Indiana we're right at the forest's edge, where the first patches of grassland reach in among hickory and oak. The low dome that makes up our part of the state divides watersheds in a big way: just north of us the St. Joseph drains toward Michigan and the lakes. Farther south we're crossed by the Tippecanoe, on its way down to meet the Wabash at Lafayette. Then there's U.S. 31, which comes up through Indianapolis to approach Delfina from the south, in past the New Holland dealer and an old pioneer cemetery.

Five miles from Delfina, four miles east of the blinking caution light on the highway, was where my dad had his place. Not that it mattered much to me; as soon as I was old enough to get away I did, following 31 clear out of Haskell County and away, up to the ore boats on the Great Lakes.

I do remember old Si Lemke in that Vo-Ag class now and then, reciting for us the rule the bankers always followed: don't make any farm loans south of the Big Four Railroad. After all the good things have been taken, there are others still in line——for my family that meant a share of that same swampy land south of the tracks nobody else had wanted. South of the Big Four turned out to be where Gerry Maars set up farming too. And that's where, after I came back from the lakes, Gerry took me on as his hired man, and where I've been ever since.

ONE

When I got home it was still early, the second week of March, as I pulled into what was left of the barn lot. Whoever'd ended up with the place had plowed to within about ten feet on the west side of the house, looped out some in back, then cut in close around the barn. It was hard to imagine there'd been a yard there once, where Byron and I conducted army campaigns, and mounted Indian resistance a century too late. Our football field had been only thirty feet wide to begin with, but now it was gone, planted to corn.

There were hogs wandering around in the pens, and I walked out to look at them. The grain bin and milk house were gone. Early spring in that part of the country is about as desolate a time as you can imagine, and I kind of missed the trees, the two in front and a long row of poplars that had run along behind the house. It made for a better view anyway, across low black fields to a distant row of brush along the ditch, and the woods that lay behind the Shaw place, a mile to the south.

A house you grew up in is supposed to have pleasant memories, I guess, but what I thought of as I went up on the porch were the whippings I'd got, for letting the screen door slam shut a couple dozen times too often. I deserved them, no doubt, but nobody likes to be whipped, and I was pleased to come up to the storm door and kick it open, splintering the frame. I stepped into the dry rot smell of an old empty farmhouse, our house, the place I was born. The door opened to the kitchen, and the same cheap paneled cabinets we'd had when I was a boy. The refrigerator and stove were gone, but there was a new water heater over in the corner, wiring coiled around its base. d-Con pellets were spread out along the floor by the pantry.

It wasn't any warmer inside, so I jammed my hands in my pockets to walk through the house. The last I'd heard, and that had been some time before, there'd been a family renting it out, a man who'd hauled steel for Continental in Kokomo. He'd hung on a couple of months after it shut down, until one night he finally packed up his family and left, still owing two months' rent. The west wall was charred from a blanket fire they'd accidentally started with a space heater, trying to save on fuel. The miracle was that the old place hadn't burned to the ground, but there it still was, cold and empty around me.

The living room floor wasn't used to people anymore, creaking under my steps. The door to the front parlor stood ajar, and I slid past it to go inside. It was the biggest room in the house, almost square, so that's where the trucker had put his pool table. I could see four deep impressions from where it had rested, and wide jagged holes in the plaster where he'd hung up, and then been in a hurry to tear off, a rack for the cues.

On the stairway was a single narrow landing. Right there, so you could see it whenever you went up or down, there'd always hung a picture of the three of us boys, me and Byron and Danny. At the top of the stairs was the room I'd shared with Danny; then, after he was killed, had to myself. Next to it was the bathroom, where the toilet and sink were ripped out and a wide yellow stain had spread across the tile. In the bathroom I pulled the shade free to look out onto wide black Indiana, heavy on flatness and mud.

Window screens were stacked in the hallway, along with a fifty-pound bag of rock salt and some spare pieces of ducting. Byron's room was down at the other end. Across from it was my dad's. I remembered well enough the way it used to be—his sagging bed and shiny comforter, always made up crisp and tidy in our house of men. I had only the faintest memories of my mother there too, propped on white pillows. I'd hung back in the doorway afraid of her, the woman who after all was almost a stranger to me, someone I'd never really known not to be sick.

There wasn't much more to see, so I went down to carry in my duffle bag, along with the groceries I'd picked up in town. The trucker had made a clean sweep of the place; even the light fixtures were gone, wires hanging twisted and bare from the ceiling. In the kitchen I plugged in a radio I'd brought. It worked, so I rigged up the drop light from the car, hanging it from one of the wires. By then it was almost dark. From the porch I looked out past the barn to Byron's, out across the sixty acres that had once been my dad's.

Byron had built his own place over on the county road, a quarter of a mile away. I'd seen it when I pulled in, a low red-brick ranch house with Bedford stone facing—not elegant particularly, but prosperous, just about right for a vice principal over at Tippy Valley. It sat alone on a four-acre lot, and to get there I walked all the way around to the crossroads, where the sun had worked through the ice earlier in the day. The road still glowed wet but the wind was raw, coming in over my shoulder.

Byron's Toyota and Bronco were in the garage. As I came up the driveway, I looked in through the picture window, lights up bright and the news playing on a color TV console just past the drapes. I watched his wife, Kendra, come out of the kitchen and stop when she saw me there standing on the porch.

It took a while for the door to open, but when it did he stood above me tall and stoop-shouldered, a large soft belly hanging over his belt. Kendy must have gotten him into the aviator glasses, bought him the sharp green sweater, but otherwise it was clearly my big brother Byron, puffy-faced and growing bald-headed, blinking as he looked down at me.

"What do you want?" he said, and it was the damnedest thing, I lost my voice. Kendra was just behind him, but he stood in the doorway in his stocking feet, blocking my way. There was a low table in front of the TV, and a blond-haired baby, my niece, steadied herself next to it.

"You back for a visit?"

"Who's got the place now?" I asked. "Everett still got it?"

Byron shook his head. "Charlie Sellars took it over. Everett had trouble, so Charlie's got it now." He had the door pushed open with his arm, newspaper in hand. "I wondered who that Camaro belonged to. You had it long?"

I told him I had, and when Kendra said something behind him, he shifted in the doorway, wiping across his chin with his fist.

"I reckon you've had dinner already."

"I don't want to put Kendy out," I said. "That's okay. I got food."

"Well, that's good. It's good you got food."

He folded the paper under his arm. I heard Kendra behind him again, and he reached back for the door. When I glanced up, though, I could see what the poor bastard was only just then realizing: he was glad to see me.

"Oh, come on in, Arthur," he said suddenly, pulling me roughly by the shoulder. I stepped past him onto a throw rug they had by the door, bulky in my heavy jacket and boots. Kendy had stayed younger than Byron, pretty and smiling, still hugging herself against the draft. She'd turned off the TV, which made the baby start crying, red-faced and unhappy, banging her fists against her legs. A boy about ten or eleven, my nephew Joey, watched me from the hall.

"Well, Kendra," I said, "I don't suppose you remember me much," but she'd already opened her arms.

"Yes, Arthur," she said, "I do."

Two

It may have taken some effort, that first evening, to leave Byron's house and go back outside. Not that we'd been having such a warm and wonderful time: we tried, but I hadn't seen any of them for five or six years. Byron never was one for a quick decision, and while he stepped back to chew over whether to let bygones be bygones, his wife took over. She showed me my niece Celeste, introduced me again to Joey. It's the kind of thing you appreciate, because even in the best of circumstances, my brother and I wouldn't have had much to say.

He was the same Byron I remembered, head bent low to the

table, concentrating on his meal. He looked up only to pick at Joey, who, excited by the visitor, squirmed in his seat until Byron sent him to his room. Celeste mashed peas into the tray of her high chair while Kendra played hostess, fussing and apologizing around us.

After dinner Byron and I settled in front of the TV, where he filled me in on who was farming what, which of our relatives had gotten rich or died, what all he was teaching at school. Tedious as it was to listen to, it meant the past was behind us, more or less, and that Byron was absorbing me back into his world. It was an effort that didn't involve me, so while he talked I watched Kendra as she cleaned up the table, got my nephew and niece ready for bed. When she brought out a pillow and blankets, I said I couldn't stay. Byron didn't press it. By the time I'd walked back around to the farmhouse, the wind had died down, the night was clear, and a solitary hog rooted in the pens next to the barn.

I'd worked the ore boats a dozen years, and for the last two or three had run with a guy named Lenny Jaynes. Lenny had gotten married right after the season, and he was wintering up in Saginaw, where his wife had a block of apartments. We were pretty close, and he told me they'd be glad to find me a place there anytime. So I just as easily could have gone back up to Michigan then. The Camaro was waiting, but instead I spent a half hour walking around by the pens. On the porch, it made me smile to see the door swinging loose in the moonlight. I liked a little air.

It was just an old house, could have been anybody's for that matter, as much difference as it would have made to me. I made camp in the kitchen, and when I'd put up my cot and slid into my sleeping bag, the drop light lit a pleasant circle around me. And from that point on that was all the world there was, three feet wide. Some people feel the need to peer out into the darkness, let their imaginations run wild, but there's no law that says you have to. The key is to put everything out of your mind. When I had I could have been in the Delfina jail or the White House, it didn't matter——I was there to sleep. Most people get scared and give in too easily, and then they wonder why they're lost.

THREE

The next morning around eight I was back out by the hog pen, where Charlie Sellars was unloading bags of feed. I'd heard the idle of his pickup as he slowed by the front porch, inspecting the door, so neither of us pretended surprise.

"Why, hello there, Arthur. Long time, no see." When I complimented his hogs, he shrugged. "Oh, they're gaining, I guess. Market's better than it will be when they're finished, though, that's what they're saying."

Charlie would have been a young man to my dad's middle age, but now he himself was nearing sixty, heavy in the chest and arms, his ears pink under a clear cold sky. He shook my hand when I offered it, but that didn't reassure him, he was already edging away from me along the pen. From what Byron told me, Charlie'd married a widow from over near Manchester and had a brand-new lease on life. He'd managed to come up with the money to buy my dad's place and at least one other, so he was doing fine.

He'd known me since I was a boy, but I still had the feeling that if I'd stamped my foot and shouted "Boo!" he would have scampered off like a calf. As it was, he settled in a few feet away, watching me warily out of the corner of his eye.

He turned to nod back to the house. "I see you got in okay. Did you find some heat in there? The thermostat's in the hall, next to the bathroom. You find it all right?"

"I found it, but I left it where it was. I don't need heat."

"I had to put a new furnace in; Byron probably told you that. That other one was plumb wore out. The heating man told me he didn't know how it lasted as long as it did. That gets kind of salty, a new furnace like that."

Charlie couldn't have expected me to feel much sympathy, and I didn't, but I knew he was just slipping on the old heartland prophylactic — nothing makes a farmer feel more secure than a recitation of his troubles. We leaned against the fence, watching his hogs nose in at the feeder. It was something I'd seen a hundred times when I was a boy, my dad and some other man leaning in together out in the barn lot. Only this time it was me, and I knew what Charlie was busy wishing was that he'd burned down this house like he had the one on his other place, so he wouldn't have Hurd Conason's thirty-year-old son back around kicking down his door. What might have comforted him was what I didn't feel like telling: I didn't want that damn farm and never had.

"You feeling okay these days, Arthur? You doing all right?"

"I'm feeling fine, Charlie."

"Ain't had no more troubles? Spells like you had?"

He was waiting for me to put him at ease, and when I didn't say anything he was forced to improvise.

"That's good you're feeling okay. Health's important. Well, anyway, I reckon you'll be shipping out again pretty soon. Them lakes thaw out before too long, don't they? That's where you're at now, up on the lakers? Good pay from what I hear, good pension, benefits, you know, a fella likes to have those things . . ."

His voice had grown too hopeful, so I let him back down.

"They took our boat off the lake, Charlie, shipping's not what it used to be. Might be a while before I get another."

"Oh," he said, frowning, and we studied the hogs.

A lot of people feel sentimental these days, or think they ought to, about owning a piece of land. Most of them are people who never had to stay up all night worrying about how to pay it off, but I guess somebody still might imagine I harbored some resentments about Charlie ending up with our place. You have to think it through, though, because after all, my dad hadn't exactly hacked it single-handedly out of the wilderness. He'd bought it from somebody else, who'd bought it from somebody else, who'd bought it from somebody else, and the vast majority of all those somebody elses were dead and gone, clear title or not. Land changes hands. I know Charlie would have agreed, and not just for selfish reasons—we weren't neither of us children, and both knew the rules. The trouble was, from Charlie's point of view, that I hadn't kept up my end of the bargain, which was to fade away and stay gone.

Out over the empty field a thin line of white smoke came up from the chimney at Byron's, so Kendra was home.

"I'll give you a hundred a month," I said to Charlie, "for the time I'm here. That sound okay?"

Charlie had an old habit I still remembered, of acting like he hadn't heard what you said. You could almost see the sound winding back into his head, and getting lost somewhere deep inside. I was patient, waiting him out.

"Lake people done drove up the prices around here, can't hardly believe what these houses go for anymore. You wouldn't believe it, Arthur."

"A hundred a month," I said, "plus take over the propane. You're heating those pipes anyway, so you might as well let me pay for it."

"Ted Marlin got offered four hundred dollars for that place of his dad's, can you imagine that? And you wouldn't believe the people that call up, wanting to know about this one. Hard to figure, ain't it? Now, look over there, Arthur, look at that gilt. See her? She's got me worried. But goddamn, I can't have a vet out here every ten minutes. They don't even want to come out no more, and when they do, the costs eat you alive."

"A hundred and fifty, then. Plus the propane."

I was rushing it, there was a rhythm to these kind of conversations that I still remembered, but if I'd followed it, we would have wound so far away from the house that in half an hour neither of us would remember that it had ever been discussed.

Charlie scratched the back of his head, his gloved fingers pushing under his cap. He took it off, rubbing his hand up over his forehead and flattop.

"You know, I remember your dad out here, all of us do. Don't seem like seven years since he died. No sir, it don't seem like it, not at all. You wouldn't wish on nobody the troubles he had out here. Nobody." He shook his head, looking at me directly for the first time. "You don't want to come back into this goddamn old house, Arthur."

It's not often another man will look at you straight on like that, and what Charlie said was so true on the face of it that for a minute I wanted to believe him. I almost forgot that he'd been working on his own plan ever since he drove up that morning, which was to get me back out of his sight forever.

"You just say how much you want for it," I told him, but I was talking to his back, he'd already climbed halfway up the fence. He straddled it with care.

"These hogs, the fuel, your equipment wears out, all these god-damn costs. It's like throwing money down a hole, Arthur. I don't know what things are coming to."

I didn't either, but a half hour later I finally did get the damn place back again, for three hundred dollars a month. My dad would have had his stroke all over again to know what I paid, and I'd realized by then that Charlie was right. I didn't really want it, even to rent, even for a month. It kept me going, though, just to see how little he wanted me there. That, and watching what a poor match he was for his greed.

Once he was officially my landlord Charlie felt free to talk my ear off, and by the time I'd finished helping him fill the feeders, I could see he was thinking he might come out ahead after all. It never hurt to have a man around who could open a couple of bags of feed. He had my three hundred-dollar bills in his shirt pocket, and maybe it was just an occupational hazard, but I noticed Charlie had taken on that same sly look that his livestock had, a look that always made me laugh at those goddamn hogs, with their narrowed eyes and smiles, because let's face it, this week's slyness is next week's bacon, nothing more.

When Charlie finally left, I went in to survey my kingdom. It was depressing enough that I couldn't even get past the kitchen. Out of the sunshine the chill from those old rooms was impressive, and with the trees gone the March winds blew up unbroken, harder than ever.

FOUR

It was hard to believe that my dad had been any poorer farmer than Charlie Sellars, or that any of us had worked any less. Maybe he forgot to pay the preacher, or just didn't hang on long enough to marry a widow from Manchester. But my dad, to be honest, never was able to get it right. He was always a step behind on everything: late to get out on his own, late to get married, late to have us boys, too, for that matter—he'd seemed like an old man even when Byron and I were kids.

He'd grown up over in Liberty Township, where his family had finally started to make a go of it by around 1910, the year he was born. He was eleven when his own dad got trampled by a team, and they'd ended up having to board him out to an Amish family. Later on he was the hired man over at the Echelbarger place. He saved up until he finally had enough to buy a couple of horses and a cultivator, and go on shares. By the late 1930s he'd bought a place over near Deland and was farming on his own.

If this sounds like a success story so far, don't be fooled, he only had that place three or four years before he was drafted into the army, getting back to Haskell County just in time to miss whatever high prices they'd had during the war. He'd begun to hire himself out again, farther behind than ever.

The high point was when he met my mother, at a Sunday school picnic up at Winona Lake. When they got married, he bought twenty acres east of Delfina, along with the house I'd just rented back. That muck ground fought him every step of the way, but I remember we were always supposed to think a little less of my Uncle Willy, who'd had the good sense to get on at GM. Generous Motors, my dad called it, handing out money with both hands. For that matter he never had much good to say about his sister's husband, Chester, either, who'd taken his last army paychecks and bought into National Homes. Within a few years Chester was living in Florida, where the decision he faced every day was a tough one: whether to fish or play golf. They hadn't done it right, somehow, but it was hard to see how we had either. If there were any good years, easy years, I came along last and missed them. I don't remember any real sweetness from back then, just too much quiet, a widow woman now and then coming in days, and me waiting for my chance to leave.

Byron was around too, of course, so he provided some company. It's funny, but what I remembered about Byron were mostly his collections: pennies, matchbooks, feed company ballpoint pens—anything that didn't take too much initiative or imagination to accumulate. We were a little short on entertainment back then, so I'd come down the hall to watch him go through them, stretching from where I sat on his bed to catch a glimpse of his "electricity box," a wood crate full of wires and insulators, and a huge black transformer that I coveted with all my heart. Whenever he would come in to find me in that crate, or see that I'd helped myself to a few of his pennies, he'd pound me dutifully but without any real enthusiasm—Byron was dull more than mean. Later he saved up for a year, sent off in the mail, and then spent the next eight months putting together what had to have been the last vacuum tube radio in America. He gave it to my dad for Christmas, and the old man still had it years later when I visited him in the nursing home, on the nightstand next to his bed.

My brother must have been as surprised as I was when he ended up with someone like Kendra. Her dad worked at the lumber company in Delfina, and she and Byron had been trapped together in the same small high school, so it made some sense—she didn't know any better. She was twice the student he was, but stayed home working at the ASCS office while he went off to college. Byron put in one year teaching down at Noblesville before he got on at Tippy Valley, and they finally got married. Women are romantic at heart, every last one of them, but it's still hard to imagine my brother as anybody's knight in shining armor. All those years that I'd seen Byron hulking through the house with his baggy underwear and thick pimply legs made it hard to believe that he'd ever gotten them between Kendra's, but the kiddies had proved me wrong twice already, at the very least.

Now she was Byron's wife twelve years over, and she'd come up to greet me that first night with a married woman's solid hug, her breasts and butt pulled back, her breath warm on my neck. Joey should have been able to remember me, but he'd shaken his head, quick to blush like his mom. When I went by that next morning after Charlie left, Joey was in school.

Joey was in school, but Kendra and my niece were there, Kendra at the stove and Celeste on the floor playing. Kendy had her sleeves rolled up, and in her western shirt and jeans she looked like any one of the new breed of farm wives you see in the magazines: a quick snapshot before they dash out to run the combine or tend to some baby calves. Except, of course, that she and Byron didn't farm anything and never would. There was coffee dripping and fresh rolls set out on the counter. Uncleness has its privileges: I'd driven by hundreds of houses on my way down from the north, and not one of them could I have come into like I did this one, to be told it was good to see me, to have my night inquired about, to sit down to a cup of coffee while a little girl played across the room on the floor. Celeste was a cool customer, though, careful in her affections, eyeing me from a distance.

With all Joey's toys out of sight and Byron at work, there was scarcely a trace of them left. A sideboard from the old house held dishes at one end of the kitchen; French doors at the other made it so bright that Kendra and I had to squint to see each other when she sat down across from me. Squinting took some of the cuteness out of her face, leaving her exactly what she was—an attractive woman, in a warm, bright kitchen, her baby safe beside her on the floor. A mouth that was a little too small, and eyes that were a touch too close together, were probably all that had kept Kendra there in Haskell County and not out in Hollywood, playing herself on TV.

Everything around us except that sideboard, which I hadn't even liked in the old place, was modern enough to fit in perfectly, the way it was supposed to. I remembered thinking as I'd come up that morning that the house was perfect too, set off by itself just like in the magazines. In the magazines the whole world is right there in the picture, a place so completely possible that almost anyone could imagine fitting in. Not long ago where we were sitting would have been mud waiting for beans, the west end of a field with drainage problems, like a lot of that muck soil had. Byron knew that much at least: he'd built up on the high ground nearest the road.

It was my brother's house, but I can't say that we missed him. If Kendra went a little overboard about things, you could understand it—she had to, being around Byron. He couldn't help it, I guess, but he soaked up energy like a sponge. With the two of us at the table she filled the kitchen with talk: when they'd last seen Willy, a card they'd gotten from Chester's trip to Bermuda, her sister's gall bladder operation in June. It didn't matter what she said: with her short blond hair, her skin that flushed so easily in front of me, it was clear that she was a lot prettier and more alive than someone like Byron really deserved.

She slipped in and out of the hostess role, jumping up to get coffee, but letting me steady jars at the counter while she poured out berries she'd been boiling down for jam. Some tar paper on their well housing had been flapping in the wind, and I went out to nail it down. A couple of taps from Byron's hammer and it was done. I didn't stay much longer, but it was long enough for Celeste to finally give in, coming up to bang on my leg as I slipped on my jacket. When I'd had her on my knee a minute, Kendra complimented me on my ease.

"Oh, I've played daddy a time or two," I told her, and I had, with girlfriends around the lakes. I didn't mind being nice to their children, but the truth was I'd never really cared for how any of them mothered, smoking around the house, drinking too much—they were just big kids themselves, shacked up with me when they should have been paying attention. Maybe she hadn't been particularly fortunate as far as a husband goes, but Kendra was the right mother, doing things the way they needed to be done.

"Joey thinks you're tops, too," she said. "He's asked and asked about you. He liked the tattoo."

I remember being embarrassed about that—impressing a ten-year-old was about all the damn thing was good for. Kendra wasn't a tiny woman, by any means, but slender, she seemed a lot smaller than I was when I reached over to hand back Celeste.

"Nobody understands all that with you and your dad," she said, "but nobody has to. It's over now."

I shrugged. The time I'd run off with him had caused nothing but hard feelings, and it wasn't a memory I cherished. Still, you could appreciate that, too, her willingness to say it out loud.

"You won't be kidnapping any of the rest of us, will you?"

My brother's wife smiled as she said it, dodging as Celeste, half-giggling, half-fussy, banged at her face.

"Oh, I don't reckon I will," I said. "Not Byron, anyway."

She laughed, backing away. I decided to take her pat on the arm as something like friendship, and turned to go back outside.

FIVE

My car was warmer than that damn kitchen at least, as I drove the next morning to a pay phone in Delfina. When I finally got through to Lenny, he said we might be out longer, until the middle of June. I didn't tell him I'd rented the house, so he re-offered the apartment—a little reluctantly, it seemed, his voice low like someone might hear. After I hung up I came back out to the old house and its kitchen, where I had lunch by myself on the floor.

I spent most of the afternoon working on the water heater. About two I was ready to trace wires to the box. There was a flashlight buried down in the trunk somewhere, but it was just as easy to walk around to Byron's and borrow his.

Joey was toward the end of the school bus line, and wouldn't be home for a while, but I didn't know that yet. Celeste was down for her nap, but I didn't know that either. Kendy met me at the door, and I waited while she went down the basement to look.

Now, the church had its way with me early, so some sense of right and wrong is like a part of you—it's the only way you know how to be. On the other hand, I'd never been one to put a check on my day-dreams, or not see things right there waiting to be seen. So sure, I'd watched Kendra color as she smiled, noticed the life in her my brother wasn't able to meet. I couldn't help following the tight stretch of denim across her bottom, might even have wanted those busy hands to touch my temple too, her attention to focus in on me the way it would on Celeste, quickly, intensely, whenever the baby had a difficulty or complaint. Maybe that morning, sweeping out that cold kitchen, I'd imagined pulling her, my brother's wife, into my arms—and more—but thoughts aren't poison, no matter what they tell you.

Kendra was gone quite awhile, and finally came back with a plastic lantern.

"It works," she said, flashing it at me once before she handed it over.

It seemed natural to hug her again, like she had me that first night. So I did. Her forearms wrapped lightly around my back, her hair soft at my cheek, and I found myself bringing her close. She stiffened, watchful, only to hesitate, rocking lightly back into my chest. It was only for the briefest of moments, stolen from a fading winter day, but for all of that moment it was really Kendra, her baby sleeping a dozen steps down the hall, who relaxed up against me. It was one of those damn houses where anything can happen, she felt soft in my arms, and she didn't push me away. I probably did hold on too long. We both knew she hadn't pushed me away.

SIX

My mistake was in coming back too soon, only an hour or so later. Anybody else would have waited, but I'd finished with the flashlight and wanted to bring it back. She must have seen me coming, because by the time I'd walked around to the crossroads and back up to Byron's, Kendra, my niece in her arms, was already coming out the door. She met me at the top of the driveway, talking me right back the way I'd come, all about her appointments in town, the groceries she still needed to buy.

When we got to the door on the passenger side, I reached for the baby.

"No, no, that's okay," Kendra said, "I've got her."

"Let me give you a hand, I can hold her while you get the door."

"I've got her," Kendy said, her little mouth set tight. Celeste was bundled in her jacket, sleepy-eyed and angry, blaming me.

"Here, I got her."

"No!" she said, so sharply I stepped back. She fastened Celeste into her car seat and slammed the door. I watched her hurry around to the other side of the car, and a moment later they were gone.

I was busy the next day anyway, running current to the bathroom, getting the hot-water pipes hooked up. I called up to the union, but they knew even less than Lenny about when we'd be going back. Kendra's car was gone the rest of that day, and most of the next. I did go over the third day, but only because the UPS truck had dropped off a package for Byron at the house.

She insisted I come inside, where there was fresh coffee waiting. I took the cup she offered me. It could have been that first morning all over again, when we'd talked so easily, except this time Kendra stayed at a distance, her voice hurried and sharp. And I do not, to this day, think I have ever heard one single person's name mentioned more times than I did my brother's, over the next quarter hour.

"Byron has more responsibilities now, but he's good at that kind of thing, administration. I know Byron is glad to have you back. He would have been over last night, only he had another meeting at school. Byron says he's glad to have his brother back. We're both really glad to have you here. Byron especially."

Meanwhile she was setting the table in front of me, three place-mats and a space for Celeste, high-chaired and protesting as she was pulled up to the table.

"Oh, Byron misses your father, I'm sure you both do. Byron's not the kind of man to let on, but I can tell. It was hard those last years, for both of us, but Byron helped out. He's so good to help with the kids, too, when he's not at work."

After the buildup I can't say I was surprised to see the man himself come in a few minutes later. Kendra kissed him with an enthusiasm that seemed to catch him off guard. When he saw me, he smiled.

"Nice to see you, Arthur, how's it going? I don't get home much for lunch, it's a long drive." He sat down next to me at the table, looking over his glasses at his wife.

"Here's your soup," Kendra announced, "eat it while it's hot. The sandwiches will be ready in a minute."

Byron nodded, wondering.

"Byron loves to come home," she said, "and I love to see him. When we were first married, he used to come home all the time, even if it was just for fifteen minutes. Byron's like that, romantic." She blushed for me, pulling on Byron's shoulder.

My brother shrugged, picking up his spoon. "I like vegetable beef," he said, and asked me to pass the salt. Kendra talked to us quickly and without stopping for the next fifteen minutes, competing with Celeste, who started crying about five minutes in, and continued nonstop until it was time for Byron to go back. Kendra saw us out together, waving with an almost frantic relief that we were out the door.

Byron turned to me when we got to his car. He had soup on his chin and was still puzzled.

"It's tough to get away from school like that and come all the way back for lunch. We only have forty minutes. My Lord, she calls at ten-thirty and expects me home at eleven, how do you figure that?" He looked at his watch and then at me. "Do you usually eat this early?"

"Not usually," I said, and walked back around toward the house.

SEVEN

When Byron came over that night, I figured he was there to give me hell about Kendra. Or try to, anyway; I was ready for him. But he just hung around for a few minutes in the kitchen, kicking at broken linoleum while he tried to think of something to say. He inspected the wiring on the water heater and pronounced it fit. He poked at my camp stove, asking how it worked. He drank a glass of water and told me about his day at Tippy Valley. As if I cared—the last day I spent in school was the last day I'd ever given it a thought—but I'd relaxed by then. Byron didn't notice anything and never would.

He didn't stay all that long, but two or three times I thought he was about to mention the two of us being back in the house again. I can't say that I encouraged him—some things are better left unsaid. However much he'd considered going into it, he had the good sense to let the moment pass, maybe because we never left the kitchen.

Kitchens are friendly that way, they let you get on with life. This one had already been through hundreds of pounds of bacon, thousands of eggs—breakfasts my mother cooked for Byron and Danny, my dad for us, and then, when we got a little older, us for us. There wasn't a trace of any of them anymore, so the one memory I did have, when I was bedding down that night, came up to surprise me. It was a quick, clear picture of toast burning, a broken plate on the floor, my dad's arm drawn back to strike. And good old Byron there, sullen, his eyes wet, forbidden to raise even his hand.

In that photograph of us that had once hung in the stairway, Byron stood with parted lips and heavy brow, serious even then. Danny, in the middle, had always seemed like a nice-enough-looking boy, whenever I'd run past him on my way up or down. Smooth skinned and smiling, he was two months from being crushed dead in a grain bin, but we didn't know that yet. As I'd aged up and away from that photograph, it got harder to recognize him. It got harder to recognize myself too, the littlest one on the end, wide-eyed and eager, still clearly tickled from something the photographer had said.

We'd known nothing back then, nothing at all. And it wasn't just us—nobody else knew anything either. All the farmers thought they could be sober, decent people, and that would be enough. They thought they could keep on doing things the way they always had, but people showed up who knew better. Young farmers came in, guys like Gerry Maars, and they passed us right by like we were standing still.

We knew absolutely nothing at all. My dad trusted that old fraud Baker in Delfina while my mother got sicker and sicker—nowadays they'd have her up at Mayo within the week. Uncle Willy was the one who got my dad to find another doctor, and he was up in Fort Wayne with him when they finally operated. My dad always thought Willy had way too much to say about things, but I wouldn't even know this much if Willy hadn't told me. He'd been with my dad in the waiting room when the doctor came out, and it was odd, Uncle Willy said, because the doctor was smiling. He had a big wide smile and was carrying something in front of him on a towel. It turned out to be my mother's uterus. The two of them stood watching while the doctor pointed out what he said was a tumor, near what he said was her cervix. The doctor was smiling because he'd been right, this had been the trouble just like he said.

My dad and Uncle Willy had smiled too, then, because they could feel his confidence. She was going to get better. On the way back down to Delfina they'd finally started to relax, but it turned out the doctor was wrong after all. My mother ended up dying a couple of months later, in the same spring that I turned three.

Ranging through the old place that week, I'd noticed something that pleased me, which was that the house wasn't all that big, wasn't all that dark, wasn't much of anything anymore. The next night I carried the cot up to what had once been my room and bedded down there. The trucker's kids had left superhero stickers all over the inside of the door, so they kept an eye on things while I slept.

The following night I spent in Byron's old room, a snap. Mice had eaten through the wire back to my dad's room, but I traced and spliced it, and on the third night that's where I settled in. No ghosts walked, and the sun came up in the morning right on time.

My dad's room was where she'd died, but even that wasn't the end of it. Back then the dead never left you for a minute. Her casket was set up downstairs, and for two or three days we'd had breakfast with my mother just behind us, across the living room in the parlor. When Danny's turn came it wasn't any different, he got his couple of nights in the parlor too.

I'd never had hard feelings toward the trucker who lived there, not like I sensed Byron and Kendra did. His family had never had an easy time of it either. For my part, I liked thinking of him playing pool there, in the room we'd found only one way to use. On the last night, it was in the very center of that abandoned parlor that I set up my cot, framed by the marks from the table. I'd picked up an *Indianapolis Star* in town, to read while I was waiting for sleep. I must have dozed off, because the next thing I knew it was the middle of the night. I got up and turned off the light. The morning dawned gray and overcast, with rain coming in on the wind.

EIGHT

My brother was a man who liked things in their places, and after three weeks I was still camped out in the old farmhouse across the road. When he ran into Gerry Maars downtown, it must have seemed like the perfect solution.

Byron was so pleased he couldn't wait to tell me, stopping by that very afternoon. He was surprised to find I was a little less impressed than he was by the mighty Gerry Maars. For my money it seemed about typical of a big-time operator like that, to go home and relax while another man played butt boy, tracking down his help.

Gerry must have been hard up, because he was on the phone to Byron twice more that same week. Finally one evening I walked over to return his call. Byron met me at the door in his own special version of a leisure suit: red baggy sweatpants and tennis shoes, pulled on under his shirt and tie from school. He'd worked for Gerry himself when he was a boy, and was so excited on the way to the kitchen that I was surprised he hadn't already turned in his chalk at the schoolhouse, and run out to jump on the tractor himself.

I didn't see Joey, who usually would have been the first out to greet me. The adventurous one of the family, he'd already stopped by on his bike a half a dozen times since I'd been back. One Saturday when the weather was good he had spent most of the day with me, watching while I went in on the Camaro. He tried to stay interested as best he could, talking nonstop about school friends and the Pacers, scrambling to hand me the wrong tool.

Kendra was washing supper dishes at the sink. It could have just as easily been a hundred years since I'd held her close; gradually I'd settled back into place as Byron's little brother, troubled but harmless. Joey's special pal. Byron was bent over the directory at the kitchen counter, reaching for the phone.

Ideas didn't visit my brother all that often, and he meant to carry this one through. He still had his vice-principal's voice strapped on from the school day, a little hearty for home consumption, but even at that a poor match for Gerry Maars, who came booming out of the receiver so hard he almost tore off my ear. He wanted to know all about me, of course, and what I'd been doing. He'd been wondering if I could give him a hand, just until he got somebody else. He wondered loud enough for the whole kitchen to hear, and while I considered it, my brother nodded eagerly at my side.

It wasn't any of her concern in the first place, but Kendra called over to Byron and me, leaning in by the phone. "Seems like he'd just be getting started, honey, and have to leave when he gets his call." She had on a baby-doll sweater, the sleeves pulled up from her wrists. "You'd be free to leave then, Arthur. You wouldn't be obligated. You could go any time you wanted."

She was smiling, and it was meant to be friendly, I guess, sisterly advice, but she'd already given it about once too often as far as I was concerned. Maybe I even felt sorry for my brother, who kept his head down, lips tightening at the sound of her voice. Through the receiver, Gerry had been glad enough to fill up the silence, and I broke in to ask if he was the one who'd ended up with the old Smiley place. He said that he had. I can't say I'd thought it through particularly, but the next time I got a word in, I said that I'd do it, I'd be willing to help him out. That made Byron smile, a rare enough occurrence. Kendra dried her hands and went back to check on the baby, leaving the kitchen to us.

NINE

We'd still called it the Bremer place when Gerry and I talked, even though he'd lived there almost twenty years himself, before they moved into town. Town was where most of the farmers had ended up, the ones who'd prospered anyway: Charlie Sellars had settled in with his widow up at the Lake, and Wendell Bardacke had a big house at the far end of a pasture he'd managed to convince people was a sub-division. Gerry Maars had his own showplace, complete with back-yard swimming pool, in Forest Meadows, on the west side of town. I'd driven by a couple of times since I'd been back, and the next morning went by again, on my way into the truckstop for breakfast. His black

Fleetwood was out in the driveway. It was gone on my way back, so I stepped on the gas—if he was anything like my dad, he'd say nine just so he could be out there at eight-thirty, complaining how nobody in the world wanted to work anymore but him.

At the Bremer place two tractors were pulled up in the barnyard. One was a big International, with dual tires mounted under a huge glassed-in cab. That was standard enough by then, and so was the planter, eight rows with a central seed drum the size of a bathtub. The other tractor was the flagship, seventy-five thousand dollars if it was a dime, a big 4586 four-wheel drive. It rose up above me huge as a house, hooked to a twenty-foot disk.

Since nobody was there yet, I walked back through the sheds. His trucks had been repainted over the winter, so even in the shadows they shone like new. He'd been quite a livestock man at one time, but the hoghouses and pens were gone. In their place a half-dozen grain storage bins stretched out along the lane, hooked up by chutes and augers to a long orange grain dryer. In the shop he had a fine set of tools.

It was a subtle kind of thing, but right there to see if you looked: the very best money could buy. Regular old gravity wasn't even progressive enough for a man like Gerry, he'd had his gas tank buried under the yard. Above ground there now stood an antique Texaco gas station pump, bright red and shiny, set in concrete at one side of the lane. No telling how many thousands of dollars a setup like that cost, just so the gas man, the seed corn salesmen, and I could all see it and agree with Byron: Gerry Maars was a heck of a guy.

It was cold that morning, with a stiff wind out of the north. Up on the lakes springtime was something I never saw enough of, so I'll have to say it felt good to have a little soil spread out in front of me again, straining to warm under a pale blue sky. I'll also have to say I felt a lot less poetic an hour later. The wind was still cold and I was still sitting on my fender waiting, with nothing to do but bounce pebbles off the tractor tires and admire that Texaco pump.

Over the next half hour a dozen cars sailed past in front of the house, and a school bus came back to park next to a double-wide trailer a quarter mile south. The Farm Bureau truck wound back and forth along the sections. I heard somebody's diesel roar off to the east, and shook my head. As far as I knew, even a hot dog like Gerry Maars couldn't get his crop out without using his tractors, and there they both were, sitting in front of me.

There was always the possibility, though, that I'd misunderstood. He might already be going somewhere else, and that wasn't exactly how I wanted to start things out, sitting for a couple of hours at the wrong place entirely. Gerry was a famous storyteller, and even that much would be enough to entertain the boys at coffee, dim-witted Hurd Conason's even more dim-witted son Arthur, sitting by himself out at the edge of the barnyard. I took my car out to tour the neighboring fields. There were farmers going, all right, but none of them were Gerry Maars. I drove into Keona, a couple of miles further east. The elevator was still in business, along with an old church on the main street of town. Midway Implement had a yard full of combines and a pop machine, where I bought myself a Coke.

Gerry's Fleetwood wasn't at the little cafe either, but about that time I realized how hard I was looking for the son of a gun, and turned for home. Misunderstanding or not, he could get his help somewhere else. On my way past the Bremer place there was a pickup pulled in behind the house, so I parked and walked up the lane. The four-wheel drive stood idling, and when I'd gone around the disk, I came upon Gerry Maars, his feet sticking out from under the blades.

"Hey there," he said, "you gonna work for me today?"

"I'd thought I was. What the hell time of day do you get started out here, anyway?"

"Oh, early if I can. Herschel Daley had some plans for the courthouse he thought couldn't wait. You see an inch-and-a-sixteenth out there?"

His voice had an echo to it, coming from under the machinery. As I handed the wrench down, I couldn't help thinking of my dad, who may not have been the best farmer in the world, may not have had any 4586 Internationals to pull his disk or a Fleetwood to drive back and forth to town, but who sure as heck would have had five hours of work done already by that time of day. I stood and watched Gerry's work shoes, heels kicking as he grunted and thrashed under the bank. He finally slid himself out to stand up, eyes moist under dust-feathered lashes.

"I called out here on the shop phone two or three times, when I knew I'd be late. There wasn't no answer, so I thought maybe you'd changed your mind. Thought maybe you'd decided to sleep in or something."

"There wasn't no phone that rang out here."

"Kind of hard to hear, though, I reckon, out on the highway. While you were out driving, you see if Wendell's going yet? I seen Harry Coyne just about finished with his beans, and I ain't even got my corn in the ground yet. What time is it, almost eleven?"

"Eleven-thirty," I told him, glad to be of help.

Gerry'd always had a reputation for a temper, but after waiting around all morning I wasn't about to let him take his troubles out on me. He rattled through the drawers in his toolbox, gave up, and began rummaging through the bed of the pickup, banging aside disk blades and jacks.

"So I can't raise you, and then that goddamn Krueger boy is supposed to come out, and he ain't showed up yet either. I was laying under that disk imagining August rolling around, and me still out here planting. That's what I was picturing, August here with me still going up and down the rows by myself."

"There weren't no calls that rang out here, but you can go ahead and think that if you want. I charge the same for standing around as I do for working, so it's all the same to me."

Gerry'd found his hammer by then, and he just grunted, turning to the disk. With my piece said I finally took a second to look him over. He was still a big good-looking guy, with a solid jaw and deep-set blue eyes. The hair left around his ears had gone mostly gray, and his bright yellow polo shirt was already stained with grease where it stretched over an impressive stomach. I was never scrawny, but as he leaned in to work on the axle, his forearms bulged huge, each the size of one of my thighs.

"These kids," he said, "they tear everything up. That Shawn, the one that quit, he'd just tear things to pieces. Look at that blade over there by the truck. It's chewed half to death, and he never even noticed. Ain't that a hell of a thing? So now while the whole damn county's planting corn, I'm climbing around on the equipment. I should have run him off the first day, I'd be a hell of a lot better off."

"So what'd you figure on me doing, anyway?"

He straightened, frowning. "Like I say, first I go into town, and Herschel Daley has to show me plans for the new furnace at the courthouse. Old Herschel don't have nothing to do anymore, so he can afford to talk. Then Irene Bremer calls, the switch on her pump's gone out. You may remember Irene, she owns this place. Poor thing's alone now, but here we are, with all these acres to plant, and I got to go play electrician. You reckon a fella like Ray Stewart is still screwing around like this? Hell no, he's been going strong for days."

Ray Stewart didn't spend all morning running around town, either, I didn't suppose, making everything in the world his business. "What did you want me to do?" I asked again.

"Oh, I reckon that'll hold, you'll have to keep an eye on it." He tossed the hammer back into the pickup and hurried around to check the oil. "You ever run one of these four-wheel drives? You've got to watch them, they've got some kind of power."

"I'll be all right."

"And that disk, it's a wide one, I got to dodge the doggone telephone poles when I move down the road, you can't hardly believe it. Equipment's a lot bigger these days, Arthur, than you might remember."

"I'll be all right, I said."

"Keep it in fourth, that way you can move right along. You want to be sure to overlap yourself. A lot of fellas don't bother, but I'm kind of particular. You may remember that about me, that I'm particular. Everybody says so. Now, you gonna be all right?"

I didn't even bother to answer, climbing past the duals to the cab. There were plenty of years I'd spent a lot more time on a tractor than I did anywhere else, but I could already tell that none of that counted. Gerry Maars was the only one who knew anything. After all, he was particular. I was just settling behind the wheel when the Krueger boy finally showed up, a pimply little hood in a denim jacket, driving a Trans Am he'd still be paying for when he retired. Gerry went over to talk to him, and when he came back the boy tagged along behind, a cigarette in one hand and a Pepsi in the other.

"Okay, Arthur, I want you to start on that field west of the ditch. Better get some fuel before you get started. You sure you're okay? You got to watch that disk, now, they're wider these days. You want me to come along with you for a round, just while you get the feel?"

Maybe I was oversensitive some, but I'd had my own dad once, and didn't much care to sit on Gerry Maars' knee while he showed me how to drive a tractor. The cab had a radio and I turned it on, hoping to drown out whatever else he might think of to yell at me.

He did yell up again, but at least he was already backing away, and I let out the clutch to swing away. The 4586 swivels in the middle to turn, but otherwise it was familiar enough; there's a secure pull and rattle to diesel that a person never really forgets. The Krueger boy had started back to the shed, with Gerry already halfway down the lane in his pickup. And that's when my right bank of disks swung head on into that damn Texaco fuel pump of his, snapping it off like a weed.

There's a sick sound of metal on metal that comes way too late to be of any help—this time long after I already had it ruined, crushed into the gravel under my blades. The Krueger boy and I watched Gerry come to a stop on the road. I turned off the radio as he drove back up the lane. He pulled around to where his antique fuel pump used to be. Then he came up alongside the cab. He pointed back to where I still had what was left of the metal housing wrapped around my disk.

"Lift 'em. Come on, lift 'em. No, the other one. The one on your left. On your left, I said. On the left! That one. Now lift it!"

My right hand offended me, shaking as I grabbed for the levers. My knees wobbled too, enough so that one foot slipped off the clutch and the tractor jerked forward, finally pulling itself free of the housing by grinding it the rest of the way into the ground. This time what the disk caught was the bumper of Gerry's pickup, swinging it around until he was looking out past an open-mouthed Billy Krueger to the shed.

As he climbed out of the truck and over the disk bank, I stayed in the cab, vaguely wishing that life could be different. Nothing grand, just that the Krueger boy hadn't been there. Or maybe that I hadn't left my car clear out by the road, where I'd have to walk all that way to get it. It's kind of pathetic, but I found myself hoping that Kendra wouldn't hear of it either, not right away. It was the last thing I wanted to do, but when I saw Gerry come up to stand below me, I opened the door.

"Damn it, Arthur, I told you them things were wide."

I looked him in the face, I couldn't very well not do that. He looked down at his crushed Texaco pump housing and back at me. I braced myself, but the next thing he did was turn to the Krueger boy.

"What the hell you lookin' at, Billy, didn't I tell you to go get seed? You see any goddamn seed around here? You see any? Where's the goddamn seed?"

He'd caught the boy by surprise, and Billy shook his head, still hypnotized by the wreckage.

"Seed don't grow in the shed, damn it, or out here in the lot, I keep telling you that. It don't grow out on the county roads, or in at the Streamliner. I need it out by the planter."

Billy didn't even have a chance to get away before Gerry'd turned to me.

"Now, Arthur, there's another fuel tank over between them bins. I didn't send you over there in the first place because it's a little on the tight side, and I don't personally like to use it. You're young, though, and like a challenge. Come on down to the field when you get finished. If Billy gets that seed out to us, we'll get some work done today after all."

Down below me Gerry kicked aside the pump housing and climbed into his pickup. He worked it until he was free of the wreckage, swung out around the disk, and without a backward glance drove away.

TEN

He hadn't been kidding about that second fuel tank; it was a tight squeeze between the bins to get up close. Eventually I'd gotten the four-wheel drive maneuvered around, filled up, and took off down the road to catch him. I started off a good fifteen acres ahead, but that's not much of a margin when he wanted the ground worked twice. To top it off, before an hour had gone by, I felt myself losing the square. By the time I got to the far side of the field, I was spending most of my time in the corner, trying to finish up.

Gerry was bearing down on me by then, planting his eight rows at a pass like he was tracing with a ruler. While he finished off the end rows, I moved across the road. It was after six-thirty and getting dark by the time he pulled in behind me, shut down his own tractor, and told me to go on home. We left everything in the field, which was fine with me. As long as I didn't have to see that damn gas tank, I could almost forget it had ever been there.

I went out early the next day, figuring to get a little ways ahead. When I pulled in along the ditch, I found that a good thirty acres had already been worked. A tractor's not a race car, and in fourth gear a person averages right at six miles an hour. It took a minute to do the figures, but before long I realized that somebody'd put in another four or five hours the night before. It had to have been Gerry, who wheeled in behind me in his pickup about ten minutes later.

"My goodness, this is a pretty day. Ain't this a pretty day? Oh, this is a corn-planting day. Come on, Arthur, we got work to do."

With the headstart at least I stayed ahead, even gaining a little ground through the morning. Once Billy Krueger got there to run seed and fertilizer, Gerry started closing on me some, but I kept a safe distance between us. About four he sent the Krueger boy away. I couldn't figure we'd be quitting quite yet, and we weren't. Billy came back with cheeseburgers from the cafe in Keona. He dropped mine off when I made my turn, and I ate them on the long pass south through the field.

By seven-thirty the sun was just settling below the horizon, red-orange from the dust that farmers had been kicking up that day all the way out to the Rockies. When I finished west of the road, I pulled up along the end rows, ready to shut it down. Instead Gerry kept the Krueger boy and had me go two miles north to sixty acres he had below the railroad. He came in behind me a couple of hours later. It was a tricky, triangle-shaped field, but even at midnight my squares still felt true. A half hour later I wasn't sure whether to trust my eyes or not, when I saw Gerry flashing his lights to signal me, and knew we were finally done for the day.

Times had changed. I remember days when my dad would come in from planting late, back when Byron and I were boys. We thought it so far out of the ordinary, imagine, all of us eating supper at ten o'clock at night! Apparently International Harvester had built their headlights to go a little later than that, and I soon found out that there were very few of the nighttime hours that Gerry didn't end up using. The third day we went past midnight again, the day after that until almost one. We finished Skidmore's a little after two the night of the fifth day. The sixth and seventh days, when the Krueger boy didn't come in, we finally realized he'd quit.

I imagine Gerry'd thought he'd run me off too, eventually, but Byron and I had been raised poor, not lazy. Once I got his schedule figured, I'd always be out there a good hour before he was, and I never came calling to leave. On breakdowns I was a pretty good hand to have, too, once I got over my surprise that they could even happen to the great Gerry Maars. All I had to get back was my patience. Sometimes a bearing would break in the most awkward place imaginable, and we'd lay out there half the afternoon, trying to work the damn thing loose. Finally Gerry'd climb up into the cab to get his glasses, and I'd run into Midway before they closed. I'd leave him there tinkering and tapping, pounding, cussing it, and nine times out of ten, by the time I got back, he had it off. We'd get the thing put back together, dig the dust out of our eyes, and make up lost time until dawn.

You've got to figure breakdowns are part of the business, especially when you're bouncing over all that ground. What I couldn't figure, not with the acreage he was carrying, were all the distractions that seemed to come with being important. It wasn't enough that he had breakfast in town; I'd watch from my tractor as a steady stream of visitors made their way out to the field. It didn't matter where we were; one of the other council members, somebody from the tax assessor's office, the deputy auditor—any one of them might be waving to him at the end of the field. Every second morning or so Irene Bremer would have something that demanded his attention too. If she missed him at home, she'd call out to the elevator. Everybody at the elevator knew her too, but they were too busy playing grab-ass to look in on her themselves, so the fertilizer truck driver would bring the message out to Gerry. Many were the days when I'd see his tractor idling at one end of the field, and the pickup truck gone. He'd be back a couple hours later, all worked up about the time he'd lost, and in more of a hurry than ever.

That meant I got a chance to get a little ways ahead, and whenever I did, I'd come back and help him pull seed. It was easy enough to understand why the Krueger boy quit: I could still remember how it felt, standing out there all sweaty and covered with dirt while the other kids drove by on their way to town. In my case I'd already *been* to town, so nighttime out in the wide empty fields of spring suited me fine. We finally came into Smiley's the third week I was there.

As far as property goes, the Smiley acreage was nothing special, poorly drained and weedy like a lot of that ground below the tracks. To my family, though, it had been about all there was to our little farm. That land we rented from Smiley was where we raised alfalfa and wheat, drove our hogs over in December to glean the corn. It was where Byron and I had kept our heads down for what seemed years at a time, eating dust all spring on the tractor and freezing half to death out with the cornpicker in the fall.

Now, with an operation like Gerry's, things went a hell of a lot easier. The fences were gone, which made for better maneuvering. We had equipment that was big enough to do the job. After a dozen cans of Freon we'd even got the air-conditioning fixed in the big four-wheel drive, so the cab was cool under all that glass. There was a high spot that I still remembered north of the ditch bank—going west on that big tractor, I could see the roof of Byron's ranch house, and beyond it the battered roof of the barn.

I don't know what mission of mercy Gerry was off on while I disked that first morning at Smiley's, but when he got back about two o'clock, he'd brought hamburgers with him. We sat back on the tailgate to eat, under sunshine and a gentle May breeze. Eventually I gathered up my trash, and when I went over to check my banks, Gerry followed.

"You know, Arthur," he said, "I remember your dad out here. I guess you probably do too."

I told him I remembered all of us, we'd spent a lot of time in that field.

"Yeah, I sure do remember your dad. Back when I was first starting out, I remember one time seeing him. It was in the spring like this, over at the Bremer place, the first year I was here. One morning I was getting my planter rigged up, and your dad came wheeling up into the field. He had that old white Dodge pickup, maybe you remember. Anyway, he came charging over like an old bull. Hell, your dad *was* a bull back then, built like a tree stump. And he said, 'Just what are you getting ready to do there, Mr. Maars?'"

Gerry laughed, remembering.

"I was a smart aleck back then, full of sass. So I come back and say, 'I don't guess maybe you've ever seen one of these before, Hurd. It's a corn planter. I'm fixing to plant myself some corn.'

"He wasn't much of a kidder, your dad. A hell of a good man, but kind of grim."

"'The hell you are,' he said.

"'The hell I ain't,' I said. Oh, I was a hothead back then. See, he was an established member of the community and all, and there I was just a young squirt, about your age. So he thought he'd just tell me how things were gonna be.

"'The hell you are,' he said again. 'The hell I ain't.' We went round and round. And it turned out it was the corn bores, see, they didn't want nobody planting until the twentieth of May. That way you broke the cycle. Ain't that something? They had it all figured out. You wait until after the twentieth. And now the whole damn county is laughing at us when they drive by and see us still on corn. Ray Stewart, Lindell, they're all proud of themselves 'cause they're damn near finished. Back then they'd just be getting started!"

"So what'd you do?"

"Do when?"

"Back then, how'd it end up? What'd you end up doing?"

"It ended up I didn't plant, I guess, I can't remember for sure. I must have had to wait, you know, that's just the way it was. You had to break the cycle. 'Course, I was glad when them chemicals came along, we all were, it made things a little easier. I can't hardly see us waiting around all spring anymore, with the kind of acreage we got now."

Gerry wasn't one to wait around when lunch was over either, but there at Smiley's I felt him still behind me while I chimed my way along the disk blades, making sure they were tight. I climbed up to throw the hammer behind the seat, and leaned out to say so long. Gerry still hadn't moved from in front of my bank. I didn't guess he would want me to disk him under with the weeds, so I climbed back down.

"See," he said, "people acted together back then. They were more of a community. That's the way life was."

"It was different back then, that's for sure."

"That's exactly right. You got what I'm saying. Things were different. You're following me."

I told him I thought I was.

"See, Arthur, I know you are. But you tell that same story to Shawn, or Billy Krueger, and they just look at you like you're speaking Chinese. They just want to drink beer and smoke that pot all night, and then come out and hot-rod around on the tractors. They don't see that people put their whole lives into these places, working things out. They don't see that."

"Well," I said, "we ain't gonna work nothing out standing around here."

Whatever it was he was driving at, Gerry still wasn't satisfied. He stood up next to me in that empty field at Smiley's, rubbing his big knuckles against his forearm as he looked out over the prairie.

"Arthur, I didn't take this place away from your dad. You know that, don't you? You know I wouldn't do that?"

"It doesn't matter," I said.

"It does to me. Gene Honnager was the one who came running down here one year when money was cheap, rented this place right out from under him. That's what happened. I know that made it hard on Hurd. I know it did. But a lot of people don't give a damn anymore. Greed drives the engine."

I couldn't help it, I laughed.

Gerry managed to look hurt. "That's the way it was, Arthur. And even then Gene couldn't work it worth a damn, he didn't have the patience. He just run on to where the money came easier. When Gene let it go, old Smiley's widow called me up, begging me to take it off her hands. So I did. That's why we're here. Your dad was already sick by then."

"It sure doesn't matter now."

"It does to me, I said, damn it, I ain't no Gene Honnager. That ain't the way I do my business. There was a time here in Haskell County when we wouldn't even have allowed what Gene done. Somebody would have kicked his ass for him. People acted together back then."

I could have told him it didn't matter again, but Gerry was back looking out over the prairie. I couldn't think of anything more foolish anyway, than for us to be standing out there in a half-planted field while he apologized for something he hadn't done. For taking on land somebody else once had rented. In modern times it didn't make much sense, and Gerry must have realized it too, about then, because he went over and climbed into his cab. He pulled past the end rows, dropped his marker, and took off to the east, sowing corn. That was the last I saw of him until after midnight. I was on my last pass back along the fence when I saw his headlights blinking, and knew that we were at the end of another day.

ELEVEN

I'd seen Kendra only a time or two that spring; most often their house sat just like all the other new ones out in the countryside, closed up to the world. One day, on the way over to Bremer's on the tractor, I was surprised to see that their garage door was open, the shiny new Toyota parked inside.

I knew she'd been spending a lot of time at her dad's—after a lifetime sucking sawdust at the lumberyard, the old man's lungs had given out, and he needed her help. On a pretty June morning, though, she was mowing the lawn, perched on a garden John Deere. She wore a light blue sunsuit with a little skirt attached, and I enjoyed watching her handle the small tractor with ease, long arms whipping the wheel around the turns. She smiled when she saw me, waving, so I pulled over to the side of the road. When I'd hopped off and come up into the yard, I saw Celeste in her playpen beside the house. That way Kendy could keep an eye on her, which is what we both did when she'd pulled up next to me and cut the engine.

"We thought maybe Gerry'd adopted you or something. We never see you around anymore."

"Well, you've got a busy family too. Everybody's busy this time of year."

"I saw you when you went by in the pickup awhile ago. You always look so serious going down the road."

"I guess I'm a serious kind of guy," I told her, and she laughed.

There was some catching up to do, about how school had come to an end and what news summer had brought. It wasn't anything out of the ordinary: Joey was putting in his hours at Bible school, and Byron was at a conference on controlling school climate. Her dad was back in the hospital again. When she asked about Gerry, I said he was doing fine.

Kendra felt comfortable as long as she was talking, and so did I, because it let me watch her a minute, there at the side of their drive-way. Her bare shoulders had gone pinkish from the sun; the blouse she'd brought out to protect them still hung from the back of the mower seat behind her. Her little smile was slow, and the soft skin around her eyes had a light purplish-rose color that I knew came from fatigue. A family makes demands. She'd nursed my dad all those years, and now with her own father wasting away—maybe I just felt sorry for her. Tiredness, if truth be told, made her seem even prettier to me, and that much easier to talk to, more like somebody real. That and the way she stood next to me in her little sunsuit and sandals, a thin line of moisture on her lip, tired eyes keeping track of her baby across the lawn.

Except for Gerry spraying a half mile to the south, we could have been the only people left in the county. All around us was a vast apron of green, a couple of square miles of it that Gerry and I'd put in ourselves. I liked the smell of grass drying beside us in the sunshine, the sound of Celeste singing to herself over in the shade. Behind me Gerry's tractor sat peacefully idling at the side of the road.

I'm not sure what awful damage it would have done for the two of us to have kept standing like that, another minute or even more, with me just liking her, but Kendra was already reaching for her blouse. She quickly wrapped it around those warm, bare shoulders, moved onto the driveway to stand between me and her house.

The rush of words and laughter that she poured out were still protective, I guess—with luck they would take care of everything. Keep me at bay, Byron's humble empire safe, her dad's lungs from filling quite as fast. With her good-byes and good wishes she would have herded me across the lawn like a calf, right up to the edge of the asphalt, but I saved her the trouble. I went back to the tractor, climbed up to put it in gear, and lumbered away down the road.

TWELVE

I still called up north now and then, but what word there was on the boats wasn't good—they'd taken two more ore carriers off the lake in June. The spraying and cultivating were finished, but even after the equipment was all put away and there was nothing to do but wait for

September, Gerry still came by for me every day.

"Doggone that Jim Fregosi," he complained, jumping from the pickup. "What do you think of that guy? Does he have a brain in his head? What would you do in that situation?"

I had to have been a disappointment to him, because it was usually only after he'd drawn out the play for me on the grass that I even knew it was baseball he was talking about, and not one of the county employees.

"Why would you have him bunt?" he demanded, shaking my arm. "He's the best doggone hitter in the league. How can you win a pennant like that?"

Gerry had been an athlete of sorts himself was what people said, and it made sense—he had an athlete's sort of confidence. He was Indiana's Outstanding Young Farmer the year Byron graduated, and won a seat on the county council the second time he ran. He'd gotten divorced soon after they moved into town.

The Bremer place had been where he'd lived with his first wife and his girls, out in the country like the rest of us. Irene Bremer had lived out there herself as a bride, but long ago had moved to nearby Keona. One week in late July we spent a week there, putting a new roof on her house. A widow a dozen years over by then, Irene was the nervous type to begin with, and the pounding made her worse. She tried to ignore me as much as possible, yelling up for Gerry even when I was right beside her on the ground.

Afternoons she'd have us down into her musty kitchen for lemonade and cookies. "She treats me just like one of her own boys," Gerry always said, and sitting around the table you could almost imagine it, if the way she treated her own boys was kind of peevishly, never quite happy with what they'd done. One of them had been killed in the Second World War, and the other had dropped dead of a heart attack just a couple of years before.

At least they might have been around when she could still remember to put sugar in the lemonade, but memory wasn't her only failing. I was surprised to see she was almost blind, running her fingers across the counter as she tried to locate fugitive crumbs or puddles of water.

Gerry didn't hurry back to work, and the sound of his voice and feel of his bulk in the little kitchen seemed to calm her. We'd sit down there for most of an hour every afternoon, cooling our heels while she would talk and worry, and he would sympathize.

One of the bonuses of being inside at Irene's was the chance to hear about her grandson Jack. From the pictures she brought out, he seemed a little young to be an investment counselor, but that's what he was, up in Chicago. Besides the photos there was a scrapbook of clippings she'd been keeping, so we picked out Jack's name among the graduates and honorees, marveled at the internships and promotions he'd managed to earn. Praising the heirs is just another cost of doing business, but Gerry seemed honestly impressed.

"I just can't hardly stand it," he told me as we climbed back up the ladder, "that you ain't ever had a chance to meet him. It's a privilege, is what it is. It's an honor. He ain't like us, Arthur, rolling around in the dirt every day. Back when he was just a little shaver he used to come out here and ride with me on that old four-row combine I had. Oh, he was a smart one even then."

Jack wasn't any older than I was, but good-looking in the relaxed, easy way that Gerry's daughters had always favored. Gaylene was only a year younger than my brother, and Perri was my grade in school, but neither Byron or I had ever been in the carloads of young people Gerry drove up to see ball games in Chicago, had been among the number dropping by for pizza and sodas on a Saturday night. Still, on those long summer days after we finished Irene's roof, it was me that Gerry'd ended up with, cleaning out culverts and mowing the side ditches, or just driving the county roads by the hour, while we studied the crops.

More often than not there'd be something he wanted to show me, like his dryer setup, or a new field entrance he'd put in the spring before. One muggy morning in late August we pushed back along the Bremer ditch bank to where he'd rigged up a kind of outdoor sump pump in one corner of the field. I'd seen it in the spring when we were cultivating, but hadn't really known what it was.

"Of course, you probably ain't gonna be all that excited by some old thing like this," he'd always say, but the truth was it did interest me some. I liked gadgets, and the little pump he'd designed seemed like a good one. We played with it for a while, Gerry triggering the float for me so I could see how it worked. He swiped at the gnats that swarmed in around us.

"You know, Arthur, the county agent told me that this here pump wouldn't even last a season, and that was damn near thirty years ago. He stood right out here where you're standing, and told me. By the next spring, he was even bringing the 4-H kids out to see it. It got written up in a lot of the farm papers, maybe you seen it over at your dad's."

I told him I guessed I'd missed it.

"It was there. I had a copy somewhere that I'd show you, but it got lost in the divorce. I've had people out here from France, Turkey, South America——Purdue used to bring them by. I had a fella from Brazil spend one night at the house with Kathryn and me just after we were married, as nice a guy as you'd want to meet. Makes you kinda proud to think you're helping somebody somewhere, that people are gonna benefit from things you've done."

When we'd roasted awhile, I followed him over to the ditch bank. That was the only high ground available, and from it we could see out across the whole hundred and twenty acres, the old Bremer house like a ghost just beyond.

"When I first came to this county, I didn't have nothing. Nothing at all. Just my name, plus a wife and two little girls that I needed to support. We had Perri in Delfina just after we come here, so I guess she's a Comet through and through. Anyway, old Harold Bremer agreed to rent this place to me, and it was a godsend, is what it was. Just a godsend. I know a lot of people think she's a bother, but that's why Irene won't never want for nothing as long as I'm alive. Her husband let me have this place when nobody else would even give me the time of day, and that's something I ain't ever gonna forget."

Gerry laughed. "I don't reckon you knew Harold. He was kind of a cultured sort of guy, taught school around here for years. But for all that learning, old Harold never could get the secret of how to work this ground. Raccoons, deer, muskrats all over—it was like a doggone wilderness out here. Now look at it. Look at all that corn."

I looked at the corn. Next to me Gerry had his hands in his pockets, big arms loose at his sides.

"Everybody laughed at me when I rented this out. Don't make no loans south of the Big Four Railroad, that's what they always said. I'll bet your own dad came in to the supper table the night he heard, told you boys there was a crazy man loose in the county. But see, where everybody else saw a damned old swamp, I could see corn growing on it. I didn't care what they said.

"The first thing I done was to take a soil sample down to Purdue. I drove it down to Lafayette myself, in that old Buick I used to have. It lacked nitrogen, of course, but a blind man could have told you that. Potash was what it really needed. See, muck don't have minerals, but old Harold was a tight son of a bitch, and wouldn't even go halves. I had to buy it myself. That was the biggest order Hostetler'd ever had. I had his trucks going back and forth all day long into town, just getting me some fertility back out here into the soil."

In front of us as far as you could see was what Gerry must have imagined, a fine stand of good hybrid field corn, twenty-five thousand plants to the acre, waving in the breeze. Since he was paying me five dollars an hour to see it, I figured he'd be watching to make sure I did. But Gerry was lost in his own world, probably way back to when he was twenty-five years old again, with his first wife and those two little girls. All of them long gone from Haskell County by then, but he was nodding as he looked out over the field.

"So I was lucky, the good Lord let me stay on here to make a home. I even got to end up serving the people of this county, and that's all a man could have asked. But back then everybody couldn't wait to tell me the news. Ain't it funny how people are sometimes? Ain't it funny how they are? They all had to tell me, every last one of them. They all said a fella couldn't raise an umbrella out here, but there's the goddamn proof right in front of you. I kept on it, got it drained right, and built this soil back to life. It took me a few years, but I got it to yield, by God. It yielded, Arthur, it yielded good."

THIRTEEN

Most of the other big farmers got going on harvest that fall about the same time we did. That didn't include Charlie Sellars for some reason, but I couldn't really figure his methods. He'd moved out his hogs in early August; one day when I was home I helped him hose down the pens for the next batch, but that second set he didn't keep more than a month. I came back one afternoon in mid-September to find them gone. It was hard to believe he'd made any money that way, but then again, Charlie had ended up the big operator, not me.

There're always a lot of little breakdowns and adjustments the first days of harvest, but gradually Gerry and I hit our pace. I still liked the ride into town, especially after an early October freeze hit hard one night and the leaves began to turn in earnest. It was something of a satisfaction, it turned out, to see the same crop we'd laid down in May going to the elevator in the fall. Gerry didn't even have to brag on himself anymore, I could see for myself. People like my dad had just never known how many bushels there really were in an acre of ground, that was their problem.

Gerry's second wife, Kathryn, had been out once in a while during the spring to help us, but I hadn't seen her much since then. I'd already known her — she'd been teaching at the high school in Delfina forever, or at least long enough to have had Byron in English once and me twice. She'd been gray-haired as long as I remembered, with the same cool eyes I'd always felt uncomfortable under back in school. In a sweatshirt and jeans, out in a muddy field pulling a wagon full of seed, she'd seemed a lot less formidable.

One night while Gerry was finishing by the ditch up at Foxie's, I started moving what I could to a forty-acre field a couple of miles west. I'd towed the mobile gas tank down and was just coming back in Gerry's pickup when I saw Kathryn in the Fleetwood coming toward me. We met on a little bridge down in one of the dips, and she motioned for me to roll down the window.

"I was just by where you're combining. Looks like you're almost finished up here."

"We're getting there," I told her.

"Well, tell Gerry to be home by ten tonight. I've got a roast in the oven."

"I think he wants to come on west here if he can. He was thinking it might rain."

She shook her head. "Uh-uh. There's no rain within five hundred miles of here. Tell him to come on home. You come, too." I hesitated, but she still had a schoolteacher's authority. "You come, too. Tell him ten o'clock, when he comes around."

I was surprised that Gerry didn't protest any; he just nodded and told me okay. The day we'd been having had put him in good spirits, and we lacked just those forty acres of being done up north. It was only nine by the time he'd finished where he was at, so we moved the combine and got the trucks into Foxie's old dairy barn. I even had time to run by the house for a quick shower, on my way over to Gerry's.

I'd been by their place in Forest Meadows a time or two by then, to drop off elevator tickets, or pick up a check for town. I came up the driveway past the pickup and Fleetwood, to the little Subaru that Kathryn drove to school. They were parked out in the driveway because the garage was full—Gerry had Byron's humble riches writ large. Two riding lawnmowers and a rototiller were jammed in next to a bass boat, backed at an angle so it'd fit. There were volleyball poles set in concrete-filled tires, a dining table piled high with boxes and lawn chairs, while along one wall were stacked what had to have been a hundred cases of soda that Gerry'd bought to help out a cheerleaders' fund-raiser a half-dozen years before. I squeezed between the Subaru and the evergreens, and wound up the long front sidewalk to the door.

The house hadn't been Kathryn's originally—it had been built with an entirely different woman in mind. She'd moved into it, though, when the time came, and made it her own. When she let me in, I came through the entryway into their wide, modern living room. Lamps turned down low put a soft cast to things, and there was music from the easy-listening station out of Marion playing soft on the stereo. Two porcelain squirrels perched on a bookcase, with a clear glass bluebird of happiness nesting under a lamp. A thick half-read book lay on the end table next to the sofa.

I liked Kathryn, but that still didn't mean I was completely used to her yet. I was glad to come up on Gerry out in the kitchen. He'd just gotten out of the shower himself, and was barefoot in a white T-shirt and old green work pants. He had a butter knife in his hand and was tinkering with the thermostat in the freezing compartment of their refrigerator.

"Doggone ice-maker," he said, "darn thing never has worked right. It gets froze up in there and won't fill." Watching over his shoulder while he worked at something was familiar enough to me, and that's what I did while I tried to stay out of Kathryn's way. It was easy to forget that she'd never raised up a family of her own when you saw her in the kitchen. She didn't waste a move, sliding pans across the stove, filling up serving bowls that she carried over to the table. She called to Gerry two or three times just to let the icebox go, and finally he did.

"Oh, my goodness, we picked some corn today," he said as we sat down at the table. "Fifty acres at least, don't you reckon? When I was a boy, a good man, a darn good one, would have picked and shucked an acre. One doggone acre. And we done fifty. You all just don't know how relieved I am to have that Fox farm about finished. Arthur, what are you waiting on? Come on, help yourself."

Gerry was still pink from his shower, and what was left of his gray hair stood fluffed out like feathers along the sides of his head. He leaned into his food with enthusiasm, his fork in his fist.

"My goodness, this is good pork. You get enough of that, Arthur? Get yourself another piece there. And these pickles come out of our garden. Pass him some of those pickles, honey. They are just out of this world. I'd put your pickles up against any doggone pickles in the world, I don't care whose they are."

It was a good pork roast, they were good potatoes, good biscuits, and the pickles were every bit as good as Gerry said. He proceeded down the line, complimenting each one in turn. I guess Kathryn already knew they were good; she watched us with what seemed to be curiosity, almost as if she was wondering who the heck these two men were that had dropped in at her kitchen table. When we were done she brought out a persimmon pie, and then leaned forward on her elbows, arms folded in front of her, to watch us eat.

"Oh, this is good pie. This is the best pie in the whole world. Have another piece, Arthur. You'll never taste any pie as good as this, I don't care if you sail the seven seas."

"You don't need another piece," she told him. "You keep eating pie like that, you won't be able to climb up to your combine."

Gerry just laughed. "Well, that's a chance I'll have to take. If I get too fat, maybe Arthur will run it for me, while I roll along behind. Pie this good don't come along that often even in this lifetime, no telling about the next."

When it became clear she wasn't going to dent his enthusiasm any, she turned to me.

"So, Arthur," she asked, "no word on your boat? That seems like a pretty undependable profession you're in, with long layoffs like that."

I agreed that it was.

"Sounds kind of like farming, don't it, honey," Gerry said. "You know, it's sad when a fella gets yields like we do, and then have prices so darn low. You get the tickets back from the elevator, and you just want to put your head down and bawl."

Kathryn still had me in her sights, and I began to feel uncomfortable. Teachers in a small town, especially ones like her who had been around forever, somehow assume they've bought into you for life. Even a poor investment like me was expected to make an accounting of himself on demand.

"You know, there's something I've been wondering about, that I didn't get a chance to ask you before. Gerry said he's never asked you about it either, which strikes me as strange."

"My gosh, that was good." Gerry patted his stomach. "That's awful nice to come home to, especially after a day like we just put in. I appreciate you thinking of us. Oh, we been working hard, Arthur and me. I don't know what I would have done without him."

Kathryn didn't get swayed too easily. She leaned forward again, watching me. "You probably know what I've been wondering."

"No," I told her truthfully, "I don't."

"What I was wondering, Arthur, is this. It's a question of why a young man would come home, pack up his sick father out of a place where they were trying to take care of him, and run halfway across the country, scaring his poor family to death. Maybe you can shed some light on that for me."

"Now, honey, maybe there's some things Arthur don't want to talk about."

"Well, why on earth not? Is that right, Arthur? Is this something you'd rather not talk about?"

I could have been fourteen all over again, called up to the front of the class. I hadn't had the right answers then, and there at the dinner table, I still didn't. I followed the same strategy, not really committing myself.

"It just seemed," I told her, "like the thing to do."

"The thing to do," she said, still watching me. "That's interesting. I wonder if Byron and Kendra thought that. It's hard to think that they did."

Gerry stood up. "Well, you two can sit around the table all evening chewing the fat if you want to, but I'm gonna sit back and relax. Me and Arthur been at it hard today, honey, pushing the limit. Kind of like that one-legged man in the ass-kicking contest, we been hopping! Come on, Arthur, let's grab them plates and get them over to the dishwasher."

I was more than ready to go on home by then, but Gerry dragged me into the living room with him, where he turned on the TV. He claimed the sofa for himself, so I sat down in the recliner. Kathryn came in long enough to pick up a stack of compositions she'd left behind, then disappeared into the back of the house.

Their TV screen was the size of a washing machine, and on it Johnny Carson was just starting his monologue. Gerry'd been cooped up by himself in the cab too much that day, so while we watched it he recapped some of the shows he'd happened to see over the years. It was almost midnight, but he was all wound up, still happy from the big day we'd had, standing to act out the different parts. I kind of hated to miss the current show, and was straining to hear it too, when I noticed I wasn't having to strain quite so hard. I looked over and saw that Gerry was laid out on the couch, softly snoring.

While I watched the rest of the Carson show, he rolled around until he lay curled up in a ball, his bald head resting on one arm. His breathing was deep and regular beside me. He'd put the best of everything in that place, so the room almost seemed to be breathing too, adjusting itself before I could even start to feel hot or cold. The house was quiet, it smelled good, the lights were down low. This was where the golden road led to. The payoff, I guess, for doing things right.

Up on top of the cabinet, and spread along the mantle above the fireplace, were pictures of Gerry's girls, of Kathryn's nieces and nephews, all of them looking happy and alert. Perri was on top of a mountain somewhere, with a smaller woman about her age at her elbow. She had high-tech sunglasses pushed high on her forehead, and there were Japanese people scattered in the background; in another shot she was posed outside a hospital in her doctor's smock, a stethoscope hanging loose in her hand. Gaylene showcased her husband and boys, standing with them on the back deck of their Seattle home.

They'd made it out of Delfina into greener pastures, nobody could fault them for that. All the children in the pictures looked happy, too, unafraid, smiling as they gathered around Christmas trees and coffee tables in living rooms every bit as nice as Gerry's. Smooth teeth and confidence, safety from want, I couldn't think of any reason why they, or Jack, or anybody else shouldn't have life a little easier starting out, and then make successes of themselves later on. That was the way of the world, it made room for energy and drive.

The next thing I knew the sun was coming in through the sliding glass doors that led out to the swimming pool. Gerry was standing over me in his town clothes, already in a hurry.

"Come on, time's a-wasting. We got corn to pick today. Ride into the restaurant with me and I'll buy you some breakfast."

I stood up quickly, blinking, embarrassed at being asleep in the chair. While I turned around, still trying to get my bearings, Gerry tossed me my jacket. There was no sign of Kathryn as we went through the kitchen and out into the frosty morning, and rode the big Fleetwood into town.

FOURTEEN

The stroke that hit my dad had come one afternoon just before Christmas, when he was out back feeding his steers. There's not a penny to be made on cattle anymore, wasn't then either, but that wouldn't have mattered to somebody as stubborn as he was. It was lucky, as it turned out, that it hadn't been hogs. They'll eat anything, and there've been more than a few heart attacks out that way where there's been nothing left to bury but a pair of shoes. Byron was the one who found him, a couple of hours later.

Since Joey was just a toddler, Byron and Kendra had their hands full, and my dad ended up in the new rest home at Wabash. I couldn't see how I'd be of any help, so even after the season was over, I didn't rush right down. Instead I spent the last week of January trying to keep the attention of a finance professor's teenage daughter up in Ann Arbor. We'd met in Traverse City the summer before, and she was willing to slum a little, going out with me. She went off with her parents to some island in the Caribbean, the first part of February, and finally I headed home.

Strokes and rest homes both sound gentle enough, especially when you're strolling along in your early twenties. Byron had given up calling me by then, and still I wasn't in any hurry, just drove my car down to Wabash when I got good and ready, walked up to the nurses' station and asked for his room. My dad had always been a big man, meaner than gunpowder. When I came in I barely recognized the old man who sat tied back in a wheelchair by the bed. Frail and trembling, he leaned forward with his hands in his lap, staring at the wall.

Byron'd said that in the three months my dad had been there, his roommates had been a black man named White, a white man named

Green, and another old guy who'd had a seizure one night, threw up a few quarts of blood, and died, while my dad watched wordlessly or slept, nobody knew. I wasn't sure whether he recognized me, but he ventured a small smile, which led me to believe he didn't. After that he settled back into his chair, and silence. That left me with his current roommate, a talkative old guy named Shaunnessey.

From then on, it was Shaunnessey who kept me company. I heard several times that he was eighty-seven years old, retired over twenty years already from work in a hardware store. We'd just about forgot all about my dad when he started getting restless, struggling to talk. Shaunnessey pitched in to try to make sense of it, but my dad just grew angrier and louder, thrashing in his chair. A nurse hurried to the rescue with his pills.

I'd seen the old man lift a grain truck transmission into place all by himself, toss hundred-pound feed bags like they were pillows. There was no more private person on the face of the earth, but a few minutes later, calm again, he stood to be undressed like a doll. They walked him to the bathroom, helped him into bed, and soon he was sound asleep, mouth open and head to the side, snoring softly.

That first night I was there had been a Sunday, when all up and down the hall there were visitors shouting out joyously, witnessing to the glories of the TV reception, insisting that everyone looked fine. By the next morning it was back to the regulars again, plus me, who showed up a little before eight. Shaunnessey was glad to see me, and my dad didn't seem to care either way, so I settled in to stay.

It was a little deceiving every morning driving up to that rest home, a low brick building on the south side of the Wabash, that looked as tranquil as a building could be. Most of the time it was tranquil, but two or three times that week, usually in late afternoon with all the visitors gone, there would come an unrest that seemed to gather along the halls. It made me think of a chicken house the way a commotion could move through the building. It was an uneasiness that was most often accompanied by women's voices from down the hall, crying out in confusion and pain.

Shaunnessey nodded knowingly. "It's their sickness, poor things. They can't help it. It's just their sickness."

Sickness or not, it would get my dad started too, complaining as he hit at his shoulders. He had never even sat still for a doctor that I remembered, but with a blood vessel burst he was helpless, shaking his head against the nurses, their injections and little paper cups. An early dinner would appear, and he'd take a few bites. He'd be trembling again, but quiet.

Every night I would leave right after the news, the next morning would be back before breakfast. They say they like to encourage company, but by the fourth morning the nurses seemed a lot less happy to see me. At one point on Wednesday the director came by to walk me down the hall for a chat, hinting that perhaps my dad needed his rest. He'd get plenty of rest in the grave, I told her, and at the rate they were going at Wabash, he'd be there soon enough.

The story they kept up was that the wheelchair was just for convenience, that my dad was just supposed to be at the rest home until he could get around a little better. That didn't seem to be the direction he was going, so I questioned Byron about it when he dropped by the next day. My brother had apparently decided that I'd long ago lost the chance for it to be any of my affair. When I pressed him on it, he just got mad. He said my dad hadn't been improving like they'd hoped, and then clammed up, like only Byron can do.

There was one time during the day when even my dad would brighten, though, and that was when Kendra came by, which she did almost every afternoon. Shaunnessey perked up, too, and so did I, for that matter. She would have been a youngster herself back then, but Kendy played it by the book, remembering who she was there to see. While Joey toddled among walkers and bed pans, she sat up close to my dad, finding occasion to touch his arm, or smooth back his hair with her fingers. I admired that she didn't just come and rush away— she put in her time. Before long they were by with my dad's medication, and he'd be out like a light before she was even gone.

On the last morning that I came in, I played it by the book too. I read the paper until breakfast was over. When Shaunnessey went in to use the bathroom, I nudged shut the door. The clothes in my dad's closet had to have been Byron's work: there were a pair of green polyester pants and a wheat-colored dress shirt, sporty like the old man had never been. When I'd gotten them on him, he looked like a stranger, but that was all right. I gave him a stranger's courtesy as I walked him down the hall, past the inmates in their shuffling walkers, dodging abandoned carts of sheets. I carried in my right hand the spiffy brown fedora with a feather that I'd found on the top shelf of his closet. The door was for emergencies only, which seemed appropriate. We came out onto a sparse scattering of Bermuda grass in back of the building, and just around the corner was my car.

The first thing, of course, was to make our break. There are a half-dozen different highways that run through Wabash, but inevitably, like the poor criminal that I was, I found myself on the one leading back toward Delfina. It was a town that had never offered much to either one of us, really, so I turned south on the bypass. When we crossed the Sycamore Road, my dad didn't bat an eye. His head was cocked to one side, and a thin line of bubbly saliva had settled on his lip. We got out onto new Highway 31, still heading south, down through the low clouds and black muddy fields along the road.

My heater was good, so it was cozy enough in the car. I'd pretty much given up on my dad saying anything that made sense, but that mattered less than a person might think. We neither one of us were big conversationalists. Just past Deer Creek a test presented itself: some poor joker had fooled around and left his corn in the field, which would have brought a comment from the old man if anything could. His hands shaking in his lap and his palsied head nodding, he watched it flash by without comment.

The highway drops down to cross the Wabash at Peru, then climbs back into the open country south of the river. Traffic was light; when we'd come back out of the valley and were passing Bunker Hill, my dad lifted his head to watch the long line of training planes, lined up next to their hangars. A few miles past the air base he turned and said to me, as clear as a bell, "Dinner will be on in a little while."

"Say what?" I asked, taken by surprise, but patience with us boys was never his long suit.

"I said dinner will be on in a little while. Now get in here! Come on, now, get on in!"

His face had gone beet red, and his voice had all the fierce authority of old. It occurred to me that maybe he was hungry. We were almost to Kokomo, so I stopped in at a Scotty's near the Delco plant. I locked all the doors and hurried inside. When I got back, the old man was madder than ever.

"Move it to the side and it'll shift, goddamn it. Move it, you goddamn fool!"

I'd put the sacks down between us, but moved them to the back out of danger. We kept a close eye on each other while I drove back through town to the city park. It seemed like a safe enough place to rest. That time of year there wouldn't be many people around, just in case he got away from me, or decided to pitch a fit.

It had stopped raining, so I parked near Old Ben, the World's Largest Steer. I'd brought along my dad's heavy jacket, and with the fedora on he'd begun to look like a dapper, withered version of his former self, sitting across from me in the pavilion. The old stuffed steer seemed to interest him. It turned out to be a way we could almost relax, sitting together and looking at livestock, our sandwiches in front of us. My dad kept shaking his head like he was trying to clear it. He didn't touch his hamburger, so I ended up eating it myself. By then it was raining again, cold scattered drops that swung in under the pavilion on the wind. I gathered our cups and wrappers, and we left.

I don't know what I'd imagined, highway patrols out to greet us, or roadblocks spread out across the state. Checkpoints in all the major cities, manned by grim-faced troopers, their revolvers and tommy guns drawn. It only slowly dawned on me that nobody even knew we were gone. Except for Shaunnessey, and they weren't used to listening to him. I drove us down through Noblesville and into Indianapolis. We came in past the big homes on Meridian to circle the Soldiers and Sailors Monument in the center of town. Three or four times around was enough for me to track down 31 again, heading off to the south.

Having my dad next to me again was hardly a pleasure, especially since he'd gotten back into his old habit of shouting out orders. It kept me tense anticipating them, bracing so he wouldn't startle me clear over into the oncoming lane. The restlessness that I'd seen in the nursing home came on again about four, and he thrashed in his seat, striking out with both arms. At one time that would have been a danger, but now it was just embarrassing. Half an hour must have passed before he finally wound down. Wiping his mouth and grumbling, he settled back into his seat.

The rainy, wooded hill country of southern Indiana had begun to depress me by then, but something about state lines kept me on the north side of the Ohio, winding along the river in the dark. Finally I did cross into Kentucky, and with no idea of what I was doing or where I would go next, I pulled in at a run-down motel. It feels foolish to even think of it now, but I registered under an assumed name. Not Smith, but something close. They sold candy bars in the office, so I bought one and put it down like you would milk next to a calf, just to see if my dad would take it. He didn't, and eventually fell back on the bed, staring at the ceiling. Even after he was asleep I sat up by myself the longest time, halfheartedly playing with the radio, trying to get something that wasn't Christian through the storm.

The next morning the old man was up with the chickens, five-thirty on the dot, even though the curtains were drawn and the room was dark as a mine. I heard him bumping around over near the bathroom, tangled in his blanket. By six we were out on the road again, plowing our way east through a steady rain.

He'd taken up moaning by then, and I wasn't in particularly good spirits myself. By Carrollton he hadn't shouted at me for a couple of hours, but I could see he was still wound up tight. I'd started to worry again about all that damn medication he'd been taking, but this time in reverse, wondering if maybe he needed something out of those pills to keep his heart beating or veins from closing up. When it dawned on me that he could very likely fall over dead next to me, I began to get nervous. I found myself listening to the radio the way bank robbers do in the movies. Apparently Louisville and Cincinnati had bigger stories to cover, and even those stations were so filled with static that I had to give up. I was left with only my wipers for company as we wound along the muddy Ohio in the rain.

The heart attack never came, but my dad spent most of the morning yawning and coughing, shifting in his seat. Going east carried us out from under the storm, and he blinked in the first rays of sunshine. He was shaking his head again, trying to get it clear. There was a noisy episode west of Maysville, and what little I could get out of it seemed to go way back, to a mule team he must have driven before the war. Only moments after that his voice grew softer, grateful. I couldn't tell, but guessed that he must have seen Kendra there somewhere out the window, keeping pace with us along the side of the road.

But the old fox was coming back to life. He would look over at me with growing recognition, and at one point said that his head hurt, clear as could be. A little while later he smiled. He still didn't know what I'd done with him exactly, but it was something he approved of. I thought about turning on the radio but finally didn't, figuring he needed all the quiet he could muster, now that he was finally getting reacquainted with his wits.

We'd never been close, my dad and me. After Byron'd left home it got worse, because there was absolutely nothing we could think of to say. For some reason I had an open mind, though, that morning. I didn't really expect him to find all his marbles again, but I figured he might come up with enough to thank me even, for getting him away. That was asking a lot, but a person never knew.

I'd come back across the river into Ohio, relieved to be in the north again, when he turned to me and said a single word: "Danny."

"Danny," was all he said, but it chilled me just the same. In all our many years together I'd never heard him mention my brother's name. He squinted, looking at me closely. "Danny?"

"Nope, Dad, Arthur. You know, me. Arthur."

"Danny," he said again.

"Dad, I'm Arthur. Another one of your sons. Arthur. There's just me and Byron now."

You feel like a fool explaining the obvious, but no matter, as far as he was concerned, his long-dead son was back. The six-year-old had slipped in between us there on the front seat, where I was still sane enough to know he didn't belong.

"Danny," my dad said again.

"I'm Arthur, Dad, come on, snap out of it. I'm Arthur. You know that."

"Danny," my dad seemed to say again, but he had a cagey look to him, and the next time I listened closer. "Be Danny," was what he was saying. "You be Danny. Be Danny."

"Be Danny?"

"You're Danny."

I laughed. "Me be Danny."

He was nodding yes. "You be Danny."

"Okay," I said, shrugging, "I'm Danny."

"You be Danny!" he commanded me, angry, his voice rising to a shout. The highway's no wider there in Ohio than it was in Kentucky, and the trucks don't care, they bear in on you hard, throwing mud and spray up over the windshield. I struggled to keep to our lane.

"I told you I'd be Danny, goddamn it," I said, tense from the two days of traffic while he sat blind to the world. "I said I'd be Danny, if that's what you want. Take it or leave it, you suit yourself."

"Danny?" He was timid again, shy to believe it was true.

"Right here. Front and center."

"Danny boy," he said, and smiled.

"Yo."

"Danny honey, Danny, I'm so sorry," is all that he could tell me, and his weak, wary eyes brimmed over. Twenty-five years vanished in a second, and my dad was more present, at that moment, to our pretend Danny, than I had ever known him to be.

"I'm so sorry, son, I'm sorry. Danny, honey, please forgive me."

"I do, Dad," I said, "I forgive you."

"Please, son," he pleaded, "please. Forgive me. I'm so very sorry."

"I forgive you," I told him again, and he broke down and wept.

I thought later it must have been the drugs, with some kind of delayed effect. It could have been the change of scenery from the rest home that set him off. Maybe it was something that professionals should have been there to deal with. I had no idea, but I couldn't have been more surprised if he'd burst into flames. The man who was my father sat beside me while tears rolled in great wet streams through the white stubble of his whiskers, and down onto the front of that ugly wheat-colored shirt.

While I drove I took counsel with myself, considering. After a while I touched his hand.

"It's all right, Dad, what's done is done. That's all in the past."

He shook his head, beyond consoling.

"Dad, you've got to get a grip on yourself. It's all over now, in the past. Come on now, settle down."

He did take my advice and settle down, but tears continued to well up and over, tumbling down his cheeks. As his pride came back, he turned his face away at least, out onto the bare Ohio hillsides. I breathed easier, but for the whole rest of the afternoon I could hear him. He'd let up once in a while, but for the most part he kept at it, now and then shaking his head.

It occurred to me somewhere along the way to get him a cup of water, and when I brought it back to the car, he drank like a camel. I filled it twice more, and got him a large lemonade for the road. In between crying spells he seemed to grow stronger. By that time I was the one wearing out, and whatever headache he'd had earlier passed on to me, settling behind my eyes.

At the motel that night I used my own name, so tired by then that they could have put it up on the marquee for all I cared. For a buck extra there was a TV, so we watched the six o'clock news out of Dayton, lying back on our beds. It was local stuff that didn't concern us any, but my dad followed it intently. About seven I stepped outside and gave a kid on his bike a ten-dollar bill to run get us some sandwiches. They do that kind of thing in the movies too, but the little shit never came back. I had to go out myself then, to a barbecue just down the highway. When I got back my dad had broken his glass on the floor, going in for more water. He was embarrassed about that, but otherwise he'd made out fine. When I'd mopped it up he seemed to feel better. It was a good thing I bought plenty of food, because he ate everything but the wrappers, and that night we both slept like the dead.

The next morning his head was still bothering him, but he sneezed in the sunlight, settling into his place on the front seat just like he'd been born there. As we drove east that morning, his face would cloud and he'd shake his head. Now and then his eyes would fill with tears. During an up time we had an early lunch at a roadside diner near Circleville. His right hand was still stubborn, so I had to cut his meat, but otherwise he was starting to act almost civilized. They'd cut off his coffee in Wabash, and he was glad to have it back. It was hard to tell that it affected him any. He slept curled on the narrow backseat while I wandered back and forth across southern Ohio. It didn't even wake him when I stopped at a gas station on U.S. 40 to look at a map. He was still peacefully sleeping, too, when I turned north toward Columbus and the interstate, and made a beeline for home.

A good son would have done something more, I guess. A good son would have done almost anything other than what I did, which was to run him around for a few days and then just drop him off again like a sack of potatoes. But I wasn't a good son. I wasn't a good brother, a good boyfriend, a good brother-in-law to have. I'd been an adequate sailor, and one day would turn out to be a pretty good hired man.

Byron had a big house rented down in Ridgeport back then. I woke my dad up twenty miles shy of it, so he'd have a chance to get his bearings. His shirt and pants were stained with gravy, but thanks to the miracle of plastics weren't even all that rumpled after three days on the road. At a gas station I got his shirttails tucked in, and brushed him off to where he wasn't too much the worse for the wear. Fields were beginning to catch his interest, finally, now that we were on the way back in. The poor fool was happy as could be to see Kendra, up on the porch of their house.

Byron was predictable, full of threats and recriminations, droning on and on about me "pulling a stunt like that." My sister-in-law ignored me, hustling my dad into the house. I didn't know it then, but the back of his old gray head and that silly green and yellow outfit would be the last I'd ever see of him, dead or alive. I don't know what we'd done with his hat.

Joey, forgotten, stood with me on the porch, watching in through the screen door. Byron came back to snatch him away, and that was the last I'd see of those two either, until the spring I came back to the house.

It's odd to think of, but when my dad had apologized to our pretend Danny, I'd had a sudden thought flash through my mind. I'm kind of a cruel guy, I guess, but when he'd said he was sorry, all I could think of was, You ought to be, you bastard. Most anyone would have felt sorry for him, but then again, most anyone would have known better than to let a six-year-old run in among the machinery, when the men were unloading grain.

A bin draws from the top. A father would know that, while his boy still probably wouldn't. While he was climbing around up on the bins, just being a kid, I guess, my brother Danny had been pulled into the corn. It runs in my mind that it took a while before anybody even noticed. By the time they did, he was gone. Up beyond the clouds, the universe may go on forever, but a life is a lot shorter than that. For some it's just long enough to make mistakes, as my dad found out.

Total it up—he'd managed to lose a wife, a son, a farm. When he finally died a couple of years later, I was asleep in my bunk on an ore boat, in the middle of Lake Michigan. There wasn't much I could do about it when they told me, and by the time we got to Gary, I'd realized there wasn't much I could do about it then, either. While we were unloading the ore, I decided to pass on the funeral. Seven hours later we were churning out of the harbor again, building to full power, bound for the north.

FIFTEEN

From Foxie's we started back south on the harvest, picking fields that had been too wet to go into on our way north. We must have finished a good two-thirds of them before we ran into our first real winter, in mid-November. The freeze made it easier to get across the last couple of muddy bean fields, and Gerry had us going later than ever, trying to finish up.

By that time I'd come down with a hellacious cold. Corn dust bothers me anyway, and bean dust is even worse, so fine that first it cuts out a place for itself in your eyes and throat, and then settles in to stay. With the dampness and then the cold, where eighteen hundred acres of dust had settled was in my lungs. Whether rolling down the road past field after field of stubble or standing beside the truck, I spent twenty minutes out of every hour coughing my fool head off. It was all for nothing, I couldn't seem to dislodge even a grain of it. With my swollen sinuses and plugged-up nose, I felt like I had a head about three times normal size, rolling back and forth on my shoulders.

We finally came up on the last field, there on the Bremer place, the first week of December. Thirty acres were all that separated us from being done, and we pushed hard through a gray afternoon. When the elevator closed I started carrying the beans over to the wet holding bin for the dryer, and we headed on into the night. By about ten-thirty the temperature had really started to drop. My cough had gotten away from me, sounding so bad that every time Gerry came up to dump, he'd tell me to go on home. My lungs and face burned, and my nose ran raw in the wind, so every time I'd say I might, but I ended up staying. I leaned against the truck between my runs, either coughing or trying to catch my breath back afterwards, while what little heat there still was in the ground rushed up around me into the nighttime sky.

We still had air running through the corn bins, so about midnight I drove over in Gerry's pickup to turn off the fans. There was a feeling of finality to climbing up and slamming shut the doors. It was possible that somewhere in the state of Indiana there were still some farmers out working, but Gerry and I had to have been among the last. From the top of the ladder I could see him moving back and forth on the far side of the field. I stood watching until the cold from the rungs worked its way in far enough to numb my fingers, and then I climbed back down.

By the time I got back to the field, Gerry couldn't have lacked more than an hour to finish. He wasn't going anywhere, though; the combine was stopped at the far end of the field. I sat on the cold vinyl of the truck seat, wiping my nose and watching. Before long he had his lights flashing, and I started off across the stubble to the other end.

When I came up on him, Gerry was crouched beside the feeder housing, one hand tugging on the belt.

"Doggone this worthless thing. If it's not one repair, it's two, right when we're just about done. Swing around so I can get some light on this here."

He was kneeling by the master belt, his breath a frosty vapor in my headlights. I could already see that wasn't his only problem. One of his lines must have broken because there was hydraulic fluid every-where, up on the sides of the combine, all over the windshields of the cab. Gerry's coveralls were already smeared with Hi-tran, and he had his bare hands up under his armpits, only then seeming to realize how damn cold it really was. He climbed into the pickup with me to warm up and complain.

"Doggone it to hell, the line to the unload auger broke, and then when I got off to look at that, I seen that my goddamn master belt's slipped. Can you believe the luck? We're about three passes from fin-ishing, and we got this damn thing broke down here in the middle of the field."

He looked at his watch. "I reckon we still got that extra hose back at the shop. It's off that old combine, so we'd have to see if it would fit. I guess a fella would have to squeeze back in under there to reach it."

"I could get in there," I told him.

"Good Lord, Arthur, listen to you. You shouldn't be getting in any-where. You ought to be home, taking care of yourself so you don't die of pneumonia, not out here in this goddamn cold field. Hell, let's just let it go."

"Suit yourself," I said, and he nodded. Gradually starting to thaw out, he slid the zipper on his coveralls down from his neck.

"'Course that hose should be all right. The fittings are the same. It can't be more than a foot longer. Then on the belt, that's not too big a deal, I've had it slip a hundred times before. The main thing's getting under the head."

I watched him study the combine, looming red above us in the glare of the pickup's brights. The backs of his hands were sliced bloody from reaching in and around the frozen stubble, and he rubbed them absently with his fingers.

"They ain't predicting no rain or heavy snow, I guess, and it ain't gonna hail. Of course, the weather's something you just can't tell about. A fella never really knows."

Nobody ever knows anything really, but I felt confident of the odds on one thing: Gerry was going to do his damnedest to get that combine fixed right then and there, whether I stayed or not.

"Yeah, you go on home, Arthur, take care of yourself. It don't matter if we do this tonight. My goodness, look at the time, it's after one already. I'll take you on up to your car."

"How about I ride along to see if we got that hose," I told him, "and then we'll take it from there."

We bounced back across the field again, and around to the Bremer place. We had the hose, so Gerry and I went back out and eventually got the other one off. It wasn't really that big a job, but everything's harder in the cold. You had about two seconds once you had your gloves off and bare fingers scraping around on the metal before they were just about useless. You'd just be hitting at the wrenches after that, using your hands like clubs. Gerry never would have gotten the hose on by himself; a man had to be a lot littler than he was to squeeze in past the duals.

Bean dust floated down my neck and into my eyes, settling over my face while I reached up to wiggle the new hose back to its connection. The hydraulic fluid was greasy in the first place, cold as could be, and I managed to get myself completely covered in a dust and Hi-tran coating in the twenty minutes it took us to do the job. We thawed out in the pickup just long enough to get our fingers moving again, and then we tackled the belt.

I held the flashlight while Gerry crawled under the grain head. My lungs were burning, and my back and legs had broken into a sweat under my ten layers of clothes. But at least I didn't have to think any-more. My job was to get the belt up over the master gear, and when Gerry said pull, to pull. He said pull, and I did, but it never yielded an inch. I coughed for a minute or two, and then pulled again. The damn Hi-tran made it hard for me to get a grip on it, and the coughing seized hold of me. Gerry lay squeezed in under the grain head, so I geared up for another pull. By the third time it was moving, and on the fifth or sixth try Gerry hollered out that he'd got it on. He stead-ied the bucket of fluid that I climbed up to pour back into the system, and by that time it was nearly three.

My hands and feet had gone dead, and I couldn't help it, I was shivering all over when we finally finished. The cold air wouldn't let my lungs alone for a second. Gerry grabbed me by the shoulder to di-rect me back toward the truck.

"Come on," he said, "we're done. I never should have had us mess with this darn thing tonight. Here, come on over here, let me get you cleaned up." He turned on the crew light and reached up to the gas tank he kept behind the cab.

"Hold out your hands. Hold 'em out. Come on, this will just take a second, hold them out." He pulled my arms out in front of me. "Now, this'll be cold."

Reaching back to pump with one hand, the hose in the other, Gerry poured out into my greasy hands a rush of gasoline. I clumped them dumbly together. As he turned to pump again, I saw his face in the crew light, gray with fatigue.

"We got it done, Arthur. We got it fixed. Ain't many who would have stuck with it on a night like this, but we did. We're just about there now. We're just about done."

The fumes from the gas rose up sharply, burning their way back through my plugged-up nose. I started coughing again, hopping like a jumping bean there at the side of the truck.

"You should have gone on home, though, I wish you would have. You're about as bad as that doggone old Gerry Maars. Never knows when to quit. Here, get the rest of that off, we got plenty of gas."

Tears had filled my eyes, and ran down over my cheeks. I tried to keep my breathing shallow, looking for some kind of break from coughing. Gerry'd found an old shop rag in the cab, and some napkins from the Streamliner. When I'd wiped my hands, I took the hose. Pumping with one hand, steadying it with the other, I poured gas into his hands. While Gerry rubbed them together, he gained energy, talking to me the whole time.

"Just keeping at it, that's the key, but a lot of folks don't understand that anymore. A person's got to keep his confidence up. My goodness, last spring I had days when I'd get so doggoned discouraged I'd want to quit. Hell, that's the way a person feels sometimes. Nothing goes right. But then, take my case, all of a sudden you come along, and we got it done. A man can do it, Arthur, if he just keeps going. You work hard, be fair to your neighbor, and keep at it. It's all in the Scripture, I guess, a fella would have to have a look in there to find it for himself."

He was wiping his hands, looking out across the fields. "Well, I don't reckon that doggone Ray Stewart is going tonight, do you?"

I shook my head.

"No, Arthur, I don't reckon he is. He ain't still out here tonight. But we are, and we've done harvested ourself a crop."

SIXTEEN

Gerry finished up those last few rows the next day, hauling them into town himself. I would have been doing it, but by then the fever had me, and I couldn't even get out of bed. I was hot, cold, and every stage in between for the next three days until the damn thing finally broke. It was a day or two more before I was ready to get back on the tractor. The pressure was off, and that was as good a place as any to gain back strength, sitting in the warm cab and listening to the radio as we went over the corn land, disking down stalks.

If it was mid-December, then Gerry had to be getting ready for Florida. It made me laugh to see how sheepish he was about it. Even as hard as he worked, he still seemed to expect to get struck down dead because he took a few weeks in the sun. He invited me two or three times to come on down to see them that winter, but I was just getting back to being human again, and wasn't ready to look that far ahead.

It was about a week before Christmas that Gerry dropped by the house. He was on his way back from town in his Fleetwood, dressed up nice, in blue slacks and a seed company windbreaker. His hair was slicked back, and he got out of his car to walk with me for a few minutes around the barn lot. I'd told him I'd take care of the last of the fall work, but it still was hard for him to finally break away. After we'd stood looking at the empty hog pens for a few minutes, I figured I might as well make some conversation.

"You seen Charlie around lately?"

"No," he said, "I ain't seen him."

"I was kind of wondering. He hasn't been around. He hasn't even been by for the rent. You reckon he's already gone south?"

Gerry had his hands in his pockets, still looking into the pens.

"He goes down to Sebring, that's what he told me once. I guess I could send the check down there."

Gerry looked up at me and shook his head. "I wouldn't send no check. Charlie ain't gonna be keeping this place no more. He's gonna let it go."

"He's retiring?"

"Yeah," he said, "I guess that's what you'd call it. He ain't gonna be farming no more. It kind of makes a fella sad. I've known Charlie a good thirty years. Knew him with his first wife. Watched his boys play ball."

We looked out over Charlie's bean stubble, past the barn to Byron's. Their house was made up cheery, with red ribbons and evergreen bunches hanging from the coach light by the road. A huge wreath was on their door. Gerry cleared his throat.

"Yeah, it's all over for Charlie. It's a damn shame, but it ain't no surprise the way farming's been going these last few years. Ain't no money left in it. I thought the widow could keep him afloat, but things didn't work out. My Lord, he owed Hostetler's alone nearly sixty thousand dollars."

64

There wasn't much more to say about it, we just stood in the sunny barnyard, our backs to the wind. It was already hard to remember that Charlie Sellars had even been there, him or his hogs, either one. The platforms and pens could have just as easily been that way forever, swept clean and empty.

"Matter of fact," Gerry said, "that's what I just been in town talking about, over at the bank. You know Al Lantz there, I think I introduced you one time. He's always been darn good to me and Kathryn, ain't asked much in return. Ain't asked nothing in return. It's been a pleasure to do business with him all these years."

I nodded, watching him.

"A man hates to see this, Arthur, he really does. Anyway, Al asked me if I'd consider taking over payments on this place. That's what he asked me to do. And it's put me in a bind, because a fella can't really afford to take it and can't really afford not to. It makes it hard." He turned to me. "Finally I told him maybe I could swing it, if I could get this young man I had helping me this year to think about staying on. You may know what young man it is that I'm talking about."

"I got some idea."

He nodded back at the house. "How much did Charlie have you paying for your dad's old place? A hundred and fifty?"

"Something like that," I told him, and he laughed.

"That doggone Charlie, he always was so damn tight he squeaked. Well, you ain't paying nothing no more. That's your place now. You live there for free."

"All right," I said, "thanks."

"I'd want to treat you right, Arthur, you know that. We'd want to get you some insurance. You still got benefits and all from the lakes?"

I shook my head.

"We'll get you insurance. Maybe you can get that doggone cough fixed up; you had me worried this fall. I'll have Dave Scott up at Mutual look into it today. I ain't got livestock no more, so I can't give you meat."

"That's all right, I don't need meat."

"So I can't get you meat. But hell, that ain't right, you ought to have meat. Joe Stahl had some calves this year, maybe he'll let me have one."

"I don't need meat," I told him, but he'd already decided.

"I'll get you meat. And that means you'll need a freezer. You got a freezer in there? I bet you don't. I'll track down a freezer for you, too, before we head south."

With tasks before him again, I could see Gerry come back to life.

"I ain't gonna have no more hogs around here. I don't reckon you'll miss them. Kendra either. Nowdays when a woman fixes her house up nice, she don't care to contend with the smell. We ain't gonna fool with no hogs. Tell Byron that when you see him, he'll be glad to hear."

"All right," I said, "I'll make sure to let him know."

"Oh yeah, one more thing. I'd like to get a phone line run out to you here, so I can get hold of you when I need to. Maybe you could keep me posted on things while I'm down in Florida. I don't want to bother you none, though, you may have different ideas. Would that bother you having a phone out here?"

I told him it wouldn't be any bother.

"I might even get one that rings out loud enough to hear, you reckon you'd like that?" Gerry laughed as he grabbed me by the arm. "Oh, I remember it like it was yesterday, you all pissed off at me that first day out behind the Bremer place. If looks could kill, I'd have been a dead man right then and there. I wasn't even used to believing my hired men anymore, Arthur, that's how bad it had got. Well, this one here will ring out loud and clear, you let me know if it doesn't."

He stopped by a last time a couple of days later. Kathryn had been ready for days, but Gerry was still dawdling, unable to break away. She must have laid down the law, because I could see that he was finally hurrying. We drove over to the Bremer place so he could do one last thing: call up a man he knew who was interested in Charlie's hog houses and pens.

Gerry was like my dad in one way, at least; he'd never gotten completely used to the phone. He'd tear into a hundred-thousand-dollar combine without a second thought, but he never seemed to quite accept that a little black box and some twenty-gauge wire could actually carry a voice. Standing next to me out in the shop, he shouted into the receiver.

"Yeah, that's right. I got a dozen of them. In real fine condition, you'll see for yourself. You'll want to look at them to be sure. No, you look at them first, and then you can decide."

It was cold in the shop, especially when you weren't dressed for it. Gerry stomped his feet in a circle as he listened, one hand in his jacket pocket.

"Well, if today ain't good, just come out when it's convenient. You decide. Okay, then, hold on for a second, let me check."

He covered the receiver. "You mind handling this for me?"

Gerry stood there whispering, still trying to fool the phone. When he raised his eyebrows, I shrugged. I shrugged, but I nodded just the same.

"Okay, Bob, that'll be fine, I'll have a man out to meet you. About ten?" He looked at me again. "Okay, ten's fine, that'll be great. I'll have my man there. Right, out there at the old Conason place. My man will be there. Look for that white pickup of mine, it'll be up in the yard. You look for my man, too, he'll be there."

Kathryn hadn't had to wait much longer; in a couple of hours she and Gerry were finally on their way to Florida. As for his man, he was out there the next morning just as promised. While I waited I sat in the pickup, listening to the radio and looking out from the rise. The phone company truck pulled up a few minutes later. Well before I'd closed the deal on the pens, they'd already gotten a line up and were stretching it tight, running it from the road back across the barnyard, and up to the house.

PART II

ONE

I've always had a soft spot in my heart for a woman in uniform, and I can still remember watching little Annie Leroux in her trim waitress whites, that February morning in the Cove Cafe, as she moved into the circle of regulars clustered around a long center table. She'd already been in and out with coffee and breakfast platters, conjured up cream servers and toast, was right then slipping past Gerry Maars with coffeepot in hand, running a quick eye over the cups spread around the table. Just settling into the rhythm of his story, Gerry patted her absently on the shoulder.

"'My Lord,' the old farmer says, 'I can't afford to buy that many roosters, I just barely had enough for the chickens. Are you sure you ain't got one a little more high-powered? I was thinking a real horny rooster, maybe, that could take care of all them hens by himself.'"

From where we sat on the east side of Main Street in Delfina we must have been a thousand miles from the nearest ocean, but somebody long ago'd decided on a seashore motif, so on the Cove's one long paneled wall there were cracked oars and starfish; high above us a green sagging fishnet hung down from a stamped metal ceiling. The other wall, the one that separated the restaurant from the tavern next door, was mirrored, reflecting back to us the cash register and my side of the table, along with a six-foot-long aquarium full of murky water in between.

The two or three fat goldfish that had managed to survive were no strangers to Gerry's stories, any more than the men who that morning sat crowded around the table: old Buck Rogers, who used to have the Chevrolet dealership in town; Bud "The Key is Keough" Keough, who handled whatever real estate managed to be sold; and Gig Walker, whose son-in-law had pretty much taken over his farming, leaving Gig to raise ill-fated racehorses for the harness tracks up north. There were three or four others bellied up to the table too. Only one was out of place, and that was me, still watching Annie as she worked her way up a row of booths against the mirrored wall.

I'd just picked Gerry up the afternoon before at the airport down in Indianapolis, but he was already back where he belonged, at the end of the table with his chair kicked back, standing for full range of motion.

"'Well,' the feed man says, 'I do got a rooster like that, a real horny son of a gun. But you don't want him.'

"'I reckon he's a pretty high-priced bird,' the old farmer says.

"'No,' the feed man says, 'as a matter of fact, I'll be glad to get rid of him, the sooner the better. But I'm telling you, you don't want that doggone thing.'

"'The hell I don't,' the old farmer says. 'Crate him on up, I'm taking him home.'"

She wasn't more than twenty-four or twenty-five, I was guessing; you wonder later whether it was that she was really attractive or just lively, with sharp features and short, wild hair, her hands and dark eyes quick as she came up to clear the table across from us. Spills were dispatched with a swipe of her rag, the change swept into the apron pouch at her waist. On most days I wouldn't have been the only one watching—men who hadn't touched their wives in a quarter century would rise every morning before daylight and come a dozen miles into town, just so a young girl like Annie could bring them their eggs.

But right then they were caught up in Gerry, every bit the reluctant feed man, who was shrugging his shoulders above me.

"'All right,' the feed man says, 'take the doggone thing. But don't say I didn't warn you. That's one horny rooster.'

"'Fine,' the old farmer says, 'I'll consider myself warned.'"

Gerry sighed. "Well, so that old farmer takes the rooster on home. It was about dark by that time, so he goes ahead and puts the rooster out in the henhouse. He has his supper and goes to bed. Of course, the first thing he done the next morning was he went out to see about the hens. And there they all were, sure enough, but by God if they weren't all scattered around out there in the chicken yard. Scattered around, lying there every last one of them, stretched out on the ground, feet up in the air, dead."

Faye Watts was another of the waitresses, as dumpy and slow as Annie was fast. Gerry waited while she worked her way past us. He nodded down to the county assessor and her assistants, having coffee under one of the starfish. He lowered his voice.

"'Why, I'll be goddamned,' the old farmer says. 'That rooster has done screwed all my hens to death!'"

That brought an appreciative laugh from around the table, and Gerry soaked it in, shaking his head.

"That old farmer couldn't believe his eyes. So he goes on over to the hog house, and there was his two old sows. Lying there stretched out in the pen, feet up in the air, dead. 'Why, you doggone horny thing,' the old farmer says. 'You done screwed my two old sows to death too.'"

He was charitable enough to raise the volume so the neighboring tables wouldn't have to strain so hard, and the old farmer managed to work his way out through the barnyard, past the pond, and into the pasture, a whole string of animals in the rooster's wake.

"And right there in the pasture, I'll be darned if that old farmer didn't find his milk cow too, lying there in the grass. Stretched out on the ground, feet up in the air, dead. Anyway, along about then that old farmer looks up in the sky and sees them." Gerry scanned the table full of eager faces. "There they were, a bunch of buzzards circling around in the sky. Just circling up there. So he runs on, and it wasn't very long at all before he come up on that old rooster himself. There that doggone thing is. Stretched out on the ground, feet up in the air, dead. And that old farmer says, 'Why, you doggone horny rooster. You goddamn horny thing, it serves you right. You finally done it. You finally done went and screwed yourself to death!' And that old rooster just lifts his head up, peeking out a little, and points to the sky."

Gerry dropped his head to peer out under a broad wrist, a finger to his lips.

"'Shh,' it says, 'buzzards!'"

Nobody liked his own jokes better than Gerry, and his high-pitched "Hee, hee, hee" rose up over the general laughter that followed. He grabbed old Bud Keough by the shoulder and turned to the table along the wall.

"He thought that old rooster was dead, but that doggone foxy thing was just waiting there! Waiting for them buzzards!" He spotted two old-timers at the table just behind him, and he called out to them, his face red and shining. "You ever have a rooster like that, Vachel? You ever see a bird do like that, John? Oh my Lord, that was one horny rooster."

He'd made his rounds on the way in that morning, slapping men's backs and shaking hands, leaning in to inquire about children and grandchildren wherever they might be. I waited while he worked his way a last time past the booths and tables, standing to join him when he got back to the front.

"Yeah," he said, "I guess it's time. Me and Arthur had better get going, got a couple more things to do. Awful good to see you boys."

"Send us a postcard when you get back to Florida," Kenny Backlund called out to him.

"Yeah," old man Keough hollered, "let us know how the fish are biting."

"Okay, Kenny, Bud, I will. You fellas at least try to be honest while I'm gone. I'll be back here soon enough to see."

Loud and laughing so that nobody could miss him, he led us on our triumphant procession out past the register, running into Davy Nelson at the door. Davy had lost his wife the year before to cancer, his right hand to a shop press a couple of months after that. Even I knew that his oldest boy was in jail. Since he still wore the stump in a cotton casing, Gerry didn't have a hand to pump. He pounded him on the back instead.

"By God, Dave, how you doing?"

"Can't complain, Gerry."

"Don't do no good, anyway, does it? You stay out of trouble now, me and Kathryn want to have you over as soon as we come back."

"You bet, Gerry. I sure will."

"Okay, we'll be seeing you now. Here, give me that check of yours, Arthur."

"I got it."

"No, damn it, don't be difficult. Come on now, give it here. 'Lo there, Mrs. Bayes, sure good to see you. Kathryn said to tell you hi. Hey there, Janine, sure good to see you, too."

He'd dug out his fat leather wallet by then, shiny over the years from being pulled out for all the fistfuls of checks he'd managed to gather up just like he had on his final tour that morning, and in a loud explosion of farewells, we were out of the restaurant and back onto the chilly, cracked sidewalks of downtown Delfina. There'd been a week of winter rain, with a cold, gray sky promising more. Still flushed, Gerry strode out ahead of me to the pickup and hopped inside. Pumping at the accelerator, he got the engine to catch, and we drove down Delfina's short main street to turn at the courthouse. His red flush of excitement was already draining away, and he coughed, hunched over the cold steering wheel. As the first drops of rain began to fall, he turned on the wipers.

"You hear them dumb bastards?" he demanded. "You hear 'em?"

I'd still been thinking of Annie Leroux, down at the end of the booths. "Hear what?"

"'Send us a card from Florida.' 'Let us know how the fish are biting.' Wouldn't you know it, that's the first thing old Keough asked when he saw me, how much longer we'd be down there. Ain't people something, how goddamn nosy they are?" He scowled. "It ain't enough to work like a dog ten months out of the year. Buck Rogers ain't worked a day in his life that I can remember, and them other guys got county jobs, or inherited some business from their dad, or work for some damn agency where another man's got the worries. Ain't a one of them could survive the kind of hours we put in, Arthur, or the pressures either one, but they got to begrudge every damn second a fella might find to relax. Oh, it's just the damn jealousy, it really is. It was the same way when me and Charlotte used to go down, it ain't no different with Kathryn. Think a fella's just goofing off down there, not like a man can save up and earn a little leisure."

By that time we were out near the underpass that was being torn down on the old railroad spur. The wet weather had driven all the workers inside, but Gerry slowed to inspect their progress. Craning his head, he studied the girders long enough to satisfy himself, then speeded back up.

"You think they don't know why I was back? You think old Keough don't know? You saw them, they couldn't hardly contain themselves. To be waiting for a goddamn government check in the first place is a doggone embarrassment, it shows where farming's ended up these days. And then to have it come in late like that, have the bank not accommodate you, how do you figure that? My doggone checks start bouncing. Mine! I ain't done business in this town for damn near forty years to have that happen, I sure as hell haven't."

He'd started brooding again, which wasn't a surprise, I'd seen it coming even before we left the restaurant. He'd already worked himself back into about as big a funk as he'd been in the afternoon before, when I'd picked him up in Indy. You'd have thought the whole state of Florida had been mass-murdered to see his face at the unloading gate; I guess he thought the world couldn't quite stay aligned in its orbit if one of his checks had to be sent through a second time. I laughed out loud to hear what the dire emergency was. But for him it was a matter of pride, and he still hadn't managed to recover.

From the torn-up underpass we cut between the old cemetery and the fairgrounds, past the new private nursing home that had gone up near the bypass, and back into town on Sixth. We turned in at the baseball park and rode up a shiny black asphalt driveway to a squat block of rest rooms. Gerry slowed, circling to check them out. Rebuilt and freshly painted, they were another project the council had allocated money for. While he brooded over his finances, Gerry took his time inspecting them, opening and closing stall doors, flushing toilets to make sure they were up to par.

It had taken a while to get the whole story, but apparently he'd barely been out of bed the morning before when he'd gotten his call from Hostetler at the elevator. A couple of hours later it was the oil man, then the seed man too, a little before noon. It must have been a hell of a morning for Kathryn, because by two o'clock that same afternoon he was already at the Orlando airport, yelling to me through the phone with the times for his plane. Twenty minutes before the bank opened that morning, the two of us had been already waiting outside Farmers and Merchants, and by nine-thirty everyone from the tellers to old Jake Evans the bank guard were lined up trying to apologize.

"Did you see what happened when Al Lantz got there?" Even in his depths, Gerry smiled at the memory. "Did you see how that goddamn smart-aleck vice president shaped up? He come in when the bank changed hands, and I never did like the arrogant little prick. Never. Oh, he tried to tell me all about it, all about the new procedures they got. My God, I had half a mind to pull my account right then and there and just walk across the street to First National. Hadn't been for Al come hurrying in right about then, I would have, it's a goddamn lucky thing they got him over there. You seen me—oh, I was mad. The little bastard was whistling a different tune after Al got through with him. He just stood there and listened. Yes, Mr. Lantz. No, Mr. Lantz. You know what Al told him? He pointed right at me, held his finger right up here to my chest, and said, 'This man here is the very heart of the community. We have to treat him right.' That's exactly what he told him. Now, it ain't the truth, really, ain't nobody in the world that important. But it makes a fella proud to know that as fine a man as Al Lantz thinks that much of you. His kidney trouble's slowed him some, but hell, Al and me are the ones that got this ballpark built over here in the first place, when the wrecking yard closed down. Him and me got that goddamn James Whitcomb Riley school built, out by the lake, back when he was on the school board. We got the new addition put on the hospital, too, when there hadn't been a bond issue passed here in a dozen years. Hospitals closing down all over the state, and there we are putting on a new wing! Oh, we done a few things, Al and me. Got a little progress pumped back into this town, while the rest of them old naysayers were still sitting around slurping up coffee."

We'd had our full look at the rest rooms by then, and it was time to move on. It would have been hard for anyone else, I imagine, who hadn't worked for Gerry some, to figure the course he set for us that morning. The James Whitcomb Riley school was next. Drainage out back had been a problem, so we idled along in the pickup to where the bread man was unloading flats of rolls at the lunchroom door. At the hospital we paid brief homage to the addition before Gerry parked the truck so we could slog a half mile around an exercise course the new administrator had hounded the council to put in.

None of it quite did the trick. There was enough community achievement out there to warm the hearts of a dozen Kiwanis, but Gerry's mood was still as dark as the day. At the new lift station by the dam, he rolled down the window to hear the pumps humming in the rain, lifting all the exclusive sewage on its first leg up from the Lake homes and over the three miles to the Tippy.

"It's like that doggone Jack," he said, after we'd listened a while.

"How's that?"

"Oh, ever since he got to be such a big shot, he can't do nothing personal no more, he's got to be drafting a letter. So I get one down in Florida right after Christmas. He's had this expert down at Purdue do one of these comparative studies, see, an analysis of all the rents across the state. Says me and his grandmother are kind of on the low end of the scale, thinks we ought to raise it. He ain't never farmed; what he don't know is that he's living in a dream world, him and that man down at Purdue both. Ain't nobody can pay the kind of rent he's talking about. Not and stay in business. Nobody. But then when I call him up, all he wants to do is argue with me. So I just say fine, and as soon as I hang up, I get on the phone to Irene. She must have jerked his chain a good one, because I ain't had no more letters. Still, it makes a fella worry. Prices getting worse, these damn troubles at the bank ..."

By that time we'd begun a broad circle back past the jailhouse, slowing as we went by the library. At the edge of town we made our leap for life across the rainy bypass, came on out Sycamore past our old place and Byron's.

"The paper ain't never liked it either," he complained, "that I make it to Florida every year. That's the only time they even mention my name anymore, to say I wasn't there for a vote. Here I am, ain't missed a meeting, not a one, in the twenty years I been on that council, except for them couple of months I'm down south. They're just all worked up, is what it is, because I ain't made up my mind on that county-wide zoning. Thing is a lot of people don't care for the idea, no matter how much the Rotary and Chamber of Commerce say we got to have it. I been around politics long enough to know a fella can get hurt on something like that, he really can."

Usually it would have comforted Gerry to be back in the country again, the wide fields of icy mud broken by bare trees and brush along the ditches. He was still irritable, though, as we moved past his own acreage and began winding south. We'd left the restaurant with barely two hours to make his flight in Indy, but he seemed to have forgotten all about it. It wasn't my plane to catch, so I just let him go on brooding. We'd gone past the gravel pit three miles south, and a big confinement hog operation that somebody'd put up back from the road. He turned left to go one road east.

"It ain't like I haven't carried my share of things out to the country," he started in again. "Ain't nobody in town can say I haven't done my share." His big face still clouded, he'd begun to brake. "Look at this, Arthur, you ain't gonna believe it."

A red dog had come running from what used to be the Holloway place, out from behind a little square prefab that somebody had thrown together. As we slowed, the dog came alongside, running hard.

"Now, look at that damn thing, what am I going, twenty miles an hour? Watch this." He began to speed up, and the dog kept pace past twenty-five, dropping back no more than a dozen yards even at thirty. Regarding him out the side mirror, Gerry shook his head.

"Every time I come by here, he's right out behind me. Dumb thing runs just to be running. Look at that, I'm damn near at thirty-five."

It wasn't too long before he stomped on the accelerator again, and the dog trailed away behind us into the ditch. I couldn't really figure what Gerry was doing down that way often enough to race farm dogs, but in another mile or so he jogged us back to the west. This time, when he slowed, it was to pull over in front of a big, muddy corner field.

"Now, that," he said, "is a pretty piece of ground. You know, a fella'd like to find out, just once in his life, what he could do with a really good farm. That doggone prairie land your dad had, that Bremer farm I been on all these years, it just ain't got the potential of a place like this. Homer Jackins has all this ground, over three hundred acres just in those two fields."

He pointed toward a small woods. "First thing I'd do is make me a pond back there. You'd lose an acre or two, but it'd help the drainage. I'd get one of the boys from the state down here, have it stocked with blue gill. Wouldn't that be the prettiest thing? All the crops up around it, corn out there about three feet over your head? Oh, this land would be worth a fortune if a man knew what to do with it."

I might have figured it would take a piece of farmland to perk him up, even a stretch of frozen old mud that belonged to somebody else. At least we finally started off in earnest to the airport. Not that the bank business didn't linger — the simple memory of it working on him might even have been what got us to Indy on time. He stepped down ever harder on the gas, pressing that old pickup to eighty and ninety down along a network of slick county roads that spilled us out near Airway with a good twenty minutes to spare. We'd just pulled up along the curb next to Delta departures when he turned to me.

"Well, I better go catch this damn thing and get back, keep Kathryn happy. Everybody's got to be happy. Oh, by the way, I was over on 31 before I left this winter, and I seen a kitchen table for you. At that furniture store beside the old drive-in. Stop in and get it sometime, it's already put aside."

"I don't need no table."

"I ain't asking your permission, particularly, I just wanted you to go by and get it. You got a birthday coming up, don't you?"

"Yeah, in July."

"Well, this'll be your present. You can't just live like a doggone cowboy, Arthur. Pick up whatever else you need, have them send the bill down to me. And cash them damn paychecks that I send you. It plays hell with the bookkeeping when you don't."

He pulled out that hard-working wallet.

"Here," he said, "here's twenty dollars. A boy like you wants some dinner before he gets home."

It took some effort, but I finally got him out of the truck with all his money. While I went around to the driver's side, he stumped over to the curbside check-in. Back in the public eye, he didn't know a stranger; on the curb all of thirty seconds, he was already shaking hands with a dapper little man in a plaid bow tie, reaching past him to greet his chubby, flattered wife.

Hemmed in by a courtesy van, I just rested there a second, back to my own company again in the airport's crowded lanes. While car trunks slammed and porters called out around me, I found myself thinking back to the Cove. The truth could have been that I was no different than those old codgers that came in every day, so sorry and lonely that I couldn't help following Annie Leroux as she moved past the booths against the wall. I'd been watching when she slowed, for what seemed the first time all morning, beside an old couple bent hesitant over their menus. It was while she stood above them, frowning into the mirrored wall, that I met her eyes, looking back down the restaurant into mine. The oldsters below her had decided, but it was another second or two at least before, still frowning, she looked away.

A sharp whistle cut across the sidewalk to bring me back to Indy. Gerry was up to the baggage chute by then, with the attendant grinning next to him, a bill sticking out of his fist. The dapper man and his wife had been joined by two or three other passengers—all of them once in a hurry, but all of them now hanging back to laugh. Gerry was bent over the counter with his arms folded in front of him, his head down, his face turned up to the side. A finger was raised to his lips, and the one eye I could see was winking out at me, while his free hand pointed up to the sky.

Two

Maybe it was my pace of cashing them, but none of my own checks from Gerry had been turned back from the bank unpaid. I got them mailed to me from Florida every week for driving the county roads, circling past fields and the different places Gerry had stored equipment. The biggest part of it, though, seemed to be to drive through Keona once or twice a day to make sure Irene's lights were still on and that smoke was coming out of her chimney. Every third day or so I'd knock on the door to see if she needed anything. If the wind blew I'd go over and pick up limbs, and when the snows came made sure her walks stayed clean.

I'd just gotten back from a trip over there one Saturday morning, a couple of weeks after Christmas, when Kendra called to invite me to dinner.

"And dress up a little," she told me, "there's someone I want you to meet."

Even when Kendra and my brother were dating, I remember her talking about a friend of hers she'd made the summer she went to Girls State, from somewhere down south by Terre Haute. It had been, as I remembered it, someone she'd been proud of, with a name she liked hearing roll off her tongue. Somebody elegant, compared to us; even after Girls State there'd been college in the picture, a sorority at IU, a junior year spent at a school in France. Someone, after all those years, that Kendra still kept track of, and who was finally coming up to my brother's house to eat.

Betsy was sitting on the sofa when I got there, but she stood to greet me, a tall, wide-mouthed girl with surprising green eyes. Attractive to begin with, she knew how to make the most of it, with a sleek dress of dark maroon, careful makeup, and a light, expensive necklace that was set off slender and bright against her long dark hair. It was no surprise, as it turned out, that the jewelry looked nice; Betsy had just become the main buyer, Kendra told me proudly, at J.C. Sipe, one of the last of the big Indianapolis jewelers. Betsy shook my hand, saying she'd been hearing all about me from Kendra.

My sister-in-law sat us at our places around a bowl of salted nuts, settling herself in on the loveseat next to Byron. She had to have been working all day long: the house had a spotless shine to it that's not easy in a house with kids. Even my brother had been brushed and polished for the occasion, looking bulky and overheated in a thick turtleneck sweater.

He probably really was overheated; I doubt that he saw many women as smooth and stylish as Betsy in his hall patrols at Tippy Valley. He sat with his lips only slightly parted, which was good, because it kept his tongue from rolling down to the floor. And Betsy was gracious, answering in a deep, warm voice to Kendra's quizzing about the better side of life. She had quite a bit to tell about, too — trips to Los Angeles and London every year, New York almost once a month. But then again, Kendra'd taken over cheerleading for both of us. Even my life sounded interesting, played back through her. Subtle Byron just kept his eyes on Betsy — I had the sense that the arm he'd put around his wife served as mooring more than anything else, to keep him from throwing himself wildly at her feet.

For her part Betsy was only too willing, when the time came for Kendra's turn to show off, to admire Celeste and Joey as they were trotted into the ring. Shy and unimpressive, his pajama bottoms clinging, my nephew hung back beside me, leaning against my shoulder while his little sister stole the show. Evidently Celeste had already taken up with Betsy before I got there and was as pleased as her mom when Betsy gasped and clapped at the sight of her again. Betsy shook her head at me in wonder that little girls can really talk.

Back whenever it was that they'd gone to Girls State, it would have been some long-ago teacher like Kathryn who had seen Kendra's brightness, had wanted to develop her full potential to lead. A half hour later she led us to the dinner table, pulled out into the center of the room. It was dinnertime for the adults, but Celeste couldn't accept that her part of the show was over, so there was a twenty-minute tantrum until she was finally put down. I could feel Joey watching from the crack in his bedroom door. Betsy was nothing if not kind: it could hardly have been the highlight of her life anymore, but at the table she joined in with Kendra's memories of that week at the dusty state fairgrounds, found interest in the tedium of Byron's vice-principal days.

I'd already noticed, out in the sunshine, how the skin under my sister-in-law's chin was beginning to sag. A recent haircut didn't flatter her either, with tattered strands of blond hair stuck out loose and tangled in a style popular with young girls at the time. Weekend makeup couldn't hide that her cheeks were broken out—Byron had told me earlier that her dad was worse, that they'd taken him to Fort Wayne in an ambulance only a couple of nights before. Better than my niece, I could accept my part for the evening: listening when I could, talking when the talk came to me, and, when Betsy got up to leave about eleven, walking her to her car. It was a cloudy night, and we went on past her car, down the driveway to the road. We walked the quarter of a mile to the stop sign, hands in our pockets, our faces turned down against the wind.

Like my brother, I'd watched Betsy during dinner. Pickings must have been slim down in Indy, or she'd just had her fill of it somehow, because by any measure she was a kind and beautiful woman. In a better world she would have had a dozen men standing in line to choose from. In that better world, certainly, she wouldn't have had to come seventy miles out into the country to a marginal friend's, just to meet somebody like me. Even granting what was obvious, that she was a sweet person, sincere really, in her own polished way, it must have been hard for her to re-imagine that distant friendship, to raise enthusiasm for all the predictable details of a Tippy Valley school day, and all of it finally for this: to pick her way down a pitch-black country road with a man who was at least taller than she was, at home in the darkness, whose shoulder she could bump up against now and again, on the way back from the stop sign to the car.

The next weekend when she came up, she parked at the old farmhouse and we went out to dinner from there.

There was the obligatory stop at Byron and Kendra's, where Kendra brought out a bottle of sparkling wine, served to us in fine glasses from their wedding set. Nominally the celebration was for news of my brother's promotion: he'd be the new middle-school principal in the fall. But for Kendra there was romance in the air, and still with her foolish haircut, her face bright with excitement, she pulled Betsy with her out to the kitchen. Ever kind, Betsy followed, leaving Byron and me where I doubt that either of us could have imagined we'd ever be—drinking sparkling wine together from crystal glasses in his living room, in what had once been the muddy forty acres east of the road.

There's not a great deal to remember from the twenty-mile trip up to Plymouth that night; we picked Plymouth because Kendra'd told us about a new Mexican restaurant there that everyone assured her was good. A lot of people in northern Indiana must have heard the same thing, because the parking lot was jammed, and we had to wait forty-five minutes in a crowded anteway before they could find us a table. A snowstorm was building, but Betsy and I sat under a large sombrero and a pair of maracas, while across the room there was a spotlighted mural of an orange sun and green cactus, with blue rocky mountains beyond. I'm no expert at Mexican dishes, but Betsy swore they were as good as she'd ever tasted. She wasn't afraid of silence; on the way back, driving down 31 under increasingly heavy skies, she sat back in the Camaro with her long legs folded beneath her, humming with the radio in the dark.

The lights at Byron and Kendra's were already off by the time we pulled up into the barnyard. Neither of us were teenagers, Betsy and I—we were a modern couple in a modern age, and she followed me up across the porch and into the old farmhouse. Kendra was equally forgotten by both of us by then, as I led us through the house to the stairs. Betsy lingered a moment at the top, admiring the clean, stark lines of the old place, the wide hallway and high ceilings, the quaint transoms set in above the doors. Glancing into the bathroom, she was taken by the old claw-foot tub. In my dad's room she imagined what kind of view there could be, if only the wall were knocked out, and a deck built out to the east. That was where we stopped, though, and her green eyes watched me come up to her. She let her breath quicken as I slid my hand through her coat, brought it down to her hip. It was awkward as hell, and noisy, but we slept together that night in the drafty old room at the end of the hall, on the creaking and battered army cot that I'd finally hauled up from the kitchen a month before.

THREE

I awoke the next morning with us still wrapped together, opening my eyes to her dress folded over one arm of a battered desk chair, to a slender brassiere that hung over the back. She always did have such pretty clothes, all the way down to her skin. That was her business, of course, pretty things. She was a person who could appreciate bone china and silver, fine furnishings and delicacy, best displayed where it was open and bright. She was stuck, though, that morning, with the grim old farmhouse.

The snowfall had come and that thrilled her, the four or five inches spread out unbroken across the fields. What had drifted up on the windowsills gave sort of an insulated feel to the place. Boat life had taught me something about orderliness, so over the winter I'd swept out cobwebs and scrubbed the floors, put linoleum down in the kitchen where the old floor had begun to crumble away. There was still nothing right about the house, or admirable, just too much me stored up from the cold months, bouncing back down to us off the walls. But Betsy's fate was to see beauty, and as we strolled down into the living room at the edge of the parlor, she tried to explain how it could work.

"That south room would be perfect for a greenhouse," she said, pointing to the far parlor wall. There was a door there that had in all my memory led to nowhere, just opened to the bare fields behind it, three feet above the ground. "You'd want to make the wall out of glass, sloping in at the top. Put a lot of green plants all around. It would be so lovely in the summer to have breakfast in there, look out into the country. Really, with that southern exposure, it'd be comfortable all the way into fall."

She'd wrapped herself in one of my blankets and had on a clean pair of my work socks. She sipped instant coffee as we went from room to room, with her pointing out where an old oak bench might look nice below the stairway, how a window on the west could be opened for light. Track lighting seemed best for the living room, she was deciding, as we climbed back upstairs on the tour.

It was only natural that a person might try to imagine it, that Betsy might try to find a way in and around me so that she could fit in too. A semi-farm girl, maybe, is how she could see herself, with a commute that wasn't impossible, and a calm place to retreat to after the bright lights of London and New York. I can still remember her voice, the deepness to it, and a bravery I had to admire.

"Of course," she said, "this room by the bathroom would make a perfect nursery, too, for when you're ready to settle down. It's away from the master bedroom, but at the head of the stairs, close enough to hear a baby cry."

"I don't think so," I said.

"I've watched you with Joey. He worships you. You'd be good for a boy."

I shook my head, trying to get past her to the stairs.

"Oh, now," she said, "you'd be a good father, you know that you would."

People can know all kinds of things and still not see the truth. I was leading her back down to the living room, but she stopped, still laughing, thinking I could be kidded after all.

"You'd be a good daddy. Babies can change a man, you'd be surprised how they do."

She was still laughing, and I turned to her, waiting until she stopped. Finally she did.

"No babies," I said, so clearly and distinctly that her wide mouth fell a mile. We both at that moment became aware of her standing foolish in front of me, wrapped in a blanket, naked except for my socks. The miserable cup of coffee rested lukewarm in her hand.

This, then, is the meaning of poise. Brought up short, she smiled, stretched luxuriously, and moved on past me on her own.

"A lot of people open up these stairways," she said. "It can be so pretty that way, when you decide to take the effort and time."

FOUR

Still a Girls Stater at heart, Betsy didn't take lovemaking lightly, and to prove it, she invited me down to Indianapolis the following weekend. And so, over that first winter, before and after Gerry's trip back to see to his banking, I would drive down every other week or so to see her. She lived on the northeast side just south of I-465, in an upscale set of apartments that looked out over a landscaped lake. The lake was a borrow pit for the interstate, really, with the highway hidden just beyond the trees. Its narrow shore was trimmed neat as a golf course; along with small bunches of obedient shrubbery scattered around, there was a decorative twelve-foot pier.

Sometimes when she'd work late on Friday I'd stroll through the Fashion Mall waiting for her. Her venerable jewelry store had followed the money from downtown out to Keystone at the Crossing, where I strolled among shops of safari clothes and evening gowns, kitchenware and ferns, soaps and powders that couldn't help but sweeten the day. It was the middle of winter outside, but there were summer T-shirts on sale, slinky tank tops and fluorescent orange shorts for the beach. In more than one store they sold shiny cloth carrots and roosters, bags of sweet-smelling herbs. In another store there was a matched set of porcelain pigs that would certainly have been less trouble than live ones, and cost only half again as much.

We went out to dinner and the movies in our evenings, one night saw a traveling version of *Cats* at the auditorium on Butler's campus. Afterwards, at a bar in Broad Ripple, we lingered over drinks. During good weather there would have been awnings to sit under out on the street, but that night we nestled back in front of the fireplace with friends of hers from the city: young lawyers and accountants who had made Indy their home. They were the kind of people who hoped to one day be her clients for diamonds and pearls, or for one of the bracelets I'd seen stretched out on velvet, made up of Hershey kisses fashioned from silver and gold. One night when they all came back to her house, we tried to find something in common. For their part they told dumb jokes about the Democrats, and looked forward to sailing on Eagle Creek. They were comfortable enough with me, as I remember it, at least until they found out what I did. Even then it wasn't really their fault: find me a place where farmhands and lawyers wrap pinkies of an evening and I'll show you a world still unknown to modern man. It wasn't anything specific even, just that some of the various certainties they spouted so easily tended to lose air almost visibly in front of us, once there was a ringer who still worked with his hands.

I don't know what Betsy was thinking, really; she liked all the better things, the better people, but maybe deep down she still carried her own doubts too, about the merits of luxury and ease. Up in her finely styled bedroom there were pictures of her family, most of whom looked like they could just as easily have come from Haskell County themselves. Even bound as they were, by sleek silver frames, the women stayed heavy and unfashionable, the men looking sunburnt and stunned. Among her friends she'd just gone on gamely trying to include me, while everyone, she and I as much as the others if truth were told, wondered what I was doing there at all. I guess it could be said that we were both of us just a little lonely. At the end of the long evening, when everyone was finally gone, we climbed back under the ruffled covers in her room. One thing in our favor, we coupled easily enough; it helps to have been around.

FIVE

By the first week of April Gerry was back, he and Kathryn towing the boat up through the jam of Hoosier farmers on their way home from Florida to the fields. They got in on a Saturday evening, and by Sunday afternoon Gerry and I were both disking on the driest land we could find, the Fox place up north of the river.

He'd managed to add another three hundred acres to the empire from down in Florida, most of it Dike Matevich's place south of Keona, after Dike had a heart attack bowling one night and died. He'd picked up the Holloway land too, a hundred and twenty acres a full eight miles south of Bremer's. I couldn't quite figure it; there were only so many days that a person could plant in the first place, and it seemed like we had just about every one of them already spoken for. Gerry'd brought back a secret weapon, though, a little black box about the size of a tobacco tin, that he plugged into the cigarette lighter up in his cab. The second night out he made me look him over carefully, when I came back with sandwiches from town.

"What do you think, Arthur, now tell me the truth. Ain't I a lot more peppy-looking than a person would expect? Come up from Florida through all that traffic, didn't get no rest. You and me go late last night. Today we been out here a good eight or nine hours already, and look at me, fresh as a daisy! That damn little machine is like a miracle, is what it is, a man don't ever have to get tired!"

It was an ionizer that he'd picked up from a chiropractor down in Florida, an old man in Lake Placid that Kathryn had been seeing about her back.

"Not that I believe in them damn old fools," he said, "but I was in there myself, having him look at this doggone shoulder, and I seen a book he had on it. Get the wrong kinds of ions, see, and you're a mess. But get the right ones, and a man don't ever want to quit. Think what we're gonna be able to do now! You and me won't hardly ever have to stop!"

We hardly ever stopped as it was, but sure enough, surrounded by more negative ions than had ever before been gathered in Haskell County, Gerry had less reason than ever to slow down. He even loaned it to me to try out, but before we'd gone two hours he was flashing his lights, begging to have it back.

Luckily the fields had started drying out some by then, and the dust that was kicked up finally plugged the needles on that damn little box, so that it quit working. Gerry was on the phone to Florida that very night, but it turned out the chiropractor had run off with one of his patients by then, and he was out of luck. With his pep gone he was on the surly side for a couple of days, but he worked through that the same way he worked through everything, going hard every minute of the day and night that the weather said we could.

"Oh, me and Arthur been putting in the hours," he assured them at breakfast. "We're so doggone wore out, we can't hardly stand it. We was out 'til midnight last night, trying to get done up north. I just thank the good Lord it's done. 'Course, now we got all that darn muck land to do, so it don't ever stop. I had to go out and get Arthur this morning, just to bring him in and get him fed. We been just like that one-legged man you hear about sometimes. You already heard about him, ain't you, Buck? Annie, you heard about that one-legged man?"

They'd heard about him all right, and I enjoyed watching Annie cross her eyes and shake her head at the prospect of hearing about it again. Gerry still had his habits of a lifetime, working all night and then lingering half the morning over coffee. He was leaning back to let Annie pour when Avis Bayes from the newsstand across the street came bustling in. She had a boy and a girl with backpacks in tow, and she told Gerry how glad she was she'd caught him in time.

"These two young people are from Germany," she was saying. "They're students, and they're traveling through Delfina right now. Very fine young people, trying to learn how we do things over here."

There had been some kind of trouble with their visas that the county clerk couldn't fix, and they looked hopefully at the big man in the DeKalb jacket, his napkin still stuck in at his neck.

"My goodness, Avis, Arthur and me done fooled away half the morning in here, and we got all that acreage still to do. Gladys turned them away? Said she wouldn't help them none?"

She'd already explained to them, apparently, that Gerry Maars would help them if anybody could, and the Germans crowded in at her shoulder.

"So I knew I had to catch you before you left. When I saw your truck, I told them not to worry, that you weren't going to just let them stand around and starve."

While all the other men at the table studied their newspapers or fumbled for tip change, Gerry frowned. "Well, I ain't gonna let nobody starve, if I can help it. I reckon there's always some phone calls to be made." He looked up to the girl. "My cousin was in the service over there in Germany during the fifties, although that would have been a little before your time. Maybe you heard of him, Kenny Perkins? Little sawed-off fella about this high. Went by the name of Perk. Any of that ring a bell?"

"A bell?" the girl repeated, coloring with the effort to understand. She started to look through her pockets.

"I say he was my cousin," Gerry repeated, raising his voice. "My cousin, a little guy, name of Perkins. Over there in the service. No, in the service. Aw hell, Avis, I guess I got time to do something. Arthur, you mind waiting a couple of minutes? You want some pie? Janine, you still got some of that coconut left? The way I been working him, he's got to keep up his strength."

As Gerry led off his international brigade, the regulars had already begun scattering, the big table emptying around me.

"You don't want that pie, do you, Arthur?" Janine called out and I shook my head. She was on the way past me to the door, which she propped open, letting the cool breeze of spring back into the cave. I had my eyes on the back booth anyway by then, because that's where Annie Leroux had settled in.

Usually, of course, Viola was still there, and she watched those poor girls like a hawk. We'd dawdled long enough, though, that she'd already gone home for her soap operas, and the waitresses were beginning to relax some in the last of the morning rush. I'd always figured too, that it was an etiquette of some kind, to leave that last booth for the help, but I didn't stop to consult with anybody, just picked up my cup and made my way back across the open floor. I went past the door that led up a short ramp to the darkened Oasis, and along the mirrored wall to where she sat.

"Howdy," I said, ever original, and Annie nodded hello.

It did feel a little like foreign territory back there, and I sensed the other waitresses watching me as I settled in and tried to act at home. Annie just looked back at me, curious. Her hands were wrapped around her coffee cup, nails broken and smudged with the last of red polish, her dark eyes taking me in. It was a little less of a distance than it had been bounced through a mirror along the wall of a restaurant, so now she could look to her heart's content, and so could I.

She seemed even younger up close and relaxing, her short hair curly in the steamy diner heat. She was sharpness everywhere— her shoulders and elbows; even her knees under the table were jutting out at mine. She was amused for some reason as she studied me. Her uniform was buttoned high, bare arms thin even after all those serving plates. She wore a watch with a thin elastic band at her wrist.

"Just leave it there," she commanded over my shoulder. "Let Ann-Marie bring it. Leave it right there on the table."

Twenty feet away from us, in front of a booth on the other wall, a little girl no older than four wobbled in a pair of high-heel shoes made of plastic. A large tumbler of soda was clutched in her hands.

"Now, you heard me, just stay over there. Or leave the root beer. One of the two. I don't want you dropping it."

The girl was as dark-headed as Annie, her hair cut shorter, but every bit as unruly. The plastic heels were too big, and she wobbled uncertainly. Once she'd gained a kind of stability, she looked into her glass and back at us. She smiled.

"Just stay there," Annie warned her again, but it was already too late; she made it all of two or three steps before her ankles gave way, one of the high heels buckling under. She staggered, and the tumbler was lost. The miracle was that she kept to her feet herself. I never remember seeing the Cove floor before that, for a million dollars couldn't have told you what was down there, but all of us from the Oasis door on back joined her in looking down at it then, and at the flood of root beer and shaved ice that spread out over the tile.

"Darn it, Moni, can't you ever listen? Come on, now. Come on." Annie waved her impatiently toward her. "Just leave it be. Come on over here. Clarence'll get it. Come on, now, it's gone."

Still committed to the heels, Moni came shuffling and sobbing across the floor to bury her face under Annie's arm. When she peeked out it was only to confirm heartbreak; the cook had summoned the old dishwasher by then, and he came limping out with a bucket. Still sobbing, she watched as he swiped at the soda, his mop filthy with cigarette butts and lint.

I called over to Ann-Marie to bring another root beer. "Just put it on my ticket," I told her. "I'll get it when I go."

"Oooo, a big spender," Annie said. "We'd better be careful, Moni, around a man like this."

In a world that doesn't stop long for anyone, a spilled soda barely gives pause, although a little girl wouldn't have noticed that at first. Still embarrassed, she hid her eyes, occasionally glaring out at me. Ann-Marie brought us the soda, and after some coaxing from Annie, she finally came back out. Wiping her eyes on her sleeve, she climbed up on her knees to sample the root beer.

"Well," Annie said, "she's not going to learn very much about spilling. Or listening to her mother, either one."

"Sorry," I said, but Annie shrugged, reaching out to ease the glass back from the table's edge.

"Oh, it's worth something to end up happy too, once in a while. There'll always be time for lessons later on."

Maybe I'd known about the little girl already, had seen her in one of those back booths at the restaurant before. I could still feel from the small-town eyes all around me that I was in a place I wasn't supposed to be, but since my companions seemed tolerant, I sat back and relaxed.

"Your boss run off and left you," she said, "and now you want company?"

"Depends on the company. Some of it I'm lucky to have. Two lovely ladies here, a man can't complain about that."

"Arthur Conason," she said, "I was remembering you just the other day. You kidnapped your own dad one time, wasn't that how it went?"

"It wasn't that big a deal."

"No," she agreed, "it really wasn't. It wasn't much at all. But I was remembering it. My mom was working over at the home there in Wabash, and I remember her telling me. You're a sailor, is that what Janine said, back home now and settled in?"

"I don't know how settled I am. Shipping may pick up."

She was stroking her little girl's back, reached up to smooth a stray curl away from the glass. "That's a job I think I'd like, out there on all that water. Is it fun like it sounds?"

"Oh yeah," I said, "it was fun."

Moni had the same dark eyes as her mother, the same wariness and curiosity, glancing up at me as she idly blew bubbles in the glass. I nodded her way.

"Maybe you and your little girl would like to go out to a movie sometime, I could see what's up in Plymouth. Drive up there some afternoon."

"To be out on the water like that," Annie said, "going places, that's what I think would be nice. The only water I've ever been on is out here at the Lake. Oh, and down in Kentucky one time, we rented a boat."

"Those small craft present their own problems," I said. "They can be pretty dangerous sometimes."

"A lot of things are dangerous," she said, watching me. She smiled, ruffling her little girl's hair. "Yeah, this headstrong one right here is mine."

Moni had dropped back to burrow up again under her mother's arm. Annie didn't seem much more than a girl herself as she stretched past her to finish the last of the root beer through her daughter's chewed-up straw.

"She's mine, along with three others, as a matter of fact, the rest of them boys. The oldest is nine, and the next one's eight. The youngest just started school this year. That makes four, in case you're counting."

She waited to see if I'd flinch. When I didn't, she went on.

"I got a husband, too, Carl Wayne. That's him right over there, the big brown-haired one in the cap." She pointed across to where the milk plant workers were just then finishing an early lunch, pushing back chairs and gathering up tickets for their pilgrimage to the front. "I got a mom, too, she works at Montgomery Ward catalog down the street. She's gonna be coming by for this one any minute. My Uncle Charles is right over there at the counter, the one giving you all the dirty looks."

I turned to glance back at a toadlike man in a battered Panama hat, swung around on his stool to glare at me. Carl Wayne, beefy and with long tangled hair under his Raiders cap, must have figured he already had his wife anchored well enough by then, because he was caught up in banter with his buddies and never even looked our way.

Annie and her little girl sat appraising me.

"I didn't mean for you to burn yourself with your coffee," she said, "rushing away, but I thought you ought to know about my family. I got one, you know."

"You've definitely got one," I said. "You and Carl Wayne must have found something to do with yourselves, those long winter nights."

She laughed. "We've had our moments. Come on, Moni, let me get your coat on. Grandma's just now coming through the door."

Six

When the weather is cool, you'll see them in their own nylon windbreakers and Lee stretch slacks: seed corn salesmen and chemical men, implement dealers, and by then, more and more as the professions developed, financial consultants and marketing specialists, all out to peddle their wares. A man had to get out pretty early in the morning not to stand in line, and Rodney Gilliland was at the Bremer place even before I got there, kind of sheepishly sidling along in his pickup to see when Gerry'd be around. I could guess as well as the next person, and told him two hours, so that's when Rodney came back, pulling a brand-new combine loaded onto the trailer of a semi. We were knee-deep in planting, so I went off for more seed, and when I came back Gerry, who after a month's solid work still had more acres unplanted than most other farmers had all told, was high in the combine's cab, wheeling it in wide circles around one end of the field.

It was a warm day toward the end of May, so Rodney had shucked his windbreaker and peeled down to a polo shirt of International Red, all part of the football-coach image that the companies were constantly trying to promote. After Gerry'd made a couple more spins, he backed a few feet, raising and lowering the pickerhead. Rodney hustled over to the foot of the ladder. "That hydrostat sounds real smooth, don't it?"

Gerry raised it high just to bring it down again, bumping an inch at a time back to the ground. "That rotor system really as good as they say?" he asked.

"You better believe it. That's all we're selling anymore, and we ain't had a complaint yet. It's the best International's ever made. You or Arthur, either one, you'd really notice the difference. When Curt told me we could deal some on this, you're the first person I thought of. Came out here as quick as I could."

Rodney had been in Byron's year in school, with red hair and the kind of complexion that doesn't tend to fare too well in the sun. What I remembered best about him was one Saturday night when he and a buddy were out fooling around in Rodney's Mustang. The whole story was never clear, but the friend had been in the backseat steering while Rodney was down on his hands and knees in the front, working the pedals with his hands, when they lost control and crashed into the front room of Ollie Williams' house out on 450 West. Now Rodney was on the International team out of Keona, standing below Gerry to point up at the cab.

"And don't that seat feel good? It's designed ergonomically is what it is, that's the way everything's gonna be from now on. Them windows are tinted too, maybe you noticed. With the kind of hours you put in, that's gotta mean a lot. That air conditioner ain't no slouch either, top of the line. Moves a hundred cubic feet a minute, air filtered pure as a hospital. They got tests that proved it over at Iowa State."

"So Curt'll throw in the grain head, that's what you're saying."

Rodney tried to keep the excitement out of his voice. "He sure will, Gerry, you bet. Like I say, he wants to deal."

"And then this glass here, I don't know that I care for it all that much. We do a lot of night work."

"Hey, that's no problem either. We got regular glass we can put in. If we ain't got it, we'll get it. Yes sir, Gerry, it's important to me and Curt both that you have what you want."

"What I want is four-dollar corn. You reckon Curt can fix that too?"

Rodney was keyed up enough to agree, but he caught himself in time. "Oh, well," he laughed, "that's one thing we can't guarantee, but I tell you, we'd like to, we really would!"

Nobody could pretend that it had been a good year for the dealers, probably hadn't been that good a year for Rodney either. Not with times the way they had been, and him in a big house not more than two or three years old, over by the golf course. Plus two kids in school already, and another one ready to start.

"You say a hundred and five, then, with the grain head."

I could almost hear Rodney's heart pounding. "I got the contract right in the truck."

"You'd be able to get it out here for me then, this fall, with them windows fixed the way I want? Financing like we talked about?"

"You bet, we'll take care of everything. Let me run get the papers, and I'll be back."

"Yeah," Gerry was saying, "it's the kind of deal a fella'd be a fool to pass up." For the first time he looked down to me. "You might as well do it, Arthur, get it over and done with. Go ahead and call me a fool."

Still smiling, Rodney turned to me too, as he tried to follow the joke.

"Come on, Arthur, you might as well say it. It's the truth. Ain't no way it isn't. A fella's a fool to let this pass. Go ahead, call me a fool. I deserve it. Go on."

When I passed on the opportunity, Rodney looked back up to Gerry, who was shaking his head.

"Well, Rodney, Arthur ain't gonna call it like it is, I guess, he's too polite. But he ought to. He ought to call me a fool for passing on this, but that's what I'm gonna do. Check back with me next year about this time, maybe I'll be ready to trade." He climbed down the ladder to the ground. "Look at this, Arthur, a man don't even have to play Tarzan on this one to get up and down."

He clapped Rodney on the back. "I sure appreciate you taking all the time to come out here and show me this. I appreciate the attention. You be sure to tell Curt that, will you? That Gerry Maars appreciates the attention."

Rodney must have been busy thinking of all the places his ten-thousand-dollar commission would have gone; at any rate, he seemed to be having trouble understanding.

"You know, we might just have that glass in stock, wouldn't have to send off for it. Let me give Curt a call."

"Yeah, make sure he knows we appreciate the attention. I remember last year during planting he was out of town one weekend, we couldn't get nobody to open up. I ain't saying a man's daughter can't get married, but during the springtime? That's when we really could have used the attention, right about then. You tell him that if you would. You want me to drive that back up on the trailer for you? I'd be glad to."

Rodney shook his head. From being all puffed up in his polo shirt he'd begun to sag, his mouth and shoulders dropping, and his stomach falling back over his belt. The combine had begun to look more and more unlikely too, all bright and polished in the wide empty fields of spring.

"And then last fall," Gerry went on, "I sent Arthur here over for some cutter blades. What's that old crippled man's name there, works in parts? Bob?"

"Old Bob," Rodney said. "Old Bob Armbruster, he's a real—"

"He's a real wise guy, is what he is, don't you reckon? See, he already had all them cutter blades put away. Now, that ain't no sin, but then he goes and tells my man here that all the good farmers were already done for the year. What do you think about that?"

"Oh, he was just joking," Rodney said quickly, "I know he was. That's just how he is, kind of smart sometimes."

"And here Arthur comes back out to the field, all crushed, thinking he's done hooked on with a horseshit operation. Took him a damn month to think otherwise. Don't know for sure that he does yet. So that's something Curt might put a little attention on too."

"I still got some room to deal," Rodney said desperately, but Gerry was already to the pickup, reaching inside. "There ain't nobody been more important to us over the years, we want to work with you any way we can. I know a man hates to go into the kind of acreage like you got this fall with less than the best."

"What I need is a Twinkie," Gerry said. "Pep me up a little. You want one, Rodney? Arthur's kind of partial to them, he must eat three or four packs a day."

"That mud hog's something we could throw in too, maybe if I talk to Curt—"

Gerry held up his hand. "Rodney, I ain't buying it. I'm sorry. That's just the way it is." He found the box of cupcakes and broke it open. "You might as well carry it around to Ray Stewart, that's the only guy I know of who's still adding on."

"He buys Deere," Rodney said glumly, and that was that.

Gerry tossed me the box. "Well, Arthur, we better get going, don't you reckon? Ain't gonna be nothing to combine even with those damned old antiques of mine unless we get it in the ground. You say hi to Elizabeth for me, Rodney, give my best to your mom. You tell Curt what I told you, now, make sure that you do."

It was a clear day for working, and we went strong on the Bremer place until almost six, when Gerry sent me into town for some dinner. We were sitting on the tailgate with our cheeseburgers before I got a chance to bring it up.

"Hell," I said, "I wouldn't even have told you about old Bob last fall if I'd known you were so touchy."

"Hmmph," Gerry said, a big bite of sandwich in his mouth. "You see old Rodney's face? I thought he was gonna shit in his pants. You see him? They all think Gerry Maars is made of money. Parts so damn high you think they'd be embarrassed to send out the bills. I reckon I have been important to them over the years, I put all Curt's kids through college just on the markup."

"That combine's been on the lot for a while."

"For a while? It's been there all winter, they tried to sell me the same damn outfit last fall. Old Curt must be desperate to send it out here this time of year." He chewed on his sandwich. "You remember Rodney, don't you?"

"Sure, he played football for the Comets. Married the Tucker girl."

"But what'd he do? What did him and his dad do?"

"They used to farm."

"That's right, they sure as hell did. They used to farm. And my goodness, it was a showplace, too, you remember? Back when I was a young man no older than you, I liked to drive by just to admire it, just to see how pretty a place could be. Now, how about that Jimmy Littlejohn, sells me seed corn. His dad had a place too, up in the north part of the county. And then there's Vic Jessup, that handles the fertilizer for Hostetler. He used to farm. The county agent, that new boy from down near Crawfordsville? His folks used to farm too. All them folks *used* to farm, and there ain't a one of them still does. But they always got a whole lot of advice, though, see what I mean?"

He balled up his wrapper and threw it into the truck bed. Somebody poking along in an old Bonneville on the road just behind us had caused a mini—traffic jam, three cars backed up in a row. Probably most of them used to be farmers too, but Gerry didn't pay them any mind, and when they'd passed the old Bonneville by, hurrying on to town, the countryside was back to us. Gerry leaned on the tailgate next to me, idly kicking at the ground.

"Yeah," he said, "it ain't Rodney, really, I never had no quarrel with him. Back when me and Charlotte used to take the ball teams out for a banquet every year, I always enjoyed him. A little banty rooster kind of player, lots of drive. I'd like to help him out now—if I was made of money I would. But my Lord, when he couldn't even keep his dad's place afloat, and it was practically given to him, you think I'm gonna spend a whole lot of time listening to what he has to say about pneumatic augers and ergonomics and who the hell knows what else? Here, look at this."

He tossed me a farm magazine, a slick little offshoot for the top-money grossers called *Farm Leaders*.

"It ain't gonna bite you, Arthur, it's just a magazine. Look there in the middle, about page twenty-six or something. See if you recognize the guy they got featured."

"You get yourself in the farm papers again?"

"Don't be asking when you can just look. Look there and tell me what you think."

It was on page twenty-six exactly—the magazine looked like it had been opened there more than a few times already. Most of the photos could have just as easily been taken anywhere around northern Indiana, except that there in the first one, under a hybrid seed corn hat with his head so big that it was almost life-size, was Ray Stewart. In another shot his three combines were behind him, looking every bit as spiffy as the one Gerry'd sent away. His two boys were up in the cabs on either end. There was a picture of Ray in front of his grain-drying setup, and another with just his boy, Carter. Carter was out in the middle of a bleached-out-looking field, with a bunch of raggedy-looking black men gathered round.

"You see that, Arthur? You see that son of a bitch? May's Model Leader. He's the pinup this month."

"I never thought of Ray as having ears that big, you don't notice it so much in person."

"He's telling the rest of us how to do it, see? Here, give me that a minute. Listen to this: 'It's been rough the last few years, but we feel good about what we have in place. We took potential losses into account and learned to live with them. We planned well.' Eloquent son of a bitch, ain't he? Oh, he's an arrogant bastard. When's the last time you seen Ray Stewart serve on a county commission? When's the last time he helped out at the doggone fair? Been a hell of a long time. And look at all that damn equipment he's got! You tell me how he pays for it! It's a doggone mystery!

"And look at this here, look here what it says by this picture: 'His two sons are active in the business too, Leonard overseeing the domestic markets, and Carter handling contracts abroad. In this photo, thirty-two-year-old Purdue graduate Carter listens to French tapes in the cab of his tractor.' Can you believe that shit? Now listen: 'In the off-season he puts his language skills to use managing the Stewart family farms in Haiti, where corn and soybeans can now be seen growing alongside more traditional crops.'"

Disgusted, Gerry tossed me back the magazine.

"I used to take Carter out too, me and Charlotte did, back when he was in high school. He wasn't much of a ballplayer, but he was on the team, and we were glad to do it. Him and Rodney both, up there clowning around, right at the front of the line."

He shook his head. "I guess Old Ray just planned well. I guess he was busy planning while the rest of us were laying around eating bon-bons or something, so he's the damn Model Leader now."

At least I knew the reason for his funk that day, although by that time it didn't help Rodney Gilliland any. One thing about field work, a man gets to think, and Gerry'd taken advantage of it, a full day brooding over Ray Stewart's fat head in the farm magazines. Even the good weather couldn't cheer him, not even the eighteen hundred acres we already had nestled in the ground, so we sat there for another ten minutes just watching the crows as they dove to get the grubs I'd been churning up with the disk.

"Well," he said, "I guess we might as well get back out there and go, that corn ain't gonna plant itself. It ain't none of my affair, anyway, how another man does his business. If Carter wants to listen to French tapes while he drives, and if Ray can manage to get a bunch of poor half-starved colored boys to do his work for him down south, then more power to him, it ain't nothing to me. It ain't gonna change nothing for us. What you and me got to do is work."

SEVEN

In late March Betsy had invited me to join her on a trip down to Mexico, a direct flight from Indy to the beaches of Cancún. I passed on it, and by the time she got back, Gerry and I were already in the fields. When I saw her a couple of weekends later, her sunburn had peeled off, and we had a hard time finding anything to say. She was another week in Dallas, with her London trip right on the heels of that. I think she might have called me a couple of times when she got back, but by that time we were planting, and I was seldom at the house. She and I had finally managed to drift apart, on the schedule that the polite and poorly suited tend to adopt.

It was almost a surprise, the second week of June, to look up and see that planting was done. With the pressure off, Gerry heard the siren call of politicking again, and ran off with Rich Taylor down to a sheriff's convention at Indian Lake. He left me with spraying to do, so one day I ended up in a stubborn field down at the Holloway place, low ground partial to weeds. We'd come into a heat spell by then—by eight in the morning it was already uncomfortable, growing steadily hotter throughout the day.

By ten my shirt and jeans were soaked black with sweat, and for the next five or six hours I would bounce over a dozen acres in the Allis, stop to mix and refill, and go back out again. All the while the air grew steadily heavier, so thick that by early afternoon the spray seemed to just hang there suspended, waiting for me on my return trips through the field.

Through the middle part of the afternoon the haze on the horizon deepened, thickening to blend with the trees. There's a precision to spraying that calls for a tradeoff: the high cost of chemicals against the last few acres before a rain. On my late-afternoon rounds I played big operator and tried to calculate, bumping the speed up to fourth. About four a first breath of cool air came out of the west. From that point the sky never quit darkening, and by a little after five, when I finally got the field done, it looked like about ten at night.

You like to have an hour for the kill to set in, so I kept an eye on my watch as I moved the tractor up onto the government acres that we'd sowed to rye. The breeze had fallen away, making room for each little squeak and rattle as I bounced the water wagon up to higher ground too. Lightning had started in the west, and angry black clouds swelled up above the trees. By the time I got the truck moved, it had been almost fifty minutes, so I spent the last ten out leaning against the bumper, watching the storm come on. It took almost exactly that long for the trees to start tossing at the far end of the field, and for the farthest rows of beans to begin to dance.

They say the rain falls on the just and unjust alike, and both of us surely got it that evening in Haskell County. The rain came like being poured from a pitcher, driven by a wind that blew ever harder until it was shaking the pickup, each new blast rocking it farther to the side. I thought of storm warnings about then, and turned on the radio. It was just static, so I sat back unadvised as sheets of water rolled down the windshield and huge bolts of lightning cracked down over the fields. Over fields I'd done right anyway, so I relaxed and let the storm blow itself past. When the rain dropped off enough to see again, I backed carefully out of the muddy rye grass and headed back north to the house.

The main part of the storm was out ahead of me by then. It looked like Delfina was catching it—a fierce black curtain was rumbling and flashing at the edge of town. Byron's had a few shingles in the grass, and a lawn chair blown all the way out to the road. When I got back to the farmhouse, the electricity had gone out. The old place clung jealously to its darkness, so I ended up carrying a flashlight back through the shower curtains, propping it between the soap dish and the wall.

For whatever reason, I'd been grateful for a day just as hot as that one. I was just that grateful for the shower, too—it felt like I'd taken on a layer of chemicals like a second skin. Outside, the rear-guard showers had passed through; gutters that I'd repaired the winter before ran gushing off the old house, and the barnyard was puddled and wet. Left behind was a half an hour or so of twilight too cool and pretty to turn my back on, so I got into the Camaro and drove to town.

I still remembered the tornado that hit when I was eleven, peeling the roof off the high school and throwing a half dozen trailer houses out into a field. This time there hadn't been any tornado that I could see, but there was water standing in all the low spots, and branches down in yards along the way. Power was still out on the north side of the road, where people stood on their front sidewalks and porches, shrugging at one another as they searched the sky.

Delfina's new transformer held the charge better than the country ones did, apparently; at least the streetlights were back on, even while water still ran fast along the gutters, backing up all along Fourth Street as I splashed my way into town. What I noticed more than anything was how old Delfina had gotten to be. The storm had washed away just enough so I could see things as they were: old brick buildings half-choked with tangled ivy, the overhanging lindens and spindly maples, a one-street downtown that had long ago given in to ValuMart and new restaurants out on the bypass.

I hadn't really thought about it being Friday night either, until I turned onto Main Street, where there were a handful of cars spread along in front of the Oasis. It was still a little early for the bar crowd, but as I parked and closed my car door, the semi-jazzy warmup of a country guitar bent out from the barroom to the street. I was glad to see that next door the Cove was still open, its door propped wide to the night.

The restaurant needed the air. Just in from the cool, clean evening, a dusty smell of dry rot seemed to be winning out over a long day's worth of gravies and grease. The only other people in there that late was an older couple in a booth toward the back, the Galloways, who owned a body shop a couple of blocks over. They'd just spent their own day under the fumes, and we nodded across the room. Behind them, a gawky busboy unloaded glasses. I took a booth while Faye Watts totaled checks at the register, and that's when I saw Annie Leroux again, just past the ramp to the Oasis door.

What I saw was the top half of her, in an oversized turquoise blouse, clowning for Faye and the busboy as she half-danced to the ragged noise from the bar.

"They'll come up with music before too long, now," Faye called out to her, "You got to be patient." She came around from the register. "You make it through the storm all right, Arthur? It about washed us away."

"We got a downpour."

"You want the chicken? If you want the chicken, I got to go back and tell them. I don't think they got the fryers broke down yet, but I better check. Iced tea while you're waiting?"

I'd grown accustomed, every six or eight nights when we got done in time, to driving in to the Cove for some of their broasted chicken. Most often it would just be the Galloways by the time I got in there, along with Faye, so she would sit and talk to me while the cook got my dinner ready in back. She wasn't an attractive woman in the first place, and had had troubles of her own: a runaway husband and a boy who'd been fondled by one of the teachers at school. On the last point, nobody cared to believe her, so she liked to complain about it to me. She hurried back to the kitchen to make sure she'd get her chance. Annie had ducked back into the bar, leaving behind a flourish of a snare drum and bass that had slipped in just before the door went closed. Down under their starfish, at the other end of the fishnets and flickering fluorescent lights, the Galloways finished their dinner and the busboy switched to unloading cups, all four of us gathered in the most closed-in and airless part of the county there was. The Oasis door swung open again, and Annie was back.

She came around the end of the booths. Besides her floppy top she had on a tight pair of blue jeans and heels. She did another quick step for the busboy and clicked across the floor to the waitress station, where she drew herself a Coke. Faye was right behind her to fill up my iced tea glass, bringing it over to me along with good news from the back.

"They said they'll go ahead and make it, I told them you were here. Robbie ain't always willing to turn that fryer back on."

"Tell him I appreciate it."

"I will, I'll tell him that. I had to talk to him a minute to convince him, but I know a man needs to eat. You and Gerry still in the field? You get some work in before the rain?"

"Yeah," I said, "I did some."

"This girl here just can't stay away." She nodded at Annie, who'd come up from the back with the Galloways, and stood across from us at the register, ringing them out.

Still swaying, Annie crossed her eyes.

"No sir," Faye pronounced, "when I get off, there's only one place for me and that's sitting down. I'll leave it to these young girls to be out at night, while they still got the energy. Let me go check on that chicken."

Annie still had the youngness, and the energy too. She seemed unable to light, going into the Oasis a time or two, back toward the serving window, and up to the register again before she finally allowed I was there. When she was ready to notice me, she did, giving one last little sway to the music from two or three tables away.

"Like my dancing?" she asked.

"I do. I like it fine."

"I like it too. Sometimes a girl just likes to dance a little. Sometimes I'm just in a dancing mood. You ever get that way?"

"Not so you'd notice," I said, and she laughed. "Where are the kiddies tonight?"

"Carl Wayne's got them over at his mom's, so it's Girls' Night Out." She came around to perch on the edge of the seat across from me, and nodded toward the bar. "Sherri's next door. You know Sherri, used to work in here? You ought to meet her. There's a good single girl for you, pretty red hair all the way down to her shoulders."

She showed me by wiggling her fingers down from her own untamed cap of black hair. I recognized those fingers, her hands. I remembered Sherri too, and realized it must have been a month ago at least that I'd seen them together, one time when I'd come into town for parts. A pretty girl in a hard-faced sort of way, she'd been with Annie and one of the other waitresses, strolling down Main Street in the sun. Annie had one of her little boys with her, and I remember Sherri laughing because the boy had his shirttail out, and Annie was pursuing him, wrestling with him to tuck it in. Waiting at the red light I'd watched him giggle helplessly, his cowboy boots kicking high as she swung him in the air, then gathered him back to be groomed.

"You get rain out your way? I talked to Carl Wayne a little while ago, and he said they had almost three inches out at his mom's."

"I didn't see the gauge, I'll have to check it when I get home."

"The lights went out there too, knocked out the TV. He was all mad about that, he goes to his mom's because they got satellite, and now he's afraid he's gonna miss a game. Me and Sherri just got in here ourselves, right ahead of the storm."

I had the chance and I took it, just to watch her there up close. Bright eyes darting, she began telling me more about Sherri, and the worthless boyfriend Sherri used to have. Deprived of her sob seat, Faye hung back by the serving window, giving us both the evil eye. She picked up a roll at the bun warmer and came through the empty tables to reach between us, my plate, wrapped with foil, in her hand.

"I just wish that band could learn another song or two," Annie was saying, "I get sick of the same old thing. Sherri don't care, though, it never bothers her, as long as Craig might come in. I'm kind of differ-ent, more on the restless side. I end up just sitting around here, no telling how long she's gonna be."

"I'd like to get you paid out, if I could," Faye broke in. "Robbie's getting anxious to close."

I knew those were the last three pieces of broasted chicken that Faye would ever go to the mat for, but I ignored her anyway. Finally she took the hint and set the plate down, backing away.

"Where do you all live?" I asked.

"Off 25, on the road up to Warsaw. A couple of miles north of town."

"You don't have to wait for Sherri."

"No?"

"I can take you by."

Her dark eyes weren't surprised, just alert, studying me. "You going out that way?"

"I reckon I can."

She nodded, still watching. The warm secret spices of the Cove's broasted chicken floated up in front of us from under the tinfoil; a surge of cheering broke in from the barroom next door. Finally she shrugged.

"Well, then, I reckon I can too."

She swept up her glass and gave the table a quick brush with her hand. "You drive the Camaro, right? It's parked across the street?"

"That's me."

"Why don't you pull it around front here, if you will. I'll go tell Sherri I got a ride."

Faye was at the register waiting for me, and while I dug out my wallet, Annie reached under the counter for her purse. We each had our three different directions to look off in, while she slung it up over her shoulder. Lips pressed tight, Faye examined the keys of the register. Annie and I went our separate ways then, and thinking back, that's the first time I ever really missed her, waiting those two or three minutes until she clicked out across the empty Delfina sidewalk, and down off the curb to my car.

EIGHT

Don't let anyone ever tell you there's no special advantage in being free. Free, of age, unbound, in America, at night, with your own car and a tank full of gas. I started out small, taking the first right to go a block over to Elm. It was one of the two one-way streets set up on either side of Main, back when the commission still thought the city might grow. The one way it went wasn't out toward 25, but when I turned there, Annie just sat slumped back looking out the window and never said a word.

It's what too few people get a chance to feel anymore, in an air-conditioned world, the sweet coolness of an evening after a rainstorm, after a day's long struggle through the heat. And even sweeter to drive slow down dark, empty streets under a black canopy of dripping tree limbs, with somebody as cute as Annie by your side.

A town like Delfina never quite had the luxury of style, or maybe it was that it suffered under too much style, successive unplanned ripples of it, reflecting back whatever was popular when somebody had the money to build. The dozen or so big Victorian houses on the two blocks south of the post office were the exception, but they soon gave way to squared-off ranch houses and bungalows, and the odd awkward farmhouse. Next to the farmhouse as likely as not might be what was meant to look like a Swiss chalet, crammed into a deep and narrow lot. Spread along under trees and dim streetlights were the modern touches: semi-trailer tractors and customized vans backed into driveways, and Trans Ams left crossways across the lawns.

There were ten or twelve blocks all told to the new Burger King by the bypass, and when I got to it, I turned east again, crossed over Main, and went back down State the other way. Annie didn't have anything to say while I wandered, just sipped at the big paper cup of Coke she'd brought along from the restaurant. Script numbers on vinyl siding graced a house on a corner lot; for the first time I felt I was seeing them, tacked next to trim plastic shutters that would never close. On the next corner a plaster menagerie had sprung up: a chipped deer browsed in a tiny front yard, and molded ducks waddled all in a line. At the waterworks park, where I turned around, an old snub-nosed jet fighter sat protected by a barbed-wire-topped fence, next to the squat cinderblock building that housed the city's wells.

We followed the railroad tracks on a long pass through the west side of town, cutting within a block of the elevator and then along the dark brick walls of the glove factory, closed down since Christmas. In the wide lot behind Precision Dynamics two warehousemen floated a Frisbee under floodlights at the end of the dock. My companion still hadn't said anything, leaning back to look out the open window, her eyes half-closed to the breeze.

I could have driven those wet streets forever, but it wasn't too long before I ran out of town. Fifty miles from the nearest college I passed the College Square apartments and was back to the railroad. Beyond was a lone sagging fence and the countryside, stretching out into the night.

There was still the Gerry Maars tour I could have taken, the underpasses and baseball park outhouses, the hospital and James Whitcomb Riley School. Still deciding, I bumped onto the tracks. From where we settled, in the center, the lights of the whole town were behind us. On either side the Big Four curled away into the brush. Creosote always had a comforting smell, coming up, like it does, after a rain. That's when Annie spoke up.

"There's the airport," she said.

"The airport?"

"The county airport. You been out there?"

"Not for a long time."

"Me either. Planes fly out from there, I can see them from my porch. People take off and land all the time."

"Well," I said, rocking us down over the crossing, "let's go out and see if one of them does."

To get to the airport you start out like you're going to Highway 25 but break away short of it, just past the turn-off to the lake. From there a gravel road runs back around the old fish hatchery and past a row of trees to the wide, grassy pasture that makes up the field. I'd been out there a time or two, on trips from grade school, and Annie said she had too; it probably had been the same old man who doubled as groundskeeper and airport manager who'd taken us through the small cinderblock hangar, had walked us along more or less the same half-dozen Piper Cubs tied down along one side of the runway. There'd been some improvements since I'd been there last: a pole barn had doubled the hangar space, and a low chain-link fence had been put in to separate the landing strip from a parking lot just recently lit up and paved. Two cars and a pickup had been left by the office. I swung past them and down off the pavement onto the gravel, just beyond reach of the lights.

"It ain't on now, but up there's the beacon," Annie said. "That's what I can see from my house."

The darkened light was on top of a tall pole that stuck up from one side of the office. On a small porch there was a soda machine; except for that and the parking lot lights, the airport was dark. With my window wide open to the cool evening, I settled back in my seat, looking out into the field.

"When Shannon was a baby is when I first remember going out on the porch to watch it. I liked to imagine the planes coming and going somewhere, that light reaching all the way to the sky."

"You ever been up in one?" I asked, and she shook her head. "Me either. I guess I never had anyplace I needed to go."

"That's not me," she said emphatically. "That's not me at all. I've always been ready to go. Take off and fly round and round, look down at everybody, I always knew how fine that would be. I'd think about it every time I'd see that beacon turn. 'Plane,' was what Shannon would say once he got old enough. 'Plane, Mommy, look. Plane.'"

There were still long cement ponds left over from the fish hatchery, so from beyond the row of trees we could hear the low thump of bullfrogs, and cicadas coming back to life after the rain. Annie gave me her hand when I reached for it, and after a little while her cold, dry fingers wrapped around mine. She let her head come under my arm. Her curly hair was softer than I expected, and I had to dodge as it tickled up into my nose.

The kiss she allowed me when I bent down was rough and quick, her lips brushing over my cheek and away. I liked it, though, and kissed her again, catching one edge of those bright eyes and the corner of her chin. She rubbed me roughly behind the neck, before pushing me away.

"That's enough kissing," she said.

"All right."

"No more kissing. That's enough. We've had enough." She scooted away from me to her window. As she retrieved her Coke, the night opened around us again, distant shadows anchored along the runway, the low fence and field, crickets and bullfrogs coming back into the car. Traffic from 25 joined in from over the trees. Annie peeled off the plastic lid to poke intently at the ice with her straw.

"It's all watery now," she said, disappointed.

She replaced the lid, peeled up one end, and tipped the cup to pour the water out her window. She stirred the ice again with the straw. When she was satisfied, she set the cup down and took up my hand.

"We've already had more than enough kissing," Annie warned me again, but a moment later she was crawling across me and into my lap, her arms around my neck. Her tongue tasted sweet from the soda, her breath was still cool from the ice. She pushed her forehead hard into my temple, rolled her cheek rough against mine.

"Okay," she said, "we'll have kissing." Her whisper was a rush past my ear, and she drew back to look at me. "We'll kiss if you want. Kissing's okay, go ahead. Just kiss me right now, if you would."

I would and gladly did; a person goes along day after day without ever knowing any different, and then suddenly to have all that life close up to him, to have Annie in my arms, to be trying out different ways to meet her lips—it was silly maybe, but we must have been an hour and a half like that, necking like a couple of teenagers at the edge of the airport lot. All day long I'd breathed the best chemical kill that money can buy, and somehow that night still got to pull into my lungs a young mother's eager breath.

Annie ground her nose into my cheek and at the end of that hour and a half dropped back to peer into me from a full two inches away. She put her fingers along one side of my cheek and rocked back considering, her ribs curled tight against my arm. And even then it was another hour and probably more before we broke apart again, finally venturing out of the Camaro and into the night.

By the fence there was a small tractor with a field mower, but its regular rounds must have been only on the landing strips. Where we walked had been mostly forgotten, a thick patch of bluegrass that led out away from the lot. Worried that her good shoes would be ruined, Annie'd slipped them off, and smaller than ever she picked her way along beside me. We ventured toward an arm of the woods and partway back, pausing every so often so I could reach down to her and she could wrap her arms one more time around my neck. With her heels off, her hips dropped down full like a mother's, plenty sufficient evidently, but still slender after all those babies. Kissing was still okay, and why not, a man can go through life and on to meet his sober Maker without ever, even once, daring to hope for a night as sweet as that.

"Oh, a lover boy," she laughed, as I stopped her yet again. It was while she was still pressed into me that I saw over her shoulder the beacon glow briefly before flashing into life. It hung staring over the trimmed-grass runways a moment, gathering energy for its tour. Annie turned to lean back into me, and we watched its bright circle, white and then green, swinging high above us and over the trees by the fish hatchery, out toward the highway, back in and across the field. The airfield had begun to blossom: first distant markers, and then, along the runways, low banks of blue and gold. Spotlights flooded a wide concrete apron that I hadn't even known was there, running from the far side of the battered office to the hangar beyond.

Annie reached back for me, running her hand up to tug at my hair. She curled one finger into my ear. "Listen," she said, and when I'd shook my ear loose I heard it: the hum of an approaching airplane. A man can feel possessive at a time like that—the county may have held title to the airport, but as far as I was concerned, it was only ours, Annie's and mine. A plane came small and blinking along the horizon and began its wide circle over the trees.

A late-model pickup had pulled up next to the office, and I recognized the young man who stepped out as Carter Stewart. He'd been one of the many boys Gerry'd been good to; now, no doubt, it was Ray's thriving international operations that brought him to the airport. He seemed at home there, slipping through the gate and onto the apron as the plane touched down a half mile out and came taxiing toward him across the field. When the engine had been cut back, he went up to the door. With the county's fine new floodlights it was easy enough to recognize who he'd come out there to meet: an apparently just-off-work and still dressed-for-success Jack Bremer.

Annie curled her fingers through my hair again, arching back so I could give her a kiss. We watched while hands were shook and greetings exchanged. Striding back from the plane, Jack and Carter looked just like what they were: successful young businessmen in a hurry, the world at their feet. Annie and I stayed in the darkness watching until they'd climbed into Carter's pickup and drove away. The lights must have been on timer, because it wasn't long after that before they began going off. First the runway markers, and then the bright banks of blue and gold, the spotlights on the apron, and finally the big beacon itself.

She'd gotten chilled from the wet grass by then, so back in the car Annie gave me her feet to dry. She sat against her door, watching me while I dried them against my shirttail, rubbing in between her toes with my sleeve. I started the car just to run the heater, another strange and sweet luxury for June, one I was glad she could have. She sat on the edge of the seat, putting on her shoes, and when I reached for her again, she shook her head.

"Arthur, I got to go home now. It's late."

The car was already started, but I wanted to hold her one last time. She let me, wrapping her own arms around my neck, pressing her cheek hard against mine. Once we'd wound out around the woods and fish hatchery, it wasn't more than a couple hundred yards more to 25, and another mile or two north to where she told me to turn. She pointed out an old frame farmhouse that stood on the right, a quarter mile away.

"It must be one or two already," she said, her voice dropping to a whisper. She balled up the straps of her purse. "Does your dome light always come on?"

"It doesn't have to, I guess," I told her, and reached up to snap off the covering. There's just one little double contact bulb inside, that I caught hold of with my finger, flipping it down so it was loose.

"Carl's probably already asleep. No, no, go on in the driveway, that's what Sherri would do. Pull up onto the lawn. Right up ahead there is fine, let me off there."

When my headlights swung across the side of her house, I caught a glimpse of the same porch she would have stood on to watch the beacon. Pulled up in front of it were two scooters made of bright molded plastic; in the middle of the yard there was a bike with a wide front basket, thrown down under a tree. A yellow plastic bucket and a Tonka toy dump truck lay on their sides in the grass. Out from behind the tree and an old tire swing, even before I could get stopped, there came bounding a big dirty collie, barking for all it was worth.

"Shut up, Shemp," Annie hissed through the window. "Darn it, get down. Down!"

We'd already used up the timeless part of the evening, I guess, because it was all hurry from there on out, as Annie snatched up her Coke cup, stuck her purse back under her arm.

"I gotta get out, Arthur, he's gonna wake up the county. I've got to go. Good night. Good-bye."

And in a second she was out the door. "Get down, darn it, Shemp. I said get down!" she was hissing as she crossed in front of the headlights, banging the collie on the nose. He liked her too, though, and left a wide trail of muddy paw prints down her blouse. The dog made it as far as the porch, and then he got left behind with me, as Annie slipped through the dark doorway and was gone.

NINE

The old cot never felt quite so soft to me as it did that Friday night in June, after I drove home from Annie Leroux's. It was after two when I got back to the house. I climbed upstairs, lay down, and for the longest time just enjoyed the coolness as it floated in and across me in the dark. I was still lingering in some kind of deep, friendly dream when a pulse began to blend in, becoming more and more demanding until it finally chased away everything but itself. I started opening things up — my mind to awakeness, my eyes to broad daylight, and finally the curtains to look down into the barn lot. Gerry had pulled up below my window in his big Fleetwood and was leaning energetically on the horn.

"So there you are," he said when I'd stumbled out onto the porch. "I didn't know if you was here or not."

"This is where I live, and there's my car," I told him. "Where the hell else did you think I'd be?"

"Oh, no telling, Arthur, a young fella like you. That was some storm you all got here yesterday; we drove up behind it all the way from Indy. I heard on the radio there was hail."

"There wasn't no hail."

"Radio said there was hail."

"I didn't see hail."

"Well, that don't mean there wasn't none. This is a big county, and spread out the way we are, you can never tell. We got to get around and look at things. Hail can ruin a fella, tight as things are now."

It was early for Gerry, just then eight o'clock, on a bright, clear morning that was already warming with the sun. I was glad to see the world still had a fine, post-Annie luster. It sparkled out in the fresh air that lingered behind the storm, floating in through the Cadillac's long windows as Gerry guided us around past his fields. He was feeling steadily happier, too, as it became clear that whatever hail he'd imagined must have missed us. His crops were safe and as good as any we saw, and maybe even just that little bit better, which is what he pointed out to me at Foxie's and out on the prairie, at Matevich's and the old Holloway place, far to the south.

At the Bremer place the loader tractor and water wagon were sitting up neat and tidy on the hill where I'd left them, with the kill already setting in along the rows. We could see, sighting down them, the light green leaves of the bean rows just beginning to peek out from the brown.

"You done good out here, Arthur, I got to tell you. That's a hell of a good job. It gives a man peace of mind to know that something's gonna be done right for a change, when he gets called away on business. Come on, we got to get them tractors switched over today, best get something to eat before we do."

Gerry and I weren't breakfast buddies as a rule, so maybe I'd forgotten, maybe never even knew, that he'd been quarreling with them over at the Cove. We stopped short of it, out on the bypass, where the new Burger King had been built.

"Here, get two or three orders," he told me at the counter. "They ain't gonna short you here." He waved to the girl at the register. "Give him another one of them pancake packs, I'm working this boy hard. We got us a full day of work planned already. It's kind of like that one-legged man, is what it is, you probably heard about him."

If she had or not, it was hard to tell—a sleepy-eyed teenager with complexion problems, she didn't stay around long enough to find out, already in a hurry to gather up our breakfast cartons and stack them in front of us on a tray. Squeezed into a tiny booth with our Styrofoam banquet between us, Gerry shook his head.

"All the years I been going to the Cove there, all the goddamn business I brought in, and they still don't know I like five strips of bacon. Out here, you get what you pay for, nothing more and nothing less. And that's the way it ought to be. Fair. And the convenience, my Lord, we're gonna be out to the field in half the time, without all that jawing around!"

I didn't figure Annie to be working that morning, anyway, so the Burger King was fine. I guess without all the Cove crowd to admire him, Gerry needed me, so Sunday and Monday he was by early too, to take me in for breakfast before we went to the fields. I called into the Cove from the shop on Tuesday morning, and they said Annie was off that day and wouldn't be in. Who was calling was a little harder to say, so I didn't. That would have made it Wednesday about eight-thirty, then, that I left the tractor and cultivator up by the ditch at Smiley's, hopped into the pickup, and drove myself in to the Cove.

Still busy with their breakfast rush, they'd seemed to survive Gerry's one-man boycott well enough: the only seat left was a little half-booth up front in Ann-Marie's section. Annie was working the back and might have glanced up at me, but that was all. The old-timers got a quick smile or a wink, a pat on the arm as she eased by; she'd join in to laugh with the other waitresses, dodging one another in the aisles. Carl Wayne came and went with his buddies from the milk plant, and Moni was stuck in at a booth toward the back with her grandmother and two other women, bent over a coloring book. Uncle Charles still held down the counter so it wouldn't float away. Even then for the next half hour I sat there, with the meager *Beacon* and my second breakfast of the morning, cooling my heels while Annie ignored me. After the restaurant cleared out she sat down in the back with her mother and the other women, so finally I went over to the register to pay out, and headed on back to the field.

Celeste's second birthday had come earlier that spring; if I hadn't already been squandering Kendra's precious gift to me so carelessly,

Betsy and I would have been invited to the party. Without us there'd been six or seven mothers all told, and their own little girls. That's not counting the clowns: not just my brother but a professional, a chunky middle-aged woman that Kendra'd hired from down in Kokomo to come up and entertain. I was disking on my dad's old acreage behind the barn, and I watched as the woman hurried up the driveway, adjusting her carrot-colored wig.

There'd been party games and favors, balloons and paper hats, a big chocolate cake. For that matter my nephew had a roomful of toys of his own, from computer games to little killer dolls that turned into race cars and back, but that cold afternoon he'd been out along the ditch bank alone, playing with sticks. I was just coming across the road, and when I did, he perked up his ears. I waved him over, and shy at first, like I couldn't possibly mean him, he'd hung back in the weeds. Then all at once he was running, across the field and around the disk banks, while I cleared out some space in the cab.

From then on he'd always had an eye out for the tractors, coming out to ride with me whenever he could. Some days I could see he'd been crying, but I didn't quiz him about it, just swung open the door to let him ride. In a world of ever-smaller family circles an uncle can be worth that much for a boy: a seat on the toolbox, freedom for a little while from inquiry, a chance to get better on his own. And invariably he would. By the end of the second or third round, he'd be looking up at me, eager for his own chance to steer.

I wasn't surprised to see him up on the tractor seat waiting for me, that morning, when I got back from watching Annie at the Cove. We rode together back and forth across those old Smiley fields. When he went home for lunch, I kept at it, moving over to join Gerry at the Bremer place a little after two.

For the rest of the week Joey's company was welcome when he sat next to me, the solitude just as welcome when he was gone. The roar of the diesel seemed cleaner and more powerful than it had been, the summer newly fresh. I spent some time imagining Annie's family, her own kids who needed her, a husband with first call on her time. I'd never been much of a pup, anyway, to go nosing for a pat on the head.

A bad one or not, that was my attitude. One I'd learned over the years to appreciate, because it always makes room for surprise. Early the following week, about six-thirty in the evening, I'd just gotten back to the house. Gerry had a council meeting, and since we were almost finished with the prairie anyway, I'd been happy enough to call it a day. Dusty and tired, I was just coming across the porch of the old house when I found it, a message that was thumbtacked to the door.

Written in wide, looping handwriting, it was on a torn piece of wide-lined notebook paper. Byron must have intercepted a dozen notes a week just like it, in his government class alone. But school was out, in my case forever, and this one had been left there for me:

> Tomorrow night's women's fellowship at my sister's church,
> I'll be out for a while. Meet me at seven-thirty at the old
> elementary school. Next to the park. Don't be late!!

"Don't" was underlined twice, while below it, scrawled quick and with a ballpoint-pen flourish, was the single letter *A.*

TEN

I shut down that next evening at six, went home and showered, and got into some clean clothes. The hot weather was back, so even with the worst of the day behind us, I was sweating under my shirt as I drove in along Sycamore to town. Once over the bypass I turned onto Sixth to go under the viaduct, and three or four blocks later came up on the old red-brick building where Byron and I had gone to school. It was closed down, but the parking lot was still in use, and people had left their cars there to go over to the Little League game in progress across the park. I figured one had to have Annie in it, and an olive-colored Nova, the back window broken out and a front fender crushed and rusting, was the one that did.

I pulled in next to where she leaned back in the driver's seat, slouched low under oversized sunglasses and a wide straw hat.

"You're late," she said.

"It's just now seven-thirty," I protested.

"It's after, Arthur, the radio says it's after. Do you have to park right up here next to me like that? Just go down to that far corner of the lot, do you think you'd mind?"

From her tone I couldn't have said whether she was likely to follow me or not, but I did as I was told. I parked in the faded yellow-striped area where the buses used to unload, just across the sidewalk from the school. The doors were chained, and in front of me there was a grassy schoolyard that gradually, after a dip scattered with pine trees, turned into a full-fledged park. Distant shouts from the ball diamond trailed after small flashes of color, reaching out across the end of a summer day.

It was a minute or two before Annie came sauntering along the sidewalk, still in her sunglasses and hat. She had on an open blouse over a tank top and loose cotton shorts, and when she came up on my car, it was like she was surprised to see it. She came down from the sidewalk to go on past the open window on the passenger side, looking around.

"What are you, undercover?"

"No, just married, and aiming to stay that way." She looked both ways one more time and swung open the door. She ducked into the car and then slid low, with only that round straw hat left for anybody to see.

"Broad daylight," she said. "That's a great time to get together. But don't be saying nothing about it, because it's the best I could do."

"I'm glad—" I began.

"A whole fat lot you care about things, anyway."

"Well," I said, "at least you're talking to me, that's an improvement."

Dropped down with her arms folded tightly in front of her, Annie flashed her sunglasses at me and snorted. "What, you mean the other day in the restaurant? Is that what you mean? You think you can just come waltzing in there whenever you please, don't you? I ain't seen you for days, and if you want to come in there like the King of Persia, that's fine. It's a public place, and I ain't got any control over that. But I got family in there, people I work with. You think I'm gonna go all moon-eyed over you there in the Cove of a morning, then you've got another think coming. You're gonna be waiting a heck of a long time."

The heat didn't help, but it took her a minute, frowning out into the schoolyard, to remember her original complaint.

"So here it is practically daytime. 'Course, that don't mean nothing to you. Why should it? It could be high noon on Main Street for all you care. Daytime or night, it's all the same. It don't matter one bit. What have you got to lose?"

Only our second time together, and there we were fighting like an old married couple. She was right, I didn't have anything to lose, but then again old married couples are generally right about each other too, but that doesn't make it any more pleasant for them to have each other around. The difference was that it *was* pleasant to be with Annie, so pleasant to have her sitting in the Camaro that I didn't care whether she was mad at me or not.

"You can't even make it to a date on time, why should I think you got any consideration of anybody else?"

"No reason in the world," I said, pleased too that that was what we were on, a date. Annie turned away from me, looking out the window and across the hot asphalt to the trees.

The new James Whitcomb Riley school had taken care of most of the students from the old school, but before giving up on it, the school board had tried to keep up with the times. Among the improvements had been black sashless windows set back into the old brick walls, giving the place a kind of strange, futuristic look. Long metal tubes still protruded at an angle from the second and third floors, the fire escape system that we'd gotten to practice every October. It was the only day of the school year I can remember looking forward to, when one after another we would launch ourselves into the tube's narrow darkness, only to tumble out onto a pile of sand at the bottom a couple of seconds later. Since Annie and I weren't talking right then, I took the time to calculate: she would have gone there too. I was one of the shy ones, the bus kids who never got used to the crush and tumble of playground life. Annie, though, I could almost see out there in front of me, wrestling and running wildly with the rest.

From her still-mad, folded-up self next to me there floated up the smell of Lifebuoy. It pleased me to think that she'd found time in and around her own family to bathe and dress not an hour before. She'd brushed and wiped and admonished and warned; then she'd come into town to me. I thought of the thumbtack she'd carried all the way from home to my porch the night before, the scrap of child's notepaper — such simple and friendly things, really, that had brought us to where we were.

We must have sat half an hour like that, as the long summer day gradually gave up its hold. Annie stayed low, leaning into the door on the passenger side, her shoes kicked off and her stubby toes kicking at the gear shift on the floor. As twilight came on, a haze began to settle over the park. Annie turned to find me watching her and shoved my leg with her heel.

"You just watch yourself," she warned, "not me."

Colors out on the diamond had been fading for some time, and with two sets of ragged cheers, they broke apart. Families, the women in summer blouses, the men already growing too stout for their muscle shirts and Bermuda shorts, herded small boys in uniform back toward cars at the far side of the lot. In twos and threes, waving to one another, they backed away until only her car was left. Across the street behind us, lights had begun coming on in living rooms and on porches, shining out dully through branches that drooped across the lawns.

Annie shifted to face me, her back against the door. Finally she slipped off her sunglasses, to consider how I might look in a lighter shade.

"We done this all wrong," she said. "The sun sets too late this time of year. We ain't got any time at all."

Enjoying her there across from me, her dark eyes watchful in the last of evening, I just nodded.

"It ain't that easy for me, I ain't all footloose and free. You've got to have some consideration."

I nodded again.

"You've just got to have some consideration," she said once more, and then paused as if to estimate whether I could. "There used to be a light up here at this end, made things bright as day. It's out now."

"I guess they ain't got around to fixing it."

"I guess not. I drove by a couple of nights ago and saw it was out. Arthur, you can hold me now, if you want. You can hold me now, here in the dark."

I opened my arms, and she came climbing across to me again, over the gear shift and onto my lap. We were awkward at first, still nervous I imagine, but there was time enough after all, I guess, because we took it, getting used to each other all over again. The light from the other end of the parking lot died long before it reached us, and the house lights, as they grew brighter, were just speckles in the distance. Her face buried in my neck, Annie murmured something I couldn't hear.

"Boy," she repeated, when I asked her. "I said I smell boy. Oh, don't get all tensed up and worried, Arthur, it don't smell bad. It's just a part of you. I can smell it on my own boys too. Stevey and Jeff, Shannon, they got it, even when they're scrubbed up clean."

I took her word for it; living right up next to a hog pen half my life had made me uncertain of that branch of my senses. But then when I lingered at her neck and along the ridge of her shoulder, down past the bar soap and floral shampoo at the edge of her hair, I found there was an Annie smell, too, one that might have been girl.

Her fingers held me close up against her.

"Moni's got it too, and she's only four. There's girl there, I can smell it already. I worry sometimes, so much, about her, because it's girl, just as sure as the world."

The night had come on to make us bolder. Annie turned to lie back against me as I ran my hand down her ribs. She shrugged and twisted, pulling away, as I brushed my fingers over her breasts.

"Uh-uh," she said, swallowing, her head pried against mine. She gave no resistance, though, as I slipped my hand under the waistband on her shorts. As I moved down to touch her, she wrapped her arms up around me. She was glad enough to see me then, risk or no risk; she pulled at my hair and ears, shivering as I touched her lightly again and again.

People rail about the laxness of the modern world, but there's an upside to things like a county too slow to get its lights replaced, or a neighborhood full of TV sets flashing on through the night. The dark summer parking lot was quick to give us back every bit of the time-lessness we'd had the week before. I learned then how little Annie would ever tire of being touched, which worked out fine, because I loved to touch her too, from that very first time that she leaned back into me, her bare feet braced against the far door of the Camaro. She pushed her shoulder into my chest as she arched her back, rubbing her cheek roughly against mine. For an uncertain minute I was both reluctant to go on and afraid to let go, her breath fast in my ear, her short broken fingernails tight against my neck.

"Oh, Arthur," she said suddenly, "you know?"

Her tone surprised me, so completely conversational that I started to pull away, but with a simple "no" she brought her knees up to squeeze them together, trapping my hand. With her face pulled up next to me, I felt against my own cheek the cool wetness of her tears.

"No, just hold me for a minute," she whispered. "Don't let go. Don't let me go for the world."

ELEVEN

That summer I came to appreciate the power the church has to work miracles in human lives. In mine and Annie's, anyway, because a late-summer surge of devotion to her sister's weekly prayer circle was met with far more indifference than suspicion back at home. Her sister, luckily enough, wasn't much taken to throwing stones.

"Holly's good people," Annie told me, "and that's all anybody has to know. They all think she's single because she's heavy, but there's more to it than that. She believes in happiness too, in being treated right. She just hasn't found it much in anybody she's seen."

It didn't always work out for us. One week Carl Wayne and Annie were fighting, so he wouldn't stay home and watch the kids. Another time Stevey got poison ivy that went into his system, and while Annie took him in to the emergency room, I sat out at the school yard unmet. We tried the fairgrounds a couple of times, and the airport again, but when we pulled in, there were already two or three carloads of teenagers, all with the same idea. We finally ended up on one of the ditch banks at the Bremer place, overlooking an old silo that stood at the far end of the field.

"Just hold me, tonight, and kiss me," Annie would whisper. "I like it that you will. Carl won't do it no more, I've missed it so much. Oh, just hold me, Arthur, it feels so good."

It's funny, all along, how little I cared to make Carl Wayne any of my affair. We liked it that way, Annie and me both; that way she could talk about him all she wanted and know I wasn't sitting there marking down points. I had no grudge against him—there are more than a few men in the world who might prefer beer, their buddies, and the old garage they hung out in to a lively and demanding little wife.

For my part I just loved holding her, and was more than glad to bend low to meet her lips. Poor seducer, I'd grown happy with just our touching, but it must be the way of adulthood that sooner or later that's not going to be enough. On an early August night of women's fellowship back in Delfina, I drove us into the country again. We left the car on the ditch bank, and I led Annie a quarter mile to the silo through the corn.

It had been a homesite once, with children and animals and fences and dogs. Gerry claimed he'd been intending all along to pull down that old glazed-brick silo, but somehow for twenty-five years he'd never gotten around to getting it done. By that time the old silo stood alone and forgotten, with no reason to be there except that it was.

The timothy at its base grew thick and wild, but I'd slipped back with Gerry's field mower a couple of days before, trimming out a patch we could use. With the nearest house a couple of miles away, we were, surrounded by Gerry's fine field corn and bound by those tangled ditches, as hidden from the rest of Haskell County as two people could possibly be. A conscientious God still could have found us, but apparently that summer had bigger fish to fry somewhere else. I spread out a blanket, and Annie and I made love for the first time with only the warm breezes above us, and a clear and untroubled sky.

It was the first time I'd been able to undress her. There was still enough twilight that she tensed as I unbuttoned her blouse and slipped it off her shoulders, held her bare chest against mine. She needn't have worried—I wasn't a schoolboy, and knew what the pull of tiny mouths could do. I just envied those greedy babies their leisure, and used my own brief turn to touch her gently, to run my knuckles lightly across her chest. I took the time to lean my ear down against her breastbone and listen to the beating of her heart.

As for the lovemaking itself, the entering and beyond, we were more than anything new to each other, trying to get it right. I was on the eager side, while Annie was just nervous, but she clung to me doggedly, and before long I heard her gasp. I lay back and held her, relaxing on my shoulder, her body going limp in my arms.

I might have envied it some, then and always, the ease with which Annie could slip over and be gone. It was dark by the time something woke her, the air as it cooled, or more likely a sudden cramp in her arm, the one that had gone to sleep under my neck. I might have been dozing myself when she finally jerked awake, lost and disoriented, trying to pull free. She sat up with a shiver, rubbing angrily at the offending wrist. It was only slowly that she seemed to recognize me, but she let me calm her, search for her blouse, draw it over her shoulders again. The night was still mild, but she trembled, drawing back under my arm.

"I got to go," she said, "it's late."

"All right," I said, but she didn't move away. She looked around us, registering the high waving corn, a dark sky above, the silo and wide clump of grass. As she looked around for her jeans, I stood to get dressed myself.

Annie caught my arm a moment later, when I reached for my shirt. She pulled me back down beside her, to my knees.

"Listen," she said, "you've got to understand something. There's something you need to know. I chose you."

"You chose me."

"I chose you. When I saw you in the restaurant last winter, there in the mirror looking back at me, I knew. I just knew, because it was like looking right back at myself. I knew."

"All right," I said, still not quite following. I started to button my shirt. "You should have told me earlier, so there wouldn't have been a whole spring's worth of church meetings we had to miss." I tried to stand up again, but Annie's fingers curled into my forearm, holding me back.

"So just wait. Listen a minute. There's something else that I know. I know there's younger girls than me now. There's girls that are cuter. I know that. There's girls that don't have these kids to work around. There's girls that got titties that aren't all pulled to pieces like mine are either, I know that too. Girls that don't have stretch marks all up and down them, I know. No, now just listen. Those girls are out there. You know it and I know it too."

She'd come up on her own knees to face me, her blouse falling open as she looked intently into my face.

"So I just don't want you diddling any of those girls. That's all. Not while you're with me. That's all I've got to say." Her dark eyes sparkled in the half moonlight as she let go of my arm. "Not while you're with me. I chose you, Arthur, I did. Now you just see if you can manage to stay chosen."

TWELVE

Even after Gerry's quarrel with the Cove had passed, I generally stayed away, and when I did go in with him, it was to watch Annie at a distance. Over time I came to be introduced at that same distance to her boys, just Stevey the first time, but then one morning all four of the kids at a back table, spread out with sodas and comic books, waiting for their mother to get free. There's a place for patience and discretion, so Carl Wayne could enjoy his breakfast too, still stunned as he was by the good fortune that as summer deepened he could fish and hunt quail again if he cared to, or stay out in the garage with his buddies as long as he wanted, and his wife no longer made a fuss.

I was glad to see her when I could. We liked that ditch bank by the Bremer place; it was shady and secluded, and after her shift changed the first week of August, there'd often be a night or two during the week when she'd get off early to meet me. It doesn't all have to be grappling—I remember more than one night sitting back there along the ditch bank and just watching while Annie counted her tips. I'd pull a hubcap out of the trunk, and she would empty her apron pockets of a day's worth of change. I liked watching her quick fingers sort down through the quarters and nickels, slipping them into paper coin rolls that she carried in her purse. The dimes were already earmarked for Shannon's birthday.

"I'm thinking of getting him a telescope, maybe, I think he'd enjoy it. He's just so serious, Arthur, he's never been quick with a smile."

"I'd smile, if I was a boy, to get a telescope."

"Oh, he'll like it. I know he will. It's kind of on the high side, but Carl won't know the difference. He'll just be glad I found the money. I think I'll go get it tomorrow."

She'd grown used to me watching her, I guess. I never tired of just noticing her, and she would talk to me about whatever crossed her mind. While she went over her various complaints and plans, I would rub her neck. Though I've never seen it on the *Star* science page, I think it's a proven fact that young mothers seldom get their recommended minimum daily amount of rubbing. I'd move along her neck and ankles, fingers and toes—Annie never seemed to quite get enough. All out around us were beans and corn domesticated to perfection, not a ragged one in the bunch. There on the tangled ditch bank or, if we had a little while, at the base of the silo, she most nights let me love her again.

I was driving her back to her car one of those evenings when she directed me just north of downtown, through the neighborhood where she grew up.

"That's my Uncle Roy's," she said, pointing to a low clapboard house. "Look in there, look, see them on the couch? They like that TV. Over there's my Uncle Lloyd's, you probably know him. He's manager over at NAPA, in charge of the parts."

We'd come past the old glass factory by then and were almost under the water tower, winding among the small frame houses and squat shade trees that were spread out around its base. It was as dark a night as our first ride, and Annie still sat low, but she'd let my hand slide up under the skirt of her uniform, to lie flat on the smooth inside of her thigh. She nodded to a small house with what looked like a permanently half-finished job of aluminum siding.

"My grandma lives there. My mom's mom. We lived with her until I was six. Next door there is where my cousin Clare's family lives."

"Anybody in town here you're not related to?"

She laughed. "I told you I have family. There's more than enough on both sides to go around, the Claytons and Yorks, you must have been in school with some of them. My grandma's maiden name was Willeford, a lot of them are still around. Carl Wayne's got family too."

On one side of her grandmother's house there was a glassed-in porch that doubled as a beauty salon. A magnetic sign reading THE LATIN QUARTER hung in the window. Somebody down the street had another sign, this one in the front yard and made out of wood. It offered miniatures for sale and saw sharpening, whichever a person might happen to prefer.

"Look," Annie said, "there's my niece Frances, coming down the street on her bike. Darn it, don't slow down, Arthur, don't! Don't!" She scooted all the way down in her seat as a chubby little girl sailed past, intent on winding in and out of the streetlights' saucered glow. Annie kicked me when we'd gone past. "Don't you dare, you creep, or you'll be sorry."

She kicked me, but settled back under my hand anyway, smiling out the window.

THIRTEEN

My own birthday came and went the last week of July. Both Moni and Stevey had picked up ear infections, so Annie wasn't able to share the occasion; instead there'd been a cupcake and a candle that I found early that morning in my mailbox, along with a leftover child's valentine. The valentine message was still there, held by a friendly-looking green worm with wire-rim glasses and a mortarboard, perched in front of a blackboard and globe. "Happy Birthday, Arthur," and "Love, A." were written on the back, in big smudged-carbon strokes.

That same afternoon Byron caught me on the way out to mow side ditches, and invited me over for cake. It was his own idea, clear enough—Kendra still hadn't forgiven me about Betsy. If not for my stubbornness, in her eyes, the four of us would have been strolling down in Indy through the old Union Station, ranging up to the Century Center to see the Judds. Byron had a big chocolate and cherry ice-cream cake he'd brought home from the store, while she'd gone to town to see her dad.

My brother dished up huge sloppy pieces while the kiddies sat around the table uncertain. Byron, for all his jolliness, seemed distracted, and between the sugar and the momentary lapse in discipline, my nephew and niece quickly grew giddy, taking advantage of the stray chance to have fun. Joey was in his last long summer of still being a boy, so he set himself to gumming the dessert for his sister's delight. Celeste threw back her head to laugh, slapped at growing puddles of ice cream with her spoon. Nobody could doubt that Kendra had hard duty, caring first for my dad and then her own, not such pleasant work watching old men slide away. Still, nobody missed her, just as nobody seemed to care that most of the second and third rounds of the ice cream ended up scattered and oozed across the table. I was still enjoying the silliness when my brother began gathering the plates, and the two of us wiped up the best we could.

Afterwards I sat down with Byron in the living room, watching as Joey and his sister lay in front of the TV. My brother frowned.

"Joey's been lost this summer," he said, "once you finished with the last of the field work. He liked being out there."

"I liked having him. He kept me alert." Joey had his head down like he wasn't listening, but his ears colored, so I knew he was positioned to receive the best kind of compliments of all, the ones halfway overheard. "He's got a knack for equipment," I told his dad, "a good steady hand."

The principal-elect considered that information as we sat back in silence. The house was too warm, but when I came in I'd let the storm door stand open, so there floated in at least a hint of the fresh summer evening just beyond. Byron and I'd begun speculating back and forth about corn prices and bond issues, passing our polite time, when my brother cleared his throat. He instinctively glanced up at the kitchen first, before turning back to me.

"Uh, Arthur," he said, "I was out to the cemetery a couple of months ago, on Memorial Day. I went out there to clean up a little. Just a little, you know, not much. They keep things real nice."

He leaned forward with his hands clasped, elbows resting on his heavy legs. He looked over his glasses again at his own children in front of the television.

"You probably remember Mom's headstone, it's real nice, red marble. It's got both their names on it now, and the family name, you know, right in the center. It's not like some of those stones that are rippled on the edge. This one's polished, on a long marble base. You might remember how it's set back a little from the creek, as you come in from the north."

Byron took his time working the long way around to it, but finally after I'd heard all over again about the groundskeeping and tombstone, he plunged ahead.

"So I was thinking, you know, last May, what a shame it was that we've never gone out there. So you could see how it looks. Gerry had you awful busy last May, but like I say, I was thinking. Would you maybe be interested in taking a ride out there with me sometime, and us having a look at the graves?"

It had all come out in a rush there at the end, but for that matter I'd been thinking some myself. It hadn't been of graveyards, particularly, but more of the kids acting silly with their ice cream, of Annie's leg bare and soft under my palm. I thought about the shade of the ditch banks, my cupcake and summer valentine, the cool breeze that was gathering just outside. I considered what a fine addition to a birthday conversation this had been too, to hear all about how a gravesite had been landscaped, the thrill of a new name added on.

"You know," I said, "that would be nice, it really would," and by the way my brother brightened, I knew he was in for a rough tenure as principal. Those kids would run circles around him every time.

"Yeah?"

"Yeah, maybe in about two thousand years. Why don't you come look me up then."

Still leaning forward earnestly, Byron blinked back at me. It had been nice to be remembered with the ice cream, I told him, as I rocked to my feet. He nodded over at the bookcase, to a small black-and-white picture on the shelf.

"Mom would have been sixty-five next week," he said. "Do you ever think about that?"

"No, Byron," I said, "never. I never once think of it at all."

FOURTEEN

During the breathing spell before harvest, Gerry still had his many and varied affairs to manage, so I kept busy mowing the side ditches and cleaning out a couple of bins. I hadn't seen him in almost a week when I ran into him down at the intersection of 14 West and the old Germantown Pike.

I was coming down from Foxie's, the field mower bouncing and rattling behind me. The little Allis doesn't have much speed, but I'd never minded; it's always a pretty drive winding along the Tippy to cross the bridge. A mile south of it I came up on Gerry's Fleetwood, pulled over at the side of the road. He'd wrestled a wooden sign out of the pile that was jammed into his trunk and was dragging it to the edge of the highway.

"Hey there," he said when I'd putted alongside. "You get finished up north?"

"Yeah, you can go pounding along up there too. I got it all trimmed up for you."

"Oh, this damn Round Barn thing," he said. "If the doggone things were all that special, they would have built more in the first place, and we wouldn't need a festival just to look at them. The Chamber thinks it's great, though, so here I am. They were going to contract it out, putting up the signs, but I told them I could do it a hell of a lot cheaper than that. Free, in fact. Here, grab that one I got laying over there in the grass, and we'll turn it toward the folks coming in from the west. Don't want 'em lost, the Burger King and Cove might lose that extra table or two of business."

We fell easily enough back into working together, just like we'd never been apart. He had one of his dress polo shirts on, his big chunks of arm bulging out, and he swung the five-pound sledge like it was a toy.

"Oh, nobody minds spending money anymore," he complained, "the council's the same damn way. Don't know if I told you about that boy we had from down at Crawfordsville, over at the jailhouse. Plenty of good places to rob down there, but no, he had to come a hundred miles north, all the way up here, where Hank Boudreau caught him breaking into Tri-County Beverage. About a month ago, maybe you heard. He was sixteen is all, so we had to put him in a private cell, separated off by himself. Anyway, damned if the little shit didn't go and get depressed, and start saying he was going to kill himself. When that got out, Rich didn't have no choice but to move him up to Warsaw, they got a twenty-four-hour unit there, where they can keep an eye on him. You know how much that damn place costs? You got any idea? Three hundred dollars a day. Three hundred! And the county picks up the tab. I about hit the ceiling when I seen the bill. And now there's four or five more, all saying they're gonna kill themselves too, see, they all want to go up to Warsaw. There's road-graders we need, street signs, and here we are paying out all that money up north. The county ain't hardly solvent as it is, so I don't know what we're going to do."

I hadn't heard Gerry complain in a while, and maybe I missed that too. As luck would have it, we'd just finished setting the sign when out in the field next to us one of Ray Stewart's new irrigation units started up. It sputtered at first, but gradually gathered force until two wide streams of water were spreading out over the corn.

"Those crops of ours look real good up north," I told him as we watched the water pipe begin its slow, high circuit around the field. "This here of Ray's ain't no better."

Gerry nodded slowly. "Yeah, a person might say that. A normal person might question putting in a half-a-million-dollar irrigation system when the rain comes for free, especially when the prices are just as damn low for him as they are for everybody else. To the average man it don't figure, not at all. But see, Arthur, Ray's different. He plans ahead. He's taken potential losses into account and learned to live with them. Low prices, weather, they don't bother him like they do most people, because he plans." He shook his head. "I don't know if I mentioned it to you, but I spent two or three days already this week with Irene. Oh, she's getting to be a handful. Don't know how much longer she's gonna be able to be alone."

"She sick again?"

"Oh, I guess so. If the doctors know, they aren't saying. And then there's Jack on the phone all the time, he'd just as soon see her in a home tomorrow. 'She listens to you, Gerry, tell her it'd be safer.' See, he just don't want to worry about her is what it is, get her socked away where she can't cause him no trouble. Hell, I'd take her in myself and be pleased to, it'd be an honor really, a woman like Irene, but it ain't quite that easy. It was really Charlotte and me that she was close to, and Kathryn never come in for that. The truth be told, I think she kind of resents it. Then with the hours we work, too, it would kind of fall to her to do the caretaking. It's not like it used to be, there ain't every woman like your sister-in-law. It ain't no mystery why Byron's making his way in the world. A wife stands behind you, there ain't no limit to what a man can do! Anyway, maybe I can keep Irene going awhile, look in on her a little more often now that she's feeling low."

The logo on the signs was a shiny black round barn, salvaged evidently from the year before, because a sticker had been placed across the bottom with a new set of dates. As we leaned in on the Fleetwood fender to watch Ray's own private rainfall, Gerry took the opportunity to frown.

"The hell of it is she knows. She knows she ain't no good, and it scares her. On the way home from the doctor's the other day in South Bend, we stopped off at Laughner's Cafeteria. She's always liked that. And it perked her up quite a little bit to go through the line, sit up there with all the other people. She was smiling some, which I was glad to see. But then on the way home, we no more got back on 31 again when I looked over and she was crying. 'Course she didn't want me to see, but I would have found out, there's things a person can't hide. The poor thing had gone and messed herself is what it is, gone to the bathroom right there in the car. It went all through her dress, down onto the seats, oh, it was a mess. Kathryn's got tickets for an ice cream social at the fire department, is expecting me home, and there I am out at the shop, cleaning up the car. It's like these signs, it gets to be kind of a lonely chore."

Every fourth car that passed on 14 would recognize us, Gerry or the Fleetwood, one. They'd honk, and he'd wave back the hammer in salute.

"A person just wears out, Arthur, is what it is. Ain't nothing goes on forever."

We both of us considered it then, trying to think of something that did. The warm breeze from the corn carried with it the swish of Ray's sprinklers as they moved away from us around the field. Low spirits or not, Gerry was never one to come in second.

"Except low prices," he said. He laughed, grabbing my arm in that big fist of his, shaking it hard once before he let go. "That's one thing, the doggone prices. They're one thing that's always been able to last."

FIFTEEN

In the middle of August Annie and I hit a bad stretch, when we had a rough time finding chances to meet. The milk plant shut down for its two-week annual cleanup, so Carl Wayne got his vacation, and they went down to Kentucky with friends. He had a fishing trip with his buddies scheduled too, but Moni came home from the south with the chicken pox, and for the rest of the month the boys got into the act, passing it around among themselves. When the plant came back on line, Carl Wayne drew four weeks of swing shift, so evenings Annie had to be home. It was hard to keep track of, and finally we ended up doing what more experienced couples would have done all along: she traded shifts herself one Saturday to get nighttime again, and we met in a Plymouth motel.

Out there in the country you're always scaring up people—the stuck hunters and four-wheelers, all of them having a wild time of it until they get caught up in the mud. Then there are the romantic ones: the fall before I'd almost run over two teenagers with the grain truck, and that spring I flushed up one of the Bareither boys and what looked to be the girls' PE teacher from over at the high school. People ought to be grateful farmers are closemouthed. While the school-teacher was busy getting dressed, the boy just looked up at me on the tractor, a cocky little guy with a big smile on his face, at peace with the world.

Still, a couple likes to think that they're onto something special. Up at the Frontier Inn in Plymouth, though, a defrocked TraveLodge that had adopted for its declining years a kind of Western motif, it was hard to maintain the conceit. Just driving through the parking lot I saw fat Jason Reid from the bank going upstairs with a secretary from the bottled gas plant; on Annie's way up to join me she ran into the new woman county attorney, pulling up in her sports car with Rodney Gilliland. To top it off, the motel was filthy, and we were both of us a little on the tidy side, liking to see things clean.

Annie had been late getting off, was still in her gravy-splattered uniform when she'd come in, dragging the Cove twenty miles north with her in the car. The boys had been sick again, and with school starting the next Tuesday, she was already on the verge of tears.

"Do you think I'm trash, Arthur?" she demanded, before I had her half-undressed on the sagging mattress. "Is that what you think?"

"Why, no," I said. "Why would I think that?"

"We don't see each other all this time, we grab an hour like this, it ain't no good. Don't you see?"

"It's okay," I said. "We're doing the best we can. Just calm down a minute."

"This damn ugly place too, it's awful, I thought you said it'd be nice. I thought we could have someplace nice."

"It's all right, honey," I said. "It's all right."

"It's all right for you, maybe, damn it, but it's just not nice. There's nothing nice about being here at all."

The truth was there wasn't, but after coming up all that way, we went ahead and made love anyway, as forced and unfocused as if we'd been together a dozen years. She had to get home right away, so, crying, she was hurrying back into her uniform almost as soon as we finished.

"I'll take you somewhere nice," I promised as she was going out the door. "You let me know when you're free. I'll take you somewhere special just for us."

Like a lot of men, though, I was firm on the promising, and a little more vague about exactly how to get things done. With the kids back in school she had to work mornings, and by that time we were into the harvest. Gerry was like the rest of the go-getters, he couldn't wait for grain to dry in the fields. We started on corn so wet that the bottom of the load looked like a big can of Niblets, and I had to practically slide down the chute myself to move it along.

I got a note or two in my mailbox again, still tried to catch a glimpse of her now and then at breakfast, but the easy days of summer were gone. Gerry had us going hard all the time, and two weeks apart had stretched into three and almost four, before headlights came up behind me in the mirror. I put up with the night-blindness as the car followed close, was surprised when it followed me on up the lane to the dryer. I was happy, then, too, to see it was Annie in the old, battered Nova, who came pulling along beside.

There was a chill in the air, and she had a black sweater pulled up over the shoulders of her uniform. It's funny how some things work: I was glad a hundred ways over to see her, but at the same time was halfway unbelieving that I'd ever held her close. She must have been feeling the same way; we stood at an uncertain distance from each other while grain tumbled down into the pit. I was dusty, but now and again would step close to put my arm around her. As I was dropping the truck bed, she came up to take my hand.

There was awkwardness to it, but that much could be expected; she'd brought good news along with her too. Carl Wayne was going up to Michigan for a special four-day bow season. Holly had agreed to keep the kids Friday night and most of Saturday, so that first half of the weekend, anyway, could finally be ours.

SIXTEEN

We'd had a pretty steady harvest from my way of thinking, but my way of thinking still tended to linger back when a few hundred acres were more than enough for any man. After a full month we'd barely made a dent on the total, and all those acres out there never ceased to weigh on Gerry's mind. He'd already started worrying and stewing about every bearing that went out or every chain that snapped apart, and there were more than a few of both. The bad days we spent running back and forth to Keona for parts; the good ones Gerry tried his best to bear down. We had a day of rain, but before that we'd managed ten days straight, always going far into the night. That still didn't make him very pleased to hear I'd be taking an evening off.

"We had two good months of summer," he complained. "Ain't that enough time to run around?"

We were at the Rawson place, on a warm Thursday evening a little before dark.

"'Course I never told you that you had to be out here. I never demanded nothing of you. You need a night off, I want you to take it."

"Good," I said, "because I'm going to."

"No sir, I ain't never expected a hired man to put in the kind of hours I do. You want to run off for a night, you just go ahead and do it. You need two nights, take 'em. Hell, take a week, it don't matter to me. You just tell me what you need."

"A night ought to about do it, plus most of the next day. We'll see. I reckon you'll still have some corn left to haul when I get back."

He had to huff and puff about it some more, but Gerry wasn't my dad and I wasn't his boy. I just went ahead with the hauling, and by the time I came back to help him move equipment, he'd already rolled once and come up the other side.

"You know," he said, "it ain't none of my business what you got planned, Arthur, none at all. Still, you make a fella think. Maybe it ain't that bad an idea if I take an evening off too, we been going at this awful hard. Kathryn might like some company for a change. A man can't expect a woman just to sit at home all fall, no matter how good a wife she is. No matter how much she understands what you're trying to do."

As the night wore on it became more and more his idea. He took the trouble to keep me posted, announcing the latest version each time I came bumping the truck alongside.

"I been thinking that if the Moose don't appeal to her, maybe we'll just stay home. Maybe she'd like that the best of all. Just order us a pizza or some of them Mexican dinners, have us a couple of Pepsis, and sit back and talk. A couple can let that part of life slip by awful easy, believe you me. I got all them channels on the TV, maybe we'll just sit back and watch one of them, have a chance to relax."

The air was cool and dry, perfect fall weather for harvest. While Gerry planned, we went until well after midnight, filling the wet holding bin up to the brim.

I got some sleep before I went back at four to turn off the dryer, grabbed a little more time in bed after that. About eleven the next morning we sheared another pin, losing a couple hours, but Gerry was still in a good mood. When three-thirty came around, though, the time we'd decided to quit, it became clear he wasn't shutting down after all.

"Oh," he said, "a man's got to get his bid in a little earlier, seems like. Kathryn done made plans already. She and some of her lady friends are going up to Fort Wayne tonight to some kind of dinner theater. That's all right, though, I wouldn't have it no other way. A woman's got her own mind, that's just the way it should be. It never hurts a fella, anyway, to get a little more corn in the hopper. We'll be mighty grateful come December."

"I'll be back out sometime late tomorrow."

"Oh my goodness, Arthur, don't worry about it. You have a good time. Here, you got money? You need a little cash? I been meaning to give you a bonus, we been going so damn hard I forgot about it. You sure you don't need a little cash? Get some gas there for your car on the way home. I'm just gonna try to get a little ways ahead here while the weather holds. You go on now and have a good time."

Maybe he thought I was waiting for his permission; at any rate it seemed to make him feel better to give it. As I pulled away along the fencerow there came the dragging down of the big diesel behind me. In the Camaro's rearview mirror there plumed up a big farewell puff of black smoke, and before I even got out to the road, the old International was moving away, Gerry heading alone back into the field.

SEVENTEEN

Gerry stayed behind, but he was the first I'd ever known to do it, break away somewhere just because he could. I still remember what a remarkable thing it was when I was a boy, that every so often when the field work was done, or in between seasons, he'd pack up his family and go off somewhere to a motel. A Holiday Inn was where they stayed, because Holiday Inns were the very best motels there were back then, and the very best was what Gerry Maars had to have.

What the modern world had brought with it, though, was a whole lot of other people who could have the very best too. Enough so that there'd sprung up a whole new half-dozen classes of motel even fancier, but I picked out a Holiday Inn just the same, fifty miles away in Marion, and I drove over that same Friday afternoon.

I guess they were used to credit cards, because the kid behind the desk handled my two fifties like they were live snakes. We only needed one bed that I knew of, but for ten dollars and the nod of my head, we magically had two. I walked past a little gift shop and the dark mahogany beams of the Baron's Table, where a sign in old English lettering announced that it would open at six. A wide carpeted hallway led me down two separate wings to Room 130, the one that had been set aside for us.

Annie had said she'd try to be there by six-thirty, which meant I'd beat her there by over an hour. I can't say that I settled in easily, making my way like a burglar past polished chrome luggage stands, a long partition and wide oval sink, a pyramid of towels on a rack. A wicker basket of shampoos and soaps had been left at the basin's edge, while for the extra dirty there was another sink, smaller, in the bathroom that opened just beyond.

Six-thirty came and went, and from the armchair where I'd settled I studied the walls. They were covered by a cream-colored fabric that softened the room, while a tasteful peach-colored stripe ran diagonally above the bed. Heavy cloth curtains did their job; over the next half hour there was only the occasional muffled voice of someone passing in the hallway, the faint slam of a car door far away. I don't know whether it was corn dust or the luxury, but I couldn't quite get adjusted to being there. A dressed-up Frontier, like any other room that people rented—that's what it was until almost seven, when there was a quick tapping at the door. I pulled it open to find Annie, who came sweeping past me into the room.

"Oh, Arthur," she said, with genuine happiness, "we're here. I can't believe we really are. This is so pretty." A quick hug was all I could hold her to before she was off on a tour of her own, smelling the towels, discovering the heat lamp, running her fingers along the smoothness of the sink. With her single suit bag in one hand and her small overnight case in the other, I followed in Annie's wake, watching while she sifted through the wicker basket's treasures, turned on and off the television, tried out the light by the bed.

She seat-dropped onto the bed, beaming. "I just can't believe it. I can't believe we're really here. You look so good to me, Arthur."

"Did you get the kids dropped off all right?"

"Yeah, but that's why I'm late. Jeff forgot his rash medicine, and we had to turn around halfway and go back to get it. This is the biggest treat in the world, to stay at their Aunt Holly's. They were so excited they fought all the way down to Caterville. I don't know who was more keyed up, them or me."

Her hair held back by a bandanna, she had on a gray zip sweatshirt over a Delfina Comets T-shirt, white sneakers, and jeans faded and flecked with paint. She bounced up to take hold of my hand and kiss me, to press her cheek quickly against mine.

"Now, you haven't seen me yet, all right? I'm just a ghost. I'm just somebody passing through. The real girl shows up in a little while." She pulled off the bandanna. "Oh, this is all so pretty. Did you put that little vanity case by the sink? I had to borrow it from Janine, I didn't even have one. Look at you, Arthur, in that nice white shirt, all cleaned up and ready. You brought a tie, didn't you? I had a half-shift early, and then getting Carl off, the kids packed . . . No, don't get close to me, I'm not here yet. You still haven't seen me at all."

She'd begun staking out the far side of the partition for herself. Her sweatshirt peeled off and tossed aside, she stepped back in long enough to give me my orders.

"You just take the next hour and do what you want, because you're still not here either. You get to see me later, not all dirty and sweaty after work, for a change."

She warned me twice more from beyond the partition to stay away. While she was showering I did go out to wander my way down the halls. The room key gave me access to the ice machine; in the stairwell I looked out on the parking lot through a small wire-reinforced window in the door. In the lobby three businessmen checked in at the desk. I stood at the front door to watch an evening's brisk business at the Amoco across the street, and a red Sunbird that had been pulled over by the cops.

Back in the room, though, was where I spent the last twenty minutes, trying to sort through the brushing and rustling from the far side of the partition. They were impossible to decipher, so I just leaned back to listen as the different sounds floated out to me, along with a steamy essence of Annie freshly washed.

"I hope you haven't got too impatient out there," she called to me. "I'm just about there. Got . . . a couple . . . of . . . things more. You hungry?"

"I'm all right."

"I'm starving to death, so you better be warned. I'm like all those other girls, saving up their appetites for their dates!"

After a false start or two, a "Darn it" and a "Wait a minute," Annie finally came around the partition to meet me. I felt myself smile then, the oddest feeling because I was so helpless against it, my own face's foolish widening to see her looking back at me, her knowing how pretty I thought she was. Still unmistakably Annie after all her sprays and brushing, still trim and tomboyish—a battler with life, really, there was no doubt about it even then—but all of it gathered up that night in a short, tight dress of red velour, nylons taking over where her dress stopped a good foot above her knees. Her lashes and eyelids were darkened, her neck bare and pale; she tottered toward me unsteadily, her heels sinking into the thick carpeting on the floor. As I took her lightly into my arms, all the sweet scents of her preparations rose up from her, and even after those weeks apart and the fifty miles that we'd wandered from home, Annie slipped into a place up against me all her own.

"Hold on," she said, "I got to make a call."

I didn't want to let go but she pushed away from me, sitting on the edge of the bed to dial. She waited, letting it ring.

"Who's this?" she said abruptly, and listened. "This is Mom. Has Dad called?" She listened again, this time for longer. She frowned. "Well, she can't. Tell her she can't. I don't care, just tell her. Tell her to behave herself or Aunt Holly's not gonna let you kids come over no more. Go on, tell her I said so."

She covered the phone. "Moni wants to do what she wants to do, and Shannon's gonna wear himself to a frazzle trying to keep her in line. Holly? Yeah, it's me. I'm here." She looked around the room. "Oh yeah, it's nice. It's just awful nice, like a picture. We're going out to eat in a couple of minutes. Yeah, I'd say so. I'd say that it does. Hold on, let me ask him." This time she didn't cover the phone. "Holly wants to know if the dress looks nice."

The truth is the only worthwhile thing in the first place, but seldom in life is it that clear and easy a thing to tell. "Just beautiful," I said.

"You hear that? You hear what he said? Yeah, that's right. Right. Oh yeah, he's pretty too." She winked at me. "He's about as pretty a man as I've ever seen. Right. Right, okay, but don't let her run wild. The boys got to live there too. That's right. Okay, we will. It's in his little fanny pack there, make him find it. Okay, we will. Bye."

I don't even know when it hit me, exactly, probably when she'd come tottering proudly around the edge of the partition, or when, despite her best efforts, that crushed velvet dress rode ever higher on her leg as she sat wrapped up in her call. Maybe it was while Shannon's plight came spilling out from the receiver, her own frown as she heard the story unfold. Whenever it was, it suddenly came to me how easily it might have happened, that I never would have seen her up close at all. In an ungoverned world how easily it could have, that fall, slipped away. She'd played absently with a dangling silver earring while she talked, brushed errant hair away from her neck: all that care and fine wrapping, and the only thing the boys want to do is muss it. When she'd hung up what I wanted was to pull her down with me onto one of those wide clean beds, to paw and press in on her, but after only the minimum amount of mussing—she'd missed me too—Annie stopped us, flushed and determined. Our first real night out and she wasn't going to let any of it go to waste. So, she patted and brushed us back into being pretty again, and we walked to the restaurant arm in arm.

EIGHTEEN

There had been a painting in our living room when I was a boy, a huge, black steam engine, high on studded wheels in an open field. Long leather belts stretched to the machinery behind it, with two or three wagons pulled close for the grain. Men stooped in golden stubble for the gathering, a woman in the foreground spread out a blanket, in the distance lay a threatening sky. They were the threshers, bent to the harvest. The other painting we'd had was right across from it, and for a certain time and people had been just as common — a straw-woven cornucopia, the simple horn of plenty. With a tail end receding into darkness, its wide mouth yielded three or four shaded apples, a handful of grapes, what might have been a small squash or pear tumbled onto the tabletop ahead.

It's kind of sad, really, that meager and half-starved notion of what abundance could really be. As Annie and I strolled into the Baron's Table that night, there were no doubt some old Hoosiers from that time, at odds with the modern bounty, scattered among the other customers. Sheepish and uncertain like my dad would have been, they'd found themselves somehow dining under crossed swords and a counterfeit coat of arms, warmed by high gas-log hearths, filing uneasily past a salad bar that was filled to overflowing with fresh lettuces and spinach, strawberries and kiwi, mushrooms trucked in from the north. Uncertain how they'd come to pay sixty-five dollars for a sleeping room, another twenty-five just to eat, maybe they were comforted some to spy a lively, young woman who was so honestly thrilled by it all, so happy with the restaurant, with herself, with me.

Whether that shock of hair was too unruly, the fuzzy dress too far out of style — how would any of us have known or cared? In a state chockful of grudges, people smiled outright to see her — that night, no one would begrudge her a single thing. Not the deep burgundy tablecloths and candlelight, or the tall blue daiquiri that a chubby-kneed cocktail waitress named Cyndi brought from the lounge next door. Leaning over a menu half her size, Annie glowed under our mutual attention. She took easily enough to being served: by Cyndi, by a nervous busboy bearing chilled butter squares and water, and finally by a tall, broad-shouldered waiter who introduced himself as Eric and boomed out the specials of the day. Under the influence of the wine that could have been Grapette for all we would have known, I turned out to be funnier than either of us remembered, and we laughed half the dinner away.

Afterwards we made our way over to the grand Holilounge, a dark, tiny bar where a combo had been set up for our listening and dancing delight. It consisted of an eager young kid with a wraparound keyboard like the cockpit of a jet fighter, and his little brother playing a tentative sort of bass. A two-piece orchestra was meant to be progress, I guess — modern times had been as hard on sidemen as it had been on farmers. Wherever the maestro led us, though, we were happy to follow, swaying together on our corner of the dance floor, necking and nuzzling like fools.

"This is so sweet," Annie whispered to me. "It's just what I thought a honeymoon would be like."

"What about yours? Didn't you have one?"

"Oh yeah, kind of. I was carrying Shannon, so I was sick most of the time. And then Carl Wayne wasn't no help, he got so drunk at the reception he couldn't stand up. We just went up to the fishing camp a couple of days. It was kind of ugly, Arthur, is what it was. Not like this. It didn't really count like no honeymoon at all."

It'd be easy enough to make fun of us, I know, the Baron's Table and the Holilounge, a motel on the far edge of town. But to us it made not the slightest difference what other restaurants might be out there, what other music might be playing in the world. Everyone should have a honeymoon, and on the way back to the room, Annie leaned up close to me, her head tucked under my chin. At our room I pushed open the door and came back to sweep her up into my arms. When I'd carried her over the threshold and set her inside, she held on tight, pulling me down so I could hear.

"Oh Arthur," she whispered, "I'm so happy. I'm the happiest girl in the world. Do you know that? Do you understand that you make me happy?"

So I finally did get to muss and pull at her, drag her down onto the bed; afterwards I might have wanted to stay awake some to watch over her, but I wasn't much of a lookout after all. The truth was that both of us had not only honeymooned for an evening, but worked the whole day and week before. On my end of things, those long nights under the combine and four o'clock drives back to the dryer had come up to take their toll. Annie was still shifting and murmuring next to me when I slipped into a daytime and nighttime both, where cornstalks flashed by in the headlights, and grain mounted slowly higher around my legs. Gentle at my ankles and knees, it came up without warning to bind me, and just that quickly I was caught. Pulled down though the swirl, grain pressing now at my waist, my chest—there rose a panic ever familiar that gripped me, a scream buried deep in my throat. Grain had already covered my face, my arms, and thrashing against the darkness that clawed at me, I burst up suddenly wide awake and alert.

It took time to realize I was free and unbound, to find breath again, to follow it that long way back to the still of a motel room. When I did, and reached out for Annie, she scooted away. I leaned up to find she was crying.

"What's the matter?" I said. "What's going on?"

She shook her head and pulled away from me, but when I reached out she let me slide up under her shoulder, scoot her back into the hollow that we made. Still crying, she lay her head on my arm.

"I woke up thinking of the kids, I guess, over at Holly's. This is the first time I ever been away from them like this. Nine years and more, if you count since Shannon got started. That's a long time."

"It is."

"I just worry about them, I guess. I don't know. Don't pay no attention to me."

"They're all fine," I said, "sleeping safe and sound at your sister's. They'll be there to greet you tomorrow."

"Arthur," she said. She rolled around to face me, her eyes brushing wet against my arm. "Now, don't be scared just because I say it, but I love you. I really do. I just can't get over how beautiful you are in my eyes."

I loved how beautiful she was in my eyes too, under my hands, through whatever sense it is that we use to feel precious life up against us in the dark. The thought occurred to me for the first time, there in that Marion motel room, that this small woman who had come all the way up from Delfina to wrap herself around me, who even then ran her fingers over my face — she meant me absolutely no harm in the world at all. Her heart wasn't set against mine in any way. I didn't know what to make of that, really, and long after she'd gone back to sleep, I listened to her breathing, idly thinking back on my own dream, and still trying to remember that odd, stubborn thing I had to keep track of, if I was going to go on being me. As the dream shifted and faded, that other thing wouldn't come back to me either. Finally I just gave up, settling back with Annie into sleep.

NINETEEN

I woke up the next morning to Annie right above me, her head propped on one elbow, studying my face.

"Didn't you ever miss people?" she asked.

"Good morning," I said.

"When you were a sailor, run off to get on them boats. Didn't you miss people?"

It turned out that she'd been awake over an hour like that, just watching me sleep. All that time to think had given her a head start, so I tried to catch up.

"Like how?"

"I don't know, how do people miss people? Like your brother and sister-in-law. Your nephew and niece. Didn't you miss them?"

"I guess not," I said, still half-asleep. As I pulled her closer, Annie elbowed her way up onto my chest to keep talking.

"I would. I know I'd miss some people a lot. Ann-Marie, Janine. I'd miss Holly too, something terrible. And my mom, I'd want to see her." She paused, considering. "I might even miss Carl some, we been together so long. To just take off like you done, I don't know that I could do it."

"I guess I'm just not much of a misser."

I was lying back with my eyes closed. When I opened them it was to see her hair, then her forehead, and finally her eyes as she edged up for a better look. Her eyes were smudged from the makeup of the night before.

"You're not scared about any of this, though, either." She said it as a fact, assessing. "You know, running around. Carl Wayne finding out and making trouble. You aren't afraid to love me like this, Arthur, are you?"

I tried to see if I was. "I guess I'm not afraid of Carl Wayne," I decided. "I never thought much about it. You planning on telling him?"

"No, I was just wondering. No, don't say that. Don't be talking about him. He's got nothing to do with this. The boys, Moni, they deserve their dad."

By that time I was awake. Having Annie up close and unhurried was a luxury, and in the small daylight that slipped in to us, I got to love her yet again, afterwards tracing between her breasts a dark blue artery, following brother and sister veins across her temples and wrists.

"You know," she said, "I got to watch you this morning. You're just the prettiest man. You really are. I can't believe I get to love you like I do."

Around nine I ordered room service, and we spent the rest of the morning in bed. Off and on, we watched TV, sharing the room with two bass fishermen on an inflatable raft, ads for breakfast cereal and wart relief, and the same cartoons that no doubt were, at the same time back in Caterville, being closely followed by her kids.

"So anyway," Annie was saying, "that's the kind of stories they been wanting me to tell lately, all about when they were babies. Even Stevey, like I say, he's the tough guy, he'll still come around for that. 'Tell us about what we did when we were babies, Mama'—that's what they all want to hear. See, Arthur, how it is? That's all the older the world is to them, they don't know no better."

I'd pulled her down beside me again. Time was already beginning to move away from us, but there was enough that she curled back against me, her head pillowed a last few minutes by my arm.

"So what do you tell them?" I asked, and she sighed.

"Oh, I just tell them how smart they were. I tell them all the brave things they done, and the adventures they had. All the monsters they killed. Jeff and Stevey, they right away start in complaining, try to tell me how Moni couldn't have killed no monsters, she still wets the bed. Can't go to sleep at night without the light. That's what they say. But I just tell them that no, the way it used to be, she was the bravest of them all. The boys need to hear that some. They don't believe me, but they need to hear it just the same."

Annie was already running late by the time she finally pulled away. She sat on the edge of the bed to rub off her nail polish, gathered all her potions into Janine's red carrying case, climbed back into her T-shirt and speckled jeans. She slid her red dress back into its bag. She had slipped off her lover's face, too, trading it for a mom's: more alert and hurried, quicker to order and frown. It was one that I was fond of anyway, so I watched her as she sat down next to me one last time.

She looked through her purse for her keys. "Maybe I'll take them all to a movie this afternoon. They been wanting to go, and with Holly it's not such a handful. I hope you can meet her sometime, you'd think she was nice. A little on the heavy side is all, but with an awful pretty face, she'll hook on with somebody before too long."

"You still trying to fix me up?" I asked, shaking her knee.

"No, you're spoken for. I hope to keep you busy enough. Carl Wayne loves that hunting and fishing, so you never can tell. You think we can do this again, sometime, Arthur, the next time I can work it out?"

I shrugged, still warm and sleepy, with the truth. "There's no reason in the world why we can't."

TWENTY

There's no telling how late Gerry worked that night I went over to Marion, but by the time I got back out there the next day, he'd finished the big field at Rawson's and had moved everything to the eighty acres south of the road. Two out of the three trucks were full and waiting, so I started right in hauling corn. He didn't say word one to me the whole time I was back, so I was surprised when he pulled around about seven-thirty or so and waved me over to the cab.

"That dryer's about caught up, ain't it? It's got some corn to do?"

"A couple of hours' worth, maybe more. It's up past the middle."

"If that GMC's empty, just leave the diesel here, you can come back and get it. I want you to come on up here a little while."

"I'll take it back down to the road."

"No, darn it, Arthur, just come on. Come on up here in the cab."

Gerry'd swung back his unload auger, and when I'd climbed over the duals to squeeze in with him, he moved back into the rows.

"So you have a good time?" he asked.

I said that I had.

"That's good. It's good you had a good time."

"I did. I had a good time."

"I know I been pushing you awful hard. You get rested, then, with a night off?"

I laughed. "I guess you could say that."

"That's good. That's just fine. A man needs a chance to get away. Now listen, I been thinking about something that I want to tell you about. I ain't been square with you. I ain't been treating you right."

The clatter of stalks went on below us, under the sharp, steady tear of the cutting plates and chains.

"How do you mean?"

"I say right. I ain't been treating you right. I get all wrapped up in my own worries, and forget that a young man needs a challenge. You ain't been getting challenged the way you should, and I'm at fault."

Gerry nodded at the wisdom of his own insight, arrived at, evidently, over all those long passes at Rawson's the night before. Halfway across the field by then, he reached over and pulled back on the throttle, bringing us to a stop. He shut down the cutting assembly and raised the picker head, backing out of the rows. Corn dust rolled up in the glare of the headlights in front of us.

"Step back for a second so I can get out of here. Go on, let me get past, I ain't as small as I used to be. We're gonna switch places here, Arthur, is what it is. You're gonna run this combine. Come on now, don't be shy, I been thinking about it. I want you to learn. There ain't no reason in the world why you can't be picking corn too."

I imagine I'd been floating along with Annie somewhere; long after she'd slipped out the door of the Holiday Inn, I was still carrying her with me in my chest. Flashes of her wiry warmth, the soft of her belly, that head of hair tucked under my chin—they'd kept me a steady sort of company as I lumbered back and forth over the county road to the Bremer place. Gerry had squeezed past me out onto the platform. While I settled behind the wheel, he creaked himself down to kneeling, trying to fit in by my side.

"I ain't never in all these years let one of my men run this damn thing before. I couldn't afford to. But you got a lot on the ball, Arthur, you ain't like all those other boys. For that matter, you ain't a boy no more, you're a man. It's easy for an old codger like me to forget that. All right, now, ease up on the throttle there, you'll feel it start to catch. Got it? Okay, good. I don't want you getting bored and running off, thinking Gerry Maars don't appreciate you, because he does. Now come in easy, you want to get a feel for it. Just sight along number five there, put that divider right down the center of the row."

I'd handled my share of power equipment over the years, for that matter had once piloted a fully loaded ore boat the length of the St. Clair River, when the first mate was too drunk to walk. To hear Gerry tell it, though, all the powers of the earth and tides themselves were in my right hand as I eased us back into the corn. Maybe I wasn't appreciating the momentousness of the occasion, but just because he'd never let me handle the combine before didn't mean that I doubted that I could.

I was a careful driver, alert to the slashing of the knives. I had an eye already quick for plug-ups, a right hand that grew steadily quicker as I got the feel.

"Now drop it a little, you're still a little high. Drop down on it some, that's right, to about there. You got it, no problem, just keep alert now. You got to be alert. Number six there, see it, it's binding, you got to back off some. See what I mean? Now ease back in on it, that's good. That's real good, Arthur, you're doing just right. Oh, Shawn and those other boys, they just begged and begged me to run these combines, but you make the first. Keep centered now as we come up on the end here. Don't forget to swing out wide enough, swing it out now, cut hard! There's that fifth row to sight on, that's right, drop her down. Drop her down now, all the way."

He coached me an hour that night, off and on, the next day made a point of climbing down for something he claimed to have forgotten, making sure I saw him turn his back to me as he clumped to the truck. I knew that as soon as he was in my blind spot he'd been following anxiously, watching every foot of my progress down the rows.

As the fall went on, his confidence grew, but whether that was a blessing for him or not, it's hard to tell——he just had more chance to break away for all his other obligations. The council was floating revenue bonds for new development, and that meant industry representatives were in town, sniffing around for their share. Irene was a worry too; in late October she called him up hysterical, claiming the whole of Keona had moved away except for her. One morning less than a week later she couldn't see that the burner was still glowing on the electric range, and burnt up a dishtowel and the bottom side of a cupboard before she finally got it out. A teenage girl that Gerry hired did manage to help out some, the week or so that she lasted.

We were making progress, though, going forward the only way Gerry knew how, full speed ahead. One night before Thanksgiving I was combining beans down at the Holloway place about eleven o'clock, when he joined me with sandwiches after his council meeting in town.

He wasn't out there to bother, he assured me; he'd take the next truck to the dryer himself. For all his good intentions, though, Gerry Maars wasn't much to sit by and watch. When he'd finished his hamburger I was gallant enough to cede him back the wheel. All puffed up from the politics and late dinner, he didn't want me to climb down, preferring to recap to me as we traded places the latest news from town.

"Oh, it's the zoning again," he said. "That don't never seem to die. And then the revenue bonds, that's something else. I ain't never been sure I really cared for the idea, ain't nobody building my barns for me, or giving me no thirty-year grace period from taxes. Nobody never did nothing like that for the glove factory or any of them other businesses downtown, but these new companies, they all got to have it before they'll even look your way. I wouldn't mind it none if they paid decent wages, but them people won't make no promises at all. Not that they got to, the chamber's bound and determined they're going to come."

The red dog from down at Holloway's had come up to join us, running in front of the headlights through the beans. Tail waving, he kept up a steady gait ahead of us, dipping and weaving just in front of the bar.

"Look at that doggone mutt," Gerry said, "running like the empty-headed thing that he is. And look at them beans flying, a fella'd like to pick some of those pods that he knocks all to hell. I'd bring out my twenty-two and be done with him, but then I always figure he's gonna get tired or run over pretty soon as it is. I combined damn near six hours here this afternoon, and he was never more than ten feet ahead of my blades."

The truth was that the dog was just partial to Gerry. I could be out there all day and barely see him, but as soon as the Fleetwood pulled up, the dog would be right alongside. He stopped ahead of us a perilous second to sniff at a gopher hole, but just in time was bounding ahead again, barking silently back to us in the combine's roar.

"Go ahead and throw the rest of that sandwich out," Gerry said when we got to the other end. "I never seen a dog that liked mustard like that one does; go ahead and throw out the whole bag. Let the damn stupid thing go through it himself."

I threw out the scraps in the end rows, and as we turned, sat back down on the toolbox, looking out into the night. It never once bothered me that Gerry wanted to be in the driver's seat; there was no doubt that's where he belonged. While he roamed back and forth over the council's business, I was just as happy to be left with a dark corner of the cab and my own thoughts, warm from the chilly evening just outside.

Annie and I had gotten together a couple of more times by then, back at Marion in mid-October, and only the week before up at South Bend. Since wet weather's as good for duck hunters as it's bad for farmers, Gerry hadn't had to suffer quite so much when Carl Wayne took off with his buddies, and Annie and I grabbed our chance to break away. Holly was a still a sport; when we'd gone to South Bend, I sent her a dozen roses just for thanks. Otherwise Annie and I'd had to make do with another quick run up to the Frontier—it made a difference when we knew that other, prettier places were still to come.

A person can be excused, once or twice a lifetime, for thinking he's at the very center of the universe, even if it ended up being on a toolbox in the corner of a combine cab, in a bean field down at the south end of Haskell County. The combine had been fighting us all fall, but for those few hours around midnight it was running free and easy. The smooth late-night drone of the engine and steady sweep of the gathering bar were hypnotizing Gerry and me both, I suppose, into believing almost anything was possible at all.

"I been thinking," Gerry said, "is what it is, but I wouldn't want you to say nothing about it. I been thinking that one day I'd like to go ahead and buy Irene out. With Al Lantz sick like he has been, I been kind of on hold, but a fella don't want to wait forever. Not the way things are now. No, I was thinking that a man with the right kind of financing could just about take over the Bremer place and make a go of it. Get some new equipment while I was at it, set up a couple of crews like Ray done. Put you in charge of one of them and I'd take the other. Keep them two combines going round the clock. Oh, my Lord, but we'd get the ground covered then! We wouldn't be out here half the winter like we still are now!"

Two or three days without breakdowns, finally making progress on the beans—from there it was a natural progression to what a fine farm a man could really build. I'll have to say I even enjoyed it, hearing Gerry plan. Not that I had any big desire to run my own crew, but it felt good, in the dark cab, to sit back and hear about it, with Gerry ever eager at the helm. For once there were no ball games on the air, so the radio was on more as afterthought, a dim murmur too faint to make out. The warm smell of dust cooking on the manifold floated in through the heater, and except for the broad window in front of us, there was only the steady rumble of machinery, closing us in.

"This here is where you sprayed, Arthur, do you remember? Would you look how damn nice it is? A fella just wonders what he could do with some farmland that was really right for him. Look down there, at how nice all this that you done turned out."

We made our turn in the end rows where I'd parked the water wagon the spring before, and started back to the south.

"See," he said, "it all depends on what kind of advantage you got. I didn't have none when I started, but then Walter Bremer gave me a chance. Al Lantz helped me along. I had Charlotte all them years until she run off. I got Kathryn now. I got you. Oh, I'm counting you on the list too, Arthur. You been a big help to me. But still, it's like a lot of things, not everybody gets a fair shot at the prize. It's like the 4-H, do you remember? There was that real fine steer you raised that one year, I still remember it. What was it, a Hereford cross? Came in second runner-up, ain't I right? Well, ain't I right? You can't believe I remember that, can you?"

Half asleep, lulled by the smooth throb of the machinery, I agreed it was hard to believe.

"Oh, I can remember it like it was yesterday. Ray Stewart's older boy come in with the Grand Champion that year, Lindell Bardacke's boy with Reserve. You was right up there at the top, though, don't think I didn't notice it. You remember that steer, don't you?"

"Yeah," I said, "I guess I do."

"The hell of it, though, see, is like I was saying. You never really had a chance. They were already at it by then, Ray, Lindell, going all over the country for the best calves to work with. Down to Ohio, over to Illinois—hell, I done it myself, back when the girls had projects. Went all the way over to Iowa just to get Perri a boar. Thing was so damn good that she never hardly gave him a thought right up until fair week, and he came in Reserve. That steer of yours, though, Arthur, you could have had it in every night with you at the dinner table, sitting right there between you and Byron, and it never would have made the grade. It's kind of cold to say so, but it's the truth. You never had a chance."

"I never gave a damn for the 4-H anyway."

Gerry had gotten worked up about it by then, just like it had happened the week before.

"But it wasn't fair, see, that's what I'm driving at. You probably never heard about it even, don't reckon nobody said nothing about it, but I came up with a plan one year to set things straight."

"On what?"

"On the doggone 4-H, for making it more fair. I had it all figured out, see, that all of us who had kids in the contest any given year, we'd just pitch our calf money into one great big pot. Then all them club members would have had the same amount to go shopping with, make it a little more of a contest. That way my girls or Ray's kids, or the rest of them, they wouldn't really have no advantage. It'd get some fairness back into it. What do you think? Wasn't that kind of a clever idea? Ain't that a better system?"

He slowed to wheel through the end rows, standing like a cowboy in the stirrups to steal a glance into the hopper. A dim yellow lightbulb told the tale: it was three-quarters of the way there, still filling under a clatter of beans.

"Anyway, I thought it was a pretty slick idea. So I brought it up, the next time the 4-H board met. My Lord, you'd have thought I'd just made a motion that we all run down and join the Communist Party. They shot that damn idea down in a hurry. No sir, that wasn't the way we were gonna do things in Haskell County, not by a long shot!"

"Sunshine," I said. "I just remembered what I named that steer. I called him Sunshine."

"Sunshine? That's a cute name, real cute." He chuckled. "Bet you took real good care of it too, am I right? See, I remember you out there, Arthur. You probably don't believe it, but I do. You must have been nine or ten that year, no bigger than this." He measured in front of me with his palm. "A tough little cuss, I admired you even then. All them other boys, when it come time to turn over their projects, they're all sniffling and crying, but that wasn't old Arthur. No way in hell. You just marched up there to get your sale check, wasn't no bawling from you."

"Some of those boys get kind of attached."

"Oh yeah, I know they do. See, they're spending all them hours with that steer or hog or whatever, and they ain't really paying attention to what's to come. All that time and effort, and then they just kind of turn it over, so it's hard. Like you say, they get attached. Them projects are designed with teaching in mind though, see. There's a lesson there, besides all the caretaking, that them kids got to learn."

I'd gone back to daydreaming about Annie again, of one night when we hadn't seen each other for almost two weeks, and she called me late to drive past her house. It must have been two o'clock in the morning, and the lights were all out, so I hadn't known what to think, slowing as I went by. I was picturing her as I first saw her that October night, coming from behind that big maple tree and Carl's scattered car collection, running out to me across the lawn. She only rode up to the next crossroad and back, but that was enough time to swing up on her knees next to me and throw her arms around my neck, to whisper she just had to see me that long at least.

So it took a while to catch up with Gerry's remembering. For that matter I must have been suffering from moral deprivation or something anyway, because it had been all of that night and day, as I calculated it, plus most of a long evening before, since Gerry'd come up with some new lesson for life. I knew it was there in the 4-H story, too, and after another hundred yards or so across the beans, I roused myself to ask.

"All right," I said. "I give up. What'd we learn from all that?"

Gerry checked once more in the hopper. "My goodness, this is a fine field of beans, hopper's damn near full already. Wouldn't even trade it for one of Ray's fields this year, May Leader or not. But see, he planned. He took his losses into account and planned." He settled back into his seat. "What'd you learn from all that? You're asking what the lesson was?"

"Yeah, what's the lesson that we all needed to learn?"

Distracted by the bean field's riches, Gerry had to consider, stumped for a minute even by himself. Finally he laughed. He laughed and reached down to shake my arm. "Why, you kids didn't go out there naming no more livestock, did you? Ain't I right? Weren't no more Sunshines coming down the pike?"

I joined him in laughing then too, because you had to admire him really, for making the effort. Still sifting through life to find all the morals that the rest of the world was just as happy to do without. That was Gerry Maars, though, the 4-H club and the fence post were alike in their abilities to take us that next step on the progressive journey, the grand march forward of Life.

At the end of the row I'd be jumping down for the grain truck, would catch up with Gerry somewhere halfway back to the other end. Poised on the toolbox those last few hundred yards, I almost hated to break the spell—even as we rode that night, without doubt the only ones in the county still out working, I knew that only a dozen miles away Annie was there. Most likely moving through her house to clean up from the day's mayhem, maybe even thinking of me. Carl Wayne, undamaged and back on days, would have bid fond farewell to his garage by then and was upstairs sleeping, dreaming toward a four A.M. start. My brother would be shifting in his heavy sleep next to faithful Kendra; Joey and Celeste slumbered safe in their beds.

There's not often time to sit back remembering, and consider where you are. I hadn't thought of that 4-H steer for a dozen years, but all through a long winter and spring I'd brought Sunshine his feed in a bucket, filled up his water with a hose. In that much I wasn't so different, because you'd have had to call that steer and me friends. He liked for me to scratch behind his ears, would nuzzle against my shoulder if I was down at the pen. He'd learned to curl out a heavy pink tongue, to lick corn from between the fingers of my hand. He stood still for all my brushing fair week, let me wax and polish his hooves. He'd followed me faithfully for hours back and forth in the barn lot, practicing for the ring.

I can't say I particularly remembered Gerry out of the sea of adult faces and bib overalls that closed in around us that afternoon, but at the auction I could understand well enough that the Oddfellows had made the purchase, and my time with Sunshine was almost done. While the farmers all clapped for the price, I led him through the crowd and back past the livestock stalls to the holding pen, at the far end of the barn. I brought him along the chute and slid open the gate, slipped off the halter to let him go.

Gerry was right: I wasn't really like those other boys and never had been. They might have been crying, but for me it'd always been different. I still kept the presence of mind to watch. Off the lead and out of the tiny pen, free for the first time of the halter, Sunshine stood for a moment to look at me. I looked at him. He took his first few tentative steps on his own. And from that point on he never looked back. The last time I saw Sunshine he was frolicking his way out across that wide slaughterhouse holding pen, cantering and capering, glad to just finally be free.

TWENTY-ONE

I lay with my head half-buried in a thick white pillow while Annie explained.

"It depended whether I had them on or not, that was the signal."

"The signal?"

"Well, we never said it out loud, exactly, but that was how he knew. If I had my panties on, he left me alone. Otherwise, you know, it was all right with me. That was the system." She plunked me on the back with her hand. "Don't be squirming around so much, you big baby. It ain't that cold. Here, I'll blow on it a little, get it warm."

The drapes at the Holiday Inn in Lafayette weren't quite the force I'd come to expect: through them came the steady drone of winter rain. The week after Thanksgiving had brought bad weather, but even at that Gerry and I'd almost made it under the wire. Would have, too, if we hadn't had to wrestle so much with the grain head; we got within a hundred and fifty acres when winter finally came. The cold weather was first, followed by rain turning quickly to sleet. Anybody who had ever farmed would look out the window, shaking his head, but Gerry and I were still out there pushing, trying to get the last of the harvest in the bins. By the time the muck land finally got soaked, there weren't more than twenty acres of corn left unpicked. They were still unpicked a week and a half later.

While winter raged around us, Annie sat back on my hips, rubbing breath-warmed Baby Magic onto my back and shoulders. "You're lucky I came along when I did, Arthur, this skin of yours might have just chapped away for good. There, that feel any better? Lift up there a little, let me get up under here aways."

Her hand slid in to glide smooth along my chest.

"So it worked? The Leroux system?"

She hit me again on the back. "You want to know everything, don't you? Why don't you just get married yourself sometime, and find out how these things work?"

"So did it?"

The silence above me got lost in the hum of the heater, laboring at the edge of the room. She shifted back onto my legs.

"It worked too good, I guess, things in a marriage can slip away. Unless he's been drinking heavy, and then it don't matter what I'm wearing or anything else. Here, turn over, let's have a look at your front."

Annie's tough little fingers had found pockets of soreness in muscles I didn't even know I had. She rose on her knees while I rolled stiffly under her, sinking back into the bed. The burdens of empire fall on the foot soldier as well as the king: all the acreage Gerry added that year had about worn me out. But instead of the cracked seats of a cold truck cab, or bean stubble on my back as I lay straining with a wrench under the combine, there was the warm tickle of Annie on my stomach as she poured lotion into her palm. The old flannel shirt she was wearing hung half open, and she lifted her cupped hands to blow into them. She looked down at me sternly.

"I don't care to be made fun of, by the way."

"I'm not making fun."

"We were both of us kids, Arthur, we didn't know nothing. I just saw him and fell in love. That's all there was to it."

"I wasn't making fun."

"Here," she said, "give me your hand."

She began rubbing lotion into it, shaking her head because my hands were the worst, chapped red and scaly, still raw from a hundred slices by the blades. I'd smashed one thumb almost flat with the hammer, and she worked carefully around the torn and blackened nail.

"The first time I saw him I was fifteen." She moved away from the thumb, rubbing intently along my wrist. "I remember seeing him on the football team the fall I was a sophomore. He was a senior, had been hurt on one of the plays or something, because he was up sitting by the fence. He could have been faking—his family all tried to tell me Carl was lazy. But I was walking along with Trudy Silvers one day, just out to be out there, and when he looked up at me I knew. Don't ask me how, but all of fifteen and I already knew. I knew he'd be the father of my babies." Her eyes narrowed as she looked down at me. "So don't make fun."

I used my softened right hand to run up her bony hip and along the edge of her ribs. "I won't make fun."

I had no grudge against Carl Wayne, but that didn't mean I wasn't curious: I was like her kiddies, wanting to hear about when she and the rest of the world were young. It pleased me somehow to know that she'd loved him. I liked that they'd teamed up to bring forth life not just once, but four times, all of it issuing from the young woman who straddled me, her dark eyes flicking warily down to mine. Finally she smiled.

"They kind of liked hanging around at first, all his friends. And I'd just had sisters, didn't know nothing about boys, so it was fun. Shannon wasn't no trouble really, but once we had Jeff, and then Stevey and Moni, I had plenty to do without all the extra. I ended up throwing the whole bunch out. They still come over; drive by any afternoon and you'll see them, after the shift at the plant." Her voice hardened. "Hanging around out in the garage till all hours, drinking beer, I don't care much for it either way now, but the kids, they don't know no better. They don't know that there's any other kind of dad than the one they got."

While she rubbed lotion into my chest, I watched her, lulled by her stories and the rain that fell harmlessly outside. She couldn't shake off a mother's ways, eyes narrowing at each little blemish or mole, fingernails quick to scrape at or pick. Finally I held out my arm and she dropped down beside me on the bed, letting her sleeves fall back so she could rub the last of the lotion into her own narrow forearms and wrists.

"So I made my bed, and I got to sleep in it. I got nobody to blame but myself. Moni, though, or the boys, too, for that matter, they're gonna have more chances than that. Ain't gonna be nobody holding them down."

With our honeymoon behind us, we'd just come at each other earlier that night, as soon as we got to the motel room. It was almost nine, after our two or three hours of reacquaintance, and I asked her if she was ready to eat.

"I'm always ready to eat, Arthur, you ought to know that. But the thing is I missed you. I've missed your touch so much. I ain't trying to be pushy, but do you think you can do it, just love me once more now again?"

When I opened my eyes the next morning, Annie was already up on one elbow, watching.

"You were dreaming," she said, "thrashing in your sleep. Something in your dreams isn't good."

"Dreams never hurt anybody."

"Something in there ain't right. Stevey has bad dreams sometimes, and I feel so sorry for him. To be little and see the world as such a scary place don't hardly seem fair." She kissed me good morning. "I'm sorry you boys have those dreams."

With both of us early risers, it was barely six. One thing about waking up early, it leaves a whole lot more of the morning to enjoy. Room service was still a treat, and we stayed in bed lounging, leafing through travel brochures that Annie'd picked up in the lobby the night before. It was one of those mornings where almost anything sounded unlikely enough to be fun, even a ride in a caged Land Rover through lions and tigers at Safariland, or a stroll through a pioneer village in Rockville, over near the Illinois line. There was a wax museum in Brown County, and a row of Victorian houses set back along a shady side street in South Bend. A leaflet that attracted both of us was for Lake Monroe down near Bloomington, nestled among quarries and hills. We lay back to enjoy glossy summer scenes of a crowded marina, deep wooded banks along the shore.

As the morning wore on I dozed on and off, dreaming or not, catching up on about three months' worth of sleep. I woke the last time to see Annie perched naked down at the end of the bed, painting her toenails while she watched some kind of how-to show on figure painting on the big swivel color TV. About eleven she roused me so we could go shopping at the new mall nearby.

She'd wanted to get a head start on the kids for Christmas, but the presents we ended up buying were all for her: a Hawaiian blouse to go with our climate, and a pair of black slacks that I thought she ought to have. We window-shopped, too; a ring that she'd admired at one of the jewelers cost three hundred dollars. While she tried on the slacks, I went back to buy it for her. It wasn't from Sipe's of Indianapolis, express-flown from London or France, but I wanted to see what it looked like on her hand. When, back at the motel room, I took it out of the box and slipped it on her finger, she cried.

"I ain't gonna be able to wear none of this stuff except with you, Arthur, but I'll keep it to one side just for us. This is the prettiest ring I've ever seen in my life."

She had to hurry, because there was nail polish to remove and presents to pack away, and by that time it was almost two. I figured I'd already bought myself another night in the motel room, so after I'd walked Annie out to the car, I came back by myself, more than halfway decided to stay. With the rain pouring down there was nothing back in Delfina to call me; the room was as warm and well-appointed as ever, the TV worked just as fine. The sheets were still soft and rumpled, but the warmth and special traces of Annie had begun to slip away. When they were finally gone, there wasn't much point in hanging around. I turned off the TV and gathered up the travel brochures, splashed my way out across the parking lot to the Camaro, and headed back up to the farm.

TWENTY-TWO

The first weeks of December Gerry hung around, cussing the weather and worrying over the last of the corn. The painful part was that somebody might drive by and see it. "How they supposed to keep sending me back to the council," he demanded, "if I can't even get my crops out of the field?"

Even with Kathryn through school, he lingered, coming by every morning so we could go out and study the mud.

"It ain't even me that needs to go down there," he said, "but Kathryn looks forward to it. All them chair jockeys at the restaurant give me hell about it, but this is the reward for her, for putting up with a farmer's life. There ain't a one of them, either, that don't show up every year or two outside my door down there, expecting to be put up. You might as well join them, Arthur, see how the warm half of the world lives."

We stared out together through the wipers at the offending twenty acres, watched the tire ruts between the rows as they filled up with rain. Out of plain restlessness Gerry started us in tearing down the engine of the Allis, a project that was destined to keep me out in the cold shop half the month of January. We both knew I could go after the corn by myself as soon as we got a hard enough freeze, so it was just stubbornness and pride that kept him hanging around. That, and a chore he finally took care of the week before Christmas, when we moved Irene out of her house in Keona and into the Good Shepherd in town.

I helped him take the furniture on a Tuesday: we loaded up the bedroom suite and two overstuffed chairs, an old washstand and her television, a box of photographs and a mantelpiece clock. We left the bed because she wanted to stay another night, and the next morning that was the first thing we broke down to carry out. Irene fretted in the narrow anteway, casting blind eyes over the box springs as we moved it out the door.

"Now, that front step might be slick," Gerry warned her. "Don't come no further. Me and Arthur got it."

"Oh, I just wonder," she said, "if maybe I couldn't just wait a little while, until after the holidays."

"But I ain't gonna be here then," Gerry said. "That's the whole point." We had the box springs halfway through the door, and set it down. "Remember how you didn't want to move out of the farmhouse either, when you and Walter come in here? And this turned out good. Maybe Good Shepherd will turn out just as fine."

Irene looked doubtful. She'd come up beside the box springs and was startled when she bumped into me.

"That's just Arthur there, Irene, the boy that's gonna look after your house. Now, I ain't telling you what to do. We carried all this furniture out here, we can just as well carry it back in. Say the word and we'll go into town and get the rest of it, have it all back in by noon. 'Course Jack's got things all lined up, and they're expecting you."

"Oh, I don't know," she said, "if you think it's best . . ."

Gerry nodded at me down at my end of the box springs, and we picked it up. "Just while I'm in Florida, and then we'll see. This house ain't going nowhere, maybe we'll get you back in here in the spring."

When we'd loaded up the mattress and box springs, slid the headboard and rails in alongside, it was Irene's turn next. She'd got her coat on, had her purse in hand, but still she backed away ahead of Gerry through the living room, until finally he got hold of her arm. Out on the porch he slammed the door shut behind us, and we started down from the porch.

I'd moved the vehicles around by that time, running the pickup out into the street and backing the Fleetwood up the drive in its place. Gerry aimed her toward the car, wedged in so that the open door was right ahead of her against the hedge. I was on one side and Gerry the other, but along about the back bumper Irene began to balk. All the time I'd watched her house for her, she never once really acknowledged me, frightened, I guess, by the world outside. With Gerry tugging away on her, though, I was the only one left who could lend an ear.

"Arnold," she said, "you probably don't even know that I'm not from around here. I'm from up in Dakota, I met Mr. Bremer up there."

Gerry was reluctant to let up once he had her moving. "Well, you sure as heck made the right move there," he said loudly. "Just shouldn't have stopped. Should have just kept going, down to someplace like Florida where it's warm. Newspaper says it's likely to sleet again tonight. Come up by the door here, I'll give you a hand."

She may have got the idea they'd moved everyone out of Keona, may have fried up the dish towel and cupboard instead of her lunch, but Irene did know one thing well enough, that where she was going memories weren't exactly at a premium.

"You know how traffic goes by on that county road out at our prairie place? Where Gerry lived? Have you seen how it goes by out there at the house?"

She kept her old eyes searching around me, until she thought she might have me fixed. I told her I'd seen how traffic went by.

"I remember being back in Dakota, when I was just a little girl, and one night seeing lights go flashing by along the section line. Now, what's that, I wondered. It moved too fast for a buggy. I knew it wasn't a train. It turned out to be a car, Allan, the first one I'd ever seen."

Gerry was still tugging on her arm. "Oh, that was up in Dakota, they were always a little backward up there. Like I say, come along here aways, and I'll help you. You just got to duck your head a little. Yeah, even an old-timer like me, there were always cars around. I just didn't know nobody who could afford one!"

Well into her last minute in her own driveway, she still seemed to expect something from me.

"We never lacked for cars," I told her, and Gerry nodded his head like I'd just said a major truth.

"Cars," he said.

"Oh my yes, cars," Irene echoed, and he squeezed her down and in through the door.

Gerry stopped by late that afternoon to say he'd gotten her settled in, and that he and Kathryn would be heading south the next morning, right after the mail. You'd have thought the prospect of a little sunshine would have pepped him up some, but his mood was sour.

"I better call Jack tonight, he's gonna be happy that job is done. He about wore me out this fall, on the phone all the time about his grandmother. He couldn't sleep for all the worry, see, wanted her over at Good Shepherd right away. Well, I guess he'll finally be glad now, one less concern for him and me both."

He tapped one side of the Allis' big block with the toe of his cowboy boot, nodded to the oily entrails spread around on the floor. "You need some help on this?" he asked, and I shook my head.

"Damned," he said, "if a fella don't hate to do it, put someone away like that, he really does."

I was his partner in crime, so maybe that much comforted him while he stewed. He poked around the shop so long just handling the tools, peeking into nail cans and seed bags, that I went back to the block. Finally he came over to stand above me where I worked.

"Well, if you don't mind getting the last of that corn in, I guess I'll be going along. I reckon you can keep an eye on things. I'll be in touch. Be awful proud to have you come and see us there at Lake Placid, any time." He brightened. "Yeah, that would be something, show you around down in Florida. Oh, that's the country for a young man, it sure is. You just tell me when you're in a mood for it, and I'll send you a ticket. You hear? Come down whenever you can."

I was too greasy for a handshake, but when I stood he reminded me one last time.

"Remember, Florida ain't but a phone call away."

The weather still didn't improve for those twenty acres, but as far as I could tell, it didn't have to: Gerry always used the best hybrid seed corn, plenty match for whatever nature threw its way. The heavy snow that had begun falling Christmas Eve didn't worry me, but early Christmas morning I drove past the field anyway, on my way to Irene's. I could have driven into Delfina to pick up Gerry's snow-blower, but it took only a few shovelfuls the old-fashioned way to make me glad I hadn't gone. Keona was a community of old people and a few scattered young families; what they shared as a community that morning was that most of them for the holidays had gone away. Red Tiebout's widow had her chimney smoking, and there was a light on at Wilbur Sutton's place next to the old town hall. Otherwise I felt like one of the last living souls left in town.

When I'd cleared out a stretch along the driveway, I stumped around the house. It looked the same empty as it had when Irene was there, except that nobody was tugging aside the curtains to spy out on me. Christmas has its advocates, but some people are best company for themselves: the steady scrape of a shovel blade up and down the driveway soothed me in a way that all the plywood reindeer and gatherings of hearty carolers never had.

Not that I didn't have a warm hearth and dinner ahead of me— I was invited over to Byron and Kendra's for Christmas afternoon. My poor brother had stuttered with embarrassment to tell me the time: his own plan to have me over for the presents that morning had apparently gone down in flames. But still I looked forward to the dinner. The kids would be fun, and whatever Kendra thought about me, I was always glad to see her. Maybe I was a little like Gerry after all, glad to see that somebody still cared. In late October she'd taped up goblins and witches to their storm door, had wished me, with orange construction-paper letters across their big picture window, a Happy Halloween. Running ahead of December snowstorms, Gerry and I had worked all of Thanksgiving Day, but for two weeks before there'd been Puritans and chubby turkeys gathered in celebration. When I walked over on Christmas afternoon, it was toward bright strings of lights along the garage door and eaves, and fresh pine wreaths wrapped with holly on the coach light and door.

Joey was right there to greet me, pulling me past a perfect Christmas tree to show off the new computer game he'd been talking about for months. Celeste held up a stuffed panda as big as a calf. There were a Tomcat jet fighter and an air hockey set, a candy-pink plastic Corvette that was girl-sized, complete with cellular phone. There were skates and shiny packs of baseball cards, a robot and games, all lined up in their boxes. Stockings full of candy that had been torn down from the chimney now were hung back in their places with care.

Byron took my coat, waving me toward a table already set for dinner. I should have noticed, though, from my brother's own care with his enthusiasm, from Joey's nervous rush, that the day had already begun to go bad. Kendra had a pretty Christmas sweater on, her own silver wreath in miniature at her breast, but her face was tense, splotched with red as she rushed food to the table. My brother's cheeks were drained white, his sad-sack eyes the giveaway as he kept careful watch on his wife. The Blue-Gray game ran sluggishly behind us on TV. Since Kendra evidently wasn't talking to my brother, he'd been trying to sulk too, apparently, only nobody cared.

The facts weren't really in dispute; they had something to do with him not bringing home the right video camera from school. Or the wrong attachments for it, I guess it was, and caring too much, Kendra seemed caught between murder and tears. Pandas and bright packs of ball cards, holly and potpourri fragrances or no, it had grown into a rough afternoon. Joey and Celeste were both crying by the time we got to the table, the baby because she'd been picked on somehow, and Joey because Byron had been quick to find out, swatting him with all his might.

A perfectly rolled pork roast was the main course, kicked off by a great broccoli-cheese soup that Joey, still sobbing, had to be threatened to eat. Celeste sat up on encyclopedia volumes, for the first time out of the high chair, but that landmark wasn't enough to keep her from tipping over her milk, an event that somehow brought Joey a pull on his hair and another swat. Even when things settled down some, that still left the three adults at a loss. With Kendra not playing, Byron and I were in the same old dilemma of nothing much to say. She put up with us as far as the main course. We leaned back as much for safety as anything else, as she banged our plates out from in front of us and away.

"It's her dad," Byron said hopefully, peering out over his glasses. "He's not good. He's not good at all."

We heard water run in the kitchen, clanks and scrapes over the sink, the dishwasher getting started on its job. The four of us who were left, two big and two small, listened carefully, like hunters at a winter dawn. Even at that, it still took us a little while to understand that she wasn't coming back.

"Well, I guess we'd best get our own dessert," Byron said. "What do you say? You kids ready for pie?"

Heartiness had never been his strong suit, but no doubt this was my brother's own worst nightmare anyway, that Christmas would somehow end up as lost and uncomfortable as it had been when we were boys. Joey was no friend of his by then, and Celeste just looked scared, her mom's close eyes pinched and confused. Byron cut into a golden cherry pie like he was rip-sawing a two-by-four, plunked down ragged pieces on our plates.

"There's ice cream," he proclaimed, "if you want it. Joey knows where it is."

But the easiness of summer ice cream was gone. Kendra's silence from the back of the house wasn't really containable; it was more alive than anything we could muster ourselves. After our hurried dessert, Byron led my niece into her brand-new Candyland game, while Joey, the lucky one, got to go outside with me. On the snow-clogged county roads he scampered ahead in pure joy and freedom, all the way around to my car.

The first place I drove us was the Bremer place, to check on the shop. When I'd bucked up through the snowdrifts, I parked so that we could stump back along the old ditch bank that ran behind the barns.

Cary Wheatly had already been by that morning to run his lines; we could see his tracks at the edge of the bank. Down between narrow shoulders of ice a slender dowel poked up where a trap had been reset for muskrat, jaws still wide open in the mud. We waited patiently for a glimpse of deer that never came.

It was almost five by then, so with our feet and pant legs wet and friendly, we came back to enjoy the car's solid heater on the way into town. Habit as much as anything took me out by the elevator, where Joey explored the Camaro's ashtray for change. The soda machines were next to the scales, and we followed the ruts of earlier customers up to get our drinks. I opened my jacket and headed us out past the airport, while Joey sipped away at his pop.

This was still before the Indiana lottery started up, back when people would drive clear over to Illinois to throw hard-earned money down the drain. There were junkets six days a week from Indy to Las Vegas or Atlantic City; Gig Walker and old Buck Rogers went out there every chance they got. I preferred to do my gambling a little closer to home. I drove past the fish hatchery to the highway, turned right and went a mile to the north. I turned at Annie's road for a quick drive-by, and that's when I saw what had a small chance to be her car, coming the other way.

It could have been Carl Wayne, of course, or her mom, or just about anyone else in the county, but it was Annie herself who came grinding along in that old green Nova. As she drew closer, I could see she had young company of her own; right up next to where she sat, with her surprised and unashamed smile, was her oldest boy, Shannon. He was caught up in the radio, bent low to work the dial. We crept alongside each other on the narrow path between snowdrifts, rolling down our windows to talk.

"Merry Christmas," she said.

"Merry Christmas. You can't keep off these slippery old roads?"

"I need some whipped cream for the pies; what we had in the refrigerator went bad. You see if Dalhart's is open?"

"The Stop and Shop is, you might try there."

Annie and her boy were both bundled up; the broken rear win-

174

dow made it drafty, and a thin layer of snow covered the ledge in back. Annie didn't care; she looked just as happy as I was to be outside in the winter air, her bare head sticking out of Carl's heavy freezer coat from the plant.

"You all had your Christmas?"

"I was over at Byron's. You know their boy Joey, don't you?"

Joey looked up at the mention of his name, but the lures of the adult world weren't quite strong enough to draw him in. They were running some kind of promotion on RC Cola that winter, where you had to look at the bottom of the can. He was twisting his up for inspection in the last cold light of late afternoon, ready to be rich.

"Just find a station and leave it," Annie said to her own partner, and turned back to me.

"Well," I said as we idled together.

"Carl Wayne was in earlier for cigarettes, but he forgot to pick up the cream. He's planning to be gone the weekend after next, it turns out, they got a special season on deer."

"The weekend after New Year's, I guess that'd be."

"Hold on a second," she instructed Shannon, who complained at her side. "We're gonna get back for your show. It's just now five-fifteen. Yeah, that's what he said. He goes up Friday after work."

I nodded, watching her words steam up in the air. "Funny, but I was thinking I might get away myself that weekend. I got some business to do, probably up in La Porte."

She smiled. "La Porte sounds nice. You do business the same place you always do?"

"I can't think of no reason to change."

She nodded toward Joey, who'd figured out by then that his can was just a can, and was leaning up next to me to watch us talk. "Little pitchers got big ears."

"No, Joey's my buddy," I told her. When I reached for his knee he giggled, squirming in his seat.

Annie and I both had one arm hanging out our open windows, and just for a moment we let our fingers touch, down low and hidden away. Balanced on the crown of that slippery old farm road, we let our forefingers clasp, a teenager's trick. Even so, through the olive drab weave of her gloves I felt the warmth and aliveness I'd been waiting for, in those few seconds before we let our hands drop away.

"Friday night," she said, "the one after New Year's. Have a good time. Don't work too hard."

"I'll try not to," I said, and pulled off first to let her get around me, on her way into town for the cream.

TWENTY-FOUR

Gerry was on the phone to me early Christmas evening. They were all of them, he and Kathryn, the girls and their families, getting ready to exchange gifts. He wanted to make sure I was having a good Christmas, and I told him I was. He asked about those twenty acres, of course, like they were liable to get up and stroll away down Highway 31. He'd had some new thoughts about what might be ailing the Allis, too. He wondered whether I might have some time to take the sweep auger on into Tattman's, so they could lay a new bead along the seam. His voice boomed out as loud and clear as ever up in Indiana; no telling how strong it was down there in Florida. Before long I began to hear complaints in the background, telling him to get off the phone.

I was used to getting a call from him every day or two, to finding out how many fish he'd caught and how pretty it was on the lake. I'm not sure how he even managed to get away from the dock: the old-timers who had settled around him down there tended toward the aged and infirm. As near as I could tell, he was forever blacktopping driveways and pruning back orange trees, cutting the same lawns that he'd been out fertilizing the week before. Never was the time that he didn't invite me down, but I was happy enough with a cold shop and the Allis, the field that I finally got harvested over New Year's, and with Annie and the new La Porte Holiday Inn, where we went the first weekend of the year.

For the special season on deer Carl had taken off Monday, not caring to question from where it might be that his special grace and leave were coming. Annie was bold enough by then to give us Saturday night too, and when she talked to Holly on the phone, her sister said the kids were doing fine. We used Sunday morning to drive the extra forty miles up to the Indiana Dunes.

It was the first time I'd seen the lake since I'd been back, and Annie and I stood on the shoreline to watch its chilly waves. Off to the east was the big Gary steel plant, behind us were hulking cinderblock bathhouses, dunes rising steep from the shore. She wore a big puffball jacket that she'd gotten for Christmas, huddling deep inside it while we strolled past abandoned lifeguard stands, kicked at frozen puddles in the sand. When we'd been iced down sufficiently by wind off the lake, we climbed into the car and made our way back to the south.

There were plenty of places to dawdle along the way, a strip mall or two in Valparaiso, coffee at a Denny's. We had dinner at a roadhouse on Highway 30, fooling around long enough that Annie was in a hurry by the time we got closer to home. She'd left her car in the parking lot of a church in Caterville, and I followed her around to Holly's little one-bedroom house on the edge of town. I watched from a distance as Annie carried the kiddies one by one to her car. A heavy, pleasant-faced girl a couple of years younger than her sister, Holly followed with handfuls of socks and fanny packs, and before long the family was on its way.

It was late by the time I got back to the farmhouse; with no reason to go to bed, I stayed up another hour or so reading the paper. In the morning I began thinking again of Gerry, that maybe I'd take him up on Florida after all. It would be a while before I'd see Annie again, and all I had to do was call—inside of two hours there would be Stubby Doore, the toupee-topped little dandy who passed for a travel agent in those parts, standing on my back porch with a ticket. I did phone down to Lake Placid, but Gerry was already at breakfast, telling tall tales at one of the Sunshine State's own versions of the Cove.

Funny, though, that morning, because as possible as Florida was for me, as close as those wide green fairways and palm-lined shopping concourses were, that's just how beautiful Indiana had come to be too, dark and brooding under the last of the Christmas snow. I admired the dark fields and low gray sky as I drove over to the Bremer place to check on the shop locks, past the old schoolhouse and the barn at Skidmore's, into Keona to check on Irene's. On Delfina's Main Street I drove under a bank temperature gauge that hovered at fifteen degrees, swung past the restaurant to enjoy all over again a world that was right where it should be, with Annie safely bustling inside.

If I hadn't been caught up in tenderness right then, for that frozen world, hadn't been busy imagining how every crow and pebble had somehow found exactly its right place and time, I might have thought something about Byron's Bronco being pulled up in his driveway across the field. I might have wondered how it was that he'd be home during the day, or how Tippy Valley could forge through a Monday morning without my brother as governor, dragging it down to speed. I wasn't noticing much of anything, I guess, never heard his car pull up in the barnyard outside. I'd just gotten in the house and my jacket off, when there came Byron's knock on the door.

He stood poorly shaven in front of me when I opened it; his eyes still showed hurt and surprise. His voice shook as he told me the news. Friday afternoon was when it happened, as near as they could figure, so that made it almost three full days by then since Kendra, sometime after her morning errands, had disappeared. She and the little Toyota were gone without a trace, he said, and nobody had seen or heard from her since.

TWENTY-FIVE

Gone without a trace. It was a phrase that somehow seemed to comfort my brother as we sat together that morning in their living room.

"There's no sign of her car, and she didn't say anything special at the cleaners when she picked up my suit. It was still in its bag when I got home. It's a goddamn mystery." Fighting back tears, he shook his head. "I don't know what I'm going to do. She's just gone without a trace."

He'd done all the right things, as near as I could tell, solid even in the confusion of getting a call from one of the women at Celeste's play group at the church, who told him Kendra'd never come by. He was at home and waiting when Joey's bus dropped him off. By dinnertime that evening he'd begun the likely calls to family and friends, people they would have known from church. Finally he phoned over to her dad's nurses at the hospital, where they too had been surprised not to have Kendra come by. At ten he finally contacted the sheriff.

With Byron something of a community leader by then, Rich rousted himself to come out to the house personally. My brother had already located a photo for him, taken in a studio down in Peru. A family picture was what they'd gone in for, but the photographer had insisted on one of Kendra alone, the result being a proof they'd bought but never copied. It was a good thing the *Beacon* didn't publish on weekends, because Byron clearly expected the picture and a banner headline spread out across the front page, proclaiming the kidnapping for all to see. It's a good thing Rich had been there to urge caution, had laboriously copied down her license plate number and description, reminded my brother there was a procedure to be followed after all. He did promise he'd call the state police and surrounding sheriffs that very evening, as soon as he got back to town. In return he got Byron to promise he wouldn't do anything on his own. That second promise was what my brother was chafing at, as he worried and complained to me through Monday afternoon.

By that time it was my turn, because Byron had just about decided to go ahead with his own plan, which was to print up two hundred copies of the block-letter flyer he'd designed, for distribution to convenience stores and gas stations all across the state. He'd left a big space for the photo, and he pulled it out to show me, Kendra pretty in her red blouse and black skirt, a gold pendant hanging from her neck as she leaned over a wooden-spoked wagon wheel, posed before an autumn facade. The first thing I did, and it wasn't easy, was get him to promise again, that he wouldn't hand out any copies until Rich had a chance to do his job.

We were just getting started then, on her fourth day of tracelessness, when we took Joey and Celeste downtown that evening for dinner. As we rode the big Bronco into town, Joey kept an eye on us, looking back and forth between his dad and me to see if he should really be scared. By that time of night on a weekday the old main street was dark and windswept, the beer signs from the tavern and the faded fluorescence from the Cove the only ports on a winter night. Faye Watts was the only waitress, indifferent to me as she greeted Byron and the kids. My brother settled in below the fishnets, chewing his lip. When I'd given Joey a handful of quarters and sent him and Celeste down to the jukebox, Byron lowered his voice.

"Rich may have something," he said, "although I hope to God it isn't true." With the kiddies safely away, my brother once again was blinking back tears. "I got a call just before we left the house. They found a woman matching her description in Kansas early this afternoon. The morgue there's going to send pictures."

"That's a goddamn waste of time," I told him. "What would she be doing in Kansas?"

"What's she doing gone?" he demanded angrily, only to look up quickly from where he sat, embarrassed even in the empty cafe. Joey strained to hear; despite his parents' fears, he was no dummy. He knew the important talk had started as soon as he was gone, and was slated to stop the very second he hurried back. So he just stood by the flashing jukebox and watched us, while Celeste, her sweater on backwards and pink sleeves smudged with grime, punched out random buttons at his side. Faye caught up to corral them by the goldfish, eager to point out a murky something in the tank.

"They could drag the river," my brother said. "That's an option, too. All Rich has to do is say the word."

"I don't doubt that they'd fish out a lot of people," I said, "but the chances of any of them being Kendra are mighty slim."

Byron scowled; he was still partial to imagining his wife naked and half-buried in a woods somewhere, or floating facedown in a ditch. Like I say, it was lucky I was around, because that night when the kiddies were in bed I finally convinced him to look more carefully through the suitcases in the garage. I led him on an expedition back to their bathroom, trolling for the odd hair dryer or curling iron that weren't to be found. There were spaces among her sweaters, too, where a couple of others once might have been.

Even when the pictures came in the next day from Kansas, of a bloated black-haired woman in her fifties, Byron wouldn't give up.

"It just doesn't make sense," he insisted, "especially with her dad so sick. I had to tell him this morning, the hardest job I think I've ever had to do. You know how he counted on her. He's just beside himself now, wild with worry that Kendra's gone."

For all his willingness to humor the new principal, Rich had begun to cool on the matter, leaving my brother adrift. I heard that harsh words were exchanged. At any rate, as far as the sheriff was concerned, it looked like the eager Boy Scouts and overgrown fire engine chasers over at the rescue squad garage would be cooling their heels a little longer. Celeste and Joey still had their school to go to the next day, and by Thursday, when there still was no trace of anyone from anywhere, my brother had no choice but to follow suit.

TWENTY-SIX

I hadn't driven south out of Keona for a week or two, and when I did, on Saturday morning, I was surprised to see that Midway Implement had closed down. The big yard that had grown ever fuller of unsold equipment was abruptly empty, the showroom windows painted over with chalk. It made me wonder about Rodney Gilliland. When I drove by his big split-level in town, the pickup was nowhere to be seen, and a big THE KEY IS KEOUGH real-estate sign was resting in one corner of the yard.

Monday afternoon I was working at something out in the barnyard when I saw Rich Taylor's squad car turn in at Byron's drive. My brother must have been alerted, because he'd come home early and was at the front door waiting as the sheriff pulled to a stop. Rich came all the way around the squad car to let Kendra out. With her tan raincoat and short blond hair, her long striding gait, she walked with her head down up the sidewalk to the porch. Byron swung open the door to let her in. He conferred a minute with Rich, and they shook hands. When the door had swung closed again, the sheriff came back to his car.

He glided through the stop sign and onto Sycamore, but instead of speeding toward town, he turned at the lane, cruising back to where I stood. I'd been surprised to see Midway closed down, had even been surprised when I'd heard a couple of days before at the elevator that the bank had changed hands yet again. For all of that, I can't say I was particularly surprised to see Gerry Maars in the front seat of the squad car, to have him come hopping out in front of me, just as soon as Rich pulled to a stop. Gerry waved good-bye, and as Rich backed away, he turned to me.

"I never knew Byron's wife was gone," he complained, by way of greeting. "How come you never told me when I called?"

"I didn't know Rich was going to mobilize the Florida reserves. What are you doing back?"

"Aw hell, I didn't plan to be, but there's county things come up. When Rich told me he had business down by the airport anyway, I figured I'd save you a trip."

Behind him out across the sixty was the lonely ranch house and its secrets, the curtains drawn and the big oak door slammed shut in Kendra's wake.

"Yeah," he said, "I didn't expect to be seeing you so soon. We worked out the budget for next year before I left, and now Rich calls down and tells me they're trying to renege on the doggone county employee raises. Tells me Hal Sanders put up a motion to reconsider. The little bastard, I got half a mind to tell him what I really think. I done my duty for Hal and all the businessmen when I carried county-wide zoning out here, went to bat for all them bonds. There's farmers that say Gerry Maars sold out to the Chamber of Commerce—well, rain on them, then, if that's what they think. But I ain't gonna stand by and let Rich and those other boys suffer, no way in the world. That's why I'm here. That and because that doggone Jack wants to meet with me, called me down in Florida just the other night. Got to see me right away. Can't do it over the phone, see, he figures everybody flies around the country all the time just like him.

"Anyway, I figured I'd drop by for the pickup. I ain't trying to hide nothing, ain't nobody in the county that don't know I stand foursquare behind Rich and the boys. Still, if the damn thing's free, it's probably better if I make it into town on my own."

"The keys are in the ignition. Help yourself."

He finally joined me in looking across the field over at Byron's. "Been awful wet, it looks like."

I nodded. "Six inches this month. That muck over east of the schoolhouse ain't gonna dry out until May."

"Yeah," he said, "Rich didn't tell me, when he called, what kind of business he had down there in Indianapolis this morning. I didn't expect it was Kendra he was after, that's for sure. Ain't many girls come along that are as just plain pretty as she is. I remember her over there at the ASCS office too, back when I was on the board. Sharp as a tack, could figure out acreages in about a tenth the time as those old biddies we'd had there for years. I always liked to talk to her, you know, she had such a sweet way about her. Never failed to brighten a fella's day. She was down at one of them motels on 465, that's where we went in to pick her up."

He shook his head. "All that water in the fields on the way up here, I commented to her about it, but she didn't have much to say. Just sat there and looked out the window. It ain't really my place, either, but along about Bunker Hill I went ahead and told her how lucky she was to have a husband like your brother. When you think about all the drinking and hell-catting around that goes on anymore, she really is."

I couldn't tell if he was appraising me or not. He watched me sure enough, but I just looked back at him until finally he shrugged.

"Well," he said, "ain't nobody lives another man's life for him. That's the long and short of it. I was thinking maybe you could give me a ride back to the airport tomorrow afternoon if you ain't too busy. You ain't too busy now? I ain't taking you away from your affairs?"

"I imagine I can squeeze you in."

"We got that meeting tonight, and then that damn Jack, I guess I'll see him. He ain't put down any gravel over there yet on those field approaches, has he? I'm gonna get on him about that, we've pussyfooted around long enough. And Arthur, I wouldn't say nothing about it if it weren't your brother, you know that. Byron's as good-hearted as they come. I wish we had a dozen more like him, boys who were willing to stay around and make this county go. Rich ain't gonna say nothing either, I told him not to. But people are funny, I wish to hell they weren't. Them principalships got all kinds of politics attached to it, and it just don't look good when a man can't keep his wife at home."

"I don't imagine that it does."

"You never know, though, sometimes it helps a woman to get away. She comes back a little fresher or something, sees things anew. You say the key's already there? Just wish I was getting back in that boat of mine and not this doggone cold-blooded pickup. Go floating again out there across the water, don't that sound good?"

I didn't get a chance to tell him about Midway or the bank, but there were only so many things even he could fix up, on his first twenty minutes back in town. He might have been longing for Florida just out of habit, because with his speech all made and a county council to set right, Gerry was marching across the barnyard like a man half his age. He pumped the old pickup into life and swung out around me, roaring down the lane toward town.

TWENTY-SEVEN

It was easy to forget that Kendra had grown up poor like we had: the lumberyard never paid much, and as I remember Byron telling it, her family never even owned a car until she was in junior high. Her dad had his pickup, but they wouldn't have taken that on the family's occasional pilgrimages down to Indianapolis. Like a whole lot of other Delfinans, she would have taken her first trip there on Trailways, chugging down on 31 to the great metropolis itself. Coming in from the north, Kendra would have been up on her knees like any one of us to peek out at the grand tree-cloaked mansions that lined wide Meridian from the White River south. Downtown they would have passed the War Memorial to come in at last to the Traction Terminal Building in the center of town. She might have spent part of her grand day in the city strolling with her mom through the Ayres department store, looking from a safe distance into the famous tearoom on the eighth floor.

It's hard to know where a poor family might have roamed. Modern trips are a little easier to trace, especially once her cash started to run low. That little plastic card may look friendly enough, but by the fifth day it was beaming an electronic trail so bright across the heavens that even Rich, no Sherlock Holmes and seventy miles away in a backwater sheriff's office, could follow her every move.

The Budget Inn was out on the interstate, but you had to figure her prowling Betsy's neighborhood at least, past shiny Keystone at the Crossing, out on 82nd to the Borrow Pit Estates itself. Like her cultured friend, Kendra liked the better things, there's no fault in that. She would have strolled through the mall, looked in at the jewelry store, maybe even daydreamed a career for herself. As near as anyone could tell, though, she never went in.

She must have lost heart, and it's too bad, because I know Betsy would have helped. By that time the credit card trail was being laid, not through Paris or London but from Shoney's to the Pizza Hut, to a Waffle House half a mile the other way. Gerry told me later that when he and Rich had knocked on the motel room door, they hadn't known what to expect, but Kendra was already packed and waiting, the room like it'd never been slept in at all. She didn't even seem surprised to see them, just picked up her coat and let Gerry take her suitcase, going ahead of them downstairs to the car.

TWENTY-EIGHT

My sister-in-law had already made her one break, I guess, because Byron left her unguarded Tuesday morning when he went back to school. Gerry couldn't have helped either; his pickup was nosed in at the curb in front of the Cove, where Annie served him his breakfast as he sat waiting for Jack. What I had on tap that morning was a bag full of laundry, so I stopped at the Dixie Lee Laundromat to run through my loads. In front of a crowded bulletin board full of listings for backhoes and baby-sitters, I sat down with the only reading material nobody'd bothered to steal: a tattered blue book of children's Bible stories. While the clothes spun dry, I began to wish I hadn't—nothing ever seemed quite as depressing to me as grown men running around the countryside in sandals and robes.

When I got back home, the pickup was already there. As I pulled up, Gerry was out by the barn dressed sharp in his windbreaker and slacks, pacing the length of its door. I left the groceries I'd bought in the backseat while I strolled out to see what he was doing.

"You got an exercise program going now? A hundred times back and forth in front of the barn door?"

He barely looked up. "I call it fourteen feet here, that sound about right? Better get the damn tape on it, though, to be sure. Grab it out from behind the seat, would you?"

By the time I came back with it, he'd already plunged into the gloom of the barn itself. I'd spent enough time slaving in and around the old heap as a boy that it had kind of lost its attraction, and doubt that I'd been in there more than a half-dozen times since I'd been back. Still, I followed, taking it slow while my eyes adjusted. I came up on Gerry a dozen paces in, shoving at the rotten slats of the old corn crib.

"This don't need to stay," he said, "it ain't been used in a hundred years. Can you think of any reason to keep it?"

I told him I couldn't.

"Then out it goes, that'll make some room." He ducked past the crib and into the old harness room, that in my time we'd always used to store seed. Past it was the long, low-ceilinged room where we'd milked. I remembered helping my dad as we'd tore down the stanchions and broke apart the mangers, filled in the manure troughs with cement the year he'd gotten rid of the cows. Gerry strode back through the cobwebs and twenty years' worth of hog dust like a man with a purpose, one he just hadn't cared yet to share. When we got to the far wall, he had me take one end of the tape while he measured the wide door that opened to the back. It hadn't been opened for so long that it fought him, bound between rust above and two or three inches of sod grown up below. Wrestling against it with my help, Gerry finally won out.

"Now, get the far end of that tape steady, there, Arthur, it's going to be close. I'm hoping we got enough room."

"What's going on?"

He craned his head back to squint at the tape. "I got thirteen, is that what it says? Let's get the vertical, it may be a problem too."

"So what's going on?" I asked again.

"It's a hell of a thing," he said, "when people in a county don't give a damn about the people who work there. Hell, a deputy can't hardly raise a family on what we'd agreed to pay him, and now those dumb bastards took it back. Four to three, with me on the losing side. It's a sorry thing, really, is what it is. Grab a block there if you need it. What do you have, eight feet even? Come on, I want to get the other side."

Gerry was in his hurrying gear, but it was one I'd never faulted him for; that's what made him a rich man in the first place. As he marched back through the darkness, he stumbled over an old rubber tire. He cussed it, and that should have been enough, but the first thing I knew he was digging down through all that old straw and frozen pig shit to get it loose. He pulled and tugged to get it free, and then only to throw it as hard as he could against the wall.

"Leave your goddamn crap behind, Charlie, let the next man break his leg. That's the way it is anymore. Whole damn town, the whole county, could go to hell, and wouldn't nobody say a thing."

"So," I ventured, "what's—"

"What's going on? What's going on?" Out of breath from his tussle with the tire, Gerry faced me for the first time. "What's going on is that he cut me loose, goddamn it. The little bastard cut me loose!"

I was still back on Charlie's tire and the ingratitude of the county fathers; it took me a second to see which way he'd gone.

"You mean Jack?"

"Who the hell else would it be? Jack cut me loose, the little son of a bitch. Ain't that something? Ain't that the damnedest thing? Climb on up there, see if you can reach the top. Now, here, take the tape. I figure we need nine feet. What do we got, eight and a half?"

"Eight foot nine. Your lease ain't up, is it?"

Gerry gave a bitter laugh. "Hell, he wishes it was. That's sure enough what he wishes, get it all handed over to Ray Stewart and his boys tomorrow. I got it another year. Wouldn't even have that much if old Al, before he got sick, hadn't hounded me to death to get something in writing. And there I was embarrassed to do it, Irene and me'd done business on just our word over all them years. But this morning I stood up in the Cove and told him, told Jack right then and there. I ain't never farmed an acre yet for a man who didn't want me. Not a one. It's too late this year, but come next Christmas he won't even know I been there. That's what I told him. Oh, it made a hell of a commotion, they're gonna be talking about it all over town."

"What's Irene got to say about all this? You go to see her?"

"Hell, that's the first thing I done. But she don't know nothing about the business, never has. I run that place for years is what it is, all she had to do was cash the doggone checks. And now Jack's got her so goddamn confused that she don't know up from down. Eighty-five years old and crying like a baby. So what do I say? That I treated her like my own mom? That I divided them crops fair and square down to the last bushel all those years, never made a load but what she got the bigger half? That I come running over to her house every ten minutes, wiped up after her, neglected my own family to tend to her? What am I supposed to do, throw her down and hog-tie her until she remembers?"

We still held the tape measure between us, the bright yellow band hanging slack across the doorway. Gerry snapped it away from me, snaking it back into its case. He was crying himself by then, tears of hurt and anger that he swiped at with the back of his hand. I helped out by keeping my own head down, following as he led us out to Charlie's pens. He waved back over his shoulder at the barn.

"Now bring that loader tractor around the side here, it'll fit anyway. Back the plows in that rear door, it don't matter if you buck up onto them end rows a little. I want them grain trucks over here, too, I don't care if they do have to sit outside. They ain't staying over at Bremer's another week. Not another day, not another minute that they don't have to. At least I got this place still, the last time I looked."

He coughed, rubbing the knit cuff of his windbreaker across his eyes. "Them tractors, too, them two 1086's. Leave the four-wheel drive and combine where they are. We'll put up a pole barn out here, I got to see the bank on that right away. I'll see if I can track old Al down, I ain't seen him in Florida this year like usual."

I didn't imagine Gerry had seen him down south, because the two or three times I'd run into Al Lantz downtown he didn't look good at all, gaunt and pale, walking gingerly against the wind. Tears were a tricky thing for a man Gerry's age; a man with the world by the tail like he had might go ten or fifteen years without any call for them, but then when they did come, they tended to have their own ideas, and he couldn't quite get them to obey. Even when he was back in charge again, leading me across the barnyard while he dictated orders, the last few kept slipping down his cheeks.

"Goddamn," he said, "this is a hell of a thing." He shook his head and cleared his throat, spitting on the ground. "Shit. Okay now, forget all this, that's what I want you to do. I'm telling you to forget it. You just get them things I told you moved, take care of it any way you see fit. We'll do our business over there this year and then get the hell off, ain't gonna be no pity parties for us. Damn fool loyalty to Irene's what kept me tied to that muck land all these years; it's time I had something for myself."

"I'll take care of it."

"A man gets complacent, is what it is. There's good land out there, the world don't end at the edge of this doggone swamp."

I nodded.

"It comes down to whether a man's got drive or not, the spunk to carry through." He turned on me. "And you, you little so and so, what are you doing, living in an igloo here? I get bills for the butane, and I can't believe it, there ain't hardly any being used. This morning early I go by the old place there, put a stick down the gas tank, and what do

I find? The damn thing's almost full! That gas is for you to use, dog-gone it, don't be paying for it in town. Don't be going without, either, not while you work for me. Got half a mind to drag you back down to Florida with me, just to get evened up some. If I didn't have all this moving for you to do, I would!"

"I'll take care of it."

"Well," he said, "I don't want to miss the plane, Kathryn'll be waiting. This here ain't no more than a setback, we're gonna roll with it. Tests a man's mettle. If it just wasn't that doggone Ray Stewart and his boys, that's what hurts. But the hell with them, let's get a move on. If we ain't running too far behind, I'll buy you dinner at that new Copper Kettle on the way."

TWENTY-NINE

"She was just unhappy," Annie told me later that same night. "Anybody could have seen that."

"Maybe," I agreed. It seemed like a judgment on Byron, so I found the best defense I could. "Lots of people are unhappy."

Annie shook her head. "A pretty girl like that, with no kind of life, no wonder she run off. You don't know. You just don't know, Arthur. When love's gone, it just ain't right."

We lay once more in a shabby bed at the Frontier, where Annie'd insisted on us going up to meet. I don't know what kind of excuse she'd used at work, but it was enough to spring her free for a couple of hours. The phone had been ringing when I got home from the air-port, telling me to meet her there at eight. She had a boy at home with an earache, and an alarm clock already set for four-thirty, but still she lingered, while I rubbed the back of her neck.

"My kids aren't gonna live that way. I'm gonna make sure of that. They're gonna know there's things to do."

I guess I should have been agreeing more enthusiastically, because Annie sprang up then, climbing to her knees beside me.

"Are you there?" she demanded. "Are you listening to what I say?" She'd thrown one leg over to straddle me, and banged her fist into my chest in frustration. "I just don't know you sometimes. Don't you understand that I love you? Can't you hear me?"

"I got ears."

"Then use them. I love you. It's you that I love. I love you more than anything else in the world."

Annie had pinned me down, black eyes aiming in at me over that pointed little nose like it was a rifle sight. Her fingers were wrapped into my chest hair, her own Annie-breath was in my face. It's funny how at a time like that almost anything else in the world can catch your attention—a card with directions for Plymouth cable set in plastic above the TV set, a whine of country-western from the room next door, the dark stain of water damage on the ceiling high above. Her fingers tightened, and I met those eyes finally, beginning to fill as her hands slowly relaxed.

"It's just that I love you," she said, "I really, really do."

"I believe you," is what I said.

The whole next week I worked on the old barn, a formidable enough task to face. I brought over the loader tractor first and started in by scooping out half-rotten bales of clover and alfalfa. When I'd torn down the corn cribs, I stacked the splintered slats out in the muddy bean stubble for burning, county-wide zoning or not. The few tons of dried manure that I scraped out got spread in a thick layer just beyond, along the edge of the field.

If the weather was any good at all that winter, Joey'd had the habit of flagging me down when he could, and coming along to the shop at the Bremer place. He'd just hang out and watch me at work on the Allis, turning out in the process to be a pretty good hand at fishing out the O ring I needed from the soak pan, or for running to the bench for a tool. When the school bus came by on Thursday, I was just torching the bonfire, so he rushed over for a look. He liked the old barn, and the next afternoon he was over again. Saturday morning he came by early, and when we'd stacked up the last of the fencing, I asked him if he was ready to learn how to drive.

It doesn't take a Ph.D. in word problems to know that you need two people to make a move, one person to drive the machinery and another to ferry him back. I could have scrounged around in town and found somebody, but I hadn't been leading Byron on, the boy did have a steady hand. We started by getting him used to the pickup, circling through the mud and gravel in front of the house. He was stretching out some, because if we sat him up on a pile of old feed bags, he didn't have trouble seeing out over the hood or reaching the pedals, either one. The braking was a little touchy at first; he about threw me through the windshield the first time he brought us to a stop. His steering was first-rate, though, and as we gained confidence, I directed him out onto the road. Our first run was down to the stop sign by his folks' place, and then beyond it straight out the deserted Sycamore Road.

As a man gets older he tends to forget about the glory of that first car or pickup you guide down the road. Joey bore in on his task like a brain surgeon, anticipating each little pothole or wiggle that we met. Once we'd gone a couple of miles, I let him have his head, relaxing back to look out the window. He was up to the task, guiding us at a steady twenty miles an hour down the center of that old cracked and pitted asphalt road.

We made two or three runs along Sycamore, slowing at the railroad crossing four miles east, then bumping over the tracks to turn around at the near edge of Keona. On the last trip I had him turn at the road to the Bremer place and pull up that old gravel driveway to the back. It was every bit as rough as Gerry had been complaining to Jack, but Joey handled it in the pickup like a champ. I climbed out, and after some pumping and priming, finally got the old GMC to start. That's what I drove as I followed Joey on his first solo, lumbering behind him all the way back to the house.

The batteries on the tractor had gone dead, so I ran a line from the barn and put them on charge while we brought over the big diesel truck. I pulled it in next to the GMC at the rear of the old barn lot, past where the milk house used to be. Then we brought the Allis down, with me putting along behind the pickup. It felt good to see the red and white of the big grain trucks as we came up the lane, to see the old barn lot gradually beginning to fill back up. When I'd pulled the Allis around to the side, I went into the house for a couple of sodas that Joey and I enjoyed in the front seat of the pickup, while we listened to the radio out of South Bend.

By that time you couldn't have pried my nephew from behind the wheel with a crowbar, so he was driving us back toward the Bremer place again when we first saw his mom. She was on foot and had made it all the way down to the stop sign, where she waved fiercely at the side of the road. Joey had seen her too, already tensing at my side, and I told him to go ahead and pull over. He did, too, after a fashion, lurching us over the shoulder and into the side ditch. The next thing I saw was Kendra's face up in the window beside him, small mouth twisting as she yelled something we couldn't hear.

"Roll down the window," I told him, easy for me to say, because she was on his side. He didn't want to, but I patted his knee. "Go ahead."

"Good little driver here," I told her. "The boy learns fast."

"I said get out, Joey. Get out right now. Go on back to the house."

Besides stretching out that winter, the boy'd grown too old for crying. All of us knew it, but his face began to crumple just the same. "Mom, I been learning to drive," he said desperately. "I'm *working*. I'm helping Uncle Arthur."

She tried to jerk the door open, but at the angle we were sitting its whole weight was in our favor. It slipped away from her, falling back closed with a bang. "Now get out," she said again, peering back in through our armor. "I'm not going to tell you again."

Joey looked at me.

"It's all right," I said. "You done good. There's plenty of driving ahead in your life. Come on, you can slide out over here."

I got out first, squeezing Joey's shoulder as he made his way past me and into the brown fall weeds along the road. It was the same shoulder that Kendra slapped not once but twice, jerking his arm as she caught up with him at the back of the bed. She swung him around to swat at him, and he danced ahead, caught between anger and shame. She pushed him hard back along the road to the house. "I'll deal with you later," she promised through gritted teeth.

Finally crying in earnest, Joey started on his way.

"I'll get pulled around here and give you a ride," I said to her back as she watched him, waving the boy on when he dared to look our way. She must have rushed out of the house without thinking, because she was bare-headed, with just a pale green knit cardigan over her blouse. "Come on," I said, "hop in. It's too cold to be out walking. We'll pick Joey up along the way."

Kendra turned to me. "Maybe," she said, "it's just lack of judgment. Or maybe you don't care. A twelve-year-old doesn't belong behind the wheel of a vehicle. Common sense ought to tell you that."

"I got some common sense," I said, "and most of it I picked up when I was his age or younger, driving equipment a hell of a lot more balky than this truck. It doesn't hurt him to be out with the men some, seeing how things are done."

She would have liked to slap me too, to shove me halfway down the road like her boy. Instead she flared back at me, her red hands buried deep under her arms. "And what's he going to see with you? That he doesn't have to pay attention to anybody but himself? That the world's just to do whatever he wants?" Her hair was loose and uncombed, her lips turned down. When I came out of the ditch toward her, she flushed angrily, backing into the truck.

"I just hadn't known," she went on, "how selfish you are. Not until you came back here again. When Byron and I were dating, I was just like he is, sorry for you. A person couldn't help it, really, to see how you were. But before long, all you see is the selfishness. I can see it now, too. Just plain selfishness. Nobody matters but you."

"Well," I said, "he's your boy. You call the shots."

"That's right," she said, "he is."

I shrugged. "Then that makes it easy. You don't want the boy out here with me, just keep him at home. That should be simple enough.

Otherwise, there's things he can do. If he keeps showing up over at the house, I'll put him to work."

That would have stung her, I imagine; she'd over the years gotten used to Byron, who'd hang his head like a damned hound dog every time she made a frown. And then there was the lesson of Indy just behind us too, that in a wide, empty world there was already a whole lot more room even for a boy like Joey, than there ever would be for her.

As for my nephew, not twenty minutes after the school bus stopped on Monday, he was running across the muddy sixty to the barn. We moved machinery together until almost six, and Kendra never said a goddamn thing.

THIRTY

The old barn had once been lively with fresh hay and shuffling animals, cement floors swept clean, seed bags stacked neat and high. With my nephew's help, it began to take on life again, as we ferried down Gerry's tractors, plows, and disks until the barnyard seemed to sprout up in the early springtime too, prickly from a distance with jutting smokestacks and glassed-in cabs. Gerry was on the phone every other day to check on our progress, and by the third week of March, he was back himself.

By that time I'd started in on the plowing. The spring had turned dry, and from Florida I'd heard glad tidings that he'd taken on even more land, in anticipation of losing the Bremer place the following year. He shouted out over the phone that he'd picked up Dean Schapp's hundred and sixty acres, land that his boy had been farming until he went into the service just after Christmas. There were another couple of parcels that he'd picked up by the Holloway place down south. How he planned to get all those acres covered was a secret all his own, but any kind of head start I could give him had to be all to the good.

By April everyone was going, Gerry and I among them, churning up ground for another year's assault. There was a lot of land to be covered, and we were still plowing the first week of May. The winter's rain had been enough to show where a tile had collapsed in the field behind the barn, so one chilly morning while Gerry was still in town at breakfast, he had me leave the tractor to go out and stand in the sixty with old Garfield Henry, while he dug around with his backhoe trying to find it.

Gar was like a lot of old-timers; he had more than enough time for gab when another man was paying the bill. It took him twenty minutes to dig a six-foot hole through the mud, but almost another hour besides to fill me in on the thumping the Comets had gotten in sectional and his boy's fading marriage over in Rensselaer. Old Gar was weather-beaten and almost toothless, with his backhoe not in the best of shape either. By the time Gerry got out there, the hole hadn't grown any deeper, but while Gar bent my ear, I'd managed to fix a new coupling on one of his hydraulic lines, tightening up the rest of them so at least they'd do the job.

Gerry came stepping lively through the mud to meet us.

"Hey, Gar," he called out cheerfully, "you get this field drained for me yet?"

"You bet, Gerry, I about got her on the run. This was a hell of a wet spot you come onto. But I got a bead on it here, won't be too much longer."

"Ain't another man in the county I'd rather see on the job. No doubt about it. First time I heard about that water, I told Arthur that Gar Henry's the only fella to call."

The old man swelled with pride. "Oh, this here is tricky work, ain't no two fields the same. You take this low ground, all mucky like it is, there's trouble setting up on it. The tractor wants to move around. Now, what I like to do—"

"You got yourself some real good help here, too," Gerry interrupted, pointing to me. "I sent my number-one man out here to give you a hand. Yes sir, I wouldn't put any other five men in the county up against the two of you, especially on a job like this. I hate to do this to you, Gar, but I need this young fella to come with me a little while. I need to show him something. You reckon you can manage on your own?"

"Hell," the old man said irritably, "I done it for twenty years, don't see why I can't do it now." He paused, though, uncertain of whether he could jettison Gerry's praise for me and still keep his own intact. He decided not to risk it. "Arthur, you go ahead with Gerry there. I reckon I got this covered. When you get done, come on back. I'll have the old tile up by then, and we can drag it off."

"Sure appreciate it, Gar. I'll try to get him back to you." Gerry was already hurrying across the mud. "Come on," he called back to me, "shake a leg. I got something I want you to see." When I finally caught up with him at the pickup, he was laughing.

"That Gar Henry, ain't he something? Got drunk three years ago and fell right off the rear end of that tractor, like to killed himself. Fractured his doggone skull, I ain't sure they quite got it all put back together yet." He threw the truck into gear, and I'd barely got the door closed before we were rocketing down the road. "I know it ain't no picnic wading around out there in the dirt with him, but I wanted you where I could find you. Oh, this is something. This is really going to tickle you, I know."

He'd been on high ever since he came back from Florida. He hummed to himself as we bore steadily south on the road that ran past the Shaw place and on to the gravel pit four miles south. Even keyed up as he was, Gerry frowned.

"There would have been a time, I reckon you remember it, when I wouldn't even have needed old Gar, would have dug that damn tile out with just a shovel. Charlotte used to get so mad at me, and then Kathryn, I don't think we'd been married too long when she come out after school one afternoon for a visit, and there I was, stripped down to my shorts and digging away. Tiled that whole east forty on the Bremer place one spring, all by myself. That was back when a man had time to fool with that kind of thing, but them days are gone forever."

Some days were gone but others had newly arrived, making him so excited that morning he could barely sit still. He seemed hardly able to let the truck keep up with him, leaning forward as he drove, both big forearms wrapped around the wheel.

"I wanted to get everything settled," he said, "before I showed you. Oh, you're going to like this, I can hardly wait for you to see."

We left the gravel pit behind, and in a few miles more had passed the turn to the Holloway place. "Where you taking us," I asked, "back to Florida?"

"Oh, we ain't too far away now, don't you worry. We ain't even out of the county yet, the line's another three miles south. Me and Lester Earle, back when he was the county surveyor, spent a lot of time down here, certifying them damn cornerstones for the state. Found a good number of them, too, before Lester got beat in the next election, and the project kind of died. We're getting close, so you better get ready. Better go ahead now and close your eyes."

"Close my eyes?"

"Just for a minute, Arthur, damn it, don't be so darn suspicious. We're getting close. Now hold 'em. Keep holding. Hold 'em just a second now."

I still had the wrench in hand that I'd used on Gar's coupling, but I covered my eyes the best I could. Before long we glided to the left, bouncing up onto the shoulder on the other side of the road.

"Just hold it a second more, I got to get stopped. Just a second now, I want to get so I can see your face. Okay, Arthur, now. We're here. You can open them eyes up now and look!"

If I'd been blindfolded and with my head in a gunny sack the whole twenty minutes, and he'd just driven around one of the sections back home, it still would have looked almost exactly the same as what I saw out the windshield in front of me: a narrow asphalt road with fall weeds in the ditches and wide muddy fields all around. There was a little more woodland on the horizon than there tended to be back on the prairie. A trim block farmhouse and white barn stood a quarter mile away. Gerry's big grin told me that the surprise was right out in front of me, waiting to be found.

"So what do you think?" he demanded. "Ain't that something?"

"It depends," I said, "on what I'm looking at."

"Why, them fields right in front of us, can't you see nothing at all? That's a full two hundred acres there on the left, drained as nice as can be. And that ain't all. On the other side of the house there's more. West of the road's a pair of eighties, and up ahead there's another sixty mostly diverted, that stand of rye. Ain't that something? You ever see such a damn pretty farm?"

"We're back at Homer Jackins'. Ain't that his barn over there?"

"Oh yeah, that's Homer's, all right. Now, look here, Arthur, pay attention to what I'm showing you. This ain't no regular place. Look how pretty it sits; there ain't all them damn low places to wrestle with. Look there at how all the fence is tore out, look at them entry-ways, all smoothed out at the corners. No more banging around like we done all the time at Bremer's. We ain't but three miles from the elevator at Onarga, so the hell with Hostetler if he can't carry me a week, we'll take our grain down across the county line. It's just a straight shot down this road."

"What do you mean?"

"What do I mean? I mean that we got this farm now, too. All this come to me. You probably figured old Gerry Maars had about gone around the bend renting that Holloway place. Thought I'd lost my damn mind getting that Schapp place too, ain't I right? But see, it's all on the way down here, the hell with that damn prairie, we'll get off there as soon as we can. Restaurant firm out of Indianapolis has all this——Foodmore, maybe you heard of them. Own half the Burger Boys in the state of Indiana, a bunch of taco stands, and I called 'em up from Florida to make the deal. Signed the papers just this morning. Old dad's still got a little life in him, I reckon. He ain't quite ready to give up yet!"

Gerry hopped out of the truck to lead me up to the edge of the field. It was a pretty farm, no doubt about it, but I was calculating that we'd come a good fifteen miles south, which made it a full thirty miles from the Fox ground north of the river.

"It puts us kind of spread out, don't it?"

"Aw hell, just for this year. We only got Irene's another season, and after that we'll be down here. I ain't so sure I'll even keep Foxie's, either, after the next couple of years."

"But how about this year? We ain't even done plowing, how are we gonna get all this planted? There aren't that many days in the whole spring and summer both. What's out there, four hundred acres?"

"Almost five. Throw in Schapp's and them other places and it's another eight hundred all told. How do we get it done? We just got to bear down, Arthur, have a little vision. I been thinking about it all morning. Maybe I'll get another planter and get you sowing too. Find another couple of boys to disk. We just got to have the pluck, damn it, and we'll be fine."

I shrugged. Gerry hadn't made his fortune listening to me or anybody else, and I didn't imagine he was about to start in that morning. I was beginning to remember the block farmhouse by then, not just from our pass by it the winter before, but from back when Homer Jackins' boys had been in the FFA the same time as me. It had the kind of look you liked to see in a farm, tidy even in that emptiest time of the year.

"We'll put up a pole barn at your place, run the combines in up there. You hear me say combines? I'm thinking more than one. We get us that second combine, form up those couple of crews I been talking about. You take charge of one while I take the other. Ain't that the way it's being done anymore? Ain't that the way Ray Stewart's going at it now?"

I'd remembered Homer Jackins by then, too, with his squeezed-up face and worried forehead, wedged in over a thick chest and arms. A short little guy, and not even all that pleasant as I remembered, but I still felt obliged to ask. "Wasn't Homer Jackins farming for that restaurant chain last year? What's he gonna do now?"

"How the hell do I know? Homer Jackins don't confide in me. Now, come on a second, come up here where you can see." Gerry led me back across the side ditch to the truck. "Look out way over there, see that little dip? Nestled back against the woods? That's where I'm gonna put the pond. It's been a long time since I even thought of something like that. Yes sir, get it stocked by the state, I reckon I still know some boys down there. Get the stocking done, and then come next July or August, you and me will be fishing out here for sure. A man works as hard as I have, he deserves a little bit of advantage in his life."

"What about Homer Jackins? I reckon he was counting on this ground. Where's he gonna hook up this late in the year?"

Gerry wheeled around at me, slamming his big hand down on the hood of the truck. "Goddamn it," he exploded, "what the hell do you or me either one have to do with Homer Jackins? What's Homer Jackins ever done for us?"

"Well," I said, "he's a neighbor, for one thing. I imagine he's—"

Gerry snorted. "Hell, he ain't done nothing, is what he's done. He's never helped me out here a damn bit. Back when I was first on the council and we had redistricting, Homer Jackins knew every bit as well as I did that we couldn't support no five grade schools in a county this size, but did he come out and admit it? Hell no, he led the fight against me. And then when this county-wide zoning come along, it was the same thing. He went around telling everybody I'd sold out to the Delfina Chamber of Commerce. Me! After all them years I done business in Keona, Deer Creek, after all I done for people out here. I don't see that as much of a neighbor, maybe you do. Maybe that's the kind of friends you like to keep."

"We come down here fifteen miles to farm."

"Twelve. I checked it on the gauge. Twelve, it won't be so bad. Three hours for a move or twice that much, it don't really matter, there's still half a day lost. We'll make it up at night."

"Twelve, then. We come down twelve, push Homer Jackins off." An anger had surged up from somewhere to surprise me, my face growing hot. "Where does Homer Jackins go then, twelve miles further on? Over to Ohio? Who's he gonna push off over there? He was counting on this place."

Gerry stood in front of me already rumpled in his shiny windbreaker, a small stain on his cuff from checking the oil on the pickup a week before. "Homer Jackins," he said slowly. "Goddamn Homer

Jackins. That's all you care about. I figure out a way to keep us going, make a deal to keep afloat for another year. I bring you all the way out here to show you a farm that for once won't just beat us down every day, that for once might be something special. Something that a man can finally be proud of. Now, listen to me close, because I'm going to tell you something. The hell with Homer Jackins. The hell with him. Homer Jackins never laid awake at night worrying about Gerry Maars. The hell with him. You're so doggone worried about Homer Jackins, you go to work for him. See how much fun it is going broke. Until then, I'm the one who signs your checks."

I still had the wrench, and for a nickel would have bashed him with it right across his fat bald head. Instead I walked back to throw it in the bed. "Well, you've signed your last one. Go ahead and keep my wages these last two weeks, you need money so damn bad."

I reached in for my work gloves from the cab, and when I ducked out, he was still standing in front of the pickup, mouth flapping open, his new southern empire laid out behind him. I looked up the empty road as I zipped my jacket. I hadn't gone a dozen yards when Gerry caught up with me, reaching out to grab my arm.

"I should have known. I sure as hell should have known."

"Get your hands off me," I told him.

"I should have known better than to show something like this to you. It's just like you, damn it, Arthur, playing the sad sack all the time when a fella tries to get ahead. You're just like your dad, is what it is, ain't nothing quite pure enough for a man to do. That was old Hurd to a T. There's a right way and a wrong way for things, and ain't nobody knew the difference but him."

"Get your goddamn greedy hands off me!"

When I'd jerked free, I turned my back and strode away. A quarter mile later he was beside me again, this time in the pickup. I stopped cold in my tracks, catching him by surprise. I walked around his battered tailgate to the other side of the road, but before long he was back, leaning out the window at my side.

"You ought to know better than anybody, Arthur. This here's a business. Ain't nobody left who thinks otherwise. It's just dollars anymore. I worked myself half to death for this county, never had nothing of my own. Now I got a chance to make something good with these Foodmore people, and it's not gonna pass me by. I ain't the kind of man who's gonna give up, you ought to know that by now. I can't just park the tractors and walk away."

He was swerving as he talked to me, and a honk surprised us both, a feed truck bearing down from the other way. Gerry waved at the driver as it rushed past, then came swinging back. A sharp tightening in my throat kept me from talking to him even if I'd wanted to, and I ignored the truck idling at my side. It was while rolling along next to me, apparently, that Gerry made up his mind.

"Yeah," he said, "ain't nothing pure enough for you, Arthur. That's what you'd like people to believe. Well, a man lives for a little while, and he knows better. I got eyes and ears. I know the sheriff pretty well, I guess you'd say, and I hear things. A man likes to keep himself informed. You come on so high and mighty with me, but it's all right to play with the girls, go running around with another man's wife while he's away. That's all just fine in your book."

The side ditch was grown over with sod, so I was lucky to find it, a piece of asphalt broken off small enough to throw. I hurled it as hard as I could into his fender.

"Get the hell out of here!" I yelled. "If you paid attention to your own business and not everybody else's, didn't have to be the big shot all the time, you'd get along fine. Pay attention to things and you might even get planted by the first of July, not have crops still out in the field after Christmas."

"I don't imagine I'd be taking on sorry boys who didn't have no place to go then, either."

"Just go to hell!" I shouted, furious. "I don't need your damn favors, and never did. I'm through with you. I'll be out of that damned old wreck of a house by the end of the month."

My voice shook, anger driving me ahead of the pickup. Gerry accelerated, bouncing through a pothole to my side.

"I might as well face it," he said, "it's the truth. You and your dad either one wouldn't have liked nothing better than to see old Gerry

Maars go down. Have him join the rest of the sorry crowd. I ain't gonna do it, though, you might as well know that right now. That ain't gonna be me." His own voice breaking, he was shouting wildly by then. "That ain't gonna be me!"

Stamping on the accelerator, he took off down the road, gravel spinning up in my face. Even at that I wasn't free. For the next mile and a half I could see him skulking ahead in the pickup, slipping back and forth on the crossroads, waiting behind a stand of trees off to the side. I kept ignoring him—the one thing he couldn't stand—until there came a last time that I looked up and he was gone.

THIRTY-ONE

They'd begun to appear more and more by then, joggers agonizing along the sections, decked out in bright-colored sweatsuits and caps. But to be out walking in the countryside, purposely, from one place to another—I couldn't have been more radical if I'd bombed the Lion's Club, or held the county assessor in chains for ransom. The two or three cars that passed slowed suspiciously and sped on, their drivers safe behind steel and tinted glass. None of it mattered; I'd begun to warm to the walking, as I swung out first one heavy boot and then the other, making my way in along the cracked, battered roads that wound those dozen miles back to the house.

It was after noon by the time the sun broke through a bank of high gray clouds. Even then I'd had a good two hours to go, but there was my selfishness to keep me company, plus a growing contentment, and my jacket opened wide to the day. Before long, I could pick out the Shaw woods on the horizon ahead. I came up on Byron's, but cut across the field like my nephew might have done, angling toward the farmhouse.

I half-expected to find Gerry's truck waiting for me in the crowded barnyard, but even if it had been, it wouldn't have mattered. I had my destination all picked out by then, well beyond that old house and barn. I went inside long enough to clean up a little bit and change my clothes. In twenty minutes I was back behind the wheel of the Camaro, driving into town.

I knew Annie was on afternoons, so I pulled up at the register, waiting until I spotted her busing a table toward the back. By year-old tradition I should have chosen the front, but this time I went back to where she was working, enjoyed her eyes first widening to see me and then narrowing at my choice of the booth she'd just finished wiping down.

Ann-Marie brought me my water and wished me a good afternoon, but I waited for Annie. She took a three o'clock breakfast to one of the deputies just going out for the day, changed filters on the coffee machine. She was bantering with a pair of city mailmen while she came my way. She reached into her wide apron pocket for her pad.

"What are you doing in this time of day? All the tractors blow up?"

"They're all fine."

"What, then, your boss man's got a fever? He decide to work regular hours?"

"He ain't decided nothing. He ain't my boss anymore, either."

That took her by surprise. "What happened?"

"Sit down with me a minute, let's talk."

She colored, looking around. It was still an hour or so too early for the white-haired dinner crowd, and the restaurant was almost empty. She lowered her voice. "Arthur, I ain't sitting down with you here."

"Sit down."

"A cheeseburger? What do you want on it, just pickles? You want fries with that too?"

I reached out a finger to catch hold of the dangling bow on her waitress uniform, set at an angle over one side of her narrow waist. With the back of my knuckles I brushed against the tight linen sheen of her belly, pressed in by the edge of the table. "Sit down," I told her again. "I want you to sit down with me a while."

Bending to her pad, she shook her head. Then she looked around again quickly, up toward the register and back along the booths against the wall, before dropping down onto the seat across from me. The clank and murmur went on around us unabated as the few patrons fed contentedly in their stalls.

"Hey," I said.

"I ain't got but a second and you know it. Viola's soap operas are over anytime now, and she'll be back. What happened with you and Gerry?"

"We had a parting of the ways. I'm through with him. I ain't gonna be working for him anymore."

Her eyes flickered around the room on their way in to rest on me. When I reached across the damp table for her hand, she let me hold it a second, even squeezed my fingers before pulling away. "I can't stay sitting here," she said.

"Sure you can. You can stay sitting here as long as you want. "

She shook her head as she stood. "I can't, Arthur, not now. Not here." Looking past me down the row of booths, she called over my shoulder. "Just a second, Herschel, I got sidetracked a second. A cheeseburger, then, Arthur? An order of fries?"

"A cheeseburger," I said, "would be great. More of you, too, whenever you get a chance."

I got the cheeseburger at least, and another minute or two of Annie when she stopped by with more tea, came back later to clear my plate. The sandwich tasted good after my hike through the countryside, and it felt good too to be where Annie could glance up at me now and then. She labored under the knowledge that I was watching, studying her as she balanced plates on her wrist, scrawled out quick totals on her bills. One of them she dropped off for me.

"Need anything else?" she asked, and then in a lower voice, "You gonna be home later on? Be somewhere around the phone if you can help it, and I'll try to get away."

"I don't need nothing special," I told her. "I just wanted dinner and a chance to watch you for a second, and I got both my wishes."

Looking one last time around her, she nodded. "You just be around the phone this evening, and I'll try to get free."

About seven that night, as I was washing the last of some dishes that had piled up, I heard her Nova come rattling into the yard.

"Your husband's got all them cars, ain't he ever gonna tune that damn thing up?" I asked her as I came down from the porch.

"This is a luxury," she answered, "coming by to find you home. I thought Gerry Maars would have hired you back by now."

"No," I told her, "we're through for good. I've had enough of his bullshit."

"You want to go for a ride and talk about it some?"

"I don't know that there's much to talk about, but I'll take you up on the ride."

Gerry had been in to get his plow by that time, spent a half hour wrestling with the same stubborn starter that I'd been telling him about for a week. He left my water jug on the porch along with my paycheck.

Annie slid over to let me drive, and I backed out through the long rows of equipment that had accumulated on either side of the barn. The Nova felt even less stable than it looked. A Popsicle stick and a bald tennis ball were jammed under the handbrake; jumbled in with sweaters and caps in the back were a popcorn bag and small white sock. On the dashboard lay two or three torn mimeographed papers. The top one had a blue-lined kite on it, and spaces for block letters below.

As I swung out onto Sycamore and accelerated, Annie slid past the gear shift to sit at my side. It was overcast again, an early spring night with the chill back into it, and the Nova just as drafty as a barn. Annie was bundled up in a gray zip sweatshirt, her dark hair bursting out from where the hood lay bunched at her neck. I felt the cool in her fingers as she put them up under my arm, squeezing tight. She told me she was sorry about the job.

"Doesn't Carl Wayne ever call up to the restaurant?" I asked.

Annie tightened her fingers. "Only when he's tired of the kids. If he does, Ann-Marie just tells him I ran out to the market for something."

"You girls all take care of each other like that?"

"We try to be friends," she said, "be on each other's side."

It had been a long time since Annie and I had been out just driving around the county together—with the monthly luxury of the Holiday Inns, I'd lost some of my resourcefulness. I ended up circling through the sections and back to the silo, pulling up onto the ditch bank above the field. The trees and brush were budding out, the fields all around still bare. As the car idled roughly beneath us, I pondered where to go next.

That afternoon I'd been determined to see her, but by evening I was already embarrassed that Annie'd made special time for me. Unable to think of what it was I'd wanted, I was just restless, reaching for the gear shift to back us out again, when she caught my hand.

"Wait," she said.

I waited.

"You got a job all picked out now? You know what you're going to do?"

"I hadn't really thought about it."

"You're really through with Gerry?"

"I'm through with him."

"You ain't going back?"

"Not in this lifetime."

"What about the house? You gonna stay there?"

It felt good to be certain, at least, about that much. "No, I'm gonna be gone. There ain't nothing for me there."

Her eyes flashed in the last of the dim sunset, her hand squeezing tight around my arm. "Arthur," she said, "let's go. You and me. Let's just get out of here once and for all."

She was flushed like she had been that afternoon moving among the tables. "Let's just go," she said, the excitement in her voice growing. "Let's do it. This ain't no kind of life. Waiting a month at a time for some happiness, sneaking around to get a few hours together. Carl Wayne ain't no kind of husband at all. Let's just go. We can make a new life together, people do it all the time."

I laughed. "Okay, where we gonna go? Where you want to head off to? Hawaii? Royal Gorge? How about the Great Smoky Mountains? What's your pleasure?"

"Anywhere. Everywhere. I don't care. I never been anyplace."

"How about Alaska? We could hunt polar bears for a living."

"Anywhere," she said with conviction. "Let's just go. I been ready for years. The boys are at a good age, and next year Moni'll be in school. Let's go, Arthur, we got a chance now to get away. I guess I'd been giving up hope these last weeks, I just didn't know how to tell you. We got a chance, though, now, to make a life."

Annie sat cross-legged in the seat next to me by that time, my hand held tight while her eyes searched my face. The car below us rattled like every last turn of the idling motor would be its last, while the ground between the ditch bank and the distant silo lay rough and unworked, still missing the plow. "Oh, don't get that long face on," she said. "Don't be looking like that. I ain't pronouncing your death sentence. It'd just be me and the kids. They ain't bad kids at all, either, you'd love them. I know you would. I know that even better than you. I could waitress anywhere, and you're handy with things. We'd get along."

"I don't reckon Carl Wayne or your family either one would care much——" I began, but Annie cut me off.

"So now I'm gonna hear about ten million reasons for why it can't be. It just so happens I don't want to hear them. We can do it. When you come into the restaurant today, when you took my hand across the table, it was just like the first day I saw you. I knew from that first day it wasn't no accident. It was just like seeing myself there, I told you already, it was like seeing myself looking back through the mirror. Now, just think about it. Think it over." She looked at me suspiciously. "Are you thinking?"

"I'm thinking."

"I ain't ready to leave tonight, so just think about it. Are you gonna think about it? Don't give in now, stay thinking."

"I'll stay thinking," I promised.

"And it's not already impossible?"

"Well," I said, and she jerked my hand.

"Just tell me it ain't impossible. Tell me once and for all, because that's all I ever hear, how impossible everything is. It's not, though, I know it. Tell me it's not impossible."

Maybe a man does get tired of playing the sad sack all the time, too close a kin to the shadows while the rest of the world grows prosperous in the sun. You might excuse that same man for counting himself fortunate that opportunity still might present itself, privileged that a young girl like Annie would end up offering him gifts like that: herself, her family, her life. You might excuse him for smiling at the possibility, on an early May evening, that things might even turn out for the good.

"It's not impossible," I said, and she threw her arms around my neck.

"Oh, I knew it wasn't, Arthur. I always knew there was a chance. Come on," she said, laughing, "let's run over to that silo a minute. I'm feeling romantic."

"There ain't no cover," I said as she pulled at my hand. "That's just an empty field. For that matter I ain't got no right to go tramping around out there. I don't work for Gerry no more."

"Take me back to the ballpark, then, or over to the fairgrounds. Rent us another motel room. You got a wild woman on your hands here, you got to take care of her. My Lord, put the car in neutral at least, Arthur, you're gonna drive us both down into the ditch."

Our teenage years were behind us, but we were still inventive enough and, more important when it came right down to it, flexible.

"That seat slides back," Annie whispered, then slipped off her jeans to straddle me, her pale knees squeezed up tight against my hips. My own pants were down around my ankles; bunched up between our chests was her sweatshirt. Soft gray arms smelling of hot dogs and Downey wrapped themselves under my chin. Night still hadn't quite settled over us as Annie rose up to press her bare scarred tummy into mine. She butted her forehead against me, rubbed her hair into my cheek.

"Just hold me a second, Arthur," she whispered. "I love you, I really do. We got a chance now — just hold me — we got a chance now to really be free."

Thirty-three

I never expected Gerry to waste time mourning me, and he didn't. Lee Fennel, who rented the house up at Foxie's, was out of work again, and the second morning after I quit he was outside my kitchen door firing up Gerry's tractors like he owned them. Gerry's dream of a second crew was still alive, too. To anchor it, he'd managed to come up with a secondhand planter and Jaron Holcomb's boy Fred, who'd just finished up the school year at Purdue. He was the kind of hand a farmer could only dream of: clean-cut and hardworking, and good with the equipment besides. Over the next week he was out every morning before seven to get started, went every night until dark.

Of course, daylight was providing only about half the hours Gerry needed to get done that season, so somewhere he dragged up Shawn again, and Shawn brought out one of his friends. He hired on Roger Good, too, a tall rangy man who preached at one of the fringe Baptist churches out on old 31. I got to see what it was like for the other tenants for a change, what Lee had put up with all those years up at Foxie's, Byron and Kendra too, for that matter, with farm equipment clattering past at all hours right under your bedroom window.

Not that I felt like complaining. There had turned out to be a whole other world out there that a person could notice, when he wasn't trying to bend it to his will. Most mornings I'd drive into the Cove about ten, figuring to miss Gerry and the rest of the breakfast crowd. The waitresses had a smile or a wink for me by then, proud of themselves as they swept by, on their way to the kitchen, to whisper in Annie's ear. I'd lean back and watch her as she slipped in and out of the last of the morning rush, glad to watch the banter and flirting she waded through to deliver the plates. I was more than generous with all the attentions that were paid her, because in a little while, when the rest of them were back on the empty highways to their trailer homes or lonely farmhouses, or putting their shoulders back to the wheel in courthouse offices and garages, when Viola had finally broken away to her condo and soap operas, I knew Annie would be slipping in across the booth with her own cup of coffee, to sit ten or fifteen minutes with me.

Out of the handful that still lingered in the restaurant those mornings, the dawdling businessmen and pensioners, the self-conscious tourists from Chicago or Detroit, I doubt that a single one wished us ill. If they thought about it at all, they might have been glad for that trim, little woman so giddy with excitement, leaning across the table to her brother, friend, extraterrestrial visitor—only a red-hot booster or an ignorant farm boy would have ever thought any different, that there was still a community out there that cared.

In the evenings, while Gerry and his crews were out sowing the scattered fields of his kingdom, she came to the farmhouse. PTA meetings and shopping trips, sick friends and shift changes—in those two or three weeks she burned through a year's worth of excuses. Every second or third night, three nights in a row during one stretch in the middle of the month, she'd come up the lane to park—we were still that careful at least—past the combine on the far side of the barn. I'd meet her on the porch and take her inside. The old house gave her the creeps, she told me, but Annie had enough energy to light up a dozen old wrecks like that and a city of five thousand besides.

"I been thinking about boarding dogs," she might say afterwards, her face moving in and out of the shadows that fell across us from where the barnyard light came through the shades. She'd propped herself on one elbow next to me, imagining our world to come. "That's a business we could do. We're gonna take Shemp along, aren't we? I'd miss him an awful lot."

"The more the merrier."

"Oh, that ain't really true, because in that case I'd take everybody. Almost everybody, anyway, Holly and Ann-Marie, my mom, I'd move us all up out of here and away. Raising puppies is something you can make money on too, if you get the right breed. I been reading in Trader Jon's some of those dog prices are out of this world."

A kennel and puppy farm, a motel office on some highway out west, dollhouses for tourists that I'd jigsaw and she'd sell by the side of the road. There were welding jobs on a pipeline project that she'd heard about, over in one of the Arab states. My pleasure was in just listening as she daydreamed, running my fingers down the arched throat where each new one formed to roll out. There would now and then be a shout from the barnyard, a pickup backing for seed, but Annie was as indifferent to the crews below us as she was to the gloom beyond the boundaries of the cot.

"Now don't be sleeping, Arthur, listen to me."

"I'm not sleeping," I'd say.

"I been thinking that I'd like to get my education. Go to night school or something, see what I can do. I just couldn't settle down the first time around. I'd be better at it now."

"Sounds fine to me."

"I'd be good at school, I help the kids all the time. I ain't no dummy, that's just Carl Wayne talking, trying to keep me down. Do you think I could go back to school?"

It would have been about that time in the spring that Kendra's father, no longer quite so wild with worry, finally gave up the ghost in his sleep. At the funeral home Byron, overcome, hugged me for the first time I could remember, while Joey hung back at my side. Kendra, now that the shoe had finally fallen, was stoic. I didn't go out to the graveyard, but at the funeral she favored me with a sullen flicker my way that lingered, before she turned back to what little the emphysema and two or three different johnny-come-lately cancers had left of her dad.

Gerry was one of the pallbearers, of course, solemn in his public duties, but I knew that as soon as they were discharged, he'd be back out to the field, complaining about all the time that had been lost. Whipping his team even harder to make it up, but I'm not sure who he would have been complaining to or whipping, either one. Shawn and his buddy came in when they cared to; I tripped over their beer cans every morning on my way out to the car. Lazy Lee Fennel was already gone, and the Purdue boy had been as true blue to the next good job offer as you might expect, grabbing a chance to do lab work for one of his professors down in West Lafayette. The second planter had been parked back next to the combine. The weather had turned dry, and Gerry had clear, warm days for working: I'd see the welders and tire men parked in the end rows, Shawn peeling out down the lane for parts.

In the morning there was Annie for me down at the restaurant; evenings I would hear her come rattling up into the yard. Maybe in those mornings I'd come to stay an extra few minutes across from her, maybe she grew a little lax those evenings about where she parked. We were like a lot of people by that time, building to that cowardly sort of carelessness lovers assume. A carelessness crafted so that even in an indifferent world their minds would sooner or later be made up for them. That, though, wasn't really my style, no more than making up motel rooms, or breeding a pack of noisy and stinking old dogs.

I'd been getting notices from the union off and on, but hadn't thought much about them until the envelope from Lenny'd arrived a couple of days before. As we came down the stairs into the bright light of the kitchen, Annie, with a mother's eye for refrigerator doors, went right to where I'd hung up the clipping that had come inside: a picture of an ore boat clearing the Two Harbors breakwater, torn out from the paper in Duluth.

It had been folded and refolded, creased by the hands of the half-dozen sailors that it passed through on its way to Lenny and finally me. "Gott to Go," was what the caption read, and a "Get Ready!" was what Lenny'd added himself, scrawling across a fading gray shore and skyline, in thick Magic Marker above the bow. Annie was taking it all in, her bright eyes still blinking from the light.

"That's the flagship," I said. "It's called the *Gott*. The boats are going again."

She nodded. "How soon for you?"

"Could be next week, could be a month. Steel's picked up again, so they need the ore. They're making their way down the roster, should be getting before long down to me."

There's a time when people are still playing, a time when they decide if they're for real. Annie talked to the clipping, taped to the white enamel of the door. "Moni's not in school yet, but she will be in the fall. I won't be needing my mom so much."

"Two Harbors is where we'll go out of, most likely. That's north of Duluth."

"I guess they got schools up there and all. People who live just like everybody else."

"Like here or anywhere, just colder is all. It's pretty with all the trees."

She looked at me, thoughtful. "I got some tips saved, but we still got our income tax check coming. I'd kind of hoped to get that. The boys are all registered for ball."

"I could go ahead," I told her, "and you come up later."

She shook her head. "No, that won't do. I don't want you leaving without me."

"Well," I said, "I'll go up Wednesday to see about it, be back in a couple of days. You might think about getting ready to go."

THIRTY-FOUR

I stopped by the restaurant a last time that Wednesday morning, on my way out of town. It was after the morning rush, but Viola had hung around gabbing with some of her cronies, leaving the Young and Restless to shift for themselves while she had another cup of coffee. There was the highway out in front of me, but while Annie worked the tables across the room, I had another cup too, waiting for my chance to say good-bye. I was just finishing it when Janine came by and told me I had a phone call.

"Not there," she said as I started toward the register. "It come in on the other line, back by the banquet room."

Banquet room was what they called it, more recently the no-smoking section, those one or two times a year when somebody wandered in to claim one. I edged between the tables, back past Viola, past the rest-room doors, and into the low, stuffy gloom of the once-a-week lair of Lions and Kiwanis. A service closet door was ajar, with a narrow yellow light that spilled out over a vacuum cleaner and a tangle of mops. Just past it Annie was waiting, coming out of the darkness to wrap her arms around my waist.

"That old woman picks this morning to stay around," she said. "I could see you getting impatient."

"She's a talker," I agreed.

Annie pressed herself up into me, darted her hard lips up to mine. "I been thinking about it," she said, "I really have. I'm ready. You just come back and tell me when."

"It shouldn't be too long. I'll have to see."

"Arthur, you haven't been having second thoughts, have you? Especially about the kids?" Tears welled up in her eyes. "I couldn't leave them. I just couldn't ever do that."

I shook my head. "The kids are all right. I don't expect you to leave them."

Annie smiled out at me with relief. "Oh, I thought so, Arthur, but you never can tell. You never know how people are gonna be." Her eyes sparkled in the yellow light. "You know I been preparing them lately, that's what I've been trying to do. I been telling them there's other places to live at, told them which way was north. When I asked Shannon if he knew who you were, he said he does. You were the one in the car we saw at Christmas. The quiet man who comes in here sometimes. He understands things, I know that he does."

She leaned back with her chatter, was watching me when suddenly she stopped.

"Arthur, where's that long face of yours come from? It scares me sometimes. Are you gonna be an old grouch when we're together?"

"I'm already an old grouch."

She nodded, regarding me seriously. Imagining what life would really be like with me, now that she was poised on the edge. "You can't be grouchy all the time around little ones. They deserve better than that. They're just getting started. It's gonna be us now, Arthur, you got to think about what that means. You and me, Moni and the boys."

I could agree they deserved better than grouchiness, and Annie held me close.

"That's union up there?" she asked. "The pay's pretty good?"

"Better than you can even imagine."

"I really would like to get my schooling if I could, once Moni gets launched. They got night classes up there and all, places I could go? There's things I need to know about, things that I want to say."

"There's plenty of schools. All manners of them. Just pick out any one you like. I'll let you know what I find out about the boats." I was pulling away, but she wouldn't let go. Viola'd already passed by the doorway twice to scowl in at us, but Annie didn't care, she was intent on me.

"Honey," she said, her eyes filling again, "listen, I want to tell you something. I've had my four babies. That's all I was ever gonna have. There's things I want to do now. But listen, if you ever feel like you want to, if it turns out we've got to, I want you to know I'll do it. I'll have your baby too."

She was crying openly by then, tears rolling down over those sharp cheeks while I hugged her as best I could. She led me to the side door that opened into the alley, wouldn't take the five-dollar bill I tried to give her for my check.

"I'll pay it out, Arthur, now go on. Just be careful there, out on the road. I'll be waiting right here. Don't worry about me now, I'll be ready."

It's funny how things go back to the beginning sometimes, how much I still liked her trimness and life—the crisp press of a linen uniform under my hands as I bent down to her, a sweet muddled smell of pancakes and coffee as I buried my face in her hair. I kissed her one last time.

"Drive careful," she instructed me, and when I promised I would, she stood by the side door, wiping her eyes and waving, while I headed up the narrow alleyway to my car.

It's not all that far into Michigan before the pines start closing in, up past the Indiana border, and the farms that spread out to the north. It was a five-hour drive to Saginaw, and that's where I found Lenny Jaynes in his apartment house paradise, so glad to see me that he almost squeezed my hand off, pounded his way clear through my back to my chest. It wasn't really personal; I gathered that when he brought me inside to meet his wife. She was a hard-looking blonde with the true soul of a landlord, already half-convinced as she sized me up that I'd be in with a hacksaw on her plumbing as soon as she turned her back. Even at best there was kind of a mean, guard-dog air to her, and it didn't take ten minutes to see that Lenny would have jumped in the lake and swam up to the first boat he could get to, if he thought it would do any good. She was on her way over to the office, but took time to chew at him in front of me for not taking out the papers. He assured her he'd get on it right away.

Instead the newspapers sat undisturbed while Lenny brewed us a fresh pot of coffee and dug out his smokes. We sat down around the kitchen table, and with his bride gone he began to relax. It didn't matter what we talked about—the weather north and south, the truck he was going to buy once we finally started getting our check. Nothing really mattered very much, as we enjoyed the sailors' simple luxury of knowing that before long we'd be gone. Both of us already sniffing at that quiet concentration in the offing, cold breezes and heavy jackets, black taconite pellets and steel. The meshed aloofness in a crew that even the young sailors come to count on, to make it through times on the shore.

We drove around for a couple of hours in his wife's smart little Sunbird, had lunch at a bar Lenny liked downtown. When we got back to the house, the two teenage kids that belonged to his wife were camped out in front of a blaring TV, their big butts holding down either end of the couch where I was slated to sleep. I was restless to move on anyway, and you could tell that Lenny didn't blame me. He walked me out to the Camaro, glancing back over his shoulder and sucking greedily at the chilly air that would be there for us in abundance, as soon as our call came in.

All the little towns and villages that I remembered so fondly stretched out along the lake—Ludington, Frankfort, Traverse City—I left alone, cutting straight up through the center of the state to reach Mackinaw at midnight, black on either side of the floodlit bridge. On the northern shore I pulled over to sleep, my windows cracked open to the night. Coming out of my dreams at dawn, the bridge loomed high above me. Somehow beneath it I still expected to see ice, but the water was bluing and clear—the straits had been open since March. It was only *my* season that was about to begin.

I spent the morning and the first part of the afternoon gliding across the broad pine forests of the northern peninsula. Duluth is where I checked in with the union, then drove over to the company offices. For once they both agreed: Lenny was thirteenth from the top, and I was at number nine. Another crew would be forming up, probably in a matter of days.

I'd come over the high bridge into Duluth about three that afternoon, past the tall cylinders of the grain elevators that guarded the port. I'd driven the clean city streets on my errands, feeling the lake out there all the while. On the twenty miles up to Two Harbors I finally found the shoreline, just off the old highway that wound through the woods. On the last of a clear afternoon the blue waters sparkled through the thick stands of pine and spruce, flashing up between old tourist cabins and fishing camps that nestled along the side of the road. By the time I came down through the train yards and out onto the docks at Two Harbors, the sun had set.

That didn't keep me from strolling out onto the huge trestled platform, climbing alongside the tracks where the ore trains were toiling—the *Gott* itself was expected later that night. After dinner in town, I came back to watch it dock, looking down as the big boat glided in silently below me, deckhands clustering at the gangway for their seven precious hours on shore. The huge ore chutes had begun lowering almost as soon as the boat stopped moving; a few seconds more and tiny pellets were already rushing by the ton down into wide hungry holds. It seemed to me a modern miracle, that somehow in our damaged heartland steel and shipping had come back yet again. Each time they rose from the grave there were fewer of us left, shaken off like a dog does fleas. But for another round I still would have a place, and with that much I came down and across the train yards to Waterfront Drive, strolled back up along it into town.

Summer afternoons would bring motor homes and tourists; in a world ever more full of restless leisure, even the north shore had gradually become popular, with Two Harbors a convenient lunch stop on the way. On a spring night it was the railroad and ore terminal town that I remembered. It grew more likely again that I really had spent two winters in an apartment above one of the downtown drugstores, and another renting, with two other sailors, an old cabin twenty miles in from the shore. Most everyone in the off season had someplace to go; remembering that I never did brought back a sweet kind of winter loneliness that still comforted, even as I drove through the town's few neighborhoods, looking for where a family might stay.

I slept in the car another night, down by the ore platform. After breakfast I set out in earnest to find a house. The paper listed one on Seventh Street, a small two-story in white clapboard. Two blocks farther east there was another, a little bigger, also up for rent. They went cheap; even with the cash I carried in my shirt pocket I could have covered those two or any of the four or five others that I visited over the rest of the morning. I found myself counting bedrooms and bathrooms, making certain they took kiddies and dogs. I inspected the quiet streets for reckless traffic, looked among cramped workman's bungalows for a backyard big enough to play in. I drove among those simple northland houses to see if there were schools nearby, and if any of them were good enough for us.

Duluth would have been a possibility, a half hour south, more prosperous and still linked to the rest of the world by ambition. But Two Harbors was more our kind of town, I decided. The truth is that a man can daydream every bit as foolishly as a girl, though a little more quietly, as a rule, and on the sly, more than halfway afraid it will come true.

In the narrower half of those daydreams I'd found myself picturing my boat coming in at the ore docks, the crew scrambling down the gangway to shore. A wave good-bye to Lenny, and the four- or five-block walk up through autumn streets to our house. The air grows chilly quick in November, as a person climbs from the lake. Ever colder all the way up Seventh Avenue, because even as I inspected the last house I knew it was the first that I was going to take, porchless but tidy, with two different bedrooms for the kids. They would have had to grow used to me by then: in seven-hour doses every few days, newness gradually has a way of wearing off. Their mother and I could even find a few minutes alone in those seven hours, while in my absence a child or even four could still grow up healthy in the northland, the summers clear and cool for playing, winters full of ski trails and ice. It all had such a sweet domestic clarity that it was embarrassing, but none of the various eager landlords that morning dared call me impostor, preferring to show off fresh-painted wallboards and linen closets, bathrooms with newly laid tile.

At that first place, then, when I went back, I peeled off four hundred-dollar bills to hand to the old widow who owned it, and who in turn promised to hold it from getting away. I doubled back once more through the streets that rose away from the lake, looping past a bandstand, the small courthouse, and a yellow-block fortress of a high school, before pronouncing the town finally fit. A little after noon I started back to the south.

I could have stayed that night or another dozen: I had my bedroll and clothes right there in the car with me. My bankbook and a couple of thousand dollars were stashed in an old tobacco tin that I'd wedged in the trunk. Of highways there's no shortage — all the way down through tidy Wisconsin they were out there, leading shamelessly in any of the four directions a person cared to go. I let one take me steadily south from Dairyland down into the congestion of Chicago, bearing east through Calumet and Gary along the lake. From that point I came east across Highway 30 into the springtime fields of north-central Indiana. I turned south at Plymouth, where the dry weather was beginning to show. It was by habit more than anything else that I broke off just before Delfina to come in past the Fox farm, and the fields that Gerry still had in the north.

Everyone can be replaced. Wisdom worth remembering sure enough, along with the sour smugness of shop teachers and gym coaches as they pronounced it, their grim pleasure in breaking eager school boys to the world. They got the same tight-lipped satisfaction, I would imagine, that I'd seen on the faces of the regulars in the restaurant that spring, speculating on the fortunes of Gerry Maars. When I'd first quit, of course, they'd been calling me over to sit by them, hoping for some handy piece of gossip they could gum over with their eggs. On that score they'd stayed disappointed, but I could still hear as I cruised north of the Tippy the way they talked on about him, while I'd waited for Annie to get free.

"He ain't touched an acre up north," was what fat Elmer Price told the circle of shaking heads, "even as dry as it's been. He had one of those damn boys disking up there, got twenty acres or so done, but since then that tractor's just been sitting there."

"He's probably working that new land down south," somebody ventured, but Elmer shook his head. "I was talking to Lee Fennel—you all know Lee, that lives in the old house up there at Fox's? My boy's sister-in-law is married to him. And Lee's pretty shrewd, he's been around. Lee told my boy that he's never in his life seen an operation as screwed up as Gerry Maars'. Equipment all wore out, ain't nobody out there when they're supposed to be, running all over like chickens with their heads cut off. It's a hell of a way to run an operation, that's what Lee told my boy."

All the rest of them at the table had to agree, that's what they'd heard too, by God, but they did their agreeing with some caution, skittish, ready to start singing his praises if Gerry'd chanced to walk in. As I drove by Foxie's, Lee Fennel was at home nursing his shrewdness, his truck pulled up in the shade. The tractor they'd all complained about was gone, but there still hadn't been any field work done to speak of, just those twenty crooked acres of disking, and the early plowing I'd done a month and a half before.

Everyone else's crops were up, of course, suffering halfway wilted under the sun. All of them suffering, that is, except Ray Stewart's; under the half a million dollars of irrigation pipes they were as green and healthy as any early corn and beans could ever be. There was no doubt about it as I came south, Gerry *did* have a lot of work still ahead: Rawson's wasn't planted, and neither was Skidmore's. The Bremer place was still spotty, as much undone as had finally been sowed.

It was almost dark by the time I came driving up into the barn-yard, where I found Gerry and what was left of his work force, clustered around the planter. They had the seed drum pulled off, and its insides spread in pieces across the grass. His two crews were down to one, with the turnover not much for the good. Even Shawn was gone, and in his place one of the Vinton boys was back. He and one of his sidekicks were standing behind Gerry with their hands in their pockets, watching him work.

I knew Ronnie Vinton and he knew me. He'd worked for us the year before, towards the end of harvest, had been out disking stalks one night when he came up on the old hemp patch back along the railroad. The boy was creative in his own way, you'd have to say, drying out leaves on the manifold as he went south from the right of way, rolling up reefer for the long ride back in the dark. Not a bad system, and it worked well enough until I caught up with him up at the road a little before midnight. The next thing he knew I was dragging his ass down from the cab, and back across the end rows to his car.

But times had changed, and now Ronnie was the right-hand man. As I came up past them to the porch, I saw him nudge his buddy. Watching Gerry do all the work wasn't quite amusing enough, so they had their own little laugh on me. The hemp was all plowed down, but they were stoned again anyway, with their sleepy eyes and silly smiles, a concern that wasn't any of mine.

There were two chicken pot pies left in the freezer, and a good quarter side still of Gerry's meat. I left the beef behind in favor of the pies. When I'd finished them, I began packing up the two or three small stray boxes that still remained. I remember thinking of Annie in her own house; the fact that she might be thinking of me too gave a

friendly sort of solidity to things, that I'd never really known or believed. That, and the almost stranger fact that I was really back for her.
a hand-scrawled receipt for the Seventh Street house doubled over in
my wallet.

Gerry and his crew were still banging at the seed drum in the
barnyard below when I, and probably Annie too, in her own separate
bed on the far side of Delfina, drifted our way into sleep.

THIRTY-SIX

I never had been much of a lie-in-bed sort of guy; take away those few
favored hours in the motel rooms with Annie, and there wouldn't have
been a handful of well mornings those last two years that found me
there much beyond sunrise. Even after it got light the next morning,
though, I lay back and looked around a few minutes, a last run around
the corners of that old upstairs room. Wood, buckling plaster, ten-
penny nails—the old place had so little to recommend it once a person was finally ready to be gone. My destination that morning was the
Frontier Inn up in Plymouth, so the house could pass on to Ronnie
Vinton and his buddies for some last-minute rock and roll, before
Gerry finally got around to tearing it down.

From the upstairs window I saw the planter down below. The
boys' cars were gone, but when I looked closer I saw that Gerry'd
never quite managed to make it home. The seed drum was back in
place and he was on his back under the frame, a droplight shining
weakly above his head. I'd carried most everything out to the car the
night before, so after I broke down the cot I shaved and showered,
packing up my razor when I was done. I put on clothes I'd saved back
for the day; the rest were already folded in my bag. I'd just finished the
last of a box of Corn Flakes, had rinsed off and packed up the bowl,
when I heard someone by the porch outside.

When I first swung the door open, I couldn't see anybody, but
that's because Gerry was standing on the ground, reaching up to rap
against the screen. I came out to look down on him, his face and hands

black with grease, the little red fox on his polo shirt locked sprinting through a ragged swamp of dust and oil. Dew had taken the shape out of his cap bill, so that it drooped down almost to his eyes.

"Don't mean to be getting you up there," he said. "I seen your light."

"You ain't getting me up."

"Hard to tell, a lot of folks like to sleep in on a Saturday. I couldn't remember if you was one of them. Mind letting me use your phone there for a minute? I got to call Kathryn before it gets any later. Just be sure to wrap it in a paper towel or something, and hand it on out. I don't want to be tracking up your floor none if I can help it. You remember the number?"

While I dialed, Gerry made his way up onto the porch. A wild patch of gray hair sprouted from his sagging shirt collar, and he wobbled as he came up the steps, stiff from kneeling all night in the grass.

"Oh, she's gonna be worried," he assured me, leaning in by the door. "Charlotte used to be like that, she'd get all worked up when I didn't get home. Where was I going to be? Out there going back and forth, just like always."

I handed him the receiver, and while it rang out in that big house back in town, we stood and looked at each other.

"Huh, she ain't answering. Maybe she's gone in to breakfast early with some of them people from school. What time is it, seven? I better give it a couple more rings. My Lord, Charlotte would have been out here with the sheriff by now, that's just the way she was."

Apparently Kathryn was a little different, because even as Gerry hung on another minute, clearing his throat and studying the doorjamb, nobody answered. Finally he handed me back the phone. His legs didn't seem too motivated to stump back down to his pickup yet, so he was still there when I'd hung up and come back to the porch. He nodded toward the planter.

"Clutch went out on that doggone final drive, the one that turns the seed drum. I was coming across there by your brother's when I seen it skipping. I sent old Ronnie flying up to Plymouth before they closed, see if we could get a part. A fella kind of misses Midway at a time like that."

"I imagine so," I said.

"So it wasn't until about seven-thirty or eight that we started breaking it down; you probably seen us there when you come in. When I finally get it apart, I stick in the new one. Put the whole thing back together. About that time, of course, those boys have to be getting home. I try it out, and the damn thing's still slipping. It was about the third time I had it apart that I seen they'd sent down a damn left-handed clutch, for the other side. Oh, I would have killed old Bob for that, but there I am about three o'clock in the morning, without no damn recourse at all. I just finished washering up the spring on the old one, maybe it'll hold."

"It ought to for a while. Them clutches are tricky."

"Goddamn right they are, you remember. A year ago was when we tore down the other side, you and me, over at the shop. You remember that? It started raining right about when we started, and by the time the weather cleared, we had it licked. Never lost a damn second. Oh, that was the way to do it."

He'd folded up the paper towel I'd given him so many times by then that it was just an oily ball of shreds. He stuck it in his pocket.

"I'll be heading out before long," I told him. "It's the thirty-first. I told you that's when I'd be gone."

"My Lord, is it the end of the month? Is that what it's got to already?"

"I ain't got but a couple more things to put in the car. It won't take me very long. If you're out in the field by then, I'll hang the keys in the barn. Up there by the fuses okay?"

"Well," he said, "I guess that's as good a place as any."

There wasn't any use in Gerry pretending he wasn't tired. I'd seen him perk up a hundred times over, for whoever might drive out to the field, but this year there'd been no wet weather to pace him, just day after day of pushing across all that acreage down south. For that matter it was only me anyway, that he'd have been trying to fool.

"Tomorrow's the first of June," he said. "Don't hardly seem possible. You probably heard everybody say it, I reckon they're all saying it right now. All about how you lose two or three bushels the acre for every day after the first. You probably heard that before."

"That's what they say."

"Maybe I told you that, you think? It might have been me."

I shrugged. "Could have been."

He laughed. "I bet it was. I sure bet it was."

"You still got corn to go before you switch over?"

It wasn't a fair question really, because from where we were standing we could both see half a warehouse full of seed bags stacked in the barn, not just a few of them corn.

Gerry laughed again. "Oh, I'd say I do. I'd say I have some to do. I got to go out and get on that tractor right now, when all I want to ride is this doggone porch."

The sun had broken down into the barn lot by then, and I was ready to go. Another ten minutes in that old house was all I'd ever need; the Camaro stood packed and waiting in the yard.

"Well," I said, "it looks like a good day anyway."

"Oh yeah," he said, rallying, "it does. A real fine day ahead. We'll get it whipped, ain't no doubt about that. That Ronnie Vinton ain't even that bad a mechanic, when he can keep his mind on it. He don't know nothing about farm machinery, but he's hell on wheels on regular engines. You heard the pickup lately? It ain't run that good since I bought it."

"Old Roger Good's been working out for you?"

"Oh yeah, and he's done fine. Real fine. 'Course we just get started of an afternoon, and he's about ready to shut it down. Got to get home to his family, see. And then there's his preaching, so Sundays and Wednesdays are out. This week he's got a tent meeting going on down in Converse, so he ain't been out at all. I ain't got no more against the good Lord than the next fella, but during planting's a hell of a time to hold a doggone revival. Guess there aren't no more farmers out here to be saved anyway."

I walked him to the edge of the porch. "Ronnie'll be here in a while."

"Yeah, I'll have those boys, whenever they get a notion to come back out. See what they can break up next. They got me running from one repair to another, while the spring's just passing us by. I crawl home at night and even when I get there I can't sleep, thinking of all them acres still to do."

"I reckon you'll get it done."

"Oh hell, yes. No doubt about that. We'll get it. I don't care if I have to do it all myself, it'll get done."

His big fingers were torn and bruised at the knuckles; he rubbed them as he squinted out at the trouble light, lost now in the morning sun. It was the first time that I realized——he wasn't going to make it.

Gerry was looking at me expectantly, while plain tiredness had let an irritation crowd back into his voice. "I say, though, that I'd just as soon not have to do that. You hear me? That's what I'm telling you. I'd just as soon not have to plant this damn crop alone. What I'm saying, Arthur, is that I could use your help out here for a few weeks. I really could."

The words came hard to him, but then again there had stood my own dad in that same barnyard before him, a man who would have just as gladly chewed glass as asked for a hand.

I shook my head. "I got other things going now."

"Oh hell, I know you do. That ain't no mystery to me. A young man like you's got his whole life ahead of him. There ain't no reason to come back with a broke-down old farmer like me. But we got a chance now, is what it is. Get out of this damn muck land once and for all. We get the right kind of breaks, we can make something out of these new places, ain't no telling where it'll all end up."

I was pretty certain that I knew, but next to me Gerry lowered his voice.

"There's something else, too, that I want you to think about. Maybe it's occurred to you, maybe not. I must have thought of it a hundred times at least, over the last year and a half. I just never said nothing, because I didn't know how you'd take it. You're kind of touchy sometimes, and a fella don't really know. But see, I don't have no boys. I ain't got boys, Charlotte's gone now, and my girls don't have no interest in farming at all. Kathryn's got her own world, she never cared much for this kind of life as it is. And I ain't even talking right now, because there ain't nothing but debt. But I'm saying someday. Someday this is the kind of operation a fella'd like to pass on. Don't turn away from me, now damn it, listen. Listen to what I've got to say."

He followed me across the porch. "Don't just shake that thick head of yours, give it some thought. There ain't nobody out here who understands anymore. There ain't nobody else I can trust."

I must have kept shaking my head, because eventually he finally fell silent behind me. A dozen steps away sat the Camaro; an hour north was a Plymouth motel room, and a long, sweet morning of waiting to give Annie a call.

We looked out through his tangle of equipment to the barn, both of us quiet so long that I guess he began to worry he was losing out.

"And damn it, I'll even give up that Foodmore land," he said finally. "There ain't no point in it, it'll just be one more farm for Ray Stewart to gobble up. But if it means so doggone much to you, I'll do it. Hand me out that receiver again and I'll call them up."

I shook my head one last time. "It doesn't matter."

"I'm serious, Arthur. Hand me out the phone. I'll call right down to them with the news."

"It doesn't matter."

"No," he said, "it really don't. That's the truth. That farm ain't going back to Homer Jackins in a hundred years, but let's get it over with. It's an Indianapolis number. I got it in my pocket here, just take me a second to find it. Let me call it out to you so you can dial." He'd pulled out his wallet and was searching through some cards.

"Forget it," I said. "Just forget it."

"It's one of these numbers, here, I just got to find it, and then—"

"Damn it, I said to forget it!"

Gerry looked up from his wallet. "Yeah?"

"I can put up with the preacher, but keep them damn potheads away. I don't want them anywhere around me."

"You know, funny you say that, I was just gonna let them go this morning. I'll be damned if I wasn't. Got the checkbook right there in the pickup to pay them out. I was there under that seed drum about four o'clock this morning, right shoulder throbbing like a goddamn toothache, and I remember saying to myself: you get rid of those boys. You'll be a whole lot better off. A fella just can't put up with careless-ness like that. That's exactly what I said."

"Another thing," I said, "my nephew Joey. Byron's boy. School's out before long and he might be able to help us. He can't go late, but he's a good little worker. He can pull up your seed."

"Oh that's just fine, Arthur, that's a hell of an idea. See, things are going better already. That's just great. Ray Stewart and all them can just go eat grass as far as I'm concerned, we're gonna get somewhere yet."

It was too much after the season he'd had to expect the fatigue to go out of his face, the sag from his shoulders, but Gerry's enthusiasm was back at least to challenge them, and the fire had returned to his voice.

"I got to go change clothes," I said.

"All right, you do that. Hell, wait a second, let's just go into town. I ain't eaten since yesterday afternoon. Come on into the Cove and I'll get us both some breakfast."

I paused at the door. You can't think much of a man—I know I didn't—who'd even wavered. Who even then couldn't stroll those dozen steps past Gerry to the Camaro, who wouldn't be up in Plymouth before the hour was out. In front of me was a doorway a lot like the one I'd just left behind in the northland, where life could still grow up free on the other side.

There hadn't been any porch in Two Harbors; there weren't many porches at all up there, it was too damn cold. I'd had little enough trouble, though, in those careless daydreams, picturing the Seventh Street house where Annie would wait. Night had already fallen on my way up from the dock, the air still with the weight of approach-ing winter as I came up the cracked sidewalk to the door. The boys were playing loud in the living room, their shouts muffled as I reached for the knob. Annie would have already come in from the kitchen by then, looking at her watch. Moni's little hands were on her hips at the rattle. There was the warmth of the oil furnace all around them, the cold of the lake at my back, Annie's lingering smile of anticipation—her part I never doubted at all. The only one always missing was me.

The door swung open to the kitchen of the old farmhouse, the living room and cold parlor beyond.

"You go ahead," I told Gerry, "I already ate. I'll get ahead some, and when you get back, we'll get some of that seed in the ground."

THIRTY-SEVEN

God only knows how much acreage Gerry still had ahead of him when I went back to work for him that spring. God and possibly old Roger Good, if it came up during one of their nightly chitchats down at the revival tent in Converse. Back in Haskell County the dry weather brought yet another workday, and I was on the tractor just like I'd never been gone.

Gerry brought back with him enough sandwiches to feed an army; we ate them in our cabs, never stopping once until almost ten that night. That's when he had a flat tire on the planter, on the eighty acres east of the ditch. A flat like that is tricky to work with, especially in the dark, but we finally got it fixed, and went straight on from then until almost three.

I'd tried to catch Annie that morning at home, without any luck. When I called the restaurant, they said she'd be working later on. The last time was at the house again late that night, when I came back to get the compressor for the tire. I hung up when I drew Carl Wayne, reprieved but suspicious, growling a hello at the other end.

Gerry would need thirty hours a day just to break even that spring; we started in again early Sunday morning, finishing the Bremer corn that evening about ten. While Gerry loaded the planter, I drove past the house for some chains. That's where Annie caught up with me, coming out from the shadows where she'd parked her car.

"Hey," I said, "I been trying to get hold of you. Where have you been?"

I reached for her, but she straight-armed me away.

"So what's the story?" she demanded.

"What story is that?"

"Damn it, Arthur, don't play dumb with me. I ain't gonna stand for it. What's the story?"

"What, about the boats?"

"Yeah, among other things. I thought you were moving out. I thought you'd be up at the motel last night."

"That's what the plan was, but it changed. Something came up."

"I see what came up. You're back working for Gerry Maars."

It was an undeniable fact on the face of it: with my seed corn hat and greasy T-shirt, I was definitely working for Gerry Maars. I shrugged. "Only for a while. There wasn't no boat quite ready anyway. I didn't see no reason not to help."

She looked up at me with suspicion, that mother's seventh or eighth sense that I'd admired from a distance, and now got to see trained on me. It was enough to make a bad boy see the error of his ways, but the truth was I wasn't a boy. "Gerry was in a bind. I thought I could help him some. It don't change nothing that I can see."

"It don't change nothing."

"Nothing at all."

"I thought you'd made your break with him. What are you doing running back?"

I didn't have an answer to that one, but I'd begun by that time to bristle. Annie didn't back down an inch.

"Darn it," she said, "don't you see? You ain't his son. You're just the hired man. I been in the restaurant almost four years, and I've seen all of them. You sure ain't the first. They sit up there like little gods, working for the great Gerry Maars. It don't mean nothing. Nothing at all."

"Maybe I don't care to just lie around a motel room, waiting for that hour or two you get away. That ain't always a whole lot of fun either."

It wasn't hard to hurt her, and when I did, she faltered.

"Anyway," I said, "what's it cost to help somebody, when I got the time? He needs my help. You're in the restaurant and you see Janine's plate up there drying out at the window, I imagine you're just gonna sit there and let it burn?"

That made Annie flare. "You ought to know by now, damn it, that I would. I definitely would. I'd let it burn and a hundred more like it, if it meant being close to you. I'd let that whole restaurant burn down, and be glad of it, to be at your side. That's the whole difference between me and you."

Tears were already coming up to betray her.

"How do you think I feel? You ever think of that? Every mile you drove up there I was with you, praying for you, imagining every step of the way. Thinking about what you might eat, where you were gonna sleep. What you were seeing out the windshield, just like I was right there to see it too. Loving you the whole way up there and back. And there I am up there in that damn ugly motel parking lot last night like a fool, waiting. So excited I could hardly sit still. Happy for each car that went by, thinking it might somehow be you."

"Hey," I said, "those boats haven't gone anywhere yet. We're still right where we were."

"I had the kids' clothes all washed. I had their suitcases laid out up in the attic. I had a book out of the library on the lakes I was reading, a map out that I'd look at late at night."

The easiest thing was just to hold her. "Come on, honey, there ain't nothing changed. I'll hear from the union when the time comes, and then we'll go. I found a place up there too, you'll like it. I'll tell you all about it when we get a chance."

She fought for a minute more but finally gave in—maybe that was another difference between her and me. She backed away finally, shrugging up a bony shoulder as she wiped her blouse sleeve across her eyes. "I reckon you'll be going at it pretty hard for a while."

"Yeah," I said, "you know how he is. Won't stop for nothing but weather, and half the time not even then."

She gave me a shove. "Don't lie to me, Arthur, I mean it. Don't play around. You tell me as soon as you get that call."

I laughed and reached out to her. "Okay, I been warned. I won't be waiting that long, though. We get a break here on the planting, I'll be calling you. I'll get hold of you as soon as I can."

She pushed away to consider me one last time, trying to decide. Still watching me, she backed to her car. I waved as she got in and circled past me, then hurried to the barn for the chains.

THIRTY-EIGHT

Rains were expected any time that spring, but while farm papers stewed and prices stuttered back and forth on the Board of Trade, we averaged a hundred acres a day for twelve days running. After a day lost when the washered-up clutch finally gave way, there followed another two weeks straight. A person may think he's using every spare hour in the first place, but that's the progressive secret: there's always another one still to be found. There was hardly a spring on record when a farmer could get into the fields thirty days straight like we did, and by the end of June, we were laying down seed through four inches of powder.

As we moved onto Holloway's the first of July, Gerry was ecstatic. "All them bastards got to race each other, see, be the first ones done. And where'd it get them? Them beans just sprouted and died, cooked right there in the soil. No sir, we didn't lose nothing by waiting this year, that's for sure. With all that muck land, I ain't so sure but what we're gonna come out ahead after all. You seen Ray's crops under all that irrigation he's got. Tell me they're any better than mine!"

I didn't tell him, but of course they were; how could they help it, with Ray sucking the water table dry twenty-four hours a day while everybody else's fields lay out in the hot sun and roasted. Still, Gerry was right in his own way, the winter had been wet, and muck land held water like a sponge. Most years it was a liability, but on this one, when he'd really needed it, Gerry'd come out ahead. The dry weather was what had given him a chance, and between him and me and twenty hours a day, we made the best of it. One hour merged into another, one week into the next, and we eventually found ourselves putting in the last of the beans down at Jackins', a full week past the Fourth of July.

Joey had been a help to us, just like I'd thought. Once school let loose he was out every day, pulling up the tractor, wrestling bags of seed, scrambling around on the auger wagon to kick down fertilizer. He couldn't go late at night, but whenever I'd come back to the barn in the daytime, he'd be waiting there with his own little water jug I'd found for him, ready to go. From my own tractor I'd see him perched up on the little Allis, waving at the occasional car that passed by, lord of all he surveyed.

It was after we were done with cultivating that I finally went back to moving Gerry out of Bremer's. The rains had finally started, and I'd use the wet parts of the day to push farther and farther back into the old sheds and barns. Summer school had started, and my nephew was one of its victims, but afternoons he'd ride his bike down the couple of miles to join me. Back in the dusty darkness of one or another of those old buildings we'd stumble onto wheat drills and manure spreaders, the odd harrow or field cultivator, an old two-row cornpicker and five-share plow. The tires were down and half rotted, the axles sprung, but one way or another Joey and I'd get them rigged up to haul out with the Allis into the yard.

There's no end to what a farmer can accumulate in a lifetime. Gerry, for all his progress, was every bit as bad as the rest. Box after box of worn couplings, buckets full of bolts, spare parts that were every one of them precision-tooled and crafted somewhere down under a dozen layers of dust and oil. There was an old hay rake and cross-cut saw, fence posts and empty feed bags, a poster for Special Sow Mitrate Cubes. Back in the corner of the shop was even a small mirror, cobwebbed above a three-legged stool. No doubt that was the place a younger and thinner Gerry Maars would have paused to check on himself, before rushing yet again into town.

I don't know if town was where he was ranging that summer; besides county business to catch up with, Al Lantz was in the hospital again, and I know Gerry'd usually stop by. He'd go by, too, to check on

Irene at the Good Shepherd. There was Foodmore to consult with, and new bankers to court, so after thirty years of at least driving by the Bremer farm every single day that he was in the county, he never seemed to make it out there at all.

That left things for the hired man and a boy. You never could tell what a person wanted to save, so I began separating things into piles. With the old house boarded up, the grass rough-cut and burned by drought, it was hard to remember that a family had once lived out there too. But back in the sheds we came upon an old fat-wheeled bicycle, the walls to a girl's playhouse as big as a car. There was a pony cart backed against the wall, and next to it a pair of figure skates and some cracked wooden stilts. It was high on a plank shelf, one morning while Joey was still being summer-schooled, that I found the tributes: the Outstanding Young Farmer plaque and a dozen Best of Show trophies, plus enough top-yield certificates to paper a room. I took the apple crate that they were stacked in, along with a pair of tassled majorette boots that I found in a cloth sack next to it, out to a separate pile just inside the door to the shop.

One Friday a little after noon Joey and I were carrying boxes out to the pickup when my brother, red-faced and out of breath, came stumping around the corner of the house.

"I parked clear down by the road. I wasn't sure where I'd find you."

"Byron," I said, "get yourself a drink of water. You look like you're about ready to keel over."

"I might have a drink at that," he puffed. "It's a lot hotter out than it looks."

Staggering under the weight of an old toolbox, half hidden under his own seed corn hat that Gerry'd given him, Joey tried to ignore his dad as much as possible. He set down the toolbox and went back for more. Byron began poking idly through the piles.

"So how's Kendra?" I asked.

"Oh, fine," he said, "coming along fine. We're all very pleased." He waited until Joey had come and gone again, then lowered his voice. "Depression's such a hard thing to fight. I think I told you we've been

236

seeing a counselor together, the pastor's wife. That, along with the medicine they've got her on now, it's beginning to show. And it wasn't just her, it was me too. There's things in myself I've got to change."

"You decide to play hooky today from school?"

He looked up over his glasses. "It's all part of what she's been telling us. I'm trying to get away some during the summer, spend time with the kids. Give Kendra a little more room for herself."

He had his chance then for time with Joey, because my nephew had come back with another crate.

"Hey there," Byron said.

Joey looked up confused; what he and his dad might be supposed to do together would have been as much a mystery to him as it was to Byron. Especially out there beside the old sheds on the Bremer place, but the boy had the advantage at least of a task in front of him, and three or four weeks on the Allis under his belt. He eased the crate onto the tailgate.

"I hope he hasn't been a bother," Byron said, reaching out to pat air. "I don't want him to be in the way."

"He's done a good job," I said. "We were lucky to have him."

Byron was squinting down into one of the boxes. "Why, here now, I remember one of these. Joey, look here at what I found!"

He'd dug down to come up with a yard-long piece of steel with clamps and levers at either end. "This is a tool that was important to people once. Your Uncle Arthur and I used to use something like this with our own dad, your granddad Conason, back when we were boys. When a fence was down, we didn't just run out and buy a new one, like you do with one of your toys. We fixed the old one. That's the way things were back then."

It must be a standard part of the education curriculum at the colleges, because every damn teacher somehow learns the trick: they manage to take the most obvious of facts and repeat them over and over again, usually kind of peevishly, until all interest is finally gone. Joey looked up at me, and then longingly over his shoulder at the shed.

"Now, let those boxes go a second, son, and pay attention. You've got to pay attention. That's why you're in summer school in the first place, and not over here playing all day long. We used to stretch fences with this. We fixed the old ones."

He wrestled the tool awkwardly in his hands. "You see how you hold it now? One end hooks on like this. Come over here a second and I'll show you how it works."

"Oh hell, Byron," I finally said, "throw that damn thing back in the box. Nobody gives a damn about a fence stretcher anymore. You might as well be showing him a collar iron."

"What's a collar iron, Uncle Arthur?"

"Ask your dad here, sometime, to show you his."

Byron blinked a time or two and dropped the contraption back into the box. A honk came from behind us, and we looked back to see Gerry roaring up the lane in his car.

"My Lord," he exclaimed as he pulled up next to us and hopped out, "look at all this junk you got piled up here. Looks like a doggone rummage sale." He clapped Byron on the back. "Why, hello there, young fella, you're looking fit. I don't ever hear nothing but good about you from over at the schoolhouse. Sounds like you're doing a bang-up job. And your boy here, I don't know how we would have made it through the year without him. Hey there, Mr. Joey, good to see you. I got to figure you make your dad awful proud."

In one smooth motion he'd managed to both squeeze Joey's shoulder and clap Byron on the back. They both of them, man and boy, blushed under his attention.

Gerry scanned the crowded barnyard. "Looks like Arthur's putting together a museum out here. Gonna go head to head with the hysterical society, I reckon, with some of these doggone antiques. You all ain't ate lunch yet, have you?"

"Well . . ." Byron said.

"Me and Joey were just getting ready to take over another load to the other place."

"And I ought to be getting back to school," my brother explained, but Gerry waved it off.

"Oh, these damn things can wait a little while. And Byron, my goodness, you're the boss over there at the middle school. If anybody has a right to be gone a couple of hours, it's you. Tell them you ran into one of the councilmen, and the old so-and-so just had to consult. I was driving just now over on 400, and it came to me right out of the blue that I could use a couple of hot dogs. Reckon any of you can eat some? I bet there's a boy here who can."

On that sunny July afternoon it was no trick for him to sweep Byron and Joey up with him. I was hungry too; while my nephew hopped in the back of the pickup, Byron and I jockeyed at the door. Finally my brother squeezed in first. It wasn't exactly a good fit; Gerry had to dig his elbow deep into Byron's belly just to get into second. It didn't slow him even a nod, though, and before long we were rocketing together down the county road going south.

"Oh yeah," he shouted over the wind that blew past us, "it ain't no surprise to me that Joey's a good little hand. His dad was too. This man sitting right here. You remember, Byron, how you come out and helped me test them hogs? Two days after Christmas, Arthur, and so damn cold that the blood froze just as soon as we pulled it out. Remember how the vet was afraid to do it? Scared to death of them damn sows, but once I got one of 'em snared, old Byron here kept her held. Wasn't a whole lot bigger than Joey, I don't reckon, and with seven hundred pounds there squirming under us, it wasn't no easy task. A grown man's job, really, was what it was, but this fella here got it done."

It was still there to see at the edge of Gerry's eyes, and in the slackness in his jaw, the fatigue that had hung on from spring. Not that my brother cared to notice: flattery isn't something that a middle-school principal tends to encounter. We drove south past the Holloway turnoff, all the way down to Onarga. Gerry was considerate enough to repeat the whole story about the hogs again for Joey, once we'd gotten to a Dairy Dell across from the run-down elevator, and settled with our lunches at a picnic table back under the shade.

"Onarga here," Gerry was telling Byron, "is where we're gonna be bringing our crops from now on. I talked to the elevator man just last week. The hell with Hostetler's, this is a whole lot closer to where we are down south. Oh, it's pretty down here, I'm glad you had a chance to see it."

My brother nodded enthusiastically as he chewed. "That sounds great, Gerry."

"I know it's a ways to go for lunch, but I kind of want to get acquainted down here this summer, have a little look around. All right, I done ate three hot dogs myself. Ain't there nobody who can do better than that?"

"Count me out," I said. "I've had enough."

"I'm supposed to be dieting," Byron apologized. "Three's all I better have."

The nice thing about a boy is that Joey was still up to the challenge, and he made it all the way to six before Gerry let him off with a tie. By that time he had the boy caught up in a game of check stub poker. It took another round of root beers, and some ice cream, but Gerry finally had four of a kind. For a while there, I think Byron even forgot his waiting world of school bells and discipline, of a wife who needed her own time away from home. In true Kiwanis fashion our luncheon activities weren't quite over even then: for our inspiration Gerry drove us back a couple of miles to the north.

"I ain't trying to take up your time, now, Byron, but there's something I want to show you over here. You ain't had a chance to see what I got going now, and I want you to tell me what you think."

He didn't have anything to say to me as we sailed by old Homer Jackins' farmhouse, slowing once we were past it so my brother could have a look. Gerry pulled over near the crossroads and led Byron to the edge of the end rows for a better view.

"These doggone crops of mine don't look so bad now, do they, after the rain? Ain't as bad as folks been telling you in town? You go back there and tell them there at the schoolhouse, when you see them, that old Gerry Maars is coming along fine."

My brother promised he would.

"And see that little bit that ain't planted yet, over to the west? Joey here's already seen it, when he helped us down here on beans. That's where I'm gonna put in that pond. I got a bulldozer scheduled for the morning, one of the county boys is gonna drop it off."

He turned to Joey, still leaning out from the bed of the pickup. "Your dad ain't never took you fishing, is that what you told me? Well, it's like I said, he's a busy man, trying to make you all a good living. Come next year this time, though, we'll all of us be out here, catching fish to beat the band. A man can't just spend his whole life working, no matter how much he thinks he should."

The next morning I drove down to the Jackins place again about eleven. I parked by the road and walked in along the edge of the field. Gerry was right, his crops were rallying; just a day later and there was already new growth on the bean plants, with the rows filling out from the rain. With any luck there'd be a full stand after all, drought or no drought, another eighty of the thousands of acres that would be waiting when fall came around. Foot-wide tracks ran along the narrow strip of government ground, back to the corner of the field.

Black smoke billowed up ahead of me as I came across the rye grass and up over a rim of tumbled dirt. At my feet Gerry rode the huge yellow road department bulldozer, wheeling it expertly around the bottom of the pit. Already a good six feet down, he was hollering as soon as he saw me there. Sweat ran off his forehead and cheeks, down into a shirt that already hung soaked and shapeless across his chest.

"Rid of it!" was all that made it up to me, until finally he cut back on the throttle so I could hear.

"I say to get rid of it all, damn it, don't be stacking it up. Just throw all that crap in the trash. All of it. Burn what you can, and call somebody to haul the rest away. Ain't nobody wants it anymore. Just get us moved out of there as soon as you can. The sooner the better, that's all I got to say."

He let the steel treads roll back, sliding him backwards down into the pit. At the bottom he called up to me again.

"You're still keeping that boy's hours, aren't you? I ain't gonna have him working for free."

"Aw hell," I said, "Joey thinks he's in heaven. I'll buy him another couple root beers when I get a chance."

"No, now," he yelled up at me, "I ain't gonna have it. You get that boy's hours totaled up and call Kathryn, have her write him out a check. And you hear me about all that stuff? I went by again last night, couldn't believe all the junk you dug up. Them crates and sacks and all, I don't want none of it, hear? That's all in the past. Gonna start a new era. Joey, your brother and me, you, we're gonna be fishing down here next summer for sure."

He threw the big Cat into reverse and backed for another run, yanking on the levers with both hands. And that's where I left him, high above the bulldozer's spinning tracks as he dug down for traction, bulling and grinding back up to the top.

THIRTY-NINE

Those first two or three weeks back, Annie'd still come out to the fields to find me. She might still be in her waitress uniform, or in shorts and a tank top on her way over to Holly's, when she'd park up at one end to wait. Some nights, if she had a few minutes, she'd ride with me on the tractor a couple of passes. That's where I told her about the Seventh Street house, and the playground I'd discovered a block away. She could imagine them just as clearly as if she'd been there herself.

The third week, though, one of the boys brought home a strep infection that he shared with the family. By that time, too, Carl Wayne had gone down, throwing his back out when he lifted a case of ice cream at the plant. Not so likely to wander off fishing, he was stuck at home all the way into the first week of August, camped out hot and cranky in a big recliner chair in the living room. With Gerry and I moving so much across the county, it got harder for her to find me, but even at that, as we neared the end of planting, I'd come back to the Camaro to find a note taped to the steering wheel, or a piece of lemon pie from the restaurant, half melted and waiting, wedged inside the screen door at the house.

Gerry and I'd had less and less to say to each other as the season wore on; day after day, we kept to our separate paths across the fields. With the drought fading, prices began to fall, so I began to gather there wouldn't be any new combine or pole building coming Gerry's way in the fall. While I finished the move from the Bremer place, he was out looking for something to replace those big holding bins and the drying setup. Without much luck—poor market or not, he had me start hauling grain from them into town the first week of August, trying to make room for fall.

By that time Holly'd found work at a container factory up at Warsaw, and if I wanted to be sure of seeing Annie, even at a distance, I had to go into the Cove. The warm welcome from the waitressing sorority had come to an end: Ann-Marie and Janine looked as likely to break the plates over my head as bring me my breakfast. Annie and I had a couple of hours together one evening in mid-July, but two weeks stretched into three and then four, when I didn't get to see her at all.

Actually I did *see* her, you'd have to say, once when she was driving the kids across town in that rattletrap Nova. Another time in line, early one evening, with Carl Wayne and the kids at the Dairy Queen, while I drove by on my way out past her house. One hot afternoon in mid-August, I broke off from hauling grain and came back to my kitchen, where I stretched out on the floor for the coolness, and dialed Annie's number on the phone.

It rang out twice before it was picked up and dropped. The receiver hit the floor with a clatter, and then Moni grabbed it up. She didn't say anything, but I guessed by the breathing it was her.

"Is your mom there?" I asked. From beyond her came the chatter of young voices, all of them talking at once. "Let me talk to your mother," I said again. There rose up a sudden cry and commotion, that Annie's tired voice broke in sharply to stop. "Now, quit it, both of you. Right now. Stevey, give it back. Give it back and leave him alone. Sit back down. Anybody who wants theirs before the pickle goes in had better speak up now!"

The receiver was dropped again onto bare wood or linoleum— whatever it was left a loud clanking echo in my ear. The hum of what must have been a floor fan rotated my way, into the bells and applause of a game show from a TV somewhere beyond. Silverware rattled on a metal table, and what sounded like a chair was dragged by in front of the phone.

"We don't need that anymore," Annie's voice came again, "she's fine up here. That's okay, just take it back," and I listened as the chair went dragging the other way.

What I heard on that hot summer afternoon was just her family gathered around at lunchtime, tuna fish and the rustle of chips. Voices rose up in protest and appeal, something was spilled; there was a scramble to find towels and fix blame. There were instructions—"take this to your daddy in the other room"—and tennis shoes that stomped past where I lay. I don't know how long it even was that I listened; Popsicles had been distributed, and I was lying on my side half-dozing, when there came a sudden rustle on the line.

"Hello?" Annie said impatiently. "Hello?" Before I could stir myself, though, there was a trailing away of "Which one of you has been playing with—" and a click. When I called back a second later, she answered herself.

"I want to see you," I said simply, and a pause like her daughter's greeted me again. "I want to see you, that's all there is to it. I want to get together just as soon as we can."

"That's not so easy," she said, her voice neutral.

"Not this minute, but when you get a chance. I've been missing you."

I could almost feel the small shake of her head. "I don't think so."

"Just whenever you can. You tell me. Anytime."

"Carl's in the other room," she said. "I got to go."

"Wait a minute," I said, "just wait."

She waited.

"I'm just saying we need to get together. I need to see you. See if you can get away."

There was a silence again at the other end. "The plant's closed next week," she said, "so we're going down to Kentucky. We probably won't be back until the last week of the month."

"Anytime you say, then. Just tell me when you're free."

"I'll think about it," she said, and hung up.

FORTY

Time passes and a woman wonders, I know. What Annie couldn't believe is that I still remembered, every bit as well as she did, the hours we'd spent together on ditch banks, the stroll to the silo, our visits to Holiday Inns across the state. Though not much for hope chests or scrapbooks, a man might still hang on to things that meant something, like I did those travel brochures from the rainy December morning we'd spent studying them in Lafayette. I called down and reserved the last week of August and first days of September at Lake Monroe, figuring to use any part of it that Annie could get free.

While she and her family vacationed in Kentucky, I spent several days around the barn lot, fixing up a shop and looking forward like a schoolgirl to when she'd be back. During those August dog days Gerry made it away too; Kathryn had tickets to a play festival up in Michigan, and they drove up the next to last weekend of the month. Even Byron took advantage of the lull before school, packing up Kendra and the kids for a quick trip over to Cincinnati. It was the kind of thing Gerry would have been good at in his prime: a ball game on Saturday, and Kings Island amusement park the next day. I happened to be outside Sunday evening when my brother's family came home. Straggling up the sidewalk, sunburned and irritable, not a one looked particularly amused.

But Annie's and my trip was still in the offing. Home a week from Kentucky, with Carl back at work and the kids just shy of school starting again, she finally said she'd go. Faithful Holly stepped forward one more time: she had a day off from the factory midway through the week. After dropping the kids off, Annie met me ten miles down the highway at the truck stop west of Peru, where, on the bubbly asphalt between high idling semis, she left the Nova.

"I hope it doesn't rain," she said, her back to me as she slammed shut her car door. "I don't want to be bailing it out."

There didn't seem to be much chance of it. The afternoon was hotter than a furnace, and there wasn't a cloud in the sky. Annie was windblown and distracted, but it was a relief to see her little red traveling case, the familiar suit bag that I spread out in the trunk. It was a relief, too, to have her next to me again in the Camaro's front seat, even as she frowned, unable to put Delfina behind.

"I don't like the way his fever was acting," she said, worried about Jeff, who'd come home sick from swimming a couple of days before. "We got him on antibiotics again. I told Holly to keep an eye on it."

"You can call as soon as we get down there, see how he's doing."

"Oh, he'll be okay. I've just got him on my mind somehow today."

With the windows wide open we had to shout. It wasn't until Kokomo that I reached for her hand. She let me take it, but was quick to pull away when I downshifted at one of the stoplights on the bypass. Frowning under her sunglasses, she looked away from me out over the fields.

"You have fun down at Kentucky Lake?" I yelled.

"Oh yeah," she shouted back. "We had a good time. Sit around a crowded houseboat for a week and watch the men get drunk. Try to keep the kids from drowning all day, stay up with them crying from sunburn half the night. It was just a ball." She shifted restlessly in her seat. "The water was nice."

In those last two weeks, waiting, I'd imagined us somehow just like we had been, floating down a summer highway wrapped up in ourselves. Real life has a way of moving on, though, slipping out of line from what a person has planned. The sun was insistent, and we still had to make our noisy way around the crowded Indy beltway. From there we spun off through an hour and a half of bleached pines and ragged fields—the drought had hung on in the south. From the interstate we wandered back through endless curves and dips, past mean-looking convenience stores and stark cinderblock churches, outposts of the Pentecostal fringe. The resort was named after the four winds, and it came up even in that parched countryside every bit as pretty as advertised, in our cozy motel room the winter before.

To my mind, for that matter, the brochure hardly did it justice—on the way in there were tennis courts and a miniature golf course, a view over the roofs to the marina, our first aqua glimpse of the pool. Still hiding behind her dark glasses, Annie stood impatiently behind me while I registered, followed me back to our room. She kept her distance at the doorway, but no sooner were we inside than I reached for her. She let me hold her for a minute, but her hands no longer cared to pull at me, falling easily away as soon as her chance came to step free.

"Well," I said brightly, "here we are!"

We'd already burned away half the atmosphere, if the papers could be believed, to refrigerate spacious motel rooms just like that one, with its wide picture window above the lake. Behind us was a cool world of banquet rooms and hallways, a lobby that opened to the pool. Unseen compressors labored mightily, and still we were not comfortable, strangers more than ever. Annie picked up her suit bag from where I'd laid it on the counter. She hung it in the open closet, straightening with a critical eye. She went in to use the bathroom, leaving me to look out onto the marina from the farther of our two standard queen-sized beds.

It was six o'clock, and we were hungry, but I still had a fine dinner in mind for somewhere off ahead of us in the misty well-daydreamed night. According to the dittoed handout next to the television, we'd already missed the group run through the obstacle course. The moonlight cruise with cocktails wasn't until nine. With the thought that it might please her, I led us back out past the swimming pool and down a long curving stairway to the docks. It was my own voice that I was hearing, but it could have just as easily been Gerry Maars', witnessing to a sullen county about the never-ending wonders of life. In my case I was pointing out the lounge windows huge against the hillside above us, the wide, sun-parched spaciousness of the grounds. I marveled at the floating wooden pier, the houseboats and pontoons tethered around it in narrow slips. The drought had taken its toll; the lake was low, growing brackish by the shore. At the end of the pier I ended up giving a ten-dollar bill to the skinny college kid who worked there, for the privilege of Annie and I ending up side by side in a small yellow paddle boat, churning our way out into the lake.

In the new order of things, a paddle boat would have to be a throwback; it was, in essence, the same unfun mechanism they would have had back at Winona Lake, where my dad and mother had courted fifty years before. They had been too little accustomed to leisure to know any better, so at least they had an excuse. I don't know what mine was: like two idiots, Annie and I sat churning our legs in unison, still not talking, and chased by the last of the afternoon sun at our backs. My pants and shirt were soon sticking to my skin. Annie sat pedaling next to me, her nose wrinkled in discomfort, as the shore on the far side of the cove became our unspoken goal. We trudged across the murky water toward it.

When we grew close and quit pedaling, the contraption glided a full foot and a half before dragging to a stop, dead in the water. Ahead of us was the wooded shore, thrust up by the drought until it was eight feet above our heads. Exposed bleaching roots were tangled with dry mud and brambles, a dank muddy lake smell floated out to us from the bank. I leaned back in the park bench that served as a seat.

"I've missed you," I said. "It seems like forever since we've been able to get away. Do you remember when we first looked at that brochure? I bet you never thought we'd get down here like this."

Annie shook her head.

"Of course, some things can't be helped. We didn't know Carl's back would go out. I didn't figure on Gerry being so far behind. The kids sick and all, Holly's job. The summer kind of slipped away."

Annie just kept shaking her head. She picked at her fingernails while I studied the shore. "You wouldn't have done any of this," she said at last.

"What do you mean?"

"Any of it. The hard parts. Running around behind Carl's back, getting the kids all rushed around. Getting ready to go last May. It was all my risk." She looked at me then, evenly. "You never risked a thing."

248

I started to protest, then shrugged. "I never had anything to risk."

That was the simple truth of it, and we considered it together as we leaned back on the bench. She could have been angry, I suppose, but her voice was softer when she finally turned back to me.

"Them boats have come and gone by now, haven't they?"

By my silence she could tell that they had. We rocked in the fading swell of a distant motor boat, slicing heedlessly across the lake at our backs. It was barely twilight, but the first early lights of the marina had come on in the distance.

"I guess I knew it," she said at last. "I just didn't want to believe it was true."

"There may be others——" I began, but she stopped me.

"No, Arthur, don't say it. Don't tell me nothing more. I feel like a big enough fool the way it is. I loved you like a husband. I made myself open to you like a wife. Didn't that ever mean nothing? Didn't I have some claim on you too?"

"I don't know," I said, and we fell back into silence. After a long time she looked up at me.

"I just wish you hadn't said it wasn't impossible. You know? You went ahead and told me it wasn't impossible, when it was just as impossible as impossible will ever be."

It's odd how people go at things sometimes, driving halfway across the state to do in five minutes what they could have just as easy accomplished at home. I'd see it later even as she tried to hide it from me, a glimpse through a closing zipper of that red velour dress in her suit bag——Annie'd had some hope for us even then. Somewhere in her tiny suitcase was the ring that I bought her, but out there on the lake there was just a sadness in her voice that I had no answer to, a truth that left nothing to say. The only thing ahead of us was our common duty, which was to turn around and start pedaling back again, splashing across the water to the pier.

I'd been thinking of Joey anyway, one morning the second week of September, as I bent over in the barnyard welding. I'd had to run a cord out from the new shop that I'd been building at one end of the old barn; next to it the big doors were slid open so that some of the gloom could spill out onto the patch of grass where I'd wrestled off one of the big duals from the combine. Late the year before it had begun shimmying on us, and with the harvest just ahead I'd finally found the problem: hairline cracks spreading out from the lug holes and across the rim.

I'd been thinking of my nephew because sometime after we'd finished cleaning out Bremer's, I'd started him welding. He took to it easily, and it had been a good way to finish the summer, idling away with my nephew while the impossible harvest lay ahead. I'd finished with the last of the cracks and was just standing to inspect my work when Kendra drove up the lane in her red Toyota. She was smiling as she got out of the car.

"Hey there," she said, "working hard?"

"Oh, some. Getting ready for the field work. There's a lot of acres out there."

"Welding?" she asked, and I nodded that she'd got that right.

She made it through the obstacle course set up around me, the toolbox and wide plastic sheath for the wrenches, the welding unit and rods, my greasy water jug and the big tire rolled flat on the ground. My sister-in-law had her hair drawn back into a ponytail, and for a last fading day of summer wore a sleeveless white blouse, open two or three buttons down from her throat. A vaccination scar the size of a quarter stood out on the smooth skin of her shoulder, reminding us that we were the same generation after all. Well-churched and counseled by then, she ducked into the shade beside me.

"The kids are both in school," she explained. "Joey started last week. Celeste's in play group again."

"That boy of yours has a good head on his shoulders," I told her. "You ought to be proud of him."

Kendra strolled slowly around the base of the big combine, stopping to look up at the cab. She came back to the axle, poised bare and exposed on a squat hydraulic jack. I watched as she knelt to inspect welds beaded like silver scar tissue across the chipped red paint of the rim.

"I reckon Byron's busy," I said, "what with classes starting and all. That's a big responsibility the way kids are now. I imagine it's a challenge."

Kendra might have nodded; from where she knelt at the rim, she looked back at me, watching as I wiped my hands on a rag.

"Does this go back on?" she asked, pointing at the tire. "Here, I'll give you a hand." She stood and began tugging at it.

"Careful," I said, "you'll get all dirty. Leave it be. I'll get to it in a little while."

She wasn't going to budge it much anyway, but bending to pull at the thick treads had brought color to her cheeks. When she left off with it and straightened, white deck pants smudged from the rubber, I was reminded again that she was a tall girl, really. Up over my shoulder, and I wasn't small. Sketched straight and black across the soft swollen skin of her eyelids were black bars of liner.

A tall girl, and fragile after all the years: wherever in the wide world she was supposed to be that early September afternoon, it wasn't out with the combine and tools, the dirt and indifference that marked off that barnyard lot. She was still smiling doggedly, and between those curling little lips and the eyeliner she peered out at me.

"You know, Kendra," I said, "I was sorry about your dad. I never had a chance to tell you, but it's a shame."

My sister-in-law looked at me suspiciously, then smiled. "I've got some lemonade over at the house," she said, "if you want some. I should have brought it over when I came."

"That's okay, I'm fine."

There was an awkward flirtatiousness when she laughed that didn't suit her, the tip of her pink tongue flicking between her teeth.

"You were always such a lonely boy." She came over to look up at me. "Watching Byron and me when we were going out, trying to keep out of the way. Do you remember that?" Her small mouth strained against her smile. "I remember a time not too long ago when you would have fallen all over yourself to come in for lemonade."

"Well," I said carefully, "I was probably thirsty. I'm not thirsty now."

"No," she said, "I don't imagine you are."

I wondered whether she'd stopped taking her medication; it seemed like the kind of thing I could ask Byron, the next time I ran into him. Past her across the sixty was their low, lonely ranch house, the double garage door open, the fields that pressed in around it thick and green.

"Is that how people do it, Arthur? How they get along?"

"How's that, by not drinking lemonade?"

Her eyes were shiny, but she pushed on. "You know what I mean. All the affairs and cheating, is that what they do? Is that how people make it in your book? Running all over the country with other people's wives? Not caring about families? Is that how it's done?"

I remember how dirty my hands were, how white her blouse. How thin her arms were as she stood hugging herself in front of me.

"You're the big man, so why don't you tell me? You aren't fooling anybody, you know. You're not near as smart as you think."

She looked past us to where the milk house had stood. Over to where Annie would have parked when she'd visited. Out of sight from the road, but easy enough to see and resent from a picture window a quarter mile away.

"Come on, Art, you're the expert on things. I want to know. Is that the way it's done? Or maybe I should go down and ask that little whore at the restaurant. Think she could tell me? Is that what I ought to do? Go see if she knows?"

Her voice had been mocking before it hardened, and as she stood in front of me, I almost laughed out loud, thinking how much like my dad she really was. Always the last to understand, triumphant with private secrets that no one else cared to know. Her throat was smooth and open, and for what it's worth she was right. I had been lonely once, still could remember the small, simple kindness that she might hold herself a moment up next to me, the warmth of those thin arms against my back.

I sighed. "I got no idea, Kendra, how people make it. I'm sorry. You're asking the wrong person. I got no idea in the world."

Her problem, though, was that she didn't believe me. Wavering uncertain in her soft cotton blouse and ponytail, she'd ended up just like everybody else, forgetful of why she was even there. I bumped past her to turn on the compressor, the rattle and broken wheeze of the cycle building up to echo in the doorway. The welds looked good, and with a jerk and pull I wrestled the big tire over to where I could work on it. Getting a tractor tire set is a job nobody envies, but I started in on it, while out of the corner of my eye I saw that Kendra's small knowing smile had faded, leaving her foolish and alone in the barnyard shade. She had no more choice then than she'd ever had, and in a minute or two more she finally gave in and went home.

FORTY-TWO

As it happened there were others just as slow to reckon as my sister-in-law—I got first evidence of it the third week of September. I'd left my car at the Bremer place one morning and came past about ten that same evening to find the Camaro's back window and windshield smashed, and huge jagged scratches across the hood. I just stood and looked at it; there wasn't much else I could do except throw seed bags over the holes and head back out to the field.

The corn was way too wet, but we were already harvesting—with all that acreage, Gerry could feel December in the air. He was caught up in his civic work too: Precision Dynamics had loaded up trucks late one night and moved out, bound for Matamoros or Tijuana, nobody at first was even sure. That set the Chamber of Commerce and councilors astir, and he had to run off to hasty all-night strategy sessions, worrying over where the county would go next. Of more importance to him right then was what kind of got lost in the shuffle—the Onarga elevator went bust that same week.

That meant long drives into the elevator, when we were able to get into the fields. After a dry spring we'd ended up with rainstorms, one of them coming a couple of days later, while we were still on the south field at Jackins! It didn't take those clay fields very long to fill up; Gerry'd been mudding his way along near the ditch about mid-morning when he finally got stuck. It was raining harder as he ferried me back to pick up the four-wheel drive for the towing. When we got to the barnyard, he climbed up to start the big tractor himself.

"Huh," he said, "damn thing won't turn over. Them batteries ain't but two years old."

At the time it was easy enough to blame his bullheadedness— instead of it all safe and dry in a shed at the Bremer place, that eighty-thousand-dollar tractor had been sitting outside all summer at my dad's. I climbed up to lean in at the cab door while he tried to coax it into life.

"Damn things don't even hold a charge anymore, and they cost about an arm and a leg. Let's pull around the truck. They must just be a little puny from sitting idle."

That big tractor was his pride, of course, but servicing it was like tending a battleship: everything awkward and twice as high as a man could reach. We hung from the ladder to uncover the three big batteries, hooked up in series at the base of the cab. While I revved up the truck for all it was worth, Gerry tried again, but the big engine never gave even a shudder.

"Goddamn thing," he complained, "now of all times. We can't hardly get along with this thing giving us trouble. It's probably the doggone electrical. I think I got my glasses over in the truck."

I've mentioned that we'd run short on things to say to each other by then; Gerry kept his own counsel and I kept mine. That didn't mean we couldn't work together, and we started in tracing the wires. We squeezed in and around that huge chassis all afternoon, bridging across breakers, looking for shorts, trying the starter again and again.

Gerry tipped back his cap, perplexed. "Damn thing acts like it's seized up or something. Wouldn't that be the shits? If a fella didn't know better, though, that's what he'd say. He'd say it was all seized up."

It was all seized up. Not that it was a truth he gave into easily, even after we found hoses cut on the combine a week later, the back tires on one of the grain trucks slashed deep with a knife. Gerry still had to pay two hundred dollars for the big tractor to be towed up to Plymouth, I don't know how much to finally get it broken down far enough to tell. We'd long since gotten the combine unstuck with one of the little tractors, and I was picking corn up at Holloway's, when Gerry came back with the news.

"Sugar in the gas tank, can you believe it? I can't quite figure it yet. I knew zoning wasn't all that popular, but surely it ain't come to this. That damn tractor's just sitting up there at Plymouth in pieces, as worthless as worthless can be. I can't figure it out."

We couldn't take time off to puzzle over it; the combine hadn't been shut down more than a few hours in a week, and we'd barely made a dent in the land he had down south. The next evening Gerry pulled up in the end rows after I dumped him, and leaned down from the cab to where I stood.

"I been thinking," he said. "It couldn't be jealousy, could it? Somebody who wanted this Jackins land too? First your car and then the tractor, all the equipment back there. Something ain't right. I ain't lived all these years in this county for this to be happening now."

Only three weeks into harvest, his face was drawn and pale. He shook his head. "We got to bear down. That's all there is to it. We can't be worrying about nothing else when winter's just around the corner. Just be careful out there on the road. I don't want nobody getting hurt on account of me."

By that time, though, I'd begun to understand. I still had to wait for a free day to look into it, and that day came within a week. Even behind as he was, Gerry'd still promised to go down to Indianapolis with Jake Hostetler, who'd got caught by the state selling off sealed bushels of corn. As soon as there was a rain day, he set off with Jake to plead his case.

"I don't know why I'm even doing it," he said. "Old Jake's cheated me for years, and his boy's just as bad. But he's in a jam, and I can't afford to get stuck today anyway. I reckon I'll be back about seven. If it dries off some, we'll start in then."

It was the kind of day when he should have rested, but instead he went running off with Jake. I knew there was no chance in the world he'd be back by seven, so after a full day of hauling grain, I took a shower and changed my clothes, went back outside to the car. I knew where I could find Carl Wayne, at the old Hoosier Lanes south of town. I mostly just felt tired by then, with the hard days and nights of work more pointless than ever. Every bit as pointless as the idleness and anger that had brought a grown man out to play silly tricks in the country, when he should have been watching things at home.

I can't think of a time that I'd ever been in that bowling alley; I didn't know one end of it from the other. It didn't take me very long to spot him, though, shaggy-haired and bulky in a red flannel shirt that hung down untucked from his pants. It was league night for the milk plant, so I sat down behind the railing to watch. And as soon as I really saw him, from the moment he turned away from the lane, I knew. His big beery smile fell away when he saw me, because he knew then that I knew too.

I'd had a little help from Annie. I still heard from her now and then; feelings sometimes take longer to fade out than they should. Not two weeks after our boat ride she'd called me after midnight, her voice low as she told about Carl.

I'd felt myself tense. "He's not hurting you, is he?"

"No, it's all right. It's fine. I just keep the kids away from him. It's ugly now, he says the ugliest things. The kids make a squeak and he's right away reaching for his belt." She still had the kindness to warn. "Be careful, Arthur, about that meanness he has. Try to stay out of his way."

I was well-warned, then, about his meanness, but maybe he just hadn't packed it along for a Tuesday night's bowling with the league. Not that it could have hurt his game; by that time he was missing pins that even I could have hit, and I'd never picked up a bowling ball in my life. There was already enough mold and dust stuffed into my lungs that the thick, blue smoke inside the bowling alley bothered me, along with the blind, drunken closeness of the crowd. I went out to wait in the lot. The rain had moved through, leaving behind a foggy mist that hung over the dark edge of the highway a hundred yards away.

When they finally came out, there were three or four of them, floating in a Budweiser haze. Carl saw me clear enough, but apparently the time wasn't right; they strolled past bragging and burping, to the far side of the lot. There was an explosion of loud farewells and bantering, just to remind themselves they'd had a good time. Carl Wayne eased away at the height of it, got into his Sting Ray and left.

The next morning I drove into town. I knew that the milk plant crew got to the Cove early for coffee, most days by a little before seven. Annie's car was around back, but it didn't really concern her anymore. I waited on the sidewalk, in front of the True Value just down the block. A couple of county commissioners went in, then Floyd Karras from the council, a couple of old farmers still early to rise. Annie's mom ducked in and out on her way to the catalog store, and the girl from the bakery came over with the rolls.

Finally Carl Wayne did come along the sidewalk, looking hung over and unready for morning, let alone the taking of revenge. It's possible that even then he could have missed me; his eyes red-rimmed and swollen, he'd found interest in his shoelaces and the sidewalk, hurrying by. I went down across the curb to the pockmarked Camaro and drove back out Sycamore in the rain.

It cleared off later on; the next day was dry enough that most everyone was in the fields. In the afternoon we had to get some of the dry corn into town, and after that long drive up there, there was another long wait at the elevator to unload. I knew Gerry was steaming full speed ahead, and that two trucks would already be filled and waiting for me by then down south. I turned right on old 31 anyway. The transmission on the grain truck was sticking, and I babied it down the slope toward the river, where the milk plant was set back against the trees. It was only ten or fifteen minutes more, so I pulled off on the shoulder to wait. They'd gone over to an electronic whistle for shift changes; when it went off I climbed down from the cab.

It was odd, really, to be out there, because I had no quarrel at all with Carl Wayne. Not a one. For that matter, I felt like I almost knew him: in and among all the stories Annie'd entertained me with on our motel weekends, there was plenty to learn about Carl. I knew about a little matchbook car collection he kept, hoarded away up in their closet from the kids. I knew that he liked biscuits at dinner, sopped with creamed frozen peas. I remember picturing it as she told me about him being so worked up and distraught over a simple dent in the fender of the Sting Ray that he picked up backing drunk from the garage. I even knew about when his own mom died. Annie and I were already seeing each other then, so she was upset too: it meant that that night she'd miss me, staying home reluctantly at his side. Even though it happens to everyone soon enough, Carl had sat beside her in their cluttered bedroom and cried like a girl, so hard she'd wondered if he was ever going to stop.

She was right, he did walk like Shannon. Or the other way around, I guess: all the three boys had that same rolling shuffle, heads up and hips rolling lazily ahead. I watched the original on its way across the loading dock, down the concrete steps, and out across the lot to his car. He had the old Mustang that day, lighting a cigarette and reaching for the radio as he circled through the lot. That's when he finally saw me for certain, waiting in my dusty coveralls up next to the truck.

I had no quarrel with Carl, but I wanted him to know he could have me, if that's what he really wanted. That way he could stop bothering Gerry and his equipment, Annie and those little kids, anybody in the world on account of me. Any place he'd cared to, he could have had his way. At the bowling alley or hardware, there by the side of the road—he could have whipped me like my own dad, made me crawl like the lowlife that I was. And all for free, because the truth was I never would have raised a hand.

But a rough guy like Carl, with his Marlboros and sports cars, his bullets and Budweisers, just couldn't get that straight. He'd slowed when he saw me, but by then he was already tromping down on the accelerator, his head tucked low as he screeched out onto the highway, swerving to miss a station wagon that bore down on him from the north. I watched as he sped out of sight, then climbed up into the grain truck and lumbered back south to the field.

I figured—rightly as it turned out—that those tricks out at the farm might finally have run their course. Carl Wayne wasn't likely to be any better husband or father than he had been, and Gerry's tractor might never come out of the shop, but that much was beyond my control. There are a lot of things that manage to get broken in a life, most of them never to be put back together again.

FORTY-THREE

Sometimes that fall it would happen: the phone would ring out and I'd stumble down through the darkness only to hear a small voice on the other end, still reaching out to talk to me, uncertain herself of even why. I would have just gotten to bed—there weren't enough hours in the day and night both to cover the harvest that year—and for those few minutes we'd still be linked. Me stupid with crop dust and plain fatigue, Annie on her way in for another day at the restaurant, pausing in her own dark kitchen to give me a call.

At times she was defiant: she told me what all she'd been hearing about California, this or the other state out west. A cosmetology school down in Florida, and another just up the road in South Bend. One predawn morning she was excited about New Zealand, and a man in the restaurant who'd been down there the year before. There were ranches in Wyoming where cowboys still roamed, and where, apparently, a woman with kids could find a job, if she cared to stay back in the kitchen and cook.

Other times, though, it was still me she thought she longed for. One stormy night in October she appeared on the porch, and we made love up in the bedroom of the old farmhouse. Afterwards she clung to me crying.

"He ain't gonna bother you no more," I soothed. "Just tell me if he does. He won't be bothering you no more at all."

She'd already turned from me by then, her narrow back curled away in the darkness. Twenty minutes later she was gone.

That rainy night was a rarity. Gerry and I kept pushing forward, so hard that it was seldom before two or three o'clock in the morning that we quit. I could catch a catnap in the truck cab between loads, another forty winks when the dryer ran full, but Gerry kept driving ever harder. He'd found a new ionizer in a catalog at the barbershop and kept it cranked up high, all the time gulping the supplements and vitamins that he got from mail order, and decongestants he bought by the cartonful in town.

His aging equipment still fought us; even in the middle of a good day we were as likely to be broke down on repairs as cutting through the grain. The weather had turned cold when the axle on the combine finally broke, shattering on one of the approaches at the Bremer place that Jack had never seen fit to grade. Ray Stewart's boys and Lindell Bardacke's hired men waved merrily as they rolled by in their grain trucks, Gerry and I down on our knees with the big combine hovering idle above us, while we pounded a replacement back on.

"Just hold steady now," is what he'd say as we rooted in the stubble. "I just about got it that time. Give me a little more on the south."

With his glasses finally yielded to and spattered, his overalls matted with mud and chaff, squeezed in to where his big fingers could only fiddle blindly with a recalcitrant bearing—you had to admire him in a way, because he still had the faith. And that faith, finally, misplaced or not, is what really carries a farmer. No archangel Gabriel, or mom and dad, no sweetheart or wife in the world was likely to sweep down and slip that heavy axle back in place.

"Doggone it to hell, it slid off. I felt her go. Come in on it again, that time we were close." Finally one of those times it did go, and by nightfall we were back moving through the beans.

"We got to just keep going," he'd say as he leaned out from the cab. "We're gonna show them. You just can't never give in, not for a minute, then a fella can make it through."

The first Saturday in November was a lot like the others, except that the grabber chains broke twice before noon, and the weather had warmed just enough to grow threatening, with rain clouds low in the south. Gerry was worked up about the delays to begin with, but early that morning I'd already promised this much: to see Annie up in Plymouth one last time.

About five I drove up and rented a room, sat and waited one last time for her to come. Waited for her to come when it would just turn out to be pointless—she cried the whole time we were there. Either cried or pulled away, her arms drawn over her chest, silent, looking everywhere in the world but at me. I was no good either, stopped up and achy, so damned tired I could barely stand up. We spent the night like snowed-in strangers, lying on top of the worn orange bedspread, her balled up under my jacket on the wall side, while I lay back worn down and sleepless, trying to breathe.

It wasn't until daylight that she deigned to talk to me, and then it was just accusations and bitterness; she'd thought that I was one of the brave ones, she told me, somebody like her. Somebody who wasn't afraid. I sat on the edge of the bed and watched her. Of all the futile things in a world chock full of them, there were few any more futile than sitting around disappointed, just because a person turned out different than you'd dreamed. Her boys and little girl were still young and needed her, there was a husband back at the house that she'd pledged herself to, rightly or wrongly, going on ten years before. Before long she was crying disconsolately, dignity and hope both thrown equally to the winds.

Recriminations aside, she looked up surprised and not really believing, to see me already on my feet. "Arthur, no. Just sit with me a minute. Don't go yet."

I looked out past the curtains to the gray light of early morning. "I got to get back."

"No, just for a second. Let me get pulled together here first. Hold on. Just a second more, please."

It was a simple enough request to grant, but I'd already picked up her coat. I tossed it across her knees. "I'm headed back," I said. "Now come on. I'll walk you back out to your car."

The third week of November brought a cold front from the north. The temperature started dropping like a lead plumb, down to fifteen the first night. For the next three days it couldn't have been more than five or ten degrees when we got out to the field, with a stiff wind that crawled up our pant legs and in past our collars, scalded our noses and wrists.

Gerry took advantage of the solid freeze to ice-skate over fields that had been troubling him with wetness, and we lumbered around bundled like Eskimos, wrapped up in every sweatshirt and jacket we could find. The machinery didn't care for the weather either; it was an hour or more every morning at least, just getting the combine to turn over and run.

"Give it another one," I'd hear Gerry call up from the cab, my signal to dig a hand out of my coveralls and squirt starting fluid into the breather. While the dry spin of the diesel whirled beneath me, I'd hunker down and look out over the fields. All that weren't Gerry's were already clear; around us the fall weeds had finally had the grace and good sense to shrivel away. The roads looked brittle and empty, with the trees in the woods and along the ditch banks stripped to the bare black of their branches by the wind.

"She's wanting to go," I'd hear from below me, "you sure you're giving it enough? Squirt the hell out of it, Arthur, there ain't no shortage of ether in the world. Give her hell!"

The big diesel would finally cough into life; while it idled, building up strength, we'd move on to the trucks. Eventually we'd be back at the harvest. There were over a thousand acres ahead of us even at that point, but Gerry knew the litany of success.

"This cold snap's only gonna help," he proclaimed. "We ain't got that trash in the fields to bother us no more. Just stay in the truck between rounds, keep out of this damn wind. We're gonna whip it yet."

Repairs don't take a holiday with the cold weather—if anything, they just got worse. The same thing seldom broke twice: it seemed like we'd been on a two-year project to rebuild that old International from scratch, a time-consuming and expensive way to get things done. I'd just dumped a load of corn over at the dryer when I came back past the field and saw Gerry out in the middle blinking his lights. I bounced across the frozen ruts to meet him, and in the sweep of prairie wind we huddled below the cab.

"The damn master drive's slipping," he told me. "I could feel it all the way down from the other end. Better grab a couple of wrenches there, and we'll see."

Nothing comes easy when your fingers won't obey, and your lungs go sulky against the cold. I slipped in past the dual, but Gerry wanted a second opinion, his own. When I came out, he took my place, wedging back under a tangle of gears and belts. At least he was out of the wind that way, and while he tinkered and cussed at it, I turned in small circles, trying to find the warmest way to stand. On one of those turns was when I saw the old Nova at the crossroad, saw it come gliding down the road toward us. I watched over the bean stubble as it pulled over and stopped.

"I guess you're right, Arthur, that bearing's out sure as the world. I don't know why this has to happen to me. You don't see Ray Stewart broke down all the time, or Lindell Bardacke standing out all winter in the cold. Them vise grips is what I'm gonna need, the damn thing's scored so bad I can't hardly get a grip on it. I say, give me them doggone grips, there's a pair right under the seat."

I already had them in hand, and dropped them in to him before I left the combine behind, clumping across to where Annie stood waiting. She'd climbed through the brown weeds in the side ditch, venturing a foot or two out onto the frozen crust of the field. She stood straight and slender against the wind, dressed up in heels and a smart pair of charcoal-gray slacks that hung straight to the ground like stovepipes. Her head was drawn back into her big puffball jacket, the same tangle of wild black hair poked out at the top.

"Hey there," I said.

"Hey."

In the old car that idled behind her, Moni was up on her knees in the front seat, frowning as she peered out at us. The boys were squeezed into the back, Stevey and Jeff lost in comic books still glossy from town. Shannon, on the near side, stared at us without expression.

"Looks like you got the whole family. Out for a drive?"

"I guess you'd have to say that. I'm going."

"You're going."

Annie couldn't have kept the excitement out of her voice if she'd tried. "I'm going. Today. Right now. We're going out west, down Texas way, maybe to Arizona. I got a cousin in Yuma. I'm gonna leave Carl Wayne and go."

"Oh," I said.

She'd been forced sideways by the wind, and brought up a small gloved hand to protect her face. Even in the minute or two she'd been out there, the wind chill had been at work, blotching her cheeks and ears an angry red.

"I know what you're thinking, Arthur, but you don't need to worry. I ain't here to bother you no more. I just came to say good-bye. I got my courage up now. I got my courage up, and we're going. I ain't never coming back."

I nodded judiciously at the Nova. "You got gas and all? The car can make it out there?"

"Ann-Marie's dad tuned it up for me yesterday. Listen. Hear it purr? It's running the best it has in years. It'll make it."

"That's good," I said. "That's good it'll make it."

It was too cold for conversation, but Annie still gave it a try. "You two about done? You got a lot of acres yet?"

"About half the state. We're gonna still be out here in July."

"Well," she said, "that sounds like Gerry Maars. Maybe I should run out and tell him that all the good farmers are done by now."

"Yeah," I said, "he'd probably appreciate that."

The horn from the Nova had begun honking at the side of the road; Moni glared out at us from behind the wheel. Annie's gloves were thin little knit things, and those dress slacks, as pretty as they were, couldn't have been much help against the wind. The ground beneath us was frozen solid, but first one and then the other of her heels would poke down through the crust, throwing her off balance.

"You look nice," I said. "All dressed up."

"Holly's going too. I called her last Monday, once I finally decided. She never hesitated a bit. She hated that damn factory."

"It's good you got company."

"We're gonna do it," she said. "We really are. There's all that country out there that we're gonna get to know. Find some warm weather first, and after that we'll think about it. Somewhere out west is where we're gonna be!"

A handful of steps to the Nova and she'd be out of the cold once and for all, but Annie braved it another minute.

"I ain't gonna bother you anymore, I told you that. I just wanted to ask, though. What was that all about, you and me? Those nights we had together. That ring you bought me down in Lafayette. Me, the kids, the plans we made. What's all that add up to for you?"

It didn't really matter how it added up, because right behind her a new life was waiting, a world full of adventures ahead. There wasn't any answer anyway, but to keep her just a little longer in front of me with her smart wool slacks, her thick puffball coat, I was willing to take a stab.

"Romance, I guess. I liked that you could be happy. I liked to make you happy when I could."

She laughed. "Oh, Arthur, I was wild about you. I don't think you're ever gonna have any idea how much. I just loved you so. You were the most beautiful thing I'd ever seen in my life."

The horn was blasting out again, short bursts into the thin, frosted chill of the countryside. Annie had started picking her way toward the road, but she stopped at the side ditch to look back. "Oh, just come on," she said. "Let's go. Just leave that damn combine and come along. Holly's a little on the chubby side, but we'll fit you in. Come on, let's go."

I hesitated, the combine across the frozen field behind me.

"Come on," she said, laughing. "You can read the map for us. That'll be your job. Get in and let's go."

"I can't."

"You can. I can, and so can you. Just come on. There ain't nothing for us here."

The horn was still honking, Moni's angry little face glowering out at us from the car. When one of the boys reached up to cuff her, a fight flared up across the seats. His thin face creased with irritation, Shannon held up one hand to block it off. The truth was that I could read a map well enough, and for a last instant a warm car full of tussling life still waited for me, poised for a dash across the plains.

It waited, but like everything else, not forever. Not much longer at all, in fact, even as Annie reached up to brush angrily at the tears that had slipped out anyway, to run down her frost-burned cheeks. When she left, it was to pick her way through the weeds in those smart slacks and heels, climbing into a car full of shrill complaints and accusations that spilled out into the gray November day. Scolding and mediating, she guided them down the road toward Holly's and Arizona, without another glance my way.

FORTY-FIVE

Al Lantz was the farmer's friend, Gerry'd always said, and by all odds he must have been the gravedigger's too, because it was just after the cold spell broke that he finally died. The ground had gone spongy again, and I was taking my time, cutting beans on the high ground over at Shaw's, when Gerry came out early with the news.

"Died during the night," he said. "Hell of a shame to lose a man like Al. Especially this time a year, when we're so damn busy. You got anything in them trucks yet?"

"I got the GMC half filled, and the diesel still to go. I don't know how long this weather's gonna hold."

Rain was clearly on the way, and Gerry looked over to the horizon to judge it, the flesh on his round face gray, hanging slack with fatigue. "I can't really afford to, but I'd best go by Al's house anyway, see Merle for a little while. That's the least a fella can do, I guess. You get finished here, just go on over to the other side of the ditch. I'll catch up to you over there."

I got in another hour or two all told, with the wind strong out of the west and a cold dampness in the air that cut right to the bone. The temperature hovered a half-dozen degrees above freezing under dark clouds that settled steadily lower, muffling the roar of the auger as I topped off the GMC at the side of the road. I'd no sooner pulled the tarp over the bed when the skies really let loose, and it didn't take long to see that Gerry wouldn't have to hurry after all. He could get his rest that morning in the widow's parlor. While puddles grew up in the fields, I started in moving all the equipment to higher ground. By the time I got the last of it up and had splashed my way back home, it had become about as chilled and miserable a November day as a person could imagine.

After all our hours that fall, the running up and down the county to the spread-out fields, it felt odd to be back in the old house in the daylight. I pulled off my boots and went in to where a dusty smell could be counted on to linger, no matter what the weather outside. There was a pile of dinner dishes in the kitchen sink I hadn't got to; I peeled off my soaked work clothes in front of them, carried the layers of sweatshirt and coveralls into the living room. I'd just finished spreading them out to dry, had just come down in a pair of jeans and a clean shirt, when there came a knock on the door. I can't say that I was completely surprised, when I opened it, to find Kendra standing out there on the other side.

I swung open the screen door so she could come past me into the kitchen, her hair wet and tangled, the padded shoulders of a long black overcoat soaked and sagging with the rain.

"I didn't hear a car," I said.

"I didn't bring one. I walked over." She smiled like that might mean something, like somehow I'd have a clue as to why she'd ended up soaked to the skin too. Still smiling, she tried to keep from shivering, drawing up her shoulders as water puddled at her feet on the kitchen tile.

I went ahead of her into the living room. "I just got home myself. Come on in where the furnace is. It's trying to kick into gear."

Besides dry rot there was the heavy smell in the dark living room of wet laundry and half-burned heating oil; the only furniture were the couple of straight-backed chairs that I'd dragged in from the kitchen to spread out my clothes. Other than that there was just an old braided rug that I'd dug up somewhere, to spread out over the warped and pitted floor. Kendra, still with her heavy coat on, stopped at its edge.

"I ain't been home so much," I said, "so my housekeeping's not what I'd like. Let me open these grates a little wider, get some more heat out here where we need it."

I succeeded in that much anyway; once the furnace was going strong, I backed up against it, palms to the flames. Under the rain's steady onslaught the long narrow windows gave even less light than usual, while the lonely sound of winter thunder broke somewhere to the west. Ever the gallant host, I tried to be polite.

"It's been a while since you been here. Not since my dad died, I'd imagine."

"The sale," Kendra said. "I was over here for that." She'd been taking a long, slow look over the room's faded wallpaper, had strolled to the closed parlor door.

"There's nothing in there," I said, and she turned back to me.

"It's been a long time," she said.

"Yeah," I agreed, "it has."

She'd drawn her arms up around her, but that couldn't have been very comfortable either, what with the coat soaked through and her pant legs still dripping onto the rug. There was a sad, angry set to her face that she tried to dress up with another smile. It was a smile meant to hold secrets, but she didn't have many, and both of us knew it.

She slipped the coat off her shoulders and dropped it, with its sky-blue satin lining, to the floor.

"That might be a little dusty," I said. "Like I say, I haven't had all that much time to be sweeping up."

"You've been too busy?" she said, still with the unsecret smile.

Under her coat she'd again worn a simple cotton blouse, soaked through on the shoulders and arms. "I know how you like to be busy."

The old heater was doing all it could, but with that wet blouse and her tight, faded blue jeans, soaked all the way down from the knees, with her wet hair hanging down like a dog's, she stood trembling by the door. To my credit or not, I did hesitate, thinking what a better man might have done. A better man would have gone for a blanket, or cleared off a chair by the fire. A more homemaking man would have started water for tea; a man with jolliness in him might have tried humor, cautioning her about pneumonia like a child. The better man would have, as soon as he could, slipped out to get his own car started, then driven her back around rain-slick county roads to her family, on the far side of the muddy field.

That better man would have spared her the humiliation, at least, of turning to me. But that old house was fresh out of better men, so instead I went up and touched her shoulder, slid my open hand down her arm. When she didn't pull away, I came up to cup her breast, loose under that damp cotton blouse. I ducked down to touch those small lips with my own, moved on to eyes clenched just as tight as her fingers, the nails digging deep into my arms. Her neck smelled of wet wool and shampoo; when I did reach for her coat, it was only to spread it out flat, over the twisted oval braids of the rug.

Her hand was ice-cold as I took it, easing her down onto her knees next to me. For all the secret smiles and saucy banter, she was stiff and awkward up close; there were soaked boots and socks to negotiate, wet, clammy blue jeans that bound. But overall you'd have to say that we managed. Not more than a minute or two later I was rolling her back onto that sky-blue satin lining, and that's where for the first time I took Kendra, on that dusty old living room floor.

FORTY-SIX

There was grain to haul on the two or three days that it rained, but as soon as the weather cleared, we were hard at it in the fields. Thanksgiving morning we finally moved onto the Bremer place for the last time, coming back through for the beans. Friday I was out early on the combine by myself, gingerly making my way across the lowlands, when Rich Taylor pulled into the field.

"Gerry's in town doing his banking," I called down to him, when I'd come around in the end rows. "Should be out here before long."

It turned out, though, that he was out there to see me, wanting to know if I'd heard from Annie. I came out to squat on the platform while he idled below me in the squad car, big stomach wedged uncomfortably behind the steering wheel. He balanced his clipboard on it while he filled me in on a story I already knew.

"So anyway, she's gone. Her sister too. You know anything about it?"

"Is that all you got to do," I said, "track down unhappy wives?"

An easygoing guy, Rich took it in stride. "No," he said, "we still got all them damn teenagers threatening to kill themselves, that's one thing. Got some sheriff sales coming up, it's getting to be that time of year. So no, unhappy wives is only about our third favorite way to pass the time. I reckon, then, that you haven't heard anything. Her husband's kind of worried."

I shook my head. "Nothing."

When he'd finished with his clipboard, he tossed it down beside him, slid his ballpoint pen back into the front pocket of his uniform. "Well, that's that, then. Thanks for your time, Arthur, I won't keep you any longer. Be sure to tell Gerry that my wife says hi. We appreciate the new washer and dryer at the jailhouse, it makes a big difference. We appreciate him standing up to the council for us like that. Tell him Darlene sends her thanks."

"All right," I promised, "I will," and we both went back to our jobs.

Gerry'd never let up on his county work; the Monday before he'd used a half hour out of a meeting to argue the councilors into new appliances for the jailhouse. He'd been lobbying for the highway workers too, and was caught up in finding new jobs to replace the ones that had run away with Precision Dynamics when he wasn't looking. He'd helped carry Al Lantz out across the cemetery lawn to his grave. The naked got clothed and the soybeans cut, but what that meant was that Gerry Maars never stopped for a minute. When the mourners went home to a warm and welcome dinner, or when the councilors settled in at home after a meeting for the eleven o'clock news, Gerry was just then climbing into his overalls for the night shift, or already wiggling under the muddy tow bar with a chain.

"We just got to keep going," he'd tell me, "that's the key. Just a little bit longer and we got it whipped."

There was too much tiredness that had settled in on both of us, though, a dullness and stupor that seemed to deepen every day. For my part I'd have been in bed an hour or two at most, choked up from bean dust and still trying to answer the bell for another day, when Kendra would come over. Byron tried to be at the middle school by seven, and the bus stopped early for Joey, just before the play-school car pool made its rounds for Celeste. Five minutes later my sister-in-law would be at the door. I'd follow her in through the kitchen and up the stairway, to the bedroom at the end of the hall.

She hadn't cared for the cot, pulling all the blankets onto the floor. That's where they stayed, and that's where she would bite her lip and come at me, pulling my shoulders, shoving me, tearing at my shirt with her hands. I don't know how many hundreds of times in the warm, unfettered privacy of my fourteen-year-old mind I'd undressed her already, but there in the cold light of a December morning, with our grown-up white bodies pressed roughly together, I'd remind myself again that this was really Kendra. They were her smooth shoulders that strained under me, her pale forearms that wrapped tight around my waist. Finally it was Kendra, naked except for her wedding rings, who pushed into me, who wrestled me forward between her legs.

With Gerry and I always in the fields, Kendra at the door when we weren't—pulling back and somehow stopping for a minute was one of the few things I really longed for. I came to cherish those times when Byron was around, and Kendra stayed closer to home.

As it was, I came back on a Saturday morning for some Hi-tran, hadn't even gotten the bucket out of the barn before my sister-in-law was there. She had her hair pulled back with a hairband, had thrown a sweatshirt over a T-shirt and an old pair of corduroy pants. She met me at the back of the pickup, and we went up onto the porch.

"Where's Byron?" I asked.

"He's gone Christmas shopping, up to South Bend."

"What about the kiddies? Aren't they at home?"

Once inside she shrugged off the sweatshirt, tossing it on the kitchen table. "Cartoons are on, so Celeste's lost in TV. Anyway, Joey's there. He can keep an eye on her."

"I ain't really got but a minute. There's a breakdown on one of the trucks. You say Joey's there to watch?"

Kendra pulled off the band to shake loose her hair.

"I told you that he was, didn't I? I said I needed to talk to his Uncle Arthur a minute, so that was okay by him. He's always thought the world of his Uncle Arthur."

"That's good," I said, "because I think the world of him."

Kendra laughed. "Come on," she said, "let's go upstairs."

I may have been held up some on my way back with the Hi-tran, was a little slower weekdays getting out to the field. Sometimes Gerry would be already out when I got there, servicing the combine himself. There was even a day or two when I dawdled longer, and the nosy bastard had to come looking me up. Kendra'd made it clear she was going to come over when she pleased, park where she wanted, but that was one thing Gerry had to find out for himself. He happened to be pulling in one morning when she was on her way down from the porch.

You have to admire how little she cared anymore: Kendra didn't hurry, never looked away. She just walked on past him on her way to the Toyota, daring him to say a word. He didn't say that word to her or me either—he may not have liked it, but the simple truth was that he needed me, me and the twenty or so other hours out of every twenty-four that I cared to send his way. He just turned around in his pickup and headed back to the field, where I caught up with him before the hour was out.

The first hints of a snowstorm came over the radio while I was at the dryer, sometime just before midnight. Gerry would have heard the same early forecasts in the combine, but by that time we were almost home free, finishing the last of his beans. There were a good four or five hundred acres of corn out there still, but they weren't a problem; a good operator like Gerry could work up fallen stalks half the winter and never lose an ear.

So at that point he should have been happy, because he'd almost made it. The beans were what he'd been worried about; the hundreds of dollars that each acre was holding hostage had driven us around the clock three times already in December, the third time only a couple of nights before. The year's worth of worry had finally narrowed to the last hundred acres on the Skidmore place, and we'd already whittled those hundred down to eighty, working through the night. By six the early disk jockeys had excitement in their voices, because the first of the big winter storms, the one that Gerry'd been looking for over his shoulder ever since March, was finally coming our way.

He had county business scheduled for later in the morning: they'd approved one factory for revenue bonds in October, and now another was in town for hearings. A vote at the council meeting was set for later that night. Irene had come up on another birthday by then, so Gerry'd ordered a cake at the bakery, which he planned to take by when he came back from town. Just before sunrise I got back from the dryer to find him already gone, so I climbed up to the combine myself.

I could have gone home for a couple of hours, but the truth was I felt glad to be up in the combine, moving into the dark field ahead. The dawn, stubborn that time of year anyway, came on about seven, highlighted by deepening clouds and a thick grayness in the air that never seemed to clear. I knew that Kendra would be looking across the field for my Camaro. She had no spiffy plans for track lighting to share, no puppy farms she wanted to start, but still had come to expect me handy once her family was gone.

Some days I managed to slip out early and miss her, but she could step lively too. I'd no more turned off Sycamore the morning before, on my first run of the day, than she was down at the end of the driveway, waving me to a stop.

I did pull over onto the shoulder, did leave that big GMC idling while I followed her up the sidewalk to their door. I could still remember when they'd built that low ranch house, still pictured the half year or more that Byron, home weekends from Noblesville, had pored over plans, the glossy catalog pages of faucets and doorbells, the cards with narrow rectangles of paint. My dad in the corner too, back then, shaking his head, but Byron'd had the good sense to ignore him. If he hadn't they never would have ended up with the Bedford stone siding, the long hallway that swept from the living room far back into the house. It was the same hallway that Kendra hurried me down to the rumple and unhappy clutter of their bedroom, where she tugged off her sweatpants and threw them on the floor.

"Come on," she said impatiently, but I faltered, hesitating at the edge of their bed. Even with brief use of it, to hear her tell the story, what with the new principal lagging behind in his homework; even though the sad failures and reproaches that had built up over the years were none of my affair and never would be, still I couldn't climb down next to her, not where Byron's heavy body had lay tossing not two or three hours before. Kendra got the laugh on my squeamishness and rolled half-naked out of bed, leading me back up the hall. We went past Celeste's little room to my nephew's, where she pulled down the tangled covers of his bed.

There was a sour and peed-on smell that hung around us, but whether that was from the yellowed sheets or the soiled clothes thrown all around, it was hard to say — things had really gone to hell around there. It's testimony to something that it still mattered to me in a little boy's room that this was really Kendra. Kendra who even then was fighting at me, pushing and hitting as I rose to take my pleasure, my face jammed into a shelf full of Bible books and plastic dinosaurs, jet fighters and dusty race cars streaked with glue. It still mattered that under me that fall it was Kendra, even through the chill and hurrying, the dryness and tearing, the anger, disappointment, and tears.

It was while I was lost in those sweet and abiding memories of romance, still guiding that bulky old eight-row International along the fencerow there at Skidmore's, that I managed to pick up a rock. It skipped along the feed auger and up into the throat before I even noticed the heavy bang and clatter—by the time I got the grain head shut down, the augers and grabber chains reined into silence, it was already jammed deep inside.

In the gray morning the clouds had dropped lower, thick with the wetness of snow. The air had grown heavier too, the first thing I noticed when I came out onto the platform. Up to that point I could still hope it would fool me, but after I'd climbed in and around the grain head for a minute, I knew. I knew and just climbed back up to the cab. The first snowflakes began to come in as I swung the big combine away from the crops, heading back to the road.

I hadn't seen Gerry get back; he must have pulled in while I was going west. As I came up on him in the end rows, he was hunched over in front of the idling Fleetwood in his town clothes, gathering up pods that the combine had missed. He threw them up onto the grain head as I swung around.

"Hey there," he said. "Sure glad to see you going. Stopped by to tell you to keep at it, don't worry none about the trucks. We got to get these beans cut. That's a hell of a storm bearing down, they got advisories out all over. I ain't gonna but stick my head in at those hearings, then as soon as I can get changed, I'll be out. There comes up a stiff wind like they're saying, and we'll lose it all."

"Gerry," I said, "I picked up a rock."

He stopped at his car door. "You say what? Got a rock you picked up? You sure it ain't in the rock catcher? You try to turn the belt?" He came back over the stubble. "There can't be no rock in there. Let me look a second, maybe I can see it. It can't be that far in."

He hadn't been convinced right away, but he could hardly afford to be, with all those acres of brittle beans waving in the gathering breeze. It must have been almost twenty minutes before he climbed down from the grain head himself, wiping his hands. His snappy windbreaker was smudged and torn, and his lips were tight.

"Okay," he said, "we got to get at it, there ain't no other choice. I got overalls in the truck. We got all the tools we need? No, just leave the damn combine here and bring over the pickup. You reckon you can manage that? You reckon you can manage a pickup without busting it all to pieces too?"

Any one of those other boys Gerry'd hired over the years would have known what to do; about that time he would have paused to look off to the horizon, kicked mud off his boots, shook his head as he reached for a smoke. A hell of a thing, really, the way rocks have a way of jumping up. I couldn't help but look back into Gerry's pale blue eyes, bloodshot and pinched as he blinked them against the loss.

"I reckon," he said, "we still got blocks in the back there, better get them out too. We'll get the head off first, and see where we go from there."

It'd been months since we'd really had anything to say to each other, and except to ask for a tool, to call for a little slack here or there or give us a count of three before we lifted away, that was the last thing he had to say to me — we worked the rest of the morning in silence. By the time he'd eased the loader tractor alongside, a heavy chain dangling from the upraised bucket, the snow flurries had thickened, settling around us as we lifted off the combine's heavy throat.

"Okay, now pull back on it. Careful, lift it off easy. You see the son of a bitch? You see it? I just hope them damn rasp bars ain't bent. Can you see back there if they are?"

It couldn't have been different, I don't imagine: the whole inside of the combine was torn to hell. We needed a new concave too, no telling how many hundreds of dollars those damn things ran, even when an implement store cared to track one down. Plymouth, when Gerry got them on the phone, allowed that they could try, and a couple of hours later one of their men wandered out with the parts. By three-thirty we were bolting them back on. Still in his cowboy boots from town, Gerry squeezed in beside me as we built back the other way, his face wind-burned and raw.

The snow had never let up, drifting steadily higher while we'd sat together in the Fleetwood, waiting for the concave and bars. As the short day of winter gave way, it never slackened, dancing in front of the headlights that we trained on the last of the job. The whole time in the car, Gerry'd never said a word—a record, I would imagine, for him. It wasn't exactly comfortable, but for my part I never faulted him; in front of us were over eight thousand dollars' worth of beans. Beans that a good farmer, one not hooked up with me anyway, would already have had tucked away in the bins.

The wind was picking up as I lay back under the grain head. Gerry eased the combine in over me, and I latched the header into place. By the time I'd rolled out from under it, he'd already climbed over the duals to drop heavily to the ground. He came around the grain head to study its steady churning and roar.

"Sounds right," he yelled. "What time is it, six? Well, them damn conferences are over anyway. We got the vote on it at seven, can't hardly afford to miss that too. Irene can just get her doggone cake tomorrow, I guess. Poor thing ain't never gonna know the difference."

We stood together watching the gathering bar sweep smoothly in front of us, the dry grind of the empty auger as it spiraled across the head. There were a hundred things he had to choose from, a dozen he might have picked out to tell me, but I already knew what Gerry was going to say.

"Well, you might as well get back up there, ain't no beans gonna get cut down here. Get on up there in the cab. Go on, damn it, there's work to do."

He'd turned his back on me to trudge out ahead, picking his way through the low, sweeping snowdrifts while I steered the combine behind. He waved me over to where we'd parked the mobile fuel tank, and I swung alongside. Before I could jump down, though, he surprised me, his big head poking up just outside the cab. Then there was the rest of him, pulling up onto the snowy platform so he could swing open the door. Puffing, he leaned inside.

"Now listen to me," he said. "Damn it, Arthur, you listen to me. I got something to say. I just get worked up sometimes, that's all there is to it. I seen you today in the car there, hanging that damn head of yours. Just let it go. Don't be hanging your head about a goddamn stupid rock. It's happened to me Lord only knows how many times, and I didn't even have no good help to dig it out. So don't be feeling bad about it, I don't want you to. I don't want you to be feeling bad about nothing, damn it, nothing at all. You hear me?"

His face was pale as he leaned in over me, his lips purple under the amber fill light from the bin.

"All right," I said, "I won't."

Gerry might have nodded; he had his head propped against the door frame, resting. I pulled up my hood.

"I'll get filled up and get started. You go ahead to your meeting."

He started. "No, now, goddamn it, you stay here and get warmed up a little. I'll pump the damn fuel. I'll take care of it." Halfway across the platform by then, he leaned back in to grab my knee. "Now, don't be worrying about that doggone rock. I told you not to."

When I promised again that I wouldn't, he made his way back to the ground.

Out in front of me through the swirling snowflakes were still those eighty acres of beans, waiting in the dark. It's easy to forget that Gerry Maars had made it a long way in life his own way, believing in pure drive and luck. His luck had held: the wind had never grown as fierce as it could have, the snow was tailing off, and with a little patience I'd probably cut some beans after all. Behind us a half-dozen miles was a warm courthouse, where the citizens of Haskell County awaited his word.

There was the unlucky side that he might have considered too, that the wind could still pick up, the snow turn to sleet, that the hours that we'd fooled away would turn out to matter after all. Already chalked up against him that day were a good two thousand dollars' worth of parts, ahead of us those five hundred acres of corn, and all Gerry Maars could think of was to get a grown man back in the driver's seat, to climb up and tell him not to worry. To run around and fill his tank for him so he wouldn't get chilled. Where there was one rock, there were bound to be more, and I had half a mind to go out and find another, twice as big if I could, three times even, one that I could jam back so far into that combine's throat that it would never come out. I wanted to do it just so I could see Gerry's fat face when I told him, see what fine lesson we could all manage to draw from that.

The relief that I felt, though, was the main thing, just the chance to be finally alone again, my fingers and feet thawing, high up and out of the wind. The heater was making enough progress that the steady sweep of the snowflakes up against the cab window had started melting, running in thin streams down the wide panes of glass. I couldn't see back to the gas tank from there; all around was just wet black and nighttime, reflecting me back at myself.

The fuel pump's motor would have been lost to me too, under the low rumble of the diesel, but as I waited I came to be listening for it all the same. I craned around in the cab, finally shouldering up my coveralls to swing open the door, to call out over the top of the hopper. I climbed out across the duals and dropped to the ground, made my slippery way back around the straw walkers to the other side.

As I came around, there was the high electric whine of the pump sure enough, running merrily on like it had forever. Gas had flooded up out of the combine's fuel tank, was pooling at the pump nozzle to pour in a steady splash and stream to the ground. It was just past the tank, then, that I finally found Gerry Maars: flat on the ground with his arms spread and feet thrown out behind him, lying facedown in the snow.

PART III

ONE

I still remember the field trips we'd take every three or four years, Hoosier public-school pilgrimages down to the Tippecanoe battlefield, where Tecumseh and the Prophet met their fates. Kendra was right about this much: I had been shy as a boy, but I still enjoyed climbing up into those long yellow buses with my schoolmates, and winding down Highway 25 to the little town of Battleground. I remember the high banks of a train grade running down the middle of a short main street, while just a few hundred yards west there was the state park itself, a cast-metal historical marker assuring that on the damp dawn of November 7, 1811, "the lofty trees looked down on William Henry Harrison and his fearless soldiers, as the state of Indiana was born."

From our tractors we'd watched, the spring before, as Homer Jackins clanked through his barnyard, heading off to wherever it was that he'd found some fields. There was a low stand of stunted poplars along the edge of some of his own ground; he'd probably planted them as a windbreak himself, or helped his dad put them in, a half a century before. It was down at their base that he parked his combine — dried-out morning glory vines had wrapped around the gathering bar was the consensus — and he'd climbed down from his cab to drag them off.

I don't know much about the land Homer Jackins had ended up with, or why he was still out there so late in the year. I do know that the big reel on a grain head looks graceful from a distance, turning gentle as a windmill on its way through a wide field of grain. Run by tempered steel chains, its job is a simple one: to bend back all that it touches against the knives. Hydraulics do their part, calm and steady, gentle as a child's history lesson, but like the chains and that gathering bar, they're hooked up most commonly to a two-hundred-horsepower diesel engine, endowed with such power and steady purpose that once they're in motion, there's no human hand on this planet that can even slow them, let alone bring it all to a stop.

There was at least one other farmer in the state, then, that December, who still had his crop in the field. No one will ever know if those old poplars were looking down on Homer Jackins or not, when he got caught up by that big grain reel and pulled into the cutting blades. Since he was working alone that day, with a full tank of fuel, it was almost four hours before somebody chanced by to find him spinning. I was picking corn south of the railroad when I saw the ambulance go by the first time, was bringing one of the trucks out, a half hour later, when I saw it come back again.

He'd been pretty much whittled down by that time, one arm and the better part of a leg were gone, but Homer Jackins was still alive. As a matter of fact, he and Gerry could have been bed buddies, bunk mates in the tiny intensive-care unit at Delfina Memorial, but Dr. Chadurri knew as soon as he climbed back into the ambulance that there wasn't enough help for him there. He'd already phoned ahead to medevac out of Fort Wayne, summoning them to the county airport little over a mile away. A good idea, but in vain: what was left of Homer Jackins died at the end of the landing strip, ten minutes before the helicopter arrived.

Gerry had been luckier. I'd managed to wrestle him into the backseat of the Fleetwood and slide him back across those snowed-over roads into town. Chadurri and Dr. Ky had both gone to work on him, finally getting him stabilized sometime around midnight. While he lolled in intensive care, Kathryn was kept busy running down to the airport to pick up the girls; they'd rushed home as soon as they heard. By that time there wasn't much use for me in the hospital hallway. So, with the family circling in, I slipped away and went back to the field at Jackins', where in a long day I got the last of the beans up away from the snow.

Two

There was a brief, awkward attempt to organize a harvesting party that fall; old Orin Altgeld came out to ask me about it, and from what I understand, a few phone calls went out around the county, and the idea got chewed over some with breakfast in town. And one Saturday Orin did make it out with his four-row corn picker, along with a couple of old-timers who wheezed around the rest of the afternoon in their grain trucks, running over almost as much corn as they hauled away. Too many were already gone to Florida was how Orin explained it, and then again he hadn't even asked people like Ray Stewart: the big operators already had the equipment put away for the year and weren't all that eager to bring it back out. The biggest problem in the operation, though, it seemed to me, was just that Gerry wasn't around to organize it. They'd taken him to Fort Wayne in an ambulance by then, and were running a whole battery of tests up there.

Kathryn kept me posted on his progress; late at night after the girls went back home she'd stop out to the field with sandwiches, and we'd have dinner together in the front seat of her car. After all those years that she'd stood tall in front of the county's young people, I still hadn't got used to the notion that she could be frightened too. Frightened and unsure, but as Gerry rallied, she began to talk hopefully about how things could be once he'd recovered. He was awake by that time, and spry enough to remember that he'd never once settled for less than the best, so for the heart surgery they flew him over to Cleveland. I would have been just finishing up on the prairie the morning they finally operated, wrestling that big consciousness under one more time, and leaving Haskell County and me all on our own.

THREE

I did get more company, as it turned out, and some good help from unexpected quarters, on those last few hundred acres of corn. I'd half-looked to see something of Joey, but the person who showed up instead was his dad. He came by one Wednesday after school, and from then on, in the evenings and on weekends, Byron was more often than not over to give me a hand. It might seem strange, in a world that comes geared without a reverse, but the week before Christmas found the two of us picking corn again out on that old Smiley ground, moving from there onto my dad's sixty acres behind the barn.

My brother watched me, of course; I'd see him looking up through his steamy glasses as I leaned out from the combine above the truck. A time or two he started to speak but remained silent—I was seeing Kendra even then. Not that we were frolicking through the meadow together, our race had about run its course. It's a poor workman who blames his tools, but one day or the other I just couldn't quite rise to the occasion, and that made it even tougher to go on. Without our mating to rely on, we were a lot like all the rest of the sorry animals of the field, not too likely to lie around and spoon. Her family's merry Christmas didn't include me, so I celebrated our Savior's birth over at Skidmore's, combining another forty acres of corn.

The day after was a Saturday, and Byron came out to help with the long move to Foxie's. We got started in up there about seven that same evening. Sunday after church he helped me again, and on Tuesday of the next week Kendra took a job at Manning Industries, the first of the new factories that the council had managed to lure. There wasn't ever anything said, but from that point on she joined two hundred other women every day in a long, open pole barn at the east edge of town, her early-morning rendezvous moving from me to a solder gun and the bright-colored wires of passing dashboard harness assemblies, bound for one of the new car plants down south.

FOUR

There were a good hundred and fifty acres up at Foxie's, and by the end of the second week of January, I about had them beat. Byron had staying power, coming out right up until we took the last load into the elevator on Saturday, on Sunday helping me move all the equipment back to the old barnyard. The combine had held together, and I'd managed to avoid rocks, so we finished, with Gerry's voice the only thing that seemed to be missing. Not that it had been turned on me much that fall, but I'd come to look for it still somewhere out there at the edges: the moralizing and chiding, his boasting and concerns, the reminders of how important every single thing in the world either was or had the potential to be. Instead, during gray afternoons there was the radio to keep me company. I listened, as I combined, to call-ins for financial advice, and nationally syndicated instructions to the lovelorn. Drive-time talk shows out of Chicago and Cincinnati run by wise guys in a hurry, still worshipful of sports scores, it seemed, but quick to make fun of everything else.

The county hadn't missed Gerry's voice all that much; the council learned that they could do without his vote that first Monday night, about the same time we were rushing in from the field. When I drove through Keona a couple of days after Byron and I'd finally finished the harvest, I saw that Irene's house was up for sale. A Christian grade school had taken over at Midway Implement, spreading out through the showroom and shop.

Kathryn brought Gerry back from Cleveland a few days later. They'd made a two-day drive out of coming over from Ohio, so it would have been Tuesday or Wednesday that she called to say he'd like to see me. I went over for dinner the following night.

It had been a long time, it seemed, since my first visit over there; after the dozens of times since then that I'd come by with tickets or for a paycheck, I'd grown accustomed to going in through the garage, in past Gerry's big bass boat and their stable full of lawn mowers and snow blowers, past the twenty or thirty cases of sodas still stacked along the wall. When I came into the kitchen, I saw Kathryn first, and for a second I could imagine what Gerry might have seen for himself, after his heart attack and brush with the knife. And that was just the simple pleasure of still being alive: of coming in from a cold night to find dinner on the stove, the windows steamy and table set, a wife there who'd been through the wars with him, and still ended up on his side.

Kathryn greeted me warmly. I imagine we both even had a certain fondness, now that Gerry was back, for those late-night suppers we'd shared at the edge of the field. She'd never had any real practice at mothering, and I wasn't much of a son, but in our own way that winter we'd got along. As Gerry had improved, she'd begun quizzing me about finances—how much we'd get for the different crops, what kind of bills to expect from the gas man, how much income might be yet to come in.

She was running water over the pressure cooker, smiling up at me through the steam, when we heard Gerry call from the other room.

"Is that Arthur I hear?" he hollered, and it didn't take either of us much longer to see that whatever talking we'd wanted to do was in the past, because Gerry, bright-faced and already pumping my hand, was back from Cleveland and the dead.

He was thinner, of course, and hadn't been to the barber yet, so his hair hung long and wispy around his ears. Without the wind burn I was used to seeing, he was paler too, but the main thing that surprised me was how instantly he'd aged. I don't know what else you'd expect, since only a couple of weeks before they'd been splitting his broad chest like a turkey's, slipping veins out of the insides of his thighs. At the table he favored us with a look at a long angry scar, displayed above his dinner plate, that divided the gray chest hairs neatly in half.

"Oh, I tell you," he said once he'd buttoned his shirt again, "that intensive care's about as depressing a place as a person can imagine. There's gonna be some changes there when I get back to them council meetings, I promise you that. I think every public official ought to spend the night there every once in a while, just like I did. Then they'd see! And it ain't those girls that work there's fault either. I couldn't believe what they got paid. I told them I'd remember them come budget time, and you better believe I will."

He slid another piece of chicken onto his plate.

"Sorry about the dinner, Arthur, but it ain't really Kathryn's fault. This damn diet they got me on, it's a fright. Boiled chicken, boiled potatoes, got some boiled string beans there without no bacon to go alongside. Everything boiled or steamed. And no pork or beef either; if it don't swim or fly, I can't eat it. That's what the doctor ordered."

"It tastes fine," I said.

"Get a little butter and salt on it there, and I'll tell you, it sure helps a lot."

Still slow to come back were his vocal cords, bruised into hoarseness from the enthusiasm of the emergency room staff right there in Delfina, trying to get the breathing tube jammed down his throat.

"And that wasn't even the worst of it, not by a long shot. Before them doctors got through with me, I had tubes in about every place a tube can go. I finally wake up the next afternoon, down in that doggone dingy basement at the hospital, Kathryn right there, a couple of those little nurses looking down, and I thought I'd done crossed over to the other side. Forty percent damage is what old Chadurri had it figured at, liked to scared poor Kathryn to death. Had me figured for a doggone invalid! I'll tell you what, I was glad to get somewhere that people knew what they were doing. And I ain't saying nothing either, because the county's damn lucky to have them, old Chadurri and Ky both, but a fella don't mind looking up and seeing an American doctor now and then. The young fella that operated on me played football right down there in Columbus, not more than a dozen years ago."

His court was a small one, but Gerry was leaning back to survey us with pleasure. He wore a bright red flannel shirt that seemed big on him; at the collar skin hung loosely from his neck.

"Once we got to Cleveland and got the operation scheduled, I wasn't so worried. But for a little while there, with Chadurri's damn verdict hanging over me, both the girls flown in to get their good-byes out of the way, well, it sobers a man, it really does. But I been on the phone to both of them since I been home, telling them they got to come back now that we can enjoy it. I been telling Kathryn we ought to all go on a big vacation somewhere, maybe a cruise. I'm gonna have Stubby bring a bunch of them Love Boat brochures on out to the house. Hell, you might as well come with us, Arthur, it'd be a pleasure to have you along."

Kathryn set her fork down. There was a tension that had come up across the table by then, although I wouldn't have been able to place it. Gerry nodded to his wife.

"Kathryn here ain't so hot on the idea, but then again she had a chance to get her visit out. I wasn't quite so lucky. I was the one that they all had figured was halfway dead. Oh, and Arthur, this'll tickle you. They been telling me I got to get more exercise. I guess doing pull-ups across those damn duals all the time, throwing seed bags, all that rolling around in the mud half the year ain't quite enough. So I got us a couple bicycles picked out, the best I could find. Me and Kathryn are gonna go riding them bikes this spring, whenever we ain't in the field. I already ordered them, should be here next week."

"We might have to be a little more careful for a while," Kathryn said, coloring as she looked up at me. "Arthur, when you get a chance, why don't you bring by the last of those tickets, and we can get the year-end totals. It's hard to understand how the prices never seemed to come up, even with the drought."

"Would you listen to that? Honey, what's all this about prices and tickets? You ain't never concerned yourself about none of that before. Let me worry about them doggone markets. There ain't been a year yet that stopped us, when we ain't been able to keep moving ahead."

Kathryn folded her napkin and set it by her plate. "I just think we should take it easy. We don't know exactly what's to come."

Gerry shook his head. "Ain't this the damnedest thing? I wasn't laid up much more than a month, and now my wife here's the expert."

For her part Kathryn seemed ready to cry. "We just don't know," she insisted, "how you're going to come back. We don't know how things are going to work out."

"Now, honey, calm down. Relax and let this nice meal you made digest in peace. I'm gonna be fine. And there ain't never been a time in farming when it ain't been like this. We just need some decent prices is all, and everything will be okay. A good crop, some decent prices, and we'll be set. You done eating, Arthur? You get enough? Don't want no boiled pie and boiled ice cream to top things off?"

"I'm fine."

"We got some sherbert in there, that's on the diet. We'll have some in a little while. First, though, there's something I want you to see. Come on, honey, let's go in and show this to Arthur."

Kathryn had started gathering the plates. "You go ahead, I'll get cleaned up in here. Go ahead without me."

"No," he said, "now, don't be that way. Don't hide away out here in the kitchen, we like your company. That's something else I been thinking about, Arthur, how a man can't afford to forget his family. Most precious thing in the world, a family is, right up there with your health. Come on, now, come in with us and see it. It wasn't all that easy to get ahold of in the first place."

When Kathryn finally agreed to join us after she got the table cleared, Gerry led me into the living room.

"You got to excuse my wife," he said when we were alone. "She kind of got a full dose of farm medicine all at once there, after I went down. The books are bad enough, but then there's the damn creditors to deal with, all afraid I'll go to the Great Beyond while they're still holding my notes. The new bank people were just as bad. There I am in doggone intensive care, and they're swarming all over her like flies. Foodmore on the phone about every third day. Oh, it can be a nightmare for a woman, lucky I come back when I did." He knelt stiffly by the television. "Okay, honey, I about got it ready! Come on in here so we can get started!"

He already knew exactly where he wanted us, me in the recliner and Kathryn on the couch against the wall. She sat back with her arms folded while Gerry fiddled with the controls on what looked to be a brand-new VCR.

"You ain't seen this yet, I guess, this here's the cassette player that I bought over in Cleveland. There was a mall right near the hospital, so when I'd get a pass, we'd go over for a stroll. And I'll be damned if there wasn't a sale going on right while we were there. They even had a deal where you get the second one half-price, so I bought us two. I put the other one back on that old console the girls used to watch, so if there's ever two things we want to see, we can. Got to plan carefully, ain't that what old Ray says? Let's see here, it ain't working right, I may need my glasses. No, no, damn it, now don't either of you get up. Make yourselves comfortable, I got it under control. A young man like you, Arthur, is gonna find this interesting. And Kathryn, of course, with an education, it means all that much more. Wait a second now, here it comes. It's just getting started here. All right now, Arthur, look! Look at that damn thing there!"

If it's not color anymore, people hardly care for a second glance, and what had come up was about as far from color as you could get, just a fuzzy black-and-white blur that only gradually sorted itself out into some kind of circle in the center of the screen. As seconds ticked by in digital hundredths in the lower right-hand corner, the circle began to take on a definite and strengthening pulse. Black borders eased back toward the edges, while all around the center there were dark loops and alleyways, curving around it and in.

"Now, ain't that something?" Gerry demanded. "Ain't that the damnedest thing?" He stepped back to admire it. "I ain't in your way, am I? Hell, they ain't even supposed to let you see these, but I got to talking to the young fella that worked in there, found out his dad used to farm himself, down near Defiance. Good cattle country over there. When I left he had this all made up for me to take."

"What is it?" I asked.

"What is it? What is it? Why, that's my doggone heart that's beating, right there on TV. That's a movie of me! They shoot that dye in, then they put a scope on it of some kind, so they can see how everything's flowing. Beforehand, I was about as stopped up as a man could be. When I told them the kind of hours we put in, the work we done this last season, they damn near came out and called me a liar. Couldn't believe it. But look at it now, just look at it! That's my damn heart, Arthur, big as life, right up there on the screen!"

"Well," I said, "it's something."

"Ain't it, though? Kathryn's seen this a dozen times already, I bet, and she still gets a kick out of it. See there, that's the aorta, like I used to stick on them Chester Whites. That there's one of the chambers, and that's the other. There's the veins they took out of my legs, see, this is after the operation, so look at them damn things flow. Look at 'em, just like a doggone twenty-year-old. That young doctor, the football player, he told me right there in Cleveland that it was a hell of a heart, about as strong as he'd seen. I ain't even convinced I had a heart attack, to tell you the truth."

"Oh, Gerry," Kathryn said, "for heaven's sake . . ."

"Well, I ain't. You show me where the damn thing's damaged. I asked the doctor the same thing, and he couldn't point it out. Said it looked good to him, real good, about as good as new." Admiration came through the hoarseness in his voice. "I ain't saying I didn't need to get them pipes rooted out a little, them bypasses put in, because I did. But look at that thing now. Good as new is what he said, and steady as a doggone clock!"

Kathryn had gotten up to go back to the kitchen, but Gerry was so caught up in the television, he never even saw her leave. It didn't matter so much, because by that time he had me back as an audience again, and I'd never seen it even once. Neither of us had to get up in the morning, so there was all the time in the world. Which was good, because with all the overdubs and re-recording—that young technician still had enough farmer in him that he didn't care for waste—there was still a good hour on the tape left to run.

FIVE

There was physical therapy scheduled three days a week at the hospital, and a nonsupervisory stroll around the new exercise track had been recommended for every afternoon, but Gerry quit doing both within a week. He preferred that I come by to take him out in the Fleetwood, circling the fields to make sure they were still in their places. Some of them weren't, of course; I don't think he could quite believe that the Bremer place had slipped away, even when he saw the grader Jack had hired smoothing out the lane and field entrances for Ray Stewart and his boys. The Fox farm was sold just after Christmas, and he'd lost the Skidmore acreage to Lindell Bardacke, while he was still over in Ohio. But even from his sickbed, Gerry'd managed to add a little bit on the plus side of the ledger too, two or three fields down past Holloway's and Jackins.' Pale, rocky land that had just been cleared, fields that even Gerry wouldn't have fooled with a half-dozen years before.

The red dog at the Holloway place was out to greet us when we drove down to look at them, coming at full gallop from behind the house to join us. I didn't have quite the heavy foot that Gerry did, and the dog managed to keep up for almost a mile before finally dropping back. Gerry watched him fade without comment; I'd noticed a moodiness that had come up to plague him again, like it did most afternoons as we drove the empty sections. It was still hanging on even as he guided the little loader tractor over the new acreage a week later, winding around while I stumped on foot just ahead of him, picking up rocks.

Rock-picking was my dad's kind of work, about as thankless a task as there is in the world. It usually means a whole day or three out in a raw winter field with no money being made, no crops sown or harvested, either one. The bigger operators just tended not to bother anymore, banging their way over whatever they'd rented, but Gerry liked his fields clean. Even when he had to sit restless in the tractor seat watching, while somebody else went out ahead doing the work.

"There's a few more right over there," he called out to me. "Let's get them too, before we go over and dump this bunch off."

It was dry enough for the little tractor, but cold, and about as gray a day as winter can bring. The wind was steady and raw, blowing from the north. After a lifetime outside Gerry'd begun to feel the weather, sitting huddled over the steering wheel in his loose coveralls and the two or three layers of jacket that he'd pulled over the top of them.

"You know," he said, "it sure is a shame we didn't get to Florida this year. It ain't so much for me, but it's something for Kathryn. There ain't many advantages to the farming life, but that's been one of them, those couple of months out of the cold. Fuzzy Welch called me last week and said they didn't even have the Haskell County breakfast this year. They didn't have no doggone master of ceremonies."

"Well," I said, lofting a chunk of granite toward the scoop, "there's always next year."

"That's what I told him. Hell, those old people aren't going nowhere. Ain't every year we'll have the kind of troubles we had this one."

He sat back idle while I tugged at a big tan rock that had decided to give me a fight. He reached down to bump the scoop a few inches lower so I could muscle it in.

"Like I say, I know you'll excuse Kathryn for the other night. Them bankers got her all worked up. Then the bills coming in—hell, they wanted damn near eighteen thousand for fixing that big four-wheel drive up at Plymouth. She ain't used to that kind of thing. You get out and drive it yet? It run all right?"

"I did some disking with it over at Shaw's. It sounds pretty good, but the transmission's still leaking. Something ain't hooked on quite right."

"Oh, we better get it back up there, then, field work's not very far away. See, all that bothers her. And then there's my doggone neighbors, they could hardly get their concern for me out of the way before they were pumping her about my landlords, wondering which way they were gonna go. Ray Stewart drove down to Foodmore himself, went all the way down there to tell 'em I was washed up. Tried to get them to take him on instead. And I'll be damned if they didn't just about drop me, too, without even so much as a fare-thee-well. I wasn't back from Cleveland four days when I had to go down and see them, try to put their minds at ease."

The big tan rock made a scoopful, so Gerry swung the little tractor around. Puffing and sweating even in the cold, I was glad enough to step up on the hitch and take a ride with him to the edge of the field. He had enough bulk left to still provide some shelter, so I ducked down behind him out of the wind.

"Tomorrow," he was promising, "or the next day, you and me are going to go for a ride. Stop in at the bank so they can see me, go out to Hostetler's, drop by the restaurant and get us some breakfast just like always. I want you with me, just so you can see those goddamn bastards when we walk in the door. From what I hear, they got me in the doggone morgue already."

He tipped the scoop over into the pile we had growing along the fencerow and swung back to the field. He shook his head.

"I don't reckon I told you, but that new vice-president from the bank was out at the house a while back, I know that's why Kathryn got so upset. A cocky little bastard, dressed real nice, coming out there with exactly how it was gonna be. I should have told him right then and there to go to hell; if I was a younger man, I would have. But it ain't quite so easy as that. I got Kathryn's money tied up in that Smiley place, and that farm of your dad's, everything financed through Farmers and Merchants back when Al still had the reins. I told him about Al, too, and what a man like that had meant to our town. I told him I didn't appreciate him coming around and throwing a scare into my wife at Christmastime, when I was still flat on my back. I told him that too."

"What'd he say?"

"Say? Say? He didn't say nothing, just sat there looking at me. There ain't gonna be no pole barn this year either, Arthur, over at your place. There ain't gonna be that new combine like we need. Won't be none of that this year, but we'll just wait and see. Everybody likes to see a man down where he can't do nothing, but just get some good prices this year, a decent yield, and then we'll see. We'll see where old Gerry Maars does his banking then!"

I'd jumped down and was out ahead of him again, clod-hopping across the dirt. "Bear a little to your left; there's one I saw over there."

"'Better management,' see, is what he kept saying, like there ain't no more to what a man does than that. Like there's something to manage with the way prices are anymore. Same thing with Foodmore. When I went down there, they had this young fella no older than one of my girls. And oh, he was a big shot too, see, general manager of all them damn restaurants. Offices in one of them business complexes, a half-dozen secretaries scattered around—a person's impressed just to see it. I know Kathryn was, she drove me down. That general manager, guy by the name of Dave, he was just as polite as a person could be. Got us both a cup of coffee, set us down in his office, and turns out he wants to talk about management, too. Works around to how disappointed they are in their returns.

"So then I got to explain how I'm disappointed too, but that this here ain't exactly like the doggone hamburger business. You got to have patience. Oh, he nodded like it all made sense, had a real friendly look for Kathryn, so she could see how he understood." He craned his head, looking out to where I was bent over a rock. "You really got hold of something there, don't you? Let me get the scoop around so it's a little closer."

"I think I got it. I felt a wiggle."

Gerry leaned forward on the steering wheel. "So there he is, real friendly, telling me how it ought to be done. Told us a little story, too, right before we left. About how the whole time he'd been in the restaurant business there was only one of his men that he'd ever had to fire. And that was when he come in one evening at their taco place down at Fairmount, just before closing, and found the manager out front mopping the floor. This boy said he fired that manager right on the spot. Had to, see. Said if the fella was out there working himself, when he could have had somebody doing it for three dollars and thirty-five cents an hour, then he sure wasn't much of a manager. Management's the key. He tells us that and sits back at his desk all smiling, like that explains it all."

He took the tractor out of gear and leaned out from the seat for a better look. "What the hell you come up on there, the doggone Rock of Gibraltar?"

By that time I was breathing hard, down on my knees in the dirt. "Damn thing's got some size on it. Maybe if I get it rocked up some here you can get the scoop down."

"I don't think you're going to make it. Here, let me have a look."

"The hell you will. Stay where you are. I'll get it."

Gerry was lowering himself stiffly to the ground. He came around the tire. "That's a damn boulder you got there, is what it is. You stay there and I'll get the other side."

"I'll go back for the chain."

"No, damn it, Arthur, you stay right there. I ain't no damn invalid, no matter what my wife says." He squatted down. "Come on and take your half, or I'm coming up alone. Put a little shoulder into it. Okay, now, on three. One, two . . . now lift!"

It was one rock that Mother Earth didn't care to part with, but with four arms pushing and four legs driving forward, we finally got it loose. Once the damn thing was moving we didn't dare let it slide back, so we kept going until we had our arms underneath, wrestling it forward. We ended up both on our prayer bones in front of it, noses pressed into the rock. Slowly we pushed ourselves back to our feet.

"Damn, that was heavy," Gerry gasped next to me. "Oh my, that was a bastard."

The day was raw anyway, and as he got his breath back, he rubbed absently at the brand-new scrapes on his hands.

"Yeah," he said, "that boy Dave had all the answers, and they sounded mighty good. Mighty good. I just wish I'd met him about forty years ago, because I've sure as hell picked a lot of three-dollar-and-thirty-five-cent rocks since then."

He took off the top two layers of jacket and tossed them onto the seat. "Well, the day gets a little warmer, anyway, when a fella gets some circulation going."

"You ain't even supposed to be breathing cold air," I told him. "Get back up on the tractor."

I had to dodge a rock that came flying toward the scoop.

"You got to step lively now," he called over, "make sure you don't get in the way. There's a real rock-picker out here now. My goodness, when I was a boy, I used to imagine these were all rubies out here, or diamonds, just waiting to be found. By God, there's another one. And here's another. At this rate we're gonna be rich in no time."

He laughed as another rock came flying my way. "Oh, don't be giving me the evil eye, Arthur, you ain't my pa or Kathryn, either one. You ain't even the general manager down at Foodmore. Look here, I got another. Jump up there and slip it into granny, we'll just let her follow us a little, while we go across this sorry field. Won't be long until we're the richest fellas this county's ever seen!"

By the time we moved into field work that spring, Gerry was up to full strength, which is to say with twice the drive and stamina of anybody else. As his voice came around, the Cove of a morning rocked with his laughter; Monday nights he was back with the council, deviling them every step of the way. His shoulders were still stiff, but it was nothing that ten or twelve hours behind a steering wheel wouldn't loosen, and by the middle of April we were finished plowing and had already begun to lay seed across the patchwork of fields he had left. After some early moisture, spring had come on with warm balmy days that already made winter hard to imagine. Gerry would have me down beside him at the field edge every other day, not praying but just marveling, both of us on our knees to sight along row upon row of green that had begun shooting up all across the springtime fields.

"This ain't the best land," he would promise me, "but it's serviceable. Ain't nobody thought that prairie land would amount to nothing either, but I reckon it did. Adversity's what tempers a man, lets him know there's still a world out there that's up for a fight. We get a good yield this fall, some prices, and there ain't no telling how far a man can go."

Kathryn still came out during the first part of the year, bringing lunch and dinner to us more often than not. As time went on, though, and Gerry started pushing harder and harder, there wasn't as much room for her anymore. There were any number of days, I would imagine, that prettiest of springtimes, when a bike ride would have been nice, but back in their cluttered garage the cartons stayed unpacked, jammed in between the mowers and boat. I saw the boxes again one Friday night when Gerry invited me back to the house to celebrate finishing the beans.

For my part I would have liked to see Kathryn, but it turned out she'd gone down to Louisville for the weekend to see one of her nieces. A car pulled up in the driveway right after mine, and Gerry, still shirtless after his shower, was paying the boy for our dinners at the front door as I came in through the garage.

"Got us our smothered burritos here, Arthur, and a couple of them Spanish hot dogs apiece just for good measure. We might as well celebrate, we done a hell of a job. Come on, though, have a look at this first. I want you to see what all I'm gonna do."

He took me in past the kitchen to show me, to spread out for my imagination the brand-new wall-to-wall carpeting that he was having installed the next day. So I could imagine it just right, he led me from the living room to the dining room, down the hall of the big house and into the bedrooms.

"Won't that be pretty?" he said. "Won't that be the damnedest thing? They're gonna put it all down tomorrow, before Kathryn gets home. She's gonna be so doggone surprised. I got new couches coming, too, cream-colored, about as nice as money can buy. I reckon old Dave Carmichael down at the Carpet House was glad enough to extend a little credit. Same for Darin Dunn down at the furniture store there, that sold me them couches. They know what the hell I stand for. That's what the bank's got to learn, a man don't work like I have all these years in a community and then get treated like a stranger. Those men still know who I am."

He frowned, thinking back over the slights that had never come, then went back to witnessing about the furniture. "You'll learn, Arthur, when you settle down for yourself, that a woman's like anybody else, she needs some consideration. It's a hell of an easy thing to forget."

We took our dinners in all their messiness into the living room; with new carpet coming the next day, we could have torn apart a transmission in there and it wouldn't have mattered. Gerry was still keyed up about getting the beans done, excited by how tickled Kathryn would be to see the rug.

"And these old sofas, they're going to your place, don't think I forgot you. Don't think I forgot how you handled things last winter, my wife kept me posted. Go ahead, try 'em out, they're yours now. I been thinking of getting that swimming pool cleaned out too, so we can start relaxing over here. We get done in decent time this spring, I'll have you help me, see if we can get things out there back in shape."

He'd picked up the remote control to the TV and was flipping through channels on the television.

"Look there on the news, Arthur, them volcanoes, over at the Philippines. And what's that colored guy there, a lawyer? A doctor? More power to 'em, that's what I say. I remember me and Charlotte always used to give money to a little colored college down in the south part of the state somewhere, used to send it every year. What in the Lord's name is that, now, ballet? Gaylene's partial to that kind of thing, her husband too. What do you reckon we did today, finishing up? Fifty acres? That's how I had it figured. That new ground's gonna fool everybody, it sure is. Get some prices, a little yield . . . look there at that little stubby guy, the one in the bow tie. I know I seen him before. What the hell's his name?"

Did I say that I'd missed his voice? They still had all the movie channels he'd bought for Kathryn, and I might have liked to watch one for more than twenty seconds at a time, but Gerry had the control firmly in hand. There wasn't a one of those channels that didn't catch his interest, but none of them in his springtime enthusiasm could hold it. After a while I just lay back on one of my new couches, propping myself up to relax.

I don't know when the dark of the old farmhouse had begun bothering me, but it was sometime that winter that sleep had begun slipping away. The old cot didn't seem to hold me, the empty rooms echoed out, and that night with Kathryn gone I settled there in Gerry's big living room, relieved not to go back to the farm. And the truth was that it did comfort me somehow, too, to have Gerry going on behind me. I took advantage of that smothered burrito and the Spanish hot dogs warm in my stomach to doze off; when I woke up he was gone, with only the light over the sink in the kitchen still on.

It would have been about two or three in the morning by then, as I stood up to move past the family pictures spread out on the TV. The only accommodation since I'd first spent the night with them was that now they clustered around the new VCR; otherwise Mt. Fuji was still in place under Perri and her girlfriend, their sunglasses still rested high on their heads. The grandkids, a couple of years older and in new outfits, smiled in their annual Christmas joy. Somewhere outside was ever-deepening springtime. The house still breathed easily around me, and as I made my way back to the bathroom, the old carpet was still plenty good enough to cushion every step, floating me lightly forward down the hall.

It was without even trying, then, that I came up on the little room in back with the old television console, where Gerry'd parked his bonus VCR. Lost in making my own way through the dark, I'd barely noticed the faint half-circle of light up ahead. Where it spilled out at the doorway, I looked inside. And there, squatting on a little footstool with his back to me, was Gerry, still awake, bathed in the glow of the old TV. Leaning forward, he never even heard me, intent as he was on the flickering black and white of that Cleveland hospital video, and his heart beating on in front of him up on the screen.

SIX

It was an easy spring overall. Even with the moving and breakdowns, the old planter balking and plugging but still managing to lay down seed, we finally that year found ourselves on par with everybody else. It took extra hours, and a whole lot less acreage than usual, but the corn was all in by the last week in May. We switched over to beans, and by the middle of June were out with Ray's boys and the rest of them, cultivating along rows of as fine an early stand as I could ever remember seeing in my life.

According to the farm papers the crops were bursting out just about everywhere that year, and from what we saw of the world, we would have had to agree. They were good on the poorer ground that Gerry had taken on down south, good back up on the prairie where Ray Stewart had about squeezed us out. Ray hadn't wasted any time that spring, tearing down the silo so he wouldn't have to work around it, plowing through the timothy for corn. He'd gone in to cut back the ditch banks, too, the better to keep their tangled shade off the corners of his swelling fields.

The Republicans had put up a running mate for Gerry that year, a woman from over at the Lake. A running mate was what they called her, but she wasn't such pleasant company to have, when only one seat was liable to be won. Gerry didn't pay any attention that I could tell, but by that time, I seldom saw him. I don't know that anyone did; if the wrappers balled up on the floor of his pickup were any indication, he'd given up on the restaurant and was most often grabbing his sausage biscuits and coffee at the Burger King out by the bypass. The moodiness had come back while we were finishing the field work, and as summer deepened he tended to keep to himself. What I remember most is that he started in fishing. He must have gotten the pond stocked sometime that spring, because many an afternoon, if I cared to, I would come up on his pickup down at Jackins', pulled in along the side of the road. Out across the bean plants was where I'd see him, standing on the bank by himself. By himself or with that red dog when it'd been able to keep up with him: if I looked close, there'd more often than not be a flash of strawberry fur bouncing in and out, bounding through the rye grass and into the beans.

He'd never broken down the dryer at the Bremer place, so I trespassed long enough that summer to load it up to haul six miles east, where he'd managed to rent some bins. Evenings I'd range in the Camaro past where the old silo had been, pulling along the ditch banks to look over Ray's smooth, unbroken rows of grain. From there I'd move out, still restless, onto highways east or west, wandering up and down 31 as far as I cared to go. Some nights I'd take a motel room along the highway; others just find a turnoff into some woods, or a truckstop where I could lay back my head. With sleep still fighting me, it was almost a pleasure to come back up the lane early one Sunday morning to find the lock to Gerry's gas tank gone, and see that there was something else that needed doing after all.

We'd come a long way from the polished Texaco gas pump, of course—all Gerry had left at my dad's place was an old gravity flow tank that sat up on rough-welded metal legs. I'd had my suspicions of gas thieves during planting, which is why I'd put the lock on in the first place. Early that next week I put on another one, and when Saturday afternoon came around, strolled around the field to Byron's.

Kendra passed me on the road right before their mailbox. As I came up the driveway, she was just stretching a long leg from the Toyota, climbing out ahead of me in a loose powder-blue work blouse and elastic-band pants, her blond hair cut short. She didn't hurry or linger at seeing me: my sister-in-law moved through those summer days in the luxury of her own hard-won brand of fatigue. The harness plant wanted them at their benches by six, but since it was on a demand basis with the assembly plants, sometimes she'd be called in early. That same morning, coming back at three from a night's idle driving, I'd seen her already heading into work.

Squinting twelve hours over smoldering solder took its toll: deep red bruises had settled in under her eyes, and lines had come up to crease either side of her mouth.

"They really got you putting in the hours over there," I offered as she slammed shut the car door.

Kendra looked at me coolly. "That's why they moved here, they wanted people who would work." She turned her back on me to reach in through the window for a little Playtime cooler. "They're not interested in loafers. Bryce and Tom have said it again and again, the first time the company hears union, it's gone."

She used the word *company* with pride, played back the words of her young managers like such gospel that I once might have thought she was trying to irritate me——for better or worse, I'd been a union man all those years on the boats. But that would have been underestimating her utter indifference to me and why I might be coming up their driveway on a July afternoon. Going up the front steps, she leaned over to examine the geraniums, rattled the handle on the screen door to see why it stuck. Left behind in the doorway, I heard her lunch box bang down on the kitchen counter.

"Has Dori called?" she hollered out as my brother came into the dining room from the garage. He was still unshaven on a Saturday, blinking to see me there. He looked into the kitchen for his sweetheart, who pushed past him as she came back out.

"Dori didn't call?" she asked, her voice fading away from us.

Byron shook his head. "No," he said, "she hasn't," as a door closed sharply behind her down the hall.

"Hello, Arthur," he said to me finally, "how have you been doing?"

"Fair enough," I said. "How about you?"

"Oh, fine. Busy with scheduling. The crops look good."

I nodded.

"Prices are still down, though. I imagine that's a concern."

"Yeah," I agreed, "it probably is," and then told him that I needed a gun.

Byron would have remembered as well as I did, our dad with one of the neighbor men, going out to guard a gas tank or some new calves at night. At any rate, I knew he was likely to have kept it, the old man's .22. I could half-see it myself, lying high on the top shelf of the pantry, could almost picture the winter afternoon when my dad took me out behind the barn so I could learn how to shoot.

"How long has it been going on?" my brother asked.

"At least a month, probably more. We were busy during planting and I didn't have a chance to check it out. Somebody came by last weekend, so they must figure the house is empty."

Byron nodded, considering. "Let me go look a minute, and I'll see what I can find."

He left me in the living room, where I could feel Kendra still, down at the end of the hall. Celeste must have been over at her Aunt Dori's, but my nephew was there, and while Byron banged around out in the garage, he came into the living room, slipping behind the recliner against the wall. He'd been out once or twice on weekends to help us, when we were first in the fields, tailing away before the season really got started.

"Hi there," I said, but the boy kept his distance, frowning, either growing nearsighted like his dad or disapproving as he watched me from across the room. "I ain't seen you for a while," I ventured again. "You got summer school this year? I figured we might pick back up on some of that welding sometime, if you cared to. I been mowing some, too, if you want to get back behind the wheel."

Finally he seemed to nod, but it may have been more toward his dad than anything else, because Byron had just come back with the guns.

There was the .22, now in adult eyes grown small and toylike. Cradled in my brother's arms next to it, though, was a bright, new 30.06 with a tooled walnut stock and polished barrel, that shone like it had never been fired.

Byron lay them both across the table and then took up the the bigger gun to slide back the bolt. He sighted down its barrel. "This is a good rifle," he said. "You better take it."

"Hell, I don't need that. This ain't TV. Probably won't even be anybody show."

"Yeah, but it's good to be prepared. It's the better weapon. That other one's just an old farm gun."

I shook my head. "The twenty-two's fine."

"Okay," my brother said, "suit yourself. I'll take the big one."

"Why? Where are you going?"

"I'm going with you."

"The hell you are. Watching for gas thieves doesn't take an army. They're probably not even in the county anymore."

"I need to check around some. I know I've got an extra box of shells someplace."

He began rooting past flashlights and fuses in the middle drawer of that ugly old sideboard. Down the hall I heard the shower running—I couldn't help thinking of Kendra's pale skin under the looseness of her blue work blouse, the two of us just a dozen paces down the hall. I told Byron again that I'd handle it, but in some things my brother was stubborn as a mule.

"You aren't doing it alone," he said, "so just put that out of your mind. What time do you think we should get out there?"

I could have argued more, I guess, to get free of him, but after all, he had the guns. I shrugged. "Eleven or eleven-thirty should be soon enough. They have to have been coming by late."

In the last drawer he finally found shells for the .22. Next he drew out the plastic casing that held the big rifle's cartridges, each of them two and a half inches of brass below a long lead-tipped point. He broke one free to snap into the chamber of the 30.06, slid back the bolt to flip it out.

"Bring your car over here, so nobody will see it," he said. "I'll come out when you pull in the drive."

SEVEN

Byron was waiting alone when I went over a little before midnight. I'd half-expected Joey, too; he may not have cared for me anymore, but before I'd even left, he'd eased out past the recliner and up to his dad, begging Byron to let him go. Byron told him no, but that wasn't the end of it. My brother told me on our walk to the barn lot that there'd been a scene. Byron had been gentle with the boy for once, reminding him that Kendra had to go in early the next morning, and that in these troubled times of gas thieves, somebody had to guard his baby sister at home.

I'd been looking forward to the boy's company; instead it was his dad and me who stumped up the dark lane to the barnyard. The farm light Charlie had added lit up between the shop door and porch, reaching the gas tank at the far side of the lane. We settled in the damp bluegrass just past where it died, in the shadows along one side of the barn. Unused to the nighttime air, my brother shifted his chair-toned body next to me, trying to find some way half-comfortable to sit.

I still couldn't figure Byron's insistence at being out there; bothered by allergies, he snuffled next to me in the dark like an old draft horse. I wasn't much better, my head still throbbing from all the bean dust I'd sucked in the fall before. By some stray miracle, though, we'd ended up out on the old place again, together, guarding another man's gas. It was an old-fashioned task, unlikely to bear fruit, but I could understand Joey's eagerness—he'd sniffed a past that Byron and I still managed to share an edge of, a time when almost any excuse would have been enough for two men to find themselves waiting alone in the darkness, rifles across their knees.

For that matter, we might have been the only two brothers in the state of Indiana—the only ones sober anyway—who had occasion to sit back on a summer night together and look at the sky. Not that our conversation particularly sparkled; over the next two hours Byron explained to me the many intricacies of the new Tippy Valley discipline manual, and an after-school science program slated for fall. I endured details of the travel trailer he meant to buy with his new principal's salary, and a North Central accreditation visit scheduled for the spring. Finally he wound into silence. Over the next half hour we enjoyed a small breeze that came in over the bean field, and a plane that we followed blinking across the sky.

"This old yard," he said to me then. "I don't know if you remember the truck patch. It used to be over there north of the house." He pointed in the darkness. "Do you remember digging potatoes in the fall? We had strawberries started when Mom was still alive. We planned to sell them at a stand along the road."

I stood up and walked away. While Byron shared his fond memories with the bluegrass, I stood by the barn to relieve myself. From there, I strolled to the edge of the field. The corn had in my lifetime never been more impressive; the beans, as I came up on them, rose almost to my waist. Behind me, my brother lapsed into silence. I made sure it was a silence we could agree on, and came back to join him in the dark.

Around three o'clock we were watching as a light came on in the bedroom of their house. We watched the little square until it went dark again. The light in their living room came on and went off. The garage door glided open a minute later for Kendra's little Toyota, which came backing quickly out to the road.

We watched his wife clear the end of the driveway, her headlights shining wide up the empty county road. She accelerated to the corner, slowed briefly, and turned to speed past us up Sycamore. We followed the low, even whine of the little Japanese engine as it faded slowly away.

The light in the garage had lingered before flickering out. I could feel Byron next to me as he shifted heavily in the grass.

"You know," he said, "I've been meaning to tell you. I appreciated the chance to work together last winter. I'm glad Joey could spend time with you too. Families the way they are anymore, it's not often a boy gets a chance like that." He paused to look across the bean field to his house. "It meant a lot to me. I wanted you to know that much at least."

I'd given up on our criminals by then, and I imagine Byron had too. We heard a car coming from the east, watched a minute later as its headlights flashed across the mailbox at the end of the lane. Byron waited until it disappeared beyond the corn.

"Arthur," he said, "I know about you and Kendra. I know what was going on."

My brother's voice had always been on the quiet side, and it came through the shadows soft and low. I considered the narrow space between us, the black line of the rifle barrel that he'd raised to my chest.

"I know that she was running around with you last winter. I know she was seeing you while we were out there working. I know what was going on."

The big gun prodded me. My own hands were empty—the .22 had ended up across the bluegrass, leaning harmlessly against the barn.

"I know you were sleeping with her."

"I don't remember," I began, but had to stop. Byron waited while I cleared my throat. "I don't recall, really," I said, "that either one of us ever did all that much sleeping."

I could imagine my brother blinking, knew that he would have colored above the gun. The darkness was there to protect him, and I was glad.

"I just wish you hadn't done it," he said.

"I did."

"But I just wish you hadn't, that's what I'm saying."

That much established, he took his own counsel, the 30.06 barrel still trained on my heart. The night breeze rustled lightly through the beans. "You know," he said, "I remember sometimes when we were just little boys. Do you remember back then? Do you ever think about that at all?"

When I stood up, the rifle followed.

"Don't run off now, Arthur, we're talking."

Byron's voice had a new sharpness as it came through the darkness. I'd remembered by then the long, polished sheathing of those 30.06 cartridges, the ugly lead thickness of their tips. A steady prod of the rifle barrel coaxed me back down.

"I kind of feel like talking tonight. I was hoping you'd be in the mood."

"I guess I'll have to get there. Talk away if it makes you happy."

"Happy," my brother said. "That's a little more to ask for." He bumped me with the gun. "About Kendra," he began, "I've got to tell you . . ." But even when he had the chance, Byron faltered. He kept the barrel steady, resettling himself in the grass. "Back when I was in college, that year in Noblesville, I used to sit and look at her picture by the hour. I couldn't believe she was really mine. Can you understand that? Can you understand what that might have meant?"

I thought I might, but Byron had the floor to himself by then.

"You say happy. What I remember from back then is feeling sad for you. You just never had the chance, Arthur, to see what happy could be. There was a time when you might have. Mom wasn't always sick, Dad was different, it wasn't all sadness like you saw. I can remember when Danny was born, how happy they both were to have another boy."

"Well," I said, "it looks like the Alzheimer's has held off on you anyway. Your memory's still sharp."

Byron nodded. "My memory's okay. I can remember when Mom first started getting sick. I remember when she died too, how when we went to the cemetery we left you behind. We left you over at the Deckers', their oldest girl taking care of you while we went into town. They kept sheep back then, up grazing in the yard."

When I rocked forward, the gun brushed my chest. "I can still see you crying in the doorway as we backed away. The funeral, out to the cemetery, all that takes time, but when we came back for you, bumping our way through all those sheep, I don't think you'd moved an inch. Still standing at the screen door crying, like your heart would break. Do you remember that?"

"No," I said.

"And then there was Danny. No, Arthur, damn it, sit down." He jabbed me with the gun. "It's my turn. I'm talking now. Right over there was where it happened. A person can't really forget a thing like that."

I joined him in looking down the narrow lane.

"A person," he said again, "doesn't forget something like that. Do you remember after Mom died how you'd come down to my bedroom? How you'd come down and crawl in with me? Do you remember that?"

No," I said again.

"I remember that." He laughed. "I remember Dad caught us one morning, with you down there in my room. Whipped me good, I know, maybe you too, I can't recall. Whatever he did, it wasn't enough, because you kept on coming. I always admired that about you, Arthur, you weren't one to give in easy. And I'd go ahead and let you climb in, I still remember that."

"Well," I said, finally pushing the barrel aside to stand, "this has been interesting."

"Right over there is where that grain bin stood. You remember that. That was the hardest thing, I think, for a young boy like you to see."

My face was hot, but my hands had gone cold. "I wasn't there."

"Oh, you were there, all right. Where else would you have been? You were right there with him. I used to be jealous of it, how we couldn't hardly ever separate you two boys."

"I wasn't there."

"See, I was supposed to be watching you," Byron said. "That was my job. But I was a lot like Joey back then, irresponsible. I was the big shot, wanting to be up with the men. So there I was climbing all over the grain truck while they loaded out corn. You remember how proud Dad was of that bin? All those men over that morning just to admire it, gathered around that old blue truck."

The night was as clear as ever, so it was only my sinus headache that had gotten worse, the congestion pressing at the edge of my eyes.

"I wasn't there."

Lost in that autumn farmyard thirty years before, Byron sounded surprised, like he was hearing me for the first time. "Why, of course you were, Arthur, that's how we finally knew where to look, when we found you squalling at the bottom of the ladder. Mad because you couldn't quite make it up to that first rung. Mad because Danny'd gone ahead by himself up the ladder, and had never come back for you.

"Of course, it was just awful then—the panic, the plain panic that goes through people at a time like that. Those men would have been our age, Arthur, most of them, no older than me, but it's like the world comes apart all of a sudden, and they were running around everywhere, men you saw downtown and at church every week, just wild, two or three up on top digging with their hands, there were others that ran for shovels; somebody came up with a pry bar so they could start in at the door. By that time I'd had an idea, though, so I was running through all the upstairs bedrooms. I'd figured out by then that it was a trick, that Danny must be hiding up there." Byron shook his head. "Of course, it wasn't a trick. When I got back downstairs and came out—just as soon as I saw them taking axes to the sides of that brand-new grain bin—I knew. I knew that it was already way too late, and that's all it was ever going to be.

"You never came down the hall to me anymore. Not ever again. I could have gone down to get you, but I didn't. I don't know why, I just didn't. I didn't, Arthur, and I'm sorry. I'm sorry that—"

"Kendra," I said, catching him in mid-regret.

"Kendra?" he said dumbly.

"Kendra. Your wife. Last winter. I was taking her whenever I wanted. Here, over at your house, wherever I cared to. That was me. I did it with her whenever I pleased."

Earnest as ever there in the bluegrass, his rifle dangling, Byron at first still seemed barely to follow. When he finally did, he just sounded dismayed.

"Oh, Arthur, what difference in the world does that make? What difference does any of that make at all?"

EIGHT

We might have seen them if we'd cared to, headlights that moved down Sycamore behind us, a low rumble of the car's muffler as it passed the old place twice, each time slowing, before it turned in at the lane. If it hadn't been for those same lights flashing over the barn wall above us, we might have stood lost in the past until daybreak. The lights were cut off, and a silver Trans Am glided by on the lane, its motor ticking softly under the hood.

Byron led the way up to the edge of the shadows, where we stood back against the rough wall of the barn. Three boys in blue jeans were already out of the car. The oldest, a blond kid, couldn't have been more than twenty. The youngest looked about fourteen, with a dark mop of hair and a tank top. They came well-prepared: the third had a bolt cutter, that he handed to the blond boy. A quick snap and a twist, and the padlock was lying worthless on the ground.

Both Byron and I were surprised to actually see somebody, I imagine, to be back in the present again. He moved first, the principal after all, accustomed to being in charge. Laying a hand on my elbow, he eased past me. They'd drawn out a couple gallons, grinning at one another for their slickness, when Byron stepped into the light.

"All right," he said, "just hold it right there. That's right, son, let go of the handle. You other two back up against the car."

All those days herding junior inmates at the middle school had finally added up to something after all. The boys looked suitably frightened, and I'll have to hand it to Byron that he looked the part, advancing huge out of the shadows with the hunting rifle raised belt-high in front of him.

"Okay, now you. Duck under the hose and come around. Duck down, I said." He motioned with a short jerk of the barrel.

The blond boy dropped under the hose, but came up smiling. "You all live here? We were wondering who to pay. I was just gonna leave the money up on the porch."

Byron came slowly around to face them. "Now all three of you turn around. Take it slow now. Nobody's in a hurry. Put your hands on the car. You too, fella, come on."

His two confederates still looked frightened, but the blond kid kept smiling. He dropped his head to look back at us under his arm.

Byron edged in behind him. "The key's in the ignition?"

The boy shook his head. "In my pocket. You want to fish for it?"

"That's all right, just toss them back here. Take your time now. Slow and easy."

The boy tossed the keys a couple of yards back onto the grass. Before Byron reached down for them, he glanced at me. "Arthur, darn it, where's your gun?"

We both knew where it was, leaning back against the wall of the barn.

"Go back and get it," he said, "I'm going to need your help."

I hurried back for the .22, fumbling in my pockets for a shell. The blond kid grinned at me as I came back into the light.

"Get a grip on yourself?" he asked.

"Shut up," Byron said, and motioned for me to cover him while he picked up the keys. Not much of a soldier, I floated the rifle barrel back and forth over those skinny young backs and fragile spines. The blond boy grinned over his shoulder as he watched me.

"You two come around here." Byron nudged the two younger boys toward the rear of the Trans Am with his rifle. Sorting through keys, he found one that opened the trunk.

"All right," he said, "get in. You go first."

"I ain't getting in there," the one with the mop haircut complained. "For all I know, you're a couple of perverts."

The blond boy turned around. "That's right. Hard to tell what these two needledicks were doing together out here in the dark." He straightened. The two boys in back had straightened too, turning to face Byron, but it was the blond boy, still grinning, who made the first move. He'd taken no more than a half-step toward me when Byron's rifle cracked out.

The boy spun to the ground, rolling at my feet. "Oh my God," he screamed, "I'm shot! Oh, God, help me, I'm shot!"

It didn't take much study of those long brass casings to know the big gun had power: the boy's faded jeans had exploded black and crimson at the knee. Already the barnyard grass had sprung up a shiny purple where he writhed. "My God. My God. Oh, my God, help me," he pleaded, rolling wild eyes up to me.

Byron had turned his attention by that time to the other two, who were already scrambling at the bumper, fighting each other to get in first.

"Don't shoot, mister, goddamn it. We was gonna pay."

The younger one was crying. "We was gonna pay, damn it. Kyle told you we was."

It was a tight fit in the sports car's tiny trunk, and while they struggled to get situated, the blond boy writhed at my feet. Byron ducked his head to see that they were set, and stepped back from the trunk.

"Watch your fingers," he said calmly, and slammed down the lid over their heads.

NINE

While we waited for the sheriff, my brother lounged next to me against the shiny hood of the Trans Am, his rifle cradled over one arm. The boy at our feet screamed as he thrashed in the grass. Byron wasn't impressed.

"Kick that mouthy little shit for me," he said, "extra hard. See if you can shut up some of those squalls."

I didn't have to kick anything, because the boy tried to choose silence, burrowing his head down and moaning softly as he grabbed for handfuls of grass. His lower leg was broken out at an awkward angle, and the way the blood soaked out into the barn lot had me trying to remember from first-aid drill how many pints it was that a person might hold. I'd took off my belt and tightened it above his knee as a tourniquet, but then Byron waved me off.

After that it was quiet again, except for the same rustle of the wind across the fields. The blond boy lay glazed-eyed in front of us, breathing shallowly, now and then licking his lips.

"Who'd you get on the phone?" Byron asked. "Was it Rich?"

"No, just the dispatcher. They said they'd get a car out as soon as they could."

"You tell them we had this boy?"

"I told them we had a man shot."

Byron nodded. "That's good. Maybe they'll put a little hurry into it, out of curiosity if nothing else."

The boy shifted spasmodically toward our feet. Byron calmly stepped over him to stroll a few feet past. He nodded across the lane.

"Yeah, right there's where the bin stood. That's where it stood the rest of the winter, too. Big gashes in the sides, the grain spilled out, tools all over the ground—Bernard Wilkie and his boys finally came in the spring and broke the damn thing down to haul away. Dad never raised a hand. Over there's where we had a kennel—you remember the year we both had pups? I remember the trees, that tire swing we used to have." Byron smiled in the vapor light. "I would sit in that old thing by the hour."

The boy at our feet had begun crying softly. The deputy who showed up in another quarter hour turned out to be Earl Richardson, who'd been in the same year with Byron and Kendra in school. He greeted us, shaking hands warmly with my brother and renewing his acquaintance with me.

"Sure, I remember," he said. "Nice to see you again, Arthur. What'd you two manage to drag up for us out here tonight?"

He knelt by the blond boy first, taking care to keep his pressed khakis clear of the blood. He took a pulse along the boy's neck, cinched the belt tighter around his leg. "Oh, I reckon he'll make it," he said when he'd stood. "You say you got the other two shut up in the trunk? Hand the keys to me there, and I'll get them out. I'll let you folks go ahead and handle the guns."

Before long we began to hear a shrill, pointless siren rolling across the sections. Earl had the two younger boys in the backseat of the squad car by the time the ambulance pulled in, siren still wailing and lights flashing wildly as they rolled up next to us in the lot. While the blond boy was being tended to, Earl led me and Byron down the lane. I'd remembered by then that Earl's dad had had a farm not that much bigger than ours was, out near the highway barn a mile south of town.

"That boy's gonna cause us some trouble," is what he told us as soon as we were off by ourselves. "I ain't no expert, but the way that leg's shattered, he might end up losing it there below the knee."

Byron shrugged. "I hadn't particularly planned to shoot him."

"Oh, you ain't gonna have no trouble from us. I know the boy, his dad's got a place over at the Lake. His mom lives in town, they're separated. The dad's a big honcho at Indiana Bell, though, that's the thing. This ain't gonna help you none over at the schoolhouse, I don't reckon."

"No," my brother said, "I imagine not."

"It definitely won't. But he was going for Arthur here, I already got that down. Made a grab for his gun, the silly son of a bitch. There ain't much else a man can do. I got all that down too. I'll get with Rich just as soon as he comes in tomorrow, and we'll see how to handle it."

Byron nodded. "I know that you'll do what you can. It's all right. Just do whatever you can."

"I will, Byron, you can count on that. Be sure to say hi to Kendra for me."

"I will. You say hi to Paula Ruth."

The first early gray of dawn was already in the sky above Byron's by the time the ambulance had gone. Earl left a few minutes later. All that was left was a bloody patch in the grass where the blond boy had writhed, an empty barnyard, and the outline of soybeans becoming ever clearer at the edge of the lot.

I looked down at the blood and back at my brother, at the big rifle he carried so casually across his arm. When he walked to the edge of the bean field, I had no choice but to follow.

"That field was fenced," he said, considering, "the whole time we were here."

I came up beside him. "I guess it was."

Byron nodded. "Yeah, it was, because I remember when Charlie tore out all the fencing. Rolled it up and carted it away, not long after he took over. You remember how we'd have the hogs out there? You have to remember that."

"I remember the hogs."

"I think sometimes of when you and I were both out here one wintertime, watching them root in the corn. You were just a little guy, maybe six. Dad was in the barn. Cold as could be, but we were out here, just watching, when you spied one of the old boars. He was ruptured pretty bad, already about gone. His insides, intestines and all, were coming out of him, you know, back behind."

Byron talked to me in the summer dawn like I was still that six-year-old, his words strangely delicate for a man so quick on the trigger. His rifle bobbed forgotten as he paused next to me to remember.

"It's kind of an ugly thing, really, to see it. You were just a little guy, but you had to know. 'Is it gonna die, Byron? Is it gonna die?'"

My brother laughed. "Just like that was the worst thing that could happen in the world. 'Is that what's gonna happen? Is it gonna die? Is that what it's gonna do?'"

He laughed again, and hoisted the gun back over his arm.

From the edge of the field, I followed him across the barnyard and down the lane. Left behind were the rescued gas tank and blood-stained grass; I still couldn't help glancing at my brother, impassive as he trudged along beside me. As beautiful a summer day as a person could ever hope for was just beginning around us as we walked together around the county roads to his house.

Still halfway back in the barnyard, I might have followed him right up his driveway and inside. At his mailbox, though, Byron stopped.

He turned to me, squinting under the low slant of morning sun that broke across his lawn. "Arthur," he said, "I meant it when I said I was glad I'd had the time with you last winter. I was glad to have that time with you last night too."

"I'm sorry to get you involved in all that," I said. "I hope it doesn't make trouble at school."

From the uphill slope of his driveway, Byron looked down at me.

"I'm happy we had that time," he said, "but it's over now. I'm not going to be seeing you from now on. I can't have you coming around here anymore."

He waited for me until I nodded.

"We've talked about it, Kendra and me, and what's past is past. There's still a lot of life ahead of us. But neither of us wants our boy around you. He's old enough now to where he understands. I still plan for us to make it through as a family, so you'll just have to go your separate way."

"All right," I said.

Byron clapped me awkwardly on the shoulder. "Good-bye," he said. "Good luck." He turned away from me then, and went up the driveway to his house.

TEN

The crops kept coming steadily that year, and not just in Haskell County, but everywhere—it was as if the world had finally decided to let every last farmer have his fill. Bean plants bulged fat with ripening pods, while the corn swelled ever thicker in the fields.

Gerry still was remote, keeping company with that old red dog, I suppose, as much as anyone. I'd see them together, the mangy red thing finally winning out to ride high in the back of Gerry's pickup as it rolled down the county road to the south. There's only so much mowing that can be done, only so much grain to haul, and during those long summer days I found myself missing the boy. At night I stood watching from the lane as the lights went out one by one over at Byron's, wandered through Gerry's scattered machinery in the yard.

I'd lied to the sheriff the winter before, because I had heard from Annie even then. It'd been just a postcard that she sent on their way down, an oil well from the capitol grounds in Oklahoma City. I heard from her a few more times after that, and all of them, cards and letters alike, had ended up in a bottom drawer down in the kitchen. It was a drawer that on those long afternoons and evenings I found myself coming back to, digging them out to look through again.

There was the well-landscaped oil well on the front; on the back were Annie's wide looping words of excitement at getting past the Ozarks and into the west. Next came a Jackalope from New Mexico, and finally a cactus-theme Christmas card from out in Yuma, where she and Holly had decided to settle their family down. In February there was a short letter with a picture of the whole group on a beach in Mexico, the old Nova still alive in the sandy distance. It was just a weekend trip; Holly'd found work cooking at a nursing home, and Annie had started waitressing at night. In the afternoons she'd gone back to school.

In March I got another snapshot, this one of her graduation ceremonies, the night she'd gotten the certificate for her GED. The school had managed to do it up right, the whole class in line and Annie with the L's right in the center, as proud of herself as could be. By the time she got the letter off, she was already studying at a community college. The kids liked their school, she reported, and Holly'd already been promoted twice.

In the Christmas card she said that she missed me, but when I looked close at the beach picture, I could see she'd been mistaken— there wasn't anyone missing at all. She'd been letting her hair grow, and at one end of the lineup it blew wildly in the foreign breeze. Holly hadn't gotten any thinner at the cafeteria, but she was laughing hard, one hand tight on Moni's shoulder as she tried to keep her still for the shot. Shannon was up over his mother's shoulder, and Jeff's toes burrowed deep in the sand. Stevey stood up close against his brother, mugging his own gap-toothed smile against the waves.

Late one evening was when I finally called her. Late when she'd be home from work or school, late when I was loneliest, late when the kiddies would all be in bed. It's a miracle really, too, that her name might be plucked from the millions, that an operator could outsmart a single initial to read me her number, that I would hold it, written on the back of a light bill, in my hand. Fifteen hundred miles of desert

320

and plain, and still I knew it was Annie instantly, answering at the other end.

" Hello?" she said, and then "Hello?" again, before pausing to listen. I lay on the kitchen floor like I had the year before, glad just to be hearing her voice, as she tried once again and hung up.

That same evening, I knelt in the bluegrass next to the lane. Even through the stubborn sod of thirty summers, my digging fingers came to it, the cement slab that had anchored the grain bin, and one of the two-inch rusted studs that held it fast. I rested alone in the barnyard darkness, listening for what my brother would have us cock an ear to: axes against bin walls, the rush and the flurry of long-dead men, cries that had risen up only to slip forever away, into the cool, vacant air of a November afternoon.

I stood to look back to the farmhouse, up to the bedrooms, across the dark living room and abandoned parlor. I thought for the hundredth time of Annie pulling up at the edge of a winter field, wondered yet again if it might even have been just that easy, to jump across a shallow side ditch and go. For anyone else it probably would be, but as I thought of her family gathered on a sunny seashore, imagined a home for them in sun-baked and regret-free Arizona, all I could think of was how good it was that they'd gotten away. It was lucky that Joey, too, now kept his distance, and that Betsy and Kendra were gone.

Remembrance was the whole point, apparently, of Byron joining me to guard the gas tank. My brother, with his leveled rifle, had just given in too easily. Maybe I could have, if I'd tried harder, conjured up the day of my mother's funeral, the plain, ruddy face of the Decker girl, the dung-streaked matted wool of the sheep. I didn't doubt that there had been a screen door that separated, a kennel for pups if he insisted, hogs set out to root in the corn.

If I wasn't quite the collector he was, as eager to pore over moldy details, that still didn't mean there wasn't something to hold onto of my own. Something that I could always come back to, that night like any other, whenever I might be tempted to forget.

Memory's not so hard; I could still see a child's coffin above the pitted parlor floor, thickened ankles and heavy work shoes, neighbor men and women pressed against floral-printed walls. The polished casket in the center, and below it me, a four-year-old not yet broken of running, bumping past the rough black of country dress pants and woolen shawls.

I'll always be grateful to Uncle Willy for this much — even with his own kids, he still had an eye out for a boy. As strong hands swept me up, I was soaring free toward the dust and hidden cobwebs along the ceiling, before Willy slid me down to his chest. I patted at the plastic pencil guard in his shirt pocket, leaned safe against the shallow pock marks and a light sheen of Aqua Velva on his neck.

This, then, is the treacherous memory that Byron would have us cling to: a gold wristwatch that pressed in as Willy bent me across his forearm, my stiff-soled Sunday shoes kicking lightly against his belt. The simple ease of being pushed forward in his hands. This, the faithless, half-remembered past — the moment that I looked into the cushioned casket and realized, for the first time, that Danny was gone.

Danny was gone, but not just from the land of the living — knowing that much was easy. The surprise was what nobody else had seemed to notice, that he'd escaped the grim parlor as well. Not, though, before ceding his place. While the sober assemblage mulled over in silence their own special regrets, I looked out from Willy's arms and saw, over the lip of the narrow coffin, that it was only selfish me who lay inside.

ELEVEN

Maybe that summer, while I thought he was fishing, Gerry was already making the rounds of the bankers, seeing who might still deal him in. There would have been a time, too, when a candidate the party put up would have come out hat in hand, asking Gerry if he minded that he ran. The Lake woman was a little more aggressive, even as she still tried to learn her way around the countryside. She stopped by one afternoon while I was out at the barn, to see if she could put one of her campaign signs at the end of the lane.

Even with her challenge, Gerry skipped the Republicans' Labor Day barbecue at the fairgrounds, the better to spend it with me in the barnyard, while we went over the combine for fall.

"Hell," he said, "every day's Labor Day for us, this time of year. We're laboring, ain't we? Getting these sieves set so we can put food on people's table — that's labor in my book anyway, I don't know about yours."

A flange deep inside the combine had come loose just as I was finishing up the winter before, so I'd spent most of that holiday afternoon squeezed back past the straw walker, digging back through a winter's accumulated bird and mouse crap to get a new one bolted on. While Gerry was still complaining about the Republicans, I climbed back out into the welcome breeze of early fall.

"No sir," he was saying, "let her run, and more power to her. That don't mean a man has to start sniffing around everybody's backsides every free minute, just to get a vote. It's demeaning is what it is. Why, I ain't put up a sign in a dozen years, and I'm not about to start. If people don't know what I done by now, then let them vote against me. That's the democratic way!"

The big harvest that we were moving into had finally shaken Gerry out of his lethargy. It was a golden outpouring that we began running through the old combine a couple of weeks later, thousands upon thousands of bushels a day. Out on the prairie, down south on that new rocky ground, at the Jackins place, all across stubborn Haskell County: the land had finally yielded up to him, granting a bounty that would have scarcely been dreamed of in days gone by.

The trouble was, of course, that miracles had long since gone public. All across the county that fall cups were running over. By nine o'clock in the morning the lines at the elevator were already ten and twenty trucks deep. The big diesel and the GMC were the runts of the class by then: with the big semis coming off Ray Stewart's and Bardacke's, it wasn't long until Hostetler's was full to overflowing.

Every morning Gerry was on the phone for an hour before he came out, calling up to Monterrey or Crawford's Point, to Kewanna and to elevators all the way down at Peru, trying to find somebody who'd still take grain. We joined the other farmers in hauling corn thirty and forty miles back and forth across the countryside, all for fifty cents less than a year ago, and seventy below the year before that.

Despite lofty promises, Plymouth had never seemed to get anywhere on the big four-wheel drive; right before we started that fall, Gerry hired a wrecker to haul it forty miles south to a dealer in Beechum. The first rainy day in October he came by for me early, to see if I wanted to go down with him to pick it up.

"By God," he said as we got out onto the highway, "it'll be good to have that big tractor back. It was bad enough not having it in the spring, putting around in those little tractors like a couple of sharecroppers. This fall, though, we're gonna need it. I didn't buy that big tractor way back when to have it waste around a year in the shop!"

Gerry was excited, dressed up for town next to me on the Fleetwood's wide front seat. Maybe it was because the tractor was finally ready, maybe just that the rain had come early enough the night before that he'd finally got some sleep. At any rate, he was in the best mood he'd been in all fall. The warm rain had a refreshing feeling to it, and we didn't see anybody else out working, so that helped his mood even more.

"How's Byron's doing?" he asked as we sped past Deer Creek.

I said I guessed they were fine.

"I'm sorry as can be how all that worked out. It can't be much fun going back to teaching after you've been the head man."

"I imagine he'll survive."

"Oh, he will, no doubt about that, but it's galling just the same. Them damn school board members, they don't listen like they used to; they see problems, they all want to hide. I called every last one of them up, but Frank Bontrager and that Patterson woman are the only ones who stuck by him once they went back to closed meeting, that's what Frank said. Here we got a young fella who's willing to stay around and help the county, and they treat him like that. You wish people were different sometimes, but they're not. Byron's troubles at home, that boy so long in the hospital, it just gives an excuse to throw stones."

The big car sailed on effortlessly as we cut down toward Beechum. We saw more and more signs of the election: posters for Larry Harsha and Big Pete Henderson, who were running for council in the district down south, bright red-and-blue signs for the Lake woman. Gerry barely seemed to notice.

"I don't reckon you knew it," he said, "but I used to know Beechum pretty well. And, oh, they knew me too. You don't figure they would, forty miles away and all, but back when I was on the extension advisory board, Purdue would have me come down here. I met with their ASCS people, too, back when I was all involved with that. Farmers down here trusted me, see, they'd see my picture in the magazines, or hear me on one of the farm shows. I showed hogs down here for years, just trying to support their fair."

Beechum is a city of bridges, winding back and forth over the two shallow rivers that meet just west of downtown. The implement company was on the far side, and when we'd made our way over to it, we splashed through the puddles to pull in among the pickups in front.

"We'll take that tractor west here," he was telling me, "get away from all the traffic. You come behind me, and I'll put my hazard lights on and lead the way."

Inside were two young guys holding court behind the counter, calling out numbers to each other as they skimmed through the manuals.

"Say there, how you doing," Gerry greeted the dozen or so farmers who were strung out in front of the parts counter. "Gerry Maars from up by Delfina, maybe you remember my name. I farm east of town up there, stretch south clear to the county line. How about this weather, ain't it awful? More rain's what they're calling for too, last I heard."

An old-timer or two at the edge may have nodded, but most of the men lined up there were more like the Stewart boys—sober as judges and half as friendly.

"I got a big tractor in the shop down here," Gerry was explaining, "a big four-wheel drive that I come by to take home."

He wasn't used to the waiting, of course; at Midway Implement they'd been accustomed to stepping lively just to see him come in the door. As the other farmers turned away, he shifted restlessly in his cowboy boots and town clothes, finally getting one of the parts men's attention long enough to tell him he needed to talk to service. The boy called back into a glassed-in office, and after another five minutes, the service manager came out. He was a little older than the countermen, with a head of curly hair cut short above a big wad gathered at his collar. He was dressed more for the beach than an implement store, in a turquoise shirt with a wide black racing stripe that ran from one shoulder down to his belt. He had his own business that he'd come out for, and it was another five minutes before he looked up to us.

"You say Maars is the name? Like the candy bar?"

"Like the planet," Gerry growled. "With one extra a. You got my tractor here and I need it back. I got work to do."

"Let's have a look at the work order."

Gerry leaned in at the counter above him. "Nice setup you got here. I don't usually come by, my hired man does. But you go ahead and deal with him just like me. Last fall we had damn near three thousand acres, and that's a handful. As much as I'd like to come down here myself, I can't always get away."

"Maars?" the man said. "Three Meadow Court? They got it in the shop right now."

"Hell, I know they got it in the shop, damn it. That's what I just told you. They've had it damn near three weeks. It's supposed to be ready."

From under his textured haircut the service manager looked at him coolly. Up in Haskell County we'd grown used to it, but only forty miles south and Gerry's voice had already swelled up too loud and aggrieved. The men down the counter looked out from their quiet, huddled groups of two or three to watch. The service man took his time, getting his papers all in order before reaching back to the phone on the wall. We could hear it ringing out twenty feet away from us, just past double doors to the shop. Nobody bothered to answer, so after a while he shook his fringed head and hung up.

"Let me finish looking up a couple of parts here, and I'll go back and check."

"Hell," Gerry said, "I'll just go on back there and have a look. I reckon I ought to recognize it."

The service manager shook his head. "Sorry, no customers in the shop. Just wait a minute and I'll get to it." He studied the book in front of him.

"What's your last name?" Gerry asked him. "Maybe I know your dad."

"I doubt it," the boy said. "Casey, you want to toss me your pen?"

The men along the counter still studied us, either afraid or looking for an advantage, it was hard anymore to tell. Gerry turned to the man next to him. "I reckon you've heard of Abe Klein. Used to be the county agent here for years. Ain't we met before somewhere? Didn't you show hogs at the fair?"

The man shook his head, and if any of the rest of them had, they didn't care to share it. A couple of stools opened up and we claimed them, so when Gerry wasn't pacing, or standing by the double doors to the shop, trying to look past the butcher paper that covered their windows, he perched up next to me while we waited. I was used to it from Plymouth, but Gerry couldn't settle down, and his good mood evaporated. The service manager finally strolled into the shop, and in another ten minutes he was back.

"I don't guess they told you on the phone," he said, "but they come up on something. That bell housing of yours is cracked. I'll have to look up in the books here to see what it runs."

"A crack in the bell housing? Hell, I brought it in here for the clutch. There wasn't no crack in the bell housing."

"It was hairline." The boy flipped through the pages. "That runs six eighty-five. With luck we could probably get it for you in a couple of days."

The only thing missing on us were the dunce caps, I guess, as Gerry and I sat there on the stools looking back at him.

"You say hairline," Gerry repeated. "They didn't say nothing about it on the phone."

"Yeah, I guess they just found it. Hairline crack, I saw it myself."

"And it's gonna cost me seven hundred dollars more to replace."

"Six eighty-five, if we can get it. Plus the labor."

Gerry stood up. "I reckon I'd best have a look at it. I'd kind of like to see what a seven-hundred-dollar crack looks like."

The service manager glanced up. "Well, I doubt that they even got it anymore. We'll try to get another one for you today, though, I know you're in a hurry. A hairline crack ain't all that easy to pick up on. I think it was Wade that worked on it. If you want, I'll call back there and—"

Gerry had already blasted off by then, banging through the double doors. I was a little slower off the mark, and in his wake ran into the big tractor right away, broken down in one corner of the shop. By the time I got back around it, Gerry already had one of the mechanics by the collar, half-lifted off the ground, while they studied a pile of rubble on the ground.

"You remember that bell housing, Arthur? You remember what it looked like when it was whole? Well, there it is."

I remembered the bell housing, and there was no doubt in the world that he'd found it. Still International Red, but now in jagged pieces, twenty or thirty of them lying on the shop room floor. Gerry looked back over his shoulder to the service manager, who had followed us in.

"So this is the goddamn hairline crack you've been telling me about? Is this the goddamn way I brought it in to you?"

The mechanic was just a little guy with a wispy blond mustache, sporting a patch on his uniform with WADE stitched in red across it. More than anything, he looked startled to be floating out at the end of Gerry's big fist, boot toes pawing the floor.

The service manager shrugged. "It was a hairline crack. Somebody just must have dropped it since then."

Wade's eyes began to bug out as Gerry tightened his grip. "That ain't what happened, not by a long shot." He looked slowly around at the other two mechanics, who had rushed up only to back carefully away. "Somebody got on it with an air wrench, is what it was. You cowboys get it on crooked, and then when you go at it with them wrenches, the damn thing shatters. Ain't I right?"

The other farmers from the parts counter had crowded in just past the sacred door to the service area, so Gerry looked around at them too, as if waiting for somebody to challenge him. The service manager's voice was even.

"It was a hairline crack, like we told you."

Gerry shook his head. "I know how cast iron is, I worked with it all my life."

"The crack was already there."

Gerry slowly let go of the mechanic's collar, and the boy hurried to back away. He stood rubbing his neck while Gerry turned to face the manager.

"I don't know what you're trying to pull down here, or who you think I am. I been on the council up in Haskell County damn near twenty years. I been farming since before you were born. This ain't the way to do business."

Forty long miles from Delfina, cool in his turquoise beach shirt, the boy had never learned to be impressed by Gerry Maars.

"And I say it's a hairline crack. You call down here all worked up, cry on my shoulder how important it is, so I go to the trouble to work you in. We got that transmission fixed, just like you wanted. If you don't like the way we do things, then just pay what you owe and tow that damn piece of junk back where it came. But if you want it to go out of here with a bell housing, it's gonna cost six hundred and eighty-five dollars. Plus labor. Apologize to Wade here, and then come out and tell me what you decide."

He left us standing by the pile of rubble. Back across the wide cement floor the other farmers had just stood there like a herd of cows, and like that same herd of cows, they were still looking back to us as they filed out the double doors. Oh, they were beginning to smile and snicker, of course, and it was easy enough to see how any one of them would have judged it: a crazy old farmer from out of town, making a fuss. Gerry was still a little louder than average, a little less willing to yield, but otherwise they turned away just like farmers had for the last fifty years. By that time down in Beechum not even embarrassed, with another man thrashing in front of them, to back off the other way.

On the way up to Delfina, Gerry sat sunk back behind the steering wheel, staring out into the wet fields along the road.

"Apologize," he finally said. "Apologize because some bastard that had it in for me dumped sugar in the engine? Apologize because after eighteen thousand dollars up in Plymouth they still couldn't get the damn transmission hooked up? Another six here, and the damn thing still ain't right? They don't care no more. They don't care no more who a man might be.

"And I ain't even saying he has to be a community leader. That shouldn't mean a thing. Everybody deserves a decent shake. That's the way it's got to be." He'd started winding up, but it must have seemed like an old refrain, even to him. He considered the black highway in front of him.

"I ain't even objecting to the money, damn it. It's just the respect that's missing, and the fairness. I'm sorry you had to see it, I really am. That's what I'm sorry about most."

It was probably hard for him to tell what he was sorry about most—there was plenty to choose from. He tried three or four other ways to come at it, one after another, until he finally gave up. For the last twenty miles there was only the flapping of the old Fleetwood's wipers to keep company with his embarrassment, as we rode back to Delfina in the rain.

TWELVE

It was less than a week later that Gerry showed up at the old house with a pickup full of plywood, and we started in painting his signs. Our inexperience showed: we got the stencil good and soaked on the first one we did, and from then on for every bold red GERRY MAARS

330

that we painted, there were three or four long streaks of paint that ran down over the white.

"The hell with it," he said, "they ain't reelecting me for my art skills. Let's get those two-by-fours cut up for braces, and we'll get these damn things out where they can be seen."

We ended up with eight all told, stacked in the pickup, drove out together to put two on the bypass, and another couple on each end of old 31 as it came into town. We pounded one in on the lot by the turnoff to Hostletler's, where farmers could see it on the way in with their loads. Keona and Deer Creek each took another, and the last one we stuck up back at the old place, the spot the Lake woman had coveted, down at the end of the lane.

For the last two weeks before the election I worked alone until it was too late for Gerry to visit rest homes or stroll through the restaurants, to sneak up on a stray herd of Moose or Elk that might be watering back in their dark, smoky lodges. The paper after three years had finally deigned to mention him, editorializing against "an entrenched old guard, who had all but lost touch with the times." Out of touch or not, he would breakfast with the Kiwanis, have lunch with the Optimists, took the last loads of an afternoon into the elevator himself, so he could make sure the corn jockeys remembered his name. I had my doubts most of them even knew there was an election, but I hadn't hired on as campaign consultant, and by that time we'd switched over to beans. I was combining late one afternoon on the Jackins acreage when I saw Ray Stewart's two boys cruising slowly by to study the field. They would have had to be impressed by the drainage, now even better on the field with the pond.

I voted early on Election Day, then went back to combining. Gerry was campaigning all day, but he came by with sandwiches once, stopping out again around eight on his way into Republican headquarters with Kathryn. While the nation picked its poisons, I was just as happy to be where I was, equally in the dark, moving back and forth along the rows. The last time I saw Gerry was about midnight, when he came out on his way back from town.

"It's a close one," he yelled up to me over the duals. "The kind that gets a fella excited. Deer Creek came in forty to six for me, can you believe it? And Keona wasn't much different, they remember a fella out there. Oh, it's gratifying, it really is."

"What about town?" I asked, and he frowned.

"Well, that's a little bit more of a problem. They had trouble with the computers and all, so the results ain't completely tallied. I ain't gonna be no top vote-getter this year either, I don't reckon. No, from what I seen, there ain't very much chance of that at all."

He was too keyed up to go home right away, so I stayed combining while he, still in his white shirt and tie under his coveralls, took the grain trucks the long drive west to the rented bins. By the time he got back from the second trip, he'd figured out exactly how it was going to be.

"Now everybody expects me to be down there about six in the morning, to see the results. Hell, they expected me to stay down there all night! Well, I ain't gonna do it. It ain't like I'm begging for the job, it's all the same to me. What I'm gonna do tomorrow morning is get back to work. You been carrying this all by yourself, Arthur, and it's about time I started pulling some weight. I just wish you had some kind of interest in the county, I'd put you on one of them damn commissions as sure as the world. Civil Defense, Courthouse Oversight, any one you thought you'd like."

Sure enough, it wasn't even eight the next morning when Gerry came wheeling up in his pickup, the earliest I'd seen him out there in weeks. He had to be up on the combine, of course, so while he set in cutting the first load, I climbed up on the GMC to open the hood. It had been missing pretty bad whenever I had any weight on it, so I had the wires all separated, and the distributor cap off, when Rich pulled in at the far end of the field. Since that figured to be good news, I wasn't in any hurry, stretched over the high fender checking plug contacts as Gerry swung around to meet him. When I strolled up there myself, a little while later, the sheriff was still explaining.

"At large is the hardest, Gerry, you know that better than anybody. You got to win everywhere. With two Republicans in there, the way it was this year, something had to give. You run again just in this district out here, nobody's gonna touch you."

It sounded logical enough, and Gerry was quick to agree, thanking Rich again and again for coming out. He laughed loud, grabbing Rich's arm, leaning in at the squad car when he said good-bye. They agreed with each other all over again, before Rich backed away, that it was one of those things, a fluke really: all he had to do was wait a couple of years, and he'd have that seat again. We stepped back as Rich spun his way out through the mud. It was only then, as his waving hand fell and Gerry turned to me, that I saw how stunned he really was.

"Oh," he was already saying, "it don't matter. Don't make any difference at all." Rich had turned at the crossroads by then, and he gave a distant toot on his horn as he sped away. "Awful nice of Rich to come out, a Democrat and all; people never did care for that, the way we were close. And that zoning hurt me some, everybody said that it would."

He'd gone past me by then, on his way back to the combine.

"Of course, being divorced never helped, but I told them. I told them the first time I run, back at the Kiwanis forum. I wasn't proud of it, but that's the way it was. A man has to do what he thinks in his heart is right. It's like I told Kathryn this morning. She was worried for me, didn't sleep good, and I told her, 'Honey, you never liked any of this in the first place. A man loses, and it gives him more time for his family.' The hell with 'em, that's what I say. People don't care no more, so the hell with 'em. I should have got off that damn council a good ten years ago. Could have spent all that time on business, where it would have done some good. A man's got to look after his own these days, that's the way it is. Adversity makes us lean. It means something in life, it really does."

He'd been on route to the combine, but led us past it, another fifty yards out into the field, before he stopped.

"Oh," he said. Gerry dropped his head, eyes squeezed shut. "Okay now, I just got to take a minute. I got to get my bearings here. Hold on just a minute." He trod a small circle in the mud. "Got to get back on track here. All right, let's see." He straightened. "A man ain't much of a man who can't face things. Okay, let's see. Oh, my. A hell of a thing."

Finally he shook his head and turned to me.

"Well, you might as well get on the combine for me, I got to get into town. You get a full load now, just take it on into Hostetler's. That doggone Andy Berkow, when he lost the assessor's race, we didn't see him the rest of the winter, but I ain't made like that. I got to find that Lake woman and shake her hand. I got grease on my face? Is that bean dust all over me? It gets in your damn nose hairs sometimes and looks a fright."

I looked him over, inspecting, reached up to run my jacket cuff across a smudge below his eye.

"I ain't dressed like I should be, but it can't be helped. You go ahead now, I'll be back."

I never doubted that he'd be back from town before too long; there wasn't much of anything left for him there. But it was a good clear day for beans, the stalks cut easy, and we were bringing loads out of that land down south like no one would ever believe. I nursed the old GMC back along the side of the field to where I could reach it, and it wasn't more than an hour before there was a full load ready to go. It turned out to have been the number-three wire that had been shorting, just like I thought, because once I'd stuck a new one on, it ran like a champ the whole way into town.

I took the same route Gerry had, and even though I'd never given a damn about politics, knew about it even less, I'd have to say I followed in the wake of what would have had to have been his surprise to find a little of my own. Somehow, even with Gerry Maars out of office, none of the county roads yawned open along the center line; no great cracks had sprung up to part the earth. A highway crew lounged over their shovels at a pull-off near the bypass. In town the schools were still open, the mail had made its rounds, and the old, ugly courthouse—shaken, no doubt, but clearly standing—still guarded the center of town. He must have found that woman's hand to shake, and had moved on to face the others, because Gerry's pickup was already pulled up in front of the Cove when I rumbled past to the elevator with his beans.

THIRTEEN

I wasn't the only one surprised that the world went on without Gerry Maars high up in its saddle. The tire men that stopped for a repair, old Gar Henry when I saw him at a crossroads, Jack Kelleher from the highway crew—not a one of them could quite figure out how he had lost. I had my doubts they'd even voted; just because a man's poorly paid doesn't make him smart.

Of course, there was his constituency that had faded too: not everyone in town cared to breakfast at the Cove. Of the old-timers that Gerry'd always had a minute for, there were a whole lot fewer left, and the ones who weren't in the nursing home listening to Irene babble on about Dakota had already headed off to Florida for the year, with their scattered absentee ballots not adding up to quite enough. The young people he'd courted, veterans of ballpark and school club visits to Cincinnati and Chicago, were by that time in Chicago themselves, had moved on to Atlanta or California, were down in Indy working for the state. And then again, of all the others who had been young once, there were some less gracious than my brother, not so content to be left back with the stock. The average person can live and die never knowing the secret grudges against his name; in public life a man has a way of finding out.

By that time Hostetler's had begun catching up to the autumn's vast harvest. The elevator boys had almost worn down the outside mounds with their little Bobcats, were sweeping out the last of the sheds. They loaded the final scoop shovels of the gravel and field corn mix from the parking lots into semis that were bound for Rochester, and the bird feed company down there.

Incoming traffic had slowed considerably by that time, the short days growing cold, so the lot men didn't particularly care to get rousted out of the warm office to take another load. The prices that had never rallied began to slip lower, and weighing in on the scale, I saw them watching me as they flipped up their sweatshirt hoods against the wind. The scale men who sang out the test weight and moisture were watching me too. No harm meant; their eyes were more than anything just curious. When I slipped Gerry's scale ticket down into the breast pocket of my coveralls, they watched that too, like I was dropping it into a well.

If most people were done by then, we still had three or four hundred acres of corn. Even after the election Gerry was most often gone during the day; he was visiting different banks that fall, all across northern Indiana. Back to the field in the evenings, he'd be clean-shaven above his coveralls, still carrying the whiff of cologne.

With Thanksgiving came Gerry's daughters, a visit planned and already paid for during the burst of his spring enthusiasm. There wasn't any hurry that I could see on the corn, but all the short week before the holiday, he pushed us hard. Tuesday we went late, until well after two, even though Perri's plane was coming in at nine the next morning, her sister's an hour after that. After he and Kathryn got everyone back to the house, he came out to join me in the field. Thanksgiving morning we got in three or four hours too, before Gerry dragged me home with him for the feast.

That much he'd insisted on, stopping me a half-dozen times over those three days to remind me—all this after we'd worked two weeks in silence, wading through our separate tasks in the cold. For whatever reason, he wanted me with him, waiting in the kitchen of the old house while I changed my clothes. When we got over to his house about one-thirty, a young man no older than me was just getting out of Gerry's Fleetwood in the drive. Sports bag in hand, he had a wet, curly head of hair free for the frosty air to ruffle it, and a face that was still flushed with warmth. He had a Cubs T-shirt on under a light jacket, and waited by the car for us to catch up.

"Hey there," he greeted Gerry, "you get finished this morning?"

Gerry moved ahead of me stiffly; he'd banged his knee on one of the combine braces the night before. On a cold morning like that the crease in his breastbone bothered him too, although he would swear on a stack of Bibles that it didn't. It was cold that the curly-haired boy seemed mostly immune to, smiling broadly at us as Gerry shook his head.

"We don't never seem to get finished, the way it seems. Norm, I don't know if you've ever got a chance to meet my hired man here, Arthur Conason. Arthur, this here's Gaylene's husband, Norm. You find the gym all right downtown?"

It turned out that Norm had used the holiday morning to track down the old A&P building, the one a Kokomo man and his wife had turned into a spa. They'd torn out the old shelving in favor of weight machines, had put down indoor-outdoor carpeting and soaped over the big windows in front. The first thing they knew, they had a little gym popular with the Bryce and Tom set, and people from the court-house who liked to work out.

"No trouble at all," he assured us. "Nice little facility."

He clapped Gerry on the shoulder after shaking my hand, walking easily in front of us to the garage. Gerry waved him ahead at the door.

"A real nice little facility you've got there," Norm told us again, never once doubting we'd be pleased.

I can't say I'd looked forward to the dinner. Kathryn greeted me warmly, and Perri suffered me well enough too, considering all the different hired men and stray cats Gerry'd probably dragged home over the years to dinners just like this one. I was introduced to a friend she'd brought from Boston with her, a small thin-faced woman who turned out to be a doctor too. I'd never really known Gaylene, but she pointed out her two boys to me, made sure I'd had a chance to meet Norm. What irritation there was in the kitchen seemed reserved more for Gerry and his going out to the field that morning, with little of it slopping over onto me.

Norm made himself useful opening bottles of wine that Perri and her friend had bought, and from the liveliness that quickly came swelling back around us, it was clear that they'd been tapped into while the girls waited for us to come in. I don't think we'd planned to throw a wet blanket on it, but I didn't feel comfortable in the first place, and Gerry, when he came out from changing his clothes, was subdued. I was used to it by then, but the girls really weren't. Kathryn had begun bringing out bowls of cut corn and mashed potatoes, long platters of turkey and ham, a basketful of fresh rolls that she reached past to set in front of me. With the rest of us shifting uncertainly around seats at the table, Kathryn asked Gerry if he'd like to say the blessing. He considered it, and then shook his head.

"No," he said, "I don't believe I care to," and everybody, glad for the comedy, laughed. He looked surprised. "No, now, I been saying it for all these years, and it's time somebody else had a shot. It's time to pass the prayer torch on to another generation."

That caused a stir of embarrassment again. We waited there awkward until finally, of the two of us left who might still remember how, Kathryn bowed her head and prayed.

I could imagine how it had been over the years, with Gerry holding court, how little chance a moment of awkward silence might have had. There wouldn't have been much room for it all those years of top yields and ball games, hog shows and county council affairs, but suddenly there'd turned up conversation frontage to spare. There was a moment when even Gaylene's boys stopped fidgeting and were waiting, to see if Grampa had something to say.

He didn't, but not even uneasiness lasts forever. Bright-eyed and still glowing from his workout, Norm couldn't help complimenting Kathryn on each loaded plate, each new relish and sauce, and Perri's girlfriend was quick to follow suit. Gaylene's older boy, Charles, almost dropped the gravy, which made his brother grin, and before long someone mentioned a movie that was showing up in South Bend, while somebody else had read a book. No more sure than anybody else how they'd ended up back home in Indiana for Thanksgiving, the girls weren't slow to fill the void: there were other movies to talk about and court cases, strange patients of Perri and her friend. She was the very same girl, I finally realized, who'd been on top of Mt. Fuji with Perri in the picture taken four or five years before. Across her brow was the same serious frown that she carried so easily, and that only then was lifting, as she began to relax there with Perri at her side.

Gerry's girls had his same blue eyes and set jaw; there was no doubt that they'd picked up his determination too, just a little more wisely applied. Two doctors and a lawyer at the table, plus Gaylene, who had a good job with the state. They moved easily through their leisure too—there were campaigns and concerts, kayaking and the Supreme Court, exercise plans like the one of Norm's they all envied. Their hands flashed with the heavy dishes that passed in front of me as I looked past them out the double dining room doors to the swimming pool, its tarp drooping low with soggy leaves. Kathryn had started slowly, out of her own worries or loyalty, but before long she gave in and glowed—why else would she have endured all those years of teaching English to students like me if not in the hope that for a few of us anyway there would be something to talk about, that the right words might come easily to mind.

I got away a half hour or so after dessert, but not before Gerry'd snapped out of his funk long enough to wrestle at Charles, who didn't care for it, and made his own escape to the TV room in back. Norm had begun helping with the dishes, and a movie had been rented, so nobody cared when I slipped away. Nobody but Gerry, who walked me first to the door and then out to my car. I was halfway surprised that he didn't climb in next to me, and ride with me back out to the farm.

As it was, I was combining by myself about seven that same evening, over at Smiley's, when he showed up at the west end of the field. He had Charles in tow, and they climbed up on the platform for a ride. They'd made friends with each other again, but after no more than a round or two the boy began to grow bored. We even let him steer, but by that time he was restless and uncomfortable, uneasy in the deepening night. Leaning out over the tumble of the ears, the snatch and pull of the chains, his grandfather could have stayed forever. The warm house and his family were waiting, though, and eventually the cold, unhappy boy won out.

The twenty acres I picked on Thanksgiving evening were the last we got in before a snowfall hit Friday morning, blanketing the county in white. It was worse up around the lakes, but we got our share too, four or five inches that crowded in around the cornstalks, and clung to the machinery like glue.

Gerry's girls were staying over until Sunday, when they'd all be flying back home. Excited by the weather, they were out with the boys early in the morning to hike along the roadway, made snow angels in the wide Forest Meadows front yards. The house would have been cozy when they got back, all set up for hot chocolate and board games around the kitchen table while they looked out on the snowy world outside. Gerry was with me on the Smiley place as much as he dared, combining above the drifts for a few hours late Friday afternoon. On Saturday he and Kathryn took the whole crew down to Indianapolis for the day, so the girls could look around the shops down there.

The snow had been wet as it fell, but by Friday night the temperature began to drop, plunging deep into full-fledged wintertime. To save a nickel or two at Hostetler's, Gerry was still drying corn, so Saturday night while I finished running my grain off the truck, I took advantage of unclaimed warmth, climbing up on the edge of the dryer to let the moist air and the warm, sweet smell of roasting corn rise up over my face.

It must have been about nine or ten when I got back out to the field, to find Gerry already there. I'd left the big combine idling while I was gone, but he'd shut it down and was on his back under the pickerhead, tugging at one of the chains.

"You seen how this damn thing keeps slipping?" he called out to me. "Can't get it to ever stay on."

"It's been slipping just like always. What are you doing out here? I thought you all went down to Indy."

"We just got back. While everyone's having a little dinner, I thought I'd come out and see how you were doing. Figured I'd tighten this up some while I was at it. This damn fifth row's been nothing but trouble all year long."

It'd been an irritant, all right, but on a cold night like that I would have just as soon left it. Instead I went back for my flashlight, and we tugged and pried a good twenty minutes until the chain finally slipped back on. When it had, we tightened everything up again, rolling in the snow to gather tools.

"Doggone that thing anyway," Gerry said. "Don't know why they can't build things to last."

"We ain't got but a couple of hundred acres left," I said. "I reckon we'll manage. There's a hose there, though, on the pickerhead that's got a weak spot. You're gonna want to pick up one of those."

"Yeah," he said, "I reckon so. Come on, we've wrestled this damn machinery long enough for one evening. Let's warm up a minute before we call it a night."

The pickup had been sitting for a long time in the cold itself by then, and Gerry had to pump at it a couple of minutes to get it to start. While the heater built up, we sat next to each other like a couple of statues, too cold to even move. Gradually, though, the warm began to win out, and we could sink back in the front seat to relax.

"Well," Gerry said, "you're probably ready to head on home."

I didn't care one way or another, but I wasn't the one with my family waiting up for me. All around us out the cab windows lay a dull, thick layer of white, pale under a deep black sky. When Gerry didn't seem in any hurry to go anywhere, I loosened my coveralls at the neck. He sat back next to me with his pant legs jammed down into rubber boots, his head hidden under an old winter cap that had cloth flaps on the sides, sticking out at the ears.

"You enjoy the kids?" he asked.

"What kids?"

"The kids, my girls. Oh, they appreciated the chance to see you, I know they did. Perri still remembers you, wanted to know what you'd been up to all these years. It's been like a tonic for Kathryn having those young people around. She couldn't care no more about them if they were her own, and that's a hell of a thing to say about anybody. Right from the first, she took to them just like they were hers.

"Gaylene's boys are fun, of course, and then that Norm, he's a hell of a nice fella too. He ain't like we used to be, feeling he has to be out making a good impression all the time. Back when I courted Charlotte, I spent more time with her damn dad than I did with her! I'd no sooner show up at their place than he'd have me working— loading out hogs, cutting silage. Why, I'd be so damn sweaty by the time I finally got a few minutes to sit down with her that I'm surprised she didn't drive me away. It ain't never been like that with old Norm. He's as likely to be reading a book as anything, or helping Kathryn get things picked up out in the kitchen. That makes it nice for a woman, it really does."

Gerry shifted behind the wheel. "Ain't Purdue up in Alaska or something, at a tournament? Let's see if they got it on."

He slipped off his gloves to fiddle with the dial, sliding through a lineup of aggrieved country singers and machined L.A. melodies to finally find the game. "I bet it's cold enough up there in Anchorage," he remarked, and only then seemed to notice that the cab had finally got warm itself. He pulled the zipper of his coveralls down to his belly.

"Yeah, they both of them girls got good professions, and that's something a fella can be proud of. Gaylene's got her husband and the boys, and that Charles is a hell of a bright kid. Goes to space camps and ocean camps and I don't know what all. I ain't forgetting Perri either, I'm just as proud of her. A doctor, of course, but I'm just glad she's got that little Carrie as a friend too. Carrie's a real *good* friend, is what I'm saying, and that's fine. People see things a little different now, so it saves on the heartbreak."

"Times have changed," I said.

"And for the better," he added reflexively, taking off his hat. He settled back in his seat. "We ain't gonna be out here long, let me just pick up the score. You ain't heard it yet, have you?"

With the combine shut down there wasn't anything else for us to do out there that night, and Gerry had his family, bright daughters and grandkids, gliding through their last hours back at the house. Still, it was me that he sat with, both of us draped in our heavy clothes and looking out into cold fields all around. The first half of the basketball game ended, and we daydreamed our separate ways through the news.

"I been working you awful hard," he said, early in the second half. "I know you're gonna want to get home." That's what he said, but still we sat idling in the pickup, listening to sweaty gym sounds and a young season's hopeful cheering half a continent away. We listened to the Boilermakers build up a lead only to lose it, before finally pulling away at the end.

"You know," Gerry said, "I appreciate you going around and getting my signs down for me like you did. That Lake woman's all set to go now, I guess. Come January they'll swear her in. I don't mind leaving all that behind, I guess I told you. Not a bit. The council license plates and crap like that, I don't need none of it anymore. The benefits were good, of course, and the insurance is something a fella kind of hates to lose. About twenty years ago the commissioners got scared about all those riots in the cities and voted us in a hell of a package, life insurance like you wouldn't believe. I guess they thought somebody was gonna go crazy in Chicago and come down here and shoot us or something."

He laughed. The post-game interview had given way to a kind of jazzy big-band sound, an old-fashioned music that still managed to hold out somehow, down at one corner of the AM dial. Gerry tapped his thick fingers in time.

"Arthur," he said, "there's been something I been meaning to ask you. Now, think about this, maybe you already do. Crack your window there for a minute and look at them stars. I want you to look at all them sitting up there."

He was waiting, so I rolled down the window far enough to see past the dashlights to the sky. The air was cold and fresh, held at bay by the heater's sturdy fan.

"I worked outside all my life, and always liked it, seeing them stars up there above me. You been to school since I have, so what are there, hundreds of them damn things?"

"Thousands," I said, considering.

"Hell, I figured I was probably on the low side. But a whole hell of a lot of them anyway. I was right about that."

I had to agree, and we leaned over to our respective windows to peer up at them, spread out above the snow.

"I don't reckon Haskell County would show up too big from out there, do you think?"

"What do you mean?"

"I mean among all them stars. Haskell County don't amount to very much. That's what I'm saying."

"Well," I said, "it depends on how you look at it."

"No, now damn it," he said, "you're beginning to sound like all them kids back at the house. I done told you how I'm looking at it. I'm talking about this goddamn little speck of Indiana. It don't add up to very much."

"All right, it doesn't."

That still didn't satisfy him, though, and he turned back around to me to scold. "You don't have to agree, for God's sake, Arthur, I'm just trying to have a little conversation. Don't be so doggone backward all the time. You got opinions, and it so happens I want to hear one. Don't feel like you have to agree with me if you don't."

"Now, why in the hell," I asked him, finally irritated, "would I feel like I have to agree with you? This time, it so happens, you got it right. Dead center. It don't amount to a goddamn thing, Haskell County. It ain't even a drop in the ocean. It don't mean nothing. Nothing at all."

No doubt I was on the backward side—it felt like more than I'd said to Gerry in half a year. It must have been enough, though, because he nodded as he leaned back behind the wheel. The station we'd been listening to had gone off the air by then, the Marine Band's national anthem spinning out while we watched the sky.

"You know," he said, "it's funny, but I ain't sleeping like I used to. There's not a farmer anymore who does, I don't reckon, but it used to be I'd just fall into bed and die. Now I got dreams and all kinds of wild things. You know what I mean? You ever have dreams like that? You ever have dreams?"

I shrugged. "I guess I've had some dreams."

344

"I had one just the other night. The other night I dreamt I was young again. Young, just starting out, with Charlotte as my bride. I mean, there Kathryn is lying right beside me—my Lord, we been married damn near fifteen years ourselves. But Charlotte was my wife, the girls were still little, and I was back on that goddamn old Bremer place in the mud. Back with a little four-share plow, new to the county, wrestling that doggone muck. All these damn hard years still ahead. And you know, the hell of it is, I was ready! I felt so goddamn full of life, Arthur, that I was ready, all set to go at it again."

I'd begun to watch him by that time, curious.

"About then, of course, along about that time of night anymore, I got to get up and use the rest room. So I march in there, all full of ginger, I turn on the light, and I'll be damned if this doggone old bald-headed man hadn't got in there first. Just standing there looking back at me. I couldn't believe my eyes; why, it took a minute to even recognize that goddamn broke old bastard there in the mirror, to figure out he was me. It just don't seem possible, not hardly possible at all."

The windshield had some of the same truth curving back in front of us, a puffy sort of green blob at the steering wheel, another one, narrower, that was me sitting off to the side. Gerry looked past us, though, out over the hood.

"And the whole time it seems like it wasn't even hardly yesterday that I was still a little boy. Out with my own dad picking rocks over there near Sharpsville, shucking corn, hurrying around to meet Charlotte after school." He frowned. "But then again I never knew all this could happen in a life. I never thought I'd ever get divorced, not in a million years. I never thought I'd have no goddamn heart attack or whatever the hell it was. I didn't think old Al Lantz would give out on me, before we got our share of things done. It don't seem possible, really, that time can leave one person so far behind."

He considered the combine at a distance, shaded black against the snow.

"I been thinking lately about Homer Jackins," he told me then. "Old Homer thought prices were bad in his lifetime, he ought to have stayed around for this. Rich told me Homer didn't have nothing at the end, not a doggone pot to cook in when he died. Farmers and Merchants had him on a doggone allowance, if you can believe it, old Homer had to go in and beg spending money like a boy. But now, see, the hell of it is that his wife won't ever want for nothing. Nothing at all. Insurance has her in an apartment across from the Burger King, about twice as nice as that old barn they lived in down south. His boy Denny don't have to fight the weather no more, he's got a body shop over in Potomac. His sister and him can look after their own families for a change. You got to give old Homer that much, he went out prepared."

The broad sky of stars lay above us forgotten as we leaned back together in the cab. Gerry'd taken on the same bulldog look that his girls had inherited, chin jutting out at the world.

"Of course, it always helps to have some old so-and-so like Gerry Maars around, to smooth things along the way. They're suspicious, them damn insurance companies — they've held on to a man's money so damn long, they start thinking it's theirs. And then Freddy Witherspoon, the coroner, he's about as picky as an old maid. I wasn't back from Cleveland a week when I had to have Kathryn take me over to his funeral home, had to go back with him into his office and explain. A couple of days later out comes the amended certificate — accidental death just as sure as the world. People forget that those kinds of things happen. They forget the way things work out."

He'd rolled up his window and was looking at me expectantly. "You see what I mean? You see how it goes?"

"What's to see? You fixed the report."

"No, damn it, not that. Freddy was just doing his job. I mean about what happened out there. Accidents. They happen."

"Accidents happen," I said. He was watching like I was on the edge of something profound. "All right, accidents happen. That ain't so hard to understand."

"You know, your foot can slip, a sleeve gets caught, them things happen. That's what I'm trying to say. It happened to old Homer Jackins, and he spent his whole life around machinery. It happened to that Ziegler boy two years ago over near Richland Center, to Bill Blaze the year before that over past Holloway's. It happens. And it can happen to —"

346

"Anybody," I said, and Gerry nodded.

"That's right, by God, you got it. It sure can. To anybody. That's exactly right. That's exactly what I was trying to say."

Whatever he'd been working around to that fall, however it was that he'd wanted me to end up out there with him that Saturday night, while his girls, tired of waiting, went off to bed back at the house, he finally seemed satisfied. He dropped the truck into gear, rocking it out of the icy dips where we'd settled. He'd gone maybe a dozen feet before he put on the brakes.

"You don't want one of them sodas back there, do you, before we go? The ones in the cooler?"

"Good Lord, Gerry," I said, "they've been frozen for hours. It's after midnight. I don't need no soda."

"Well, I don't want you going thirsty now, that's for sure. Not when I got all those damn things bought and paid for, just sitting back there in the garage. I thought we'd use up some over the holidays, but Perri and them don't seem to care for pop like they used to. Don't want the boys drinking it, either, all that sugar's bad for the teeth. But I don't want you or Kathryn, I don't want nobody, wanting anything on my account. Stop by and pick up a whole case of them sometime, if you want to, whether I'm around the house there or not."

For all the different reasons a man might linger, and even then not be ready to go home, sooner or later there comes a time when he has to. I could have walked easy enough to my car, but Gerry must have wanted me with him that much longer, anyway, because he wouldn't let me climb out. Instead he wheeled a wide circle around on the snow, sliding us the hundred yards back along the end rows to where I'd parked.

FIFTEEN

Their bright auger wagons and grain trucks were all in the sheds, but Ray Stewart's boys were still managing to get a little field work done that December before they fled to the islands. I saw them at a distance putting behind them the fall plowing, while Gerry and I made the move to the south. It's a long way down there from Tippy Valley, so I was surprised late one afternoon, while combining on the Jackins acres, to see Byron's Bronco pull into the field. The seasons had changed twice since I'd last talked to my brother that bright early morning in July. Bundled in his down winter coat and a navy stocking cap, he waited for me in the end rows until I pulled around.

"Gerry gone?"

I nodded. "He's run off on business somewhere again. Hasn't been out here all day."

"You working alone?"

I looked around. "I'll be darned. I guess I am."

My brother nodded. "I was thinking maybe you were."

He shuffled back and forth below me in the snow, his school shoes wet and glistening. Finally I swung open the door.

"You want to just stand out there, or you want to come along? I'd like to get this field in tonight if I can."

Byron mounted the muddy duals to squeeze in too, his shoulder digging into my ribs as he settled onto the unlucky toolbox. He unzipped his jacket, watching as I moved through the corn.

"Good-looking crop," he observed, and I agreed.

"The family all right?"

"Oh yeah," he said, "they're doing fine."

With that much established, we rode in silence to the far end of the field. I braked just short of the fencerow, swung east twenty feet, and started back south.

"How's Gerry doing?" he asked, still looking straight ahead.

"Seems all right, just that stiff shoulder bothering him at night. His girls were in town, and then we went late yesterday, after we got moved down here. If the weather holds, we should get done before long. There's the field work, all the disking, probably move into that sometime next week."

"They're calling him in," my brother said.

"It's just the size of the crop that's kept us out here. Look how thick that corn is. You ever remember seeing corn like that?"

"Arthur, it's true. The bank's going to call Gerry's loan."

I kept the pickerhead steady, backing out and then in again to buck through a low spot. "Just damn rumors, Byron, we've been hearing them all our lives."

"This time it's going to happen. You know Carol Sue Eller that I work with? Teaches French? Her husband Mickey's at the bank. He told her for sure. They're calling him in."

"Is that the big talk around the teachers' table, then? Gerry going broke?"

"It's been mentioned. People can't help but wonder."

I checked over my shoulder to the hopper. "So how is it, anyway, back in front of the classroom? You making them mind?"

Checked momentarily, Byron paused to think. "It's all right. Not as many headaches. We count on Kendra's hours more now than we used to. That Lake boy's walking again, but all the litigation's made it hard. Arthur, you ought to listen to me a minute. It's true about Gerry. Carol Sue knows."

"I imagine there's other banks."

On his own easy terms with disasters, my brother shook his head. "I kind of doubt it. The auditors had a fit this fall, is what Mickey told her. It was hundreds of thousands of dollars he was into them for, well over a million. He couldn't even keep up the interest these last few years."

You think sometimes about why anyone would be a French teacher way out there in the country, other than to lord it over the rest. Then there was Mickey Eller to keep her company, a stuck-up bastard in his own right, thinking the world should bow down to him just because he shuffles papers at the bank. Secretaries are supposed to have something to do with secrets, and bank tellers never tell, but people will still somehow get their bones to chew on anyway, never uncurious to see the next one go down.

"His houses are still free and clear? That land down in Florida?"

"Oh, no," Byron said. He shook his head. "It's all of it gone. Gone, gone. Mortgaged two and three times over, these last few years, just to keep crops in the field. A man Gerry's age could go the rest of his life trying to work it down and never make a dent. The bank's going to get hit hard enough the way it is. Nobody can figure what Al Lantz was thinking all those years.

"Rich won't serve the papers, none of his deputies will either, so it's made for a lot of commotion down at the courthouse. Carol Lee said they've called all the way up to Warsaw, trying to get somebody from there."

We rode together another hundred yards. It was hard to believe how good that corn had turned out to be, down south, every bit as fine as Gerry dreamed. When I craned my neck up to look in the grain hopper, it was already halfway full. I slowed to a stop.

"You want to drive?"

Byron rustled his quilted coat next to me to hold up his palms. "Oh no, Arthur, go ahead. I've never driven anything like this."

"It ain't so hard," I said, throttling down. "Come on, damn it, it's gonna be the bank's anyway, if Mickey Eller has his way. Just come over here and drive. You won't hurt anything."

Embarrassed, my brother laughed. "No, really, I can't. I haven't picked corn in twenty years."

He protested some more, but considering his natural slowness about things, didn't waste all that much time getting behind the wheel. There's a first and last chance for everything, and I guess he finally figured out it was likely to be both. He could drive the combine or not, but even if he lived like a Buddhist a hundred lifetimes, a place for him high up behind that steering wheel would never come open again. Still in that silly stocking cap, he settled into the seat. I got him used to the hydrostat as we rolled back and forth across the stubble. When he was ready, I reached across to throw the big diesel into gear.

"Take it a little lower even, if you want to," I told him after our first fifty yards, "just watch for the plug-ups," and then settled back on the toolbox to watch.

Byron, like his boy, always did have a good steady hand. That much you could grant him; he sat hunched forward with his lips pursed, concentrating on the dry stalks below. He expected me any minute to take over again, but I guess it was my own turn, finally, to be comforted. Either that or I was getting as bad as Gerry Maars, not willing to let another man break away. For his part Byron was so caught up in that old International that we unloaded not once but three or four times more, while his dinner hour receded behind him. We must have gone a good two hours together down there at Jackins' before my brother finally got his fill, climbed down past me to his Bronco, and went home.

SIXTEEN

It takes a good couple of lifetimes, you have to figure, to build up an operation; a hell of a lot less when it begins to fall apart. When I got back to the farmhouse that night, the barnyard was dark, but it wasn't until I got into the house that I found out the electricity had been shut off at the box. It was too late to do anything then, so I waited until the next morning to re-hook the line myself. It's always a little tricky when the wires are live, and I might have preferred it a little warmer for my numbing fingers, but in twenty minutes I had it licked. A farmer's a little like an old hog: he might prefer the slop brought down to his pen, but still can get by pretty handsome out there ranging on his own.

After breakfast I didn't go out to combine right away: I'd seen again, dumping Byron's loads, that the hose holding up the pickerhead had gotten worse. Puffed white with fatigue, it was a danger, and when I didn't hear from Gerry, I drove up to Plymouth to get another one. I was accustomed enough to spending his money, I guess, still slow to believe it was gone. Others weren't so faithful: word traveled fast enough that the countermen balked when I tried to put it on account. I ending up just paying for it myself.

I don't know whether he'd had to play electrician at his own house that morning, but when I got back down to Jackins', Gerry was already there and dressed for field work, trudging out to the combine. As I pulled in I saw Kathryn's car too. She'd parked the little Subaru on the side ditch, to follow him out into the mud.

She'd caught up just short of the combine, but then he broke away. He threw his water jug up onto the platform, and was just starting to pull himself up when he saw me. He dropped back to the ground.

"And say, there," he called back to her, "you still got that checkbook? You got it? Give Arthur his check, write it out to him right now. Arthur, just throw that damn hose in the pickup. I'm going out to pick corn. You go on into town. Kathryn's gonna give you your check. Take it right on in there and cash it. Don't loll around now, take it in and get it cashed."

When I looked over at Kathryn, she was crying.

"Honey, now," he said, "don't be like that. It don't do no good to hang our heads. Get Arthur his check. Don't forget to put down all his hours, either. Put down the other night, when I had him out late. Make sure you get that down too."

He started climbing again, bellying his way stiffly up over the muddy dual. He yelled back to me when he'd made it to the cab. "And fill that damn car of yours up, I don't want you burning your own gas. Fill it up!"

He squeezed inside and slammed the door. "Go on!" we saw him mouthing, shooing us like a couple of sheep. The diesel roared up in front of us, and he spun away into the field.

"I don't need no check," I told her as soon as the combine had moved away.

Kathryn was still crying, walking out ahead of me, pulling to find an edge of the Kleenex that she'd balled up in her hand. Finally she gave up, wiping across her eyes with her sleeve. At the Subaru she reached under the seat for their big looseleaf book of checks.

"I don't need a check," I told her again, but she shook her head angrily.

"You might as well have it," she said, "it doesn't matter now. All morning he's been after me. 'Make sure Arthur gets his check. As soon as we see him, make sure he gets it.' There's a bonus there too, so take it. No, take it. Cash it at Hostetler's, they still have our grain. Take the pickup like he said."

I stood there for a minute in the end rows with Kathryn crying next to me, while we watched the combine far out across the field. Then I doubled the check to fit in my breast pocket and rode Gerry's pickup into town.

SEVENTEEN

When I got back out to the field, Gerry almost had another truck filled. While I took it over to the drying setup, he moved to the next field south. We only worked until about nine that night, and the next two days I worked alone. Indifferent as they were to finance, bearings would still shatter, and pins tend to shear, but I made the repairs and kept going. Gerry was back the third day and still nothing happened, but when you think back, it makes plenty of sense. The bank owned a fair number of the county's combines, one way or another, but Carol Lee's Mickey wasn't too likely to round up the other loan officers so they could come out and pick field corn themselves. That much of the fall's bounty was left to us.

The third day when Gerry came out he sent me back to the prairie, to start disking stalks up there. I worked another full day while the combine sat idle, with Gerry, dressed for business, ranging off in his Fleetwood yet again. I was on my dad's old acreage the next afternoon, making a turn at the road near Byron's, when I saw him, back in his coveralls, waiting up next to the barn.

After the fits and starts of harvesting it had felt good to be moving easily again, locked in a steady fourth gear of the tractor as I turned frozen ground in my wake. Gerry raised up a hand to flag me down.

"Hey there," he called, "how's it going?"

"Fine. No excitement to speak of. Just getting this field put away."

"That's good. Hell of a day, don't you think? Don't often get pretty days like this."

I looked around. The December morning had dawned clear enough, but by noon the winter sun had been crowded out by a low cover of clouds. In its absence the day was growing cold. I dropped back on the tractor's idle and jumped down.

"I'm on my way back down to the Jackins place," he said, "so I thought I might come by and see if you needed anything. I thought I'd stop by and see if you were okay."

"I might as well come haul for you a while. There ain't no hurry on these stalks."

"No, no," he said quickly, "I got it. I don't want you running all over the county. You go ahead and finish this. Oh, and you know that hose? The one you brought back from Plymouth? I'm gonna take that with me. Gonna put it on this morning."

For some reason I remember that it especially irritated me, just the foolishness of it, me up in the warm cab disking while he wrestled with a dirty job like a hose. "I told you I'd put that damn thing on, I been wanting to all week. Let me take care of it."

"No, now, it's okay. I'm gonna do it. I know you would have, but I had it with me in the car there, so you never had a chance. I been saying, though, off and on all week, that I was gonna get to it. You probably heard me say that."

"Maybe," I said, curious.

Hands in his pockets, Gerry rocked back and forth in the stubble. "I'm gonna put that new one on, that's what I'm planning. But then again, I may do a couple of rounds. Any number of fellas might do that." He checked me out of the corner of his eye. "I say a lot of folks do that very same thing. Put it off."

He was already nodding for me, so I joined him. "They do."

"They do. It ain't wise, but they do. I don't know hardly anybody who could say different. Then, of course, there's that chain that's been nagging us. We been fighting that fifth row on the pickerhead all season long."

The last and slowest disciple, it was only gradually that I understood. I remember wondering a funny thing: how a person picks out what he's going to wear on a day like that. I guess with a farmer it's easy enough: Gerry had on his same old coveralls, drawn up over an old hooded sweatshirt. He'd always been partial to that sweatshirt, it seemed like, never failing to fish it out of the pile of quilted vests and jackets he kept jammed under the front seat of the truck. I looked Gerry in the eye then and nodded.

He sighed, in relief maybe, to know that I understood. He nodded toward the barn.

"I was sitting up on the lane there just now, thinking about the field of beans we had out here. I was thinking how I wish your dad could have seen them. I wish he could have seen some of that damn corn we had out here too. He never would have believed it in a million years."

"No," I said, "I doubt that he would have."

He stepped up beside me. "You and me have had our differences on things, I know. We ain't always seen things exactly the same. But a man never knows what blessings the good Lord's gonna send. He sent me you, these last two or three years. I'll always appreciate you coming back and helping me that spring. I always will. I appreciate you staying on the summer before last, I know it wasn't an easy thing to do. Helping out after I went down last year. I just wish I could thank you somehow, had something to pass on that would be yours. A fella'd feel like he'd done something if he could just do that."

"I never wanted a damn thing," I told him, and Gerry laughed.

"Well, you come to the right place, then, anyway, that's for sure. And hell, it would have just caused problems anyway. My family, Kathryn, they ain't got nothing to fight over now. And oh, they might have. Gaylene and Perri got a lot of Charlotte in them, they really do."

He looked over the empty field, up the low winter slope toward Byron's.

"My girls," he said, "young people, I wanted them to have confidence about things. I just wanted them to get a kick out of life. Not be so afraid of it all the time. And the way they turned out, they're different. They ain't like we used to be. For my girls, for a lot of them anymore, there just ain't no damn limits on things. It's all supposed to work out, see. There ain't supposed to be nothing go wrong in their world at all.

"I never had to baby you none, Arthur, you already knew the

score. You already knew how things can turn out. A fella appreciates that when it comes to a pinch." He looked at me a last time, appraising. "'Course, you knew how to work, too, and a man's always grateful for that."

The four-wheel drive may still have been in pieces down in Beechum, but the old 1086 rumbled on peacefully beside us; there's a certain pleasure in having one piece of machinery that still did its job. Gerry took a minute to stand under it with me before he finally moved away.

"Well, ain't nothing getting done this way, I guess. A fella gets a little older, he just don't want to get to his chores. You seen that I got that hose now, and that I was going to put it on. I had that in mind the last time you seen me."

I nodded, but that wasn't good enough for Gerry Maars, he still had to coach me. "You seen me just this afternoon. I told you when I stopped out here that I was going to replace it. I'd been planning to all along."

"That's what you told me, damn it, I heard you. I ain't a damn fool. That's what you said you were going to do."

"I can count on you, then. It means something to me that I can."

"Yes," I told him, "you can."

"Well, then," he said, "be good. Give Kathryn a hand for a little while, if you would, until things get straightened around some. It shouldn't take too long. Keep an eye on that Hi-tran on this tractor too; I seen last evening that it was leaking by the seal. You got to check it now and then."

"I will."

"Don't trust the gauge, it ain't worth a damn. You think if a fella puts out forty thousand dollars for something, it might last for a while."

With that final complaint, then, he left me, stumping back across the end rows to his car.

EIGHTEEN

There was probably a handful still in the tractor cab somewhere, or out in the glove compartment of the pickup, buried down under the bills. I'd found one not two or three weeks earlier, as a matter of fact, when I was digging down to look for a fuse: one of the cards that Gerry had handed out in an earlier campaign, eight or twelve years before. Business card–sized, it sported a picture of him — thinner and with more hair, back then not even completely gray. The bold text next to it was standard too, trumpeting Gerry Maars for council on the Republican ticket. The back of it, though, is what I would have liked to see. In those idle three and a half inches Gerry'd managed to squeeze in the Pyramid of Success, a miniaturized version of what he'd copied down from the great Johnny Wooden, at a seed company dinner the winter before.

It made sense in a way, too, because Johnny Wooden had been a Hoosier farm boy himself, long before basketball brought him fame in the west. There were small blocks in the triangle for Industriousness and Friendship, for Loyalty and Cooperation, with Enthusiasm making five at the base. Just above were Self-Control and Alertness, Initiative and Intentness; Team Spirit, Confidence, and Skill. Faith, Fight and Patience, Integrity and Poise — they led up like certain stair steps to the pinnacle of Competitive Greatness, alone at the top of the heap. Johnny Wooden had retired to the banquet circuit in time to imagine that all those fine qualities might still mean something, while Gerry'd hung on just a little longer than that.

I churned steadily east toward Byron's, bounced up the disk blades as I turned, and made my way back to the west. The county seemed deserted; it was hard not to think of the people who had still been streaming out to catch Gerry's ear when I'd first been back from the boats, how they'd lined up to talk to him in the fields. In fairness, a lot of them were already gone themselves, and for that matter he would have been a lot harder to find, ranging from the prairie down through his scattered acreage to the south. Down into neighborhoods that weren't his, that for that matter weren't really anybody's. Ahead of me back on the prairie was Byron's closed-up little ranch house. When I turned to go west, there was the old barn of my dad's and the rest of Gerry's machinery, scattered around the lot. I bumped up the blades as I came over the end rows and started back across to the east.

The clouds had settled lower above the ditch bank; the prairie closed in black and tumbled around the cab. A string of sparrows with their special providence had settled on the phone wires along the roadside. As I came up on my passes in front of Byron's, they would scatter, settling in again when I'd swung back away. When twenty more minutes had passed, there was finally some sign of humanity: one of the big trucks from Tattman's Welding rose up to bump across the Big Four tracks, slowing at the stop sign before crossing in front of Byron's just ahead. It was Roger Richardson or Wilbur Sutton most likely, but I couldn't, from the cab, make out which. Almost within hailing distance, whoever it was accelerated, rumbling past Shaw's Woods and out of sight. As I disked I imagined the big truck making its own steady way down through the county, until I'd finally lost track of it in my mind's eye as well.

I didn't fault Gerry Maars: it was hard to imagine him lurking in the background at a sheriff's sale, standing back while other men climbed on his equipment or went sifting through his tools. The odd thing, I suppose, is to know that I wasn't all that much different from those other boys after all, Byron and the rest. I admired Gerry too, if truth be told, his eagerness and ministry, his insistence on himself in the face of the world. If only I could have believed, I would have been scrambling up those pyramid steps right behind him, up past the sky to the sun. As it was, some come late to their calling, and mine in this vast unwatched workplace had turned out to be the simplest of all: to go steadily forward without weakening, back and forth across an empty winter field.

By that time, though, I was already hurrying. Byron's was closer, but it would have been locked up anyway, and I swung through those east end rows, dropping the transmission into eighth. The big diesel rocked in complaint; as I let out on the throttle, a black, oily fog of half-burnt fuel rolled up and over the cab. Faithfully, though, the old tractor built back up against its load, until I was crashing through the dry stalks ahead of me, disk blades bouncing and sliding, the engine raised high to a whine. It was still shaking and shuddering at the other end as I slid to a stop in the barn lot and leaped out, half-falling to the ground.

My first stop was the shop phone, where I spun out the familiar number to Tattman's in town. Dale Junior was doing the dispatching, and no less than the Plymouth countermen, he grew wary when he heard it was me.

"Gerry still picking corn?" he said carefully. "I heard he was done."

"Dale," I said, "I saw Wilbur Sutton go by here a little while ago, him or Roger Richardson, one. Somebody else in the cab, too, heading out 600 East. Can you reach them on the radio?"

"Well," he said, "I might, but they got a call they're going out to. Can't really say when they'd get done. We're kind of booked up right now, is what it is."

"You've got to get them on the radio right away. Get them turned around and back to the old Jackins place, the field that sits south of the ditch. Just hurry. You've got to hurry. You got to get them out there right away."

It helps to never, over a lifetime, have asked a favor: people tend to listen a little closer when you do. It didn't take Dale Junior all that long to decide.

"You gonna meet them there? All right, Arthur, damn it, I'm calling them. You go ahead. I'll get them out there just as fast as I can."

NINETEEN

Not since the early spring day when Gerry'd taken me down to show off that new Jackins land had it really mattered to me how far away it was that he'd moved. I'd walked it that day, of course, strolling north, but now I was pushing the old pickup like Gerry Maars himself, impatiently standing hard on the accelerator to speed ever faster along narrow and abandoned blacktop roads. Four miles south was the gravel pit; another mile farther and the road jogged right, the two dozen or so yards needed to fit in another section as the earth widened out. A blue heron that had settled on a ditch bridge was slow to respond, rousing itself to just clear the windshield as I bore down on it and past. An old schoolhouse flashed by in a blur of winter brambles and weeds; there was the occasional bleak farmhouse — the whole countryside lay fallow by then except for me, racing that rattling pickup as fast as I could.

The Jackins house had been rented out: an old Dodge van and two stripped-down Harleys camped out on the unmowed front lawn. An orange blanket that hung over the wide front window did the work of curtains, a rusted metal swing set lay on its side by the drive. At one crossroad I was already scanning for the next, and from the Holloway turn on I'd been searching the roads and distant fencerows for the big tan-colored welder's truck. Dale Junior must have hung up and just gone back to his account books, because there was nothing to be seen at half a mile, only Gerry's Fleetwood and the old red combine pulled in close along the ditch bank, pointed out into the field.

As I jumped from the cab, the red dog was up to greet me, bouncing through the beans from the front of the combine, waving its burr-matted tail like a flag. Its good-natured *woof* was lost in the huge roar of the combine's diesel, revved up as high as it could go. I pushed past the dog and the deserted cab to the pickerhead, raised high and quivering, shaking with the engine's strain against itself.

Gerry hadn't gone broke because of footwear, anyway. I came up that afternoon on the same pair of old work shoes that had been sticking out from beneath the disk at the Bremer place the day I first went to work. Only now they were under the pickerhead, a clever setup really; Ray Stewart wasn't the only one who could think ahead. The worn hose was still in place, its weak spot bulging ever wider as the whole heavy pickerhead rocked back against the combine, forced ever harder at the end of its reach. When the red dog bumped off me and into Gerry's legs, the work shoes kicked out to keep it away. I dropped down to peer under the row guides, only to run into Gerry's face glaring out at me from the gloom.

"Go on, get out of here!" is what he must have been shouting, his words swallowed up long before they got to me. In one hand he held a wrench, while with the free one he waved me away from him, kicked up his heels in my face.

I looked up to the combine and back to him.

"Go on!" he was yelling. "Go on!"

There's no doubt we come into the world the hard way, choking and fighting for the light. It's the odd man who would, I suppose, of his own volition, go back to the narrow and dark. I was a little worse trained, though, as it turned out, than a forgotten old farm dog. Less trustworthy, when it came right down to it, than Shawn, or Ronnie Vinton, because I left Old Red outside and climbed underneath the pickerhead myself.

I had to come in past those kicking old work shoes, slide past a free-swinging wrench. If not a heavy pickerhead bouncing above us, then what once might have scared a boy was the face Gerry Maars turned on me right about then, jaw jutting and bloodshot red eyes bugged out and blazing, a layer of corn dust shaken over him like a mask.

"Get the hell out of here!" he shouted. "What are you doing? I told you to stay on the job."

I wiggled back until we were shoulder to shoulder. "That chain slipping again?"

"The hell with the chain. I done told you how it was. Now get out of here!"

Without old Gerry Maars to run interference, with insurance running out and the bank closing in, he'd had to be crafty. The tools were spread out on either side of him; a new link kit was shrink-wrapped in its plastic package on the ground.

Even cheek to cheek with him, I had to shout to be heard. "Hand me that seven-eighths that you got on the other side there. I'll give it a turn while you push up."

The engine roared above us so hard it made my ears ache all the way down to my throat, and our eyes teared from the steady drizzle of dust.

"Damn it," he shouted, "I got it. Get out! Go on now, I'm telling you, get out!"

The pickerhead jerked hard and dropped; the hose must have ballooned out another inch, because the steel struts and chains fell a half a foot above us. I lay back to study the cool, shadowed logic of the cutting assembly as it shook above my head. It was a miracle, really, the combine, developed over all those years just so one man could finally be alone.

Gerry kicked again at the red dog, who ducked in, exuberant, at our feet. He even tapped at the chain a couple times, pretending for all of two seconds before he turned back on me. "Damn it, I don't need you here, go on! I don't want you around!" He jerked his head to the side. "Go get me a pry bar out of the truck if you want to be useful. That's what the hell I need. Hurry up and go for it. Now! Go on!"

The pickerhead danced above us while next to me Gerry wiggled, making like he was about to roll out. "I'll go get it myself if I have to. Damn it, go ahead, and I'm coming. You go on first, I'm right behind."

"Nobody's stopping you," I yelled back. "Go ahead."

By that time he'd managed to get a fat knee up into my back and was shoving at my shoulder with his hand. I wasn't any wilting daisy myself, though, had grown up over the years to be a man. Able enough to hold my own that he was still wrestling at me a minute later when we saw, in the thin slice of outside that remained to us, the big welding truck as it bounced up into the field.

"What the hell we got now, a goddamn convention? Is that what we got? All right now. All right. I'm coming. Go on ahead and get out."

I went on ahead and got out, rolling into the gray cold of late afternoon. A moment later Gerry followed; we stood for a moment half-dazed before the angry scream of the motor, rocking against its bolts above the cab. Wilbur Sutton, strolling toward us around the duals, grabbed playfully at the red dog's ears, slapping at him with his leather gloves.

"Hey, Gerry," he shouted, "Arthur. How goes it?"

His face drained of color beneath the corn-dust mask, Gerry

looked back at him with hollow eyes. It's one thing to have it all figured down to your last minutes alive under a pickerhead, another to
be facing daylight and other people again, fresh air all around. Wilbur
reached down to pound Old Red on the flanks.

"Kind of loud, ain't it? I say, ain't it kind of loud?"

Gerry looked at him blankly.

Wilbur pointed up to the cab. "You sure you want the idle set that
high? The idle on that diesel! That how you want it set?"

Gerry stared at him, and back over at me then, for the longest
time, until finally he shook his head.

"Go on up and shut it down, damn it, Arthur. Shut it down all the
way."

Of course, a wise man would have done that first, as soon as he'd
got out to the field, but the thought had never even crossed my mind.
I was pulling myself up onto the platform when the hydraulic line
finally burst, spraying like a fire hose over the row guides and ground,
spinning up to soak down the front of the cab. The head fell with a
solid four-ton crash into the dirt. There came a rushing in of the quiet
winter world around us, as I cut back on the engine until it died.

Wilbur shook his head, hitting at his ears as if to clear them.
"That's kind of an improvement, don't you reckon? It ain't quite so
hard to hear yourself think." He couldn't help looking at Gerry and
back up to me, past us to the fallen pickerhead and ruptured hose, as
it drained steaming Hi-tran into the mud.

"Um," he said, "Dale Junior said you had some kind of job out
here."

"Hell, ask Arthur," Gerry said sourly. "He's the one deciding how
things ought to be done."

He turned his back on us and stumped away. It was while I was
climbing down again across the duals that I saw the boy, hanging back
by the truck. He must have been sixteen or seventeen, with limp
blond hair that hung down from a ragged wool cap that might have
been a poor cousin of Byron's. Shivering in a jean jacket, he looked
every bit as unhappy as Gerry was that the four of us had found ourselves together in the late-afternoon cold.

"Well," I said, "since I'm the one deciding, we might as well put some heat on this shaft back here. There's a bearing going out, and the ring hasn't quite wanted to budge."

Under the circumstances it was a repair that could have waited, probably forever, but I didn't want Wilbur to leave. The boy kept a wide berth as the welder brushed past him on his way back to the truck, watching with hooded eyes as he ranged through his metal lockers for a torch. He climbed up into the bed when Wilbur told him to, wrestling the acetylene tank back to the lift.

The shaft bearing that had occurred to me was back behind one of the rear wheels. While I got the drive cover off, Wilbur divided his time between adjusting his flame and glancing back over his shoulder at Gerry, pale and slump-shouldered a dozen yards away. In their trips across the countryside welders and tiremen got to see about every kind of situation possible, but I don't imagine that Wilbur, any more than the rest of them, had ever found Gerry Maars with nothing to say. Checking back toward Gerry one last time, he lowered the torch to the bearing, gas tip bending into steel. When the ring had glowed orange for half a minute, Wilbur backed away.

"You want to tap it there, Arthur, see if it's loose?"

It was more frozen than I would have thought, because I was just hitting it halfway at first, before finally leaning back to pound on it full strength. The bearing held fast, so Wilbur heated it again, and I beat on it some more, with no more luck than I'd had. Wilbur called back to the boy.

"Get me that medium sledge out of the truck. No, not over there, on this side. Use your head for a change. The far one there on the left."

Gerry in his aimlessness had wandered back, close enough to look from a few paces away at the drive shaft, the bearing still glowing bright against the day. Behind him was the pickerhead half-buried in the ground. Crouching above the shaft, Wilbur shrugged his shoulders and craned his neck, uneasy with the silence that Gerry finally broke.

"That there's your boy?" he said hoarsely.

"Yeah, Gerry, it sure is. That's Del, my youngest. Got Christmas vacation he just started, so he thinks he ought to be able to lie around the house all day. I don't quite see it like that."

We all took a look at Del, who scowled.

The welder stood, sweeping the hose around for more play. "Sorry about his manners. He's mad now, but he'll be glad again. Don't pay him no mind."

Nobody else would have needed any advice on that score, but while Wilbur bent down to the bearing, Gerry watched the boy.

"You an athlete, Del? You play sports?"

"Hell," Wilbur growled, "he was out for football, but then he quit. Didn't care for it somehow. He's like a lot of these boys, he don't care for nothing. That's half his problem."

The boy stood defiantly, hands buried in his pockets, while his dad brought the torch in yet again.

"Well," Gerry said mildly, "he's a good-looking young man, that's for sure. He's got the build for an athlete, that's why I asked."

"Brace that son of a bitch a little higher, Arthur, so I can get around on it all the way."

One hand on the rear end of the combine, Gerry watched us through red-rimmed eyes. Maybe it was just the somehow normal that I aspired to: if not for the hose and pickerhead, and the strained silence that surrounded them, we could have been on any number of shafts that we'd crouched above over the years. Except that Gerry for once wasn't right in the middle of it, moving away instead of closer when Wilbur took up the sledge from the boy.

"Yeah, Del," Gerry said above us, still hoarse, "a man's got to find what pleases him. I was kind of the odd one, I guess. All I ever wanted to do was grow corn."

Wilbur paused with hammer to metal, measuring for his swing.

"It's been awful hard for you fellas, ain't nobody in the world who doubts it. Nobody thinks nothing bad about it, though, Gerry, you got to know that. Hold it solid there, Arthur, while I give it a try."

He'd traded Del the torch, and now leaned full force into the task. It was a five-pound sledge and Wilbur gave it his all, pounding a good minute before he had to rest. He put on more heat and pounded again. We were both of us bent over the stubborn bearing, studying it, when the boy finally spoke up from behind.

"I might go out for baseball this spring. I been thinking about it."

We were all surprised to hear from him; a sullen boy like that usually doesn't have too much to say. Gerry, though, nodded, preferring to look past me and Wilbur to Del.

"You got the right size for it, all right. Is your arm any good? A good arm and you'd have a chance for shortstop. That's the very heart of things, see, where everything's happening. Here, Wilbur, might as well give me that goddamn sledge. Might as well let me get a chance to pound on it some myself."

Already stepping up to go at it again, the welder might have hesitated a second, but quickly stood aside to make room. Gerry picked up the hammer as if he was surprised it had weight. He closed his big fist around the handle, measured his own distance, and set in pounding. He'd driven many a bearing off in his day, and that much he seemed to remember, how to bring steel against steel. He pounded, grunting, driving the head harder and harder against the ring.

"Shortstop, second base," Del said behind us, suddenly talkative. "That's what I was thinking." Dodging the sledge's backswing, he leaned close so Gerry could hear. "The coach, Mr. Kelleher, he don't think I can do it, all he ever had me do was shag flies. But shortstop was what I was thinking too, that maybe that's where I ought to be."

"Goddamn it, goddamn . . . this . . . goddamn . . . thing," Gerry was muttering, raising the hammer again and again. "Come on, I said, damn it, you just better come now. Come on . . . I said . . . you better . . . come on. Come on, now, I just about, just about, damn it . . . by God, I *got* you, you stubborn son of a bitch."

He did have it, too, the ring shifting just a hair at first, but finally moving. Another dozen blows and it was loose. Gerry sat back on his heels, panting.

"But even third would be okay," Del was saying, "just so I could get a chance. I was thinking—"

"Oh, my Lord," Gerry gasped. "I *got* that son of a gun. Did you see how that damn thing fought me? Did you see how it fought me all the way?"

Wilbur laughed. "You got it, all right." He worked the bearing down the shaft into the thick leather palm of his glove. "You got the new one somewhere, Arthur? Pound 'em off and pound 'em back on again, that's the way a day goes by. What's the matter, you ain't got the new one?" Wilbur wasn't a young man either, I noticed, as he climbed back stiffly to his feet. "Well, I reckon I'll leave that to you." He glanced one last time over at the pickerhead and back at me. "You ain't got nothing else out here you wanted me to do?"

Still on his knees, Gerry studied the shaft. His face red from the exertion, he ran his fingers along the rusted metal. He seemed reluctant to let go of the sledge, too, even after the sharp echo of hammer blows had faded into the gray light of late afternoon. He didn't have any use for me at all, so when he stood up it was to his public, the welder and his boy, that he turned.

"You know, Del," he said. "Or Wilbur, I don't know if you fellas ever heard about that old man they found downtown a few weeks ago. Either one of you hear about him?"

With his back to me, it could have been just the three of them, standing together in one corner of the field. Wilbur had been coiling his hose, and he stopped expectantly. The boy, still flushed from his brief burst of enthusiasm, shook his head.

"You ain't heard of him either, Del? I'm surprised. Anyway, there was this old man, see, just terrible old, about my age. A real old-timer, and some folks were going along one day when they seen him out there standing on the street corner. Standing right out in broad daylight, crying to beat the band."

"Crying," Wilbur echoed.

"That's right, just a-bawling away. Crying like a baby. So these people go up to him, and they ask what the matter is. 'Oh,' the old man says, 'I just got married a while back, a few months ago. I married this young woman, see, thirty-five or forty years old. Real young and pretty. And all she ever wants to do is make love.'"

"There you go," Wilbur said, "that's the way it ought to be. That don't sound like no problem to me."

"Well," Gerry said, turning just enough to avoid me, "it didn't sound like no problem to them either. So they look back and forth at each other, and finally one of them goes ahead and asks him. 'Mister,' he says, 'that don't sound so bad, a young pretty wife waiting there all eager when you get home. So what's the problem? Why are you crying?' And that old man, still a-bawling away, says, ''Cause I forgot where I live!'"

Wilbur started in with his haw-haw at that, practiced over hundreds of farmers' visits spread out over the miles and years. Del brushed back his dirty hair and smiled.

"Forgot where he lives!" Wilbur repeated, shaking his head. "That old man's sure in a fix."

Gerry had always laughed hardest at his own jokes, but this time he just nodded, watching the boy.

"Oh, he's in a hell of a fix, all right. He sure is. You reckon that's ever gonna happen to you, Del?" He grabbed the boy's arm. "You ever gonna get old and worn out like that? The way science is, you might have come along just right, and get to go on forever. Wouldn't that be something, a boy like you jus. living on forever?"

Del, his smile fading, pulled away; it had never even occurred to him that he wouldn't.

Gerry reached back for his wallet. "Say there, Wilbur, I reckon Dale Senior's gonna want cash for that."

Wilbur shook his head. "Keep your goddamn money."

"No, now the way things are, you never can tell. I want to get you paid."

"And I want you to know I ain't taking it. You been a customer all these years, that's good enough for me. Dale Junior don't even need to know I found you."

Gerry looked up from his wallet. "Well, Wilbur, all right. The truth is I appreciate it. I ain't got the cash here on me anyway, would have had to have Arthur run all the way back for the checkbook. I appreciate it, I really do. Keep your head down on them grounders now,

Del, like this. You got to challenge them damn things, that's the key."

The boy had been vaguely smiling still, but once the advice started, a dull look settled back into his eyes. Evening was coming on, and while Wilbur slammed shut the truck lockers, Del shuffled impatiently. It had no doubt already occurred to him by then that he wouldn't be on the baseball team, wouldn't ever get to be shortstop, and even if by some miracle he did, any advice that he might pick up from a stooped-over, dirty-faced old farmer moving back and forth in the cornstalks wasn't too likely to help.

Gerry left me to walk Wilbur and his boy as far as their truck cab, the red dog trotting at his heels. He waved them good-bye. Laughing and waving too, they backed from the field, to lumber out of sight up the road. His own smile fading, the first thing Gerry did as he came back past the pickup was to hit me in the chest, his big fist landing so hard against my breastbone that it felt like I'd been kicked by a mule.

"Little bastard," he snarled as I staggered back. "You meddling little shit. Think you know something. You think you might know how it's gonna be. You don't know nothing. Just keep away from me, damn it, I don't want you around." He swung wild again and missed, then picked up a dirt clod to hurl past my head. "Just keep the damn hell away."

Old Red barked and jumped at his hand, sensing a game. Gerry fired off another clod that hit me in the shoulder. He had a good arm himself still, and it stung. "Get your worthless ass away from here," he yelled. "I don't never want to see you again. Get out of here and leave me the hell alone."

It wasn't very likely, though, that I would. I didn't have a new bearing close at hand, but the hose I'd paid cash for was in the car, and in the short winter twilight granted to us, I already had it planned to carry it out there to the pickerhead, to take off the old one and fling it just as far over the ditch bank as I could. I got the new hose and made it as far as getting the old one off, but by that time my hands were shaking so bad I couldn't hold them steady, couldn't even fit the wrench head around the nut.

Thinking back now, I still can remember when Touby Willets and his dad, back when we were kids, got hit by one of the Big Four freight trains up at the crossing. They were on their way into town with a calf, and the train was just getting up speed as it topped the moraine. So it wasn't going that fast yet, and managed to hit them a couple of feet behind the cab. The calf got killed, but Touby Willets and his dad were thrown free.

It wasn't until a couple of days later, then, when we were in school one morning, that Touby Willets finally began to shake. It threw him right out of his chair, and before long he was trembling so bad that the teacher got scared herself. She couldn't stop him, the principal either, and finally his dad had to come in from the country and take him home. His sister told us later that he'd shook like that day and night for a couple of days, before he finally was able to stop.

The wrench head wouldn't hold the bolt, my fingers the wrench; as it fell to the ground, my legs were shaking too, knees wobbling so bad that I could barely stand up. Over by the pickup Gerry stood alone, and as I went back I could see he was crying. I took up my own spot again beside the combine. Out of dirt clod range, but otherwise just as close as I could get to him all the same.

Warm Hi-tran cooled on my fingers, the broken hose was cast aside; ten feet from the sunken pickerhead I stood and shook like I would never stop. Rebellious muscles rose up against me, and in a world not always noted for its favors, all of it came to me at once: the tug of a seed cap, the grimy weathered red of the combine, a binding of coveralls across my back. A cool line of orange between nighttime and the ragged ditch bank, chilly topsoil slick with clay—far down below it, science could assure us, there would be rock and still more rock to encounter, packed around a fiery and raging core. In the sophisticated times that we had stumbled into, only Gerry Maars would have still hoped to break loose of it, the conceit to pit himself and Haskell County against the stars. Unsuccessful even in sacrifice, he was back to just being worn out and broke again, leaning against the pickup with his head down, while I shook twenty yards away like a fool.

That was all I could offer either one of us, just to shake out of control like little Touby Willets as darkness settled in. The red dog had picked up a scent of some kind by then, and bounded through the cornstalks to the woods. There was the cool glass of the cab above me, a faint dry rustle from the wind; it had been just that plain damn self-ishness again, and nothing more, that had wanted Gerry Maars not to die. Failed in my narrow duties, I just stood there and trembled, a warmth that had started in my legs moving up into my chest and arms. Somewhere out there would have been memory too: Annie running across the lawn for a three-minute ride to the crossroads, her swinging up next to me, on bended knees, to hug my neck. Somewhere back there a mother, if Byron wanted. Sheep outside the screen door, axes against a bin; the brush of a cool hand on my forehead, that might even once have been hers.

I felt Gerry by that time more than saw him, leaning alone in the darkness against the truck. Alone but not unaccompanied—growing accustomed to unsteadiness, I would stay out there all that night and a dozen others if I had to, and besides, there was plenty of company to be had. More than enough to fill the wide countryside that surrounded us: duty and enterprise, memories, regrets, a dog's distant bark in the woods. The warmth of blood that still stubbornly cared to flow through us, a farm light in the distance, the cool, muffled bareness of winter air. Hydraulics, hope, market prices, mystery, with all of it wound through the prickliness of a human nature made for both orneriness and acceptance after all. The better, it seemed, in an ever more impatient world, to venture on anyway—unheralded and unprofitable; mortal, but still unaccountably alive.

AVON BOOKS TRADE PAPERBACKS

MEMOIR FROM ANTPROOF CASE 72733-1/$14.00 US/$19.00 Can
by Mark Heplrin

A SOLDIER OF THE GREAT WAR 72736-6/$15.00 US/$20.00 Can
by Mark Heplrin

THE LONGEST MEMORY 72700-5/$10.00 US
by Fred D'Aguiar

COCONUTS FOR THE SAINT 72630-0/$11.00 US/$15.00 Can
by Debra Spark

WOMEN AND GHOSTS 72501-0/$9.00 US/$12.00 Can
by Alison Lurie

BRAZZAVILLE BEACH 78049-6/$11.00 US
by William Boyd

COYOTE BLUE 72523-1/$10.00 US/$13.00 Can
by Christopher Moore

TASTING LIFE TWICE: LITERARY 78123-9/$10.00 US/$13.00 Can
LESBIAN FICTION BY NEW
AMERICAN WRITERS
Edited by E. J. Levy

CHARMS FOR THE EASY LIFE 72557-6/$12.00 US/$16.00 Can
by Kaye Gibbons

THE MEN AND THE GIRLS 72408-1/$10.00 US
by Joanna Trollope